THE SECRET LIVES OF THE KUDZU DEBUTANTES

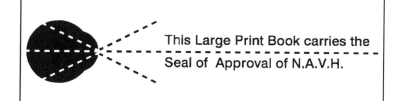

This Large Print Book carries the
Seal of Approval of N.A.V.H.

THE SECRET LIVES OF THE KUDZU DEBUTANTES

CATHY HOLTON

THORNDIKE PRESS

An imprint of Thomson Gale, a part of The Thomson Corporation

THOMSON

™

GALE

Detroit • New York • San Francisco • New Haven, Conn. • Waterville, Maine • London

LIBRARY OF CONGRESS CATALOGING-IN-PUBLICATION DATA

Holton, Cathy.
    The secret lives of the kudzu debutantes / by Cathy Holton.
      p. cm. — (Thorndike press large print laugh lines)
    ISBN-13: 978-0-7862-9929-4 (hardcover : alk. paper)
    ISBN-10: 0-7862-9929-0 (hardcover : alk. paper)
    1. Women — Southern States — Fiction. 2. Southern States — Fiction. 3.
Large type books. I. Title.
PS3608.O494434S43 2007b
813'.6—dc22
                                     2007031848

Published in 2007 by arrangement with The Ballantine Publishing Group, a division of Random House, Inc.
Printed in the United States of America on permanent paper
10 9 8 7 6 5 4 3 2 1

For Sam, Lauren, and Jordan —
always watch out for the elk

CHAPTER ONE

Virginia Broadwell was angry. And anyone who knew Virginia, knew she was a dangerous woman when riled. Her first husband, the Judge, had learned this lesson long before he died, and her only son, Charles, had experienced the sting of her self-contained fury enough times over his forty-five years to be gun-shy. And her new husband would learn it, too, although Virginia would wait until the last thank-you note had been written and the ring was securely settled on her finger before showing Redmon that side of her nature. She would give him a chance to settle into the traces and take the bit firmly between his teeth before applying the whip the first time.

Downstairs she could hear the wedding guests milling about. She looked around the flowered chintz bedroom she had shared with the Judge for nearly twenty-six years, and then spent the next twenty years enjoying in solitary bliss. It would be sad to leave this house, the one she had insisted the Judge build for her all those years ago, before she would agree to marry him. The scene of so many of her social triumphs, the place where she had plotted and schemed her way to the top of the wobbly Ithaca social ladder, and which now, sadly, must be sold to pay her debts. Redmon, like the wily redneck businessman he was, had insisted she enter the marriage debt-free. He had insisted she sign a prenuptial agreement. Despite herself, Virginia had felt a kind of grudging admiration for him then. She would have done the same thing had their circumstances been reversed.

She had survived an unfortunate childhood, widowhood, scandal, near financial ruin, and now Y2K, and it had seemed only fitting that she set her wedding date for January 20, 2000. Let others worry about computer crashes and social anarchy; Virginia had endured enough turmoil in her life to know that victory belonged to the bold and the cunning.

There was a knock on the door and her son, Charles, stuck his head in. "Mother, are you ready?" He wore the same whipped-dog expression he had worn since his meek wife of sixteen years walked out of his life a

8

little over a year ago, taking with her his children, his pride, and nearly six hundred thousand dollars of his assets. His defeatism irritated Virginia beyond words.

"Yes, I'm ready," she said. "I'm ready to do my duty, to do whatever is necessary to hold this family together —"

"Good." He knew where this was headed and he wanted no part of it. "I'll give the signal then." He tried to close the door but Virginia inserted her slim little foot. Charles sighed and swung the door open again. "Yes, Mother?" he said, rolling his eyes skyward like a martyr on his way to the stake.

"Come in and close the door behind you," she said fiercely. He did as he was told and followed her into the center of the room, where she stood looking at herself in a cheval glass. She lifted a well-manicured hand, indicating a wingback chair by the window.

"Do we really have to do this now?" he said, and when she said nothing, only stared at him steadily in the glass, he sighed and slumped down with his feet stretched in front of him.

"You brought this on yourself," she said. She sniffed, looking at herself critically in the mirror. There weren't many women her age who could still wear designer clothes and heels. Hadn't she caught the bag boy at the Piggly Wiggly staring at her legs yesterday as he loaded her groceries into the car? And hadn't some ruffians in a pickup truck whistled at her last week as she crossed the street in front of the Courthouse?

Charles slumped in his chair and stared despondently at a spot in the center of the oriental carpet. It was his newest technique, this passive-aggressive slumping, this lumpish inertia, like a sack of grain propped against a table leg. Virginia frowned at him in the glass. "You won't return my phone calls, you hide behind locked doors when I show up at your condo — don't think I haven't seen you peering from behind the blinds — you refuse to see me when I show up at that ratty little place you call an office."

Good. She had drawn blood. She noted the way his ears flushed, the way he lurched forward with his elbows pinned to the arms of the chair. "That ratty little office is all I can afford," he said tersely.

"Whose fault is that?"

"Surely, Mother, you're not blaming me for the breakup of Boone and Broadwell." He lifted his top lip, looking more like the old Charles, more like the surly, sarcastic boy she had raised and tutored, so much like his father, but so much more like her.

"Who should I blame?" she said, lifting one eyebrow. "Who should I blame for the breakup of your father's law firm, for the loss of my annual income and partnership assets?"

He smirked in a way she found particularly offensive. He said, "Well, you're managing to survive pretty well, considering you're marrying one of the wealthiest men in Georgia."

"I'm doing what I have to do given the circumstances," she snapped. "And you'd be well advised to do the same."

His eyes clouded suddenly and he shrugged and went limp again, and in that moment of surrender Virginia knew the breakup of Boone & Broadwell had something to do with Nita. Something had happened between Charles and his soon-to-be-remarried ex-wife. Something secret but underhanded — and Virginia knew a thing or two about secrets, not to mention under-handedness.

"Speaking of marriage," she said, smoothing her hair with one hand. "I understand Nita is getting remarried next week."

Charles stared at his feet. A muscle moved along his jaw. "So I heard," he said evenly.

"You should have put a stop to all that when you had a chance."

"This isn't the dark ages, Mother. I couldn't have stopped her from divorcing me if she wanted to."

"Yes, but you could have made it more difficult for her. You could have tied the case up in court for years and bled her dry, financially and emotionally. You're a good attorney, or at least you used to be."

He laughed bitterly and put his hands on the arm of the chair as if to rise. "Are we about finished here?"

She looked at him suspiciously. Why hadn't he opposed the divorce? Why hadn't he stopped Nita from running off with that good-looking young carpenter she hired to fix her pool house, an action that made the Broadwells the laughingstock of Ithaca, Georgia?

Virginia smelled a rat.

And she knew it had something to do with Nita and her two devious friends — Eadie Boone and Lavonne Zibolsky. Some scheme they had cooked up a year ago when Nita and Lavonne left their husbands, and Eadie ran off to New Orleans with her husband, Trevor, to live the life of bohemian artists.

Virginia adjusted the sleeves of her jacket. "Tell them to give me five minutes and then start the wedding march. You can wait for me at the foot of the stairs. And for God's sake, stand up straight and stop slouching."

Charles went out without another word, pulling the door closed firmly behind him. No, it had been a bad year for everyone but Nita, Lavonne, and Eadie, who had somehow managed to turn everyone else's bad luck to their advantage. And Virginia was determined to get to the bottom of what had happened no matter what it took. But first she must put her own affairs in order. She tucked her bobbed hair behind one ear and looked at her smooth skin appreciatively. *Keep your face out of the sun.* It was the one bit of childhood advice her mother had given her that actually proved useful, besides her admonition to Virginia on her wedding night, to "close your eyes and think of something pleasant." Virginia had laughed bitterly then, and she laughed bitterly now, remembering.

She stared at herself in the mirror, somewhat disgusted at the predicament she found herself in now — a bride at sixty-five. Still, beggars can't be choosers, she reminded herself. Desperate times call for desperate measures. She had married beneath herself both times, first, to the Judge, the son of a sharecropper, and now to Redmon, the son of a pine barren hog farmer, but she had done what well-brought-up women of her generation were taught to do: she had married for money. She had her work cut out for her this time, though. Redmon didn't seem the type likely to submit to the crop and bridle of matrimony, although Virginia was certain she would prevail in the end.

She would prevail in bringing her new husband to heel and then she would turn her attention to Nita and her renegade girlfriends. Virginia had never, in her entire life, let anyone get the best of her, and she wasn't about to start now. She stared balefully at herself in the mirror, trying to remember that brides should appear virginal and not homicidal. Her tiny hands curled into fists. Her tiny teeth clenched. Twin spots of color appeared on her cheeks. Below her the wedding march began, low and plaintive as a cow stuck in a bog, slow and ponderous as a funeral dirge.

Virginia forced a bright, artificial grin. She checked her teeth for lipstick stains.

Vengeance is mine, saith the Lord, but Virginia had never been one to turn her responsibilities over to someone else.

Somewhere deep in the house, a phone was

ringing. Eadie awakened from a dream about crickets chirping, and sat up on her elbow to listen. It was her cell phone, but she couldn't remember where she had dropped it the night before. This house was too big. Too damn big, and too damn lonely. The ringing stopped, and then began again, insistently. It was probably Trevor, calling to tell her he'd been delayed in New York. Again.

Eadie sighed, and rolled over in bed.

Outside the long windows, a soft New Orleans rain was falling. Beyond the wrought-iron balcony the garden glistened, a jungle of greenery, banana plants, ferns, bougainvillea, and thick clusters of trailing vines. Through the lush foliage the old bricked wall rose protectively above the courtyard, built in 1737 when the house had been a convent erected on the outskirts of Nouvelle Orleans, and the city itself was nothing but a backwoods settlement laid out in French military outpost style along the swampy banks of the Mississippi. Later, it had been a boys' orphanage. Trevor had wanted the house from the moment he first saw it. He had been entranced with the mystery and tragic history of the place, with its fourteen-foot ceilings and chandeliers that dangled like golden fruit. They had attended a cocktail party here soon after arriving in New Orleans, and standing on the balcony overlooking the moonlit garden, Trevor had taken Eadie in his arms and kissed her. "I can *write* here," he said fiercely. These words had proved prophetic.

Eadie plumped the pillows behind her and reached for the TV remote. She scrolled through the stations several times but nothing caught her eye. Thunder rumbled in the distance. She picked up an opened box of Mondo Log Candies and rummaged through the empty wrapper looking for any sticky chocolate pieces she might have missed during last night's binge. Nothing. The box was empty. Eadie tossed it over the side of the bed.

She switched off the TV and then lay back on the bed. A water stain spread slowly across the ceiling like a giant inkblot. Eadie saw a profile of Elvis Presley, the slim Elvis, not the fat one, and then she saw two girls fighting. Finally, weary and exhausted, she did what she always did when she was bored these days and out of Mondo Logs. She picked up the phone beside the bed and called Lavonne.

"Hey, what are you doing?"

"I'm working. Or at least I'm getting ready to work. I'm sitting in the back room drink-

16

ing a cup of coffee and reading the morning newspaper."

"I've been thinking about the way Myra Redmon kicked the bucket," Eadie said.

"Look, Eadie, if you're going to call me every day we need to get on one of those shared-minute plans. You're eating up my minutes."

"I mean, considering Myra was such a pain in the ass, how ironic was the way she died? And can you believe Virginia actually married Redmon?"

"Yeah, I know. How desperate did she have to be."

"Pretty damn desperate. Myra must be spinning in her grave."

"Now there's a happy thought." Lavonne took a sip, opened the paper, and snorted suddenly, spewing coffee.

"What's so funny?"

"Speak of the devil. I'm sitting here looking at a photo of Virginia in the wedding section of the newspaper. Just so you know, it was the Social Event of the Season."

"Did the bride wear chain mail and carry a battleax?"

"No, interestingly enough, she appears to be unarmed. She's described as being 'graceful as a swan' and 'slender as a willow.'"

"I'll bet Virginia wrote that herself."

"Actually, they've got Lumineria writing the wedding and engagement section these days, in addition to the 'Town Tattler.' "

"Oh shit," Eadie said.

"Town Tattler" was the gossip column of the *Ithaca Daily News* written by Lumineria Crabb. Lumineria had taught Sunday school for thirty years and she could never bring herself to say anything ugly about anyone, so most of the gossip was pretty tame. *Guess which former Cotillion Queen is celebrating another birthday? And she doesn't look a day over twenty! I heard it from a little bird one husband, J.T., bought his lovely wife, L.T., an anniversary ring and a trip to Paris. Isn't he the sweetest?* That kind of thing. When Eadie announced she and Trevor were moving to New Orleans, a photo of her taken the day after her Let's Get the Hell Out of Ithaca Party appeared in the "Town Tattler" with the caption, "Guess which little love birds are flying the coop?" The photo, showing a very disheveled and obviously intoxicated Eadie, was probably the only bad picture she had ever taken. Lavonne referred to it as Eadie's Meth Bust Photo and gave her shit every chance she got.

"Well, at least it's not as bad as your Meth Bust Photo."

"Very funny," Eadie said.

"Actually Virginia looks really good. Amazingly good."

"Yeah, well, that's what happens when you bathe in the blood of virgins."

"I'll have to try that."

"Speaking of looks, there's something I've been meaning to ask you." Eadie put her hand behind her shoulders and probed with her fingers. "There might be something wrong with my back. It feels like I have a lump there, where my neck comes in."

"A Dowager's Hump," Lavonne said. "We all get them. It's part of aging."

"Remind me not to call you when I'm depressed."

"Are you depressed?"

"I wasn't until you mentioned the Meth Bust Photo and the Dowager's Hump." Eadie slumped down in the pillows. She raised her legs into the air, admiring their long lean shapes, pointing with her toes toward the ceiling. Except for the slight paunch around her midsection, her figure was still good, which was amazing considering her recent inactivity and constant candy cravings. "And speaking of depression, I'm out of Mondo Logs. I need you to order me a case and I'll pick them up when I get to town."

A Mondo Log was a pecan log covered in chocolate with a marshmallow center. It had been known to cause Type II diabetes after just one slice. The logs were made by the Mondo Candy Company out of Stations-of-the-Cross, Georgia, and were rumored to have a special secret ingredient known only to the Mondo family. Eadie suspected heroin. She had been addicted since childhood but she had held her addiction at bay for nearly twenty years. Since she moved to New Orleans, however, her Mondo Log habit had returned with a vengeance and now she ordered cases of the stuff.

Lavonne, who'd grown up in Cleveland, and even after twenty years in the South, had yet to assimilate Southern culture said, "I'm not going down to the Mondo Candy Factory to buy you a case of Mondo Logs. I'm not enabling you to continue this disgusting and unhealthy habit."

"You know, Lavonne, now that you've lost seventy-five pounds, you're not near as much fun as you used to be."

"You'll be down for Nita's wedding in a few days. Just pick up a box when you get here."

"They'll be sold out by then! You know they only turn out a limited number of logs and then they close down till September."

The reason for Eadie's repeated phone calls became suddenly, glaringly apparent to Lavonne. She grinned, leaning back in her chair. "Oh my God," she said, "you're homesick. You're homesick for Ithaca, Georgia."

"Don't be ridiculous," Eadie said, a little too forcefully. "I live in the greatest city in the world. I can get any alcoholic drink imaginable at three in the morning, read the *New York Times* in the Quarter over café au lait and beignets, eat in a different restaurant every night and not hit the same one twice."

"But you can't get a Mondo Log."

"Are you going to order it or not."

Lavonne folded the newspaper and used it to blot up the spilled coffee on her desk. "How does Trevor feel about this latest addiction of yours?"

"Who?"

"Trevor. Your husband. The man you left town with a little over a year ago."

"Oh him," Eadie said.

Lavonne crumpled the wet paper and threw it into the trash can. "Trouble in paradise?" she said.

Eadie yawned and stared at the inkblot water stain. It reminded her now of a witch riding on a broomstick. "You'd have to be here to understand what's going on. It's hard being married to a celebrity."

"You sound jealous."

"Not jealous. Just bored."

"Oh shit. That can't be good."

Eadie frowned and put her hand over her eyes so she wouldn't have to look at the inkblot water stain. "He signed that two-book deal with Random House and now he's up in New York meeting with the publicity boys to plan his book tour."

"So let me see if I've got this right," Lavonne said. She tapped her computer screen and waited while it booted up. "You spend twenty years hounding Trevor to quit practicing law and finish his novel, and now that he's done it, and managed to sell it to one of the biggest publishing houses in the world, you're depressed? You're married to a smart, good-looking man who adores you, and you're not happy?"

"Well, you know what they say," Eadie said, yawning. "Be careful what you wish for. You just might get it."

"Remind me to smack you the next time I see you." Lavonne went online to check the e-mails on her Shofar So Good Deli web-site. She scrolled down the list, holding her cell phone against her ear with one shoulder.

"About the wedding," Eadie said, dropping her legs and rolling over on her stomach. "Are you sure it's okay if I stay with you? Are you sure Ashley won't mind?"

"Ashley's on winter break and Louise doesn't go back to Tulane until next week. They're down in Florida with Leonard and his trophy wife."

"Funny, you don't sound bitter. Why don't you sound bitter?"

Lavonne grinned. "Because now the trophy wife's stuck with Leonard. And I'm not."

From deep within the house, Eadie could hear whispering. In French. She turned her head to listen, and after a minute, it stopped. "I think my house is haunted," she said. She was pretty sure it was a child. She had, several times, caught something small and fleeting out of the corner of her eye. "Lights go on and off. I hear whispering all the time, like someone is standing behind me and when I turn around, there's no one there. Sometimes I hear footsteps on the stairs."

"What does Trevor say?"

"He says I'm crazy. He says I spend too much time shut up in the house, alone."

On the other side of the wall, the old mixer made a *wump, wump* sound as it mixed the dough. Lavonne could hear Little

Moses Shapiro, her partner's son, moving around the kitchen, taking bread loaves out of the ovens and sliding them onto the cooling trays. "Look, Eadie, I've got to go. We're catering Nita's wedding and I've got a lot to do before next Saturday. E-mail me your flight plan and I'll pick you up at the airport on Wednesday."

"Is Nita having a bachelorette party?"

"She says she doesn't want one. She's acting kind of weird about the whole thing. I'm starting to think she might be getting cold feet."

"What do you mean? Is something wrong with her and Jimmy Lee?"

"Oh no, they're as happy as ever. I just get the feeling she doesn't want to get married. I don't know, I could be wrong."

"Well, let's you and me take her out to Bad Bob's and see if we can ply her with tequila and find out what's going on."

Lavonne said, "Well, that might be a problem since Bad Bob's is no more. Two guys named Thom and Petor moved down from Atlanta and bought the place. They decorated it to look like a New York loft, put up a screen of trellises to hide the concrete plant, and built a deck overlooking the river. Now it's a wine bar called Malveux Robert."

"Shit, what's happening to that town?"

"You'll see when you get here," Lavonne said, and hung up.

Eadie hung up the phone, yawned, and rolled over in bed. The house was quiet again. The ghost had gone. The rain had stopped and the sun now peeked from behind a bank of low clouds, slanting through the long windows. A patch of blue sky appeared above the neighbor's roofline. They had bought the house on Prytania Street soon after they sold Trevor's ancestral home in Ithaca and moved to New Orleans. Most of their furniture was still in storage back in Georgia, and except for the bedroom, the kitchen, and the library, the mansion was empty. They had gambled that everything would work out over their first year there. That was all the time Trevor had given himself to finish his novel.

"If it doesn't work out, we can always go back to Georgia," he said. "I can always go back to practicing law. And you can work anywhere. It doesn't matter where we live."

But, apparently, it did. There were art galleries all along Magazine Street and Eadie told herself that she would work again, but instead she fussed over Trevor like an overbearing mother. She would wake him every morning and bring him café au lait in the garden, watching anxiously from the French doors until he began, tentatively at first, and then with a steady tapping of his fingers over the keyboard, to write. He would break for lunch and then go back to the garden. Eadie would allow no one to visit until four o'clock in the afternoon, cocktail hour in New Orleans, and then the garden would be crowded with neighbors and college professors and lawyers who had graduated from Tulane but never practiced law a day in their lives. Gradually, Eadie succumbed to the easy charm of the place, the dusty bookstores along Carrollton Avenue, the cafés of Maple Street, the bon vivant attitude and wit of the people she met at cocktail parties and art galleries and book signings. A general feeling of sloth and lassitude overtook her. She set up her studio in the dining room but kept the door closed and locked. Instead, she began to take long naps in the afternoon.

Trevor, on the other hand, seemed energized by the place. He worked feverishly, and after two months had a rough draft of the novel, a legal thriller, completed. By then he had landed an agent, based on his outline and the first three chapters. Four months later he had signed a two-book

26

contract with Random House. It had all gone as perfectly and predictably as a Hollywood movie plot. The novel was due out in May and Eadie had no doubt it would become an overnight bestseller. That was the way her luck was running these days.

In a little over a year, Trevor had become a local Literary Figure. He had succumbed completely to the siren's song of adulation and praise. Eadie was consumed by jealousy, not of the women who threw themselves at her husband at cocktail parties and gallery openings, but of the fact that Trevor could work and she could not.

And now, lying in the house on Prytania Street and yawning in her antique bed, Eadie was overcome by a numbing sense of boredom.

Jealousy and boredom. Always a dangerous combination for Eadie Boone.

Now that her wedding was less than a week away, Nita was not even sure she wanted to get married again. She sat out on the screened porch drinking coffee in the mornings after Jimmy Lee had gone to work and the children had left for school, wondering if she was doing the right thing. Steam rose off the surface of the Black Warrior River and catfish the size of terriers splashed in the dark pools between the cypress trunks. Nita loved the quiet isolation of the place, their little cabin in the woods. Jimmy Lee had bought it soon after she left Charles Broadwell for good and moved in with him. She brought her two children with her, Whitney and Logan. They liked to take the boat out on the river or feed the catfish from its pine-strewn banks. In the summer, they swam in the dark water, cavorting like otters, enjoying themselves in a way they had never done when they lived in the big house in River Oaks with its kidney-shaped swimming pool. Jimmy Lee hung a rope swing from the top of a tall tree and watching the three of them swing out over the water, laughing and twirling and kicking their feet, Nita realized she had what she had always wanted — a happy family.

They lived simply and frugally on the money Jimmy Lee made as a self-employed carpenter. The children went to public school now and seemed much happier than they ever were attending the prestigious Barron Hall School. Nita herself had gone back to school, taking classes at the small college in town where she was trying to decide whether to major in elementary education or women's studies. The money she had taken from Charles Broadwell sat untouched in her bank account, insurance against Charles ever filing a custody suit to take the children away from her. Her love life with Jimmy Lee, thirteen years her junior, was passionate and intensely satisfying. All in all, Nita's life was turning out to be everything she had ever dreamed it could be, and she was hesitant to upset that delicate, happy balance by marrying Jimmy Lee.

Already there were ominous signs. He had begun to hint at fatherhood although Nita had told him that, at forty, and with her own children nearly grown, she did not want more children. He said he understood, but she saw the way he looked at young mothers pushing babies in the grocery store. And lately he had begun to grumble about money, to insist, despite her assurances to the contrary, that a man with a family must do more to provide for them than work as a self-employed carpenter.

Nita, who was writing a college research paper on the histories of black women who worked as domestics in the South in the 1930s and 1940s, had begun to question how long her happiness would last. On Tuesday and Thursday afternoons she went out to the Suck Creek Retirement Home with her tape recorder and notebook and boxes of chocolate that she handed out to the women she interviewed. There she heard tales of social injustice and love gone bad, stories of the cruelty of nature and the capriciousness of fate. Immersing herself in the histories of these sad women made Nita realize how fleeting and illusionary moments of genuine happiness can be, and she could not shake the feeling that her happiness, too, was doomed to failure.

But then Jimmy Lee would come home from work and take her in his arms, and she would forget all that. Then her doubts would be nothing more than a slight gnawing sensation in the pit of her stomach. She would go about the small cabin planning her wedding and feeling like she was pushing something large and heavy up a hill, and if she stopped, it would roll back down and crush her. She hurried through her days. The flowers were ordered. The menu was decided upon. She loved Jimmy Lee and she knew he loved her. But there was a part of her, a cynical part born of sixteen years of marriage to Charles Broadwell, which knew that a wedding ring is not always the blossoming of a love affair.

Sometimes it's the death knell.

Once she had swindled her ex-husband,

Leonard, out of his dream home and embarked on her career as a small-business owner, Lavonne Zibolsky was amazed at how quickly success came. In a little over a year, she and her business partner, Mona Shapiro, had increased the revenue of their Shofar So Good Deli thirty percent, and had even turned a small profit in their first year. Which was pretty good considering the amount of equipment and advertising they had bought, not to mention the expensive website they had paid a company out of Atlanta to design. Leonard's participation in all this had, of course, been forced, which was unfortunate but unavoidable, given the circumstances. Survival of the fittest was applicable not only to Darwinian theory, it would seem, but also to matrimony. Lavonne was the only divorced woman she knew whose standard of living had *not* gone down after the divorce, and it was only because she had been willing to do whatever was necessary to protect herself *before* the first petition was filed. She had taken the steps necessary, however unethical, morally questionable, or potentially criminal they might be, to ensure that she didn't spend her golden years living in a mobile home eating Feline Delight for breakfast, lunch, and dinner.

Besides, Leonard had only gotten what he deserved.

She stood at the counter of the Shofar So Good Deli on a rainy Tuesday morning, contemplating this. Lavonne used to daydream about moving to the south of France with Leonard after the girls were grown. She used to daydream about writing a series of travel cookbooks. But perhaps a book on protecting yourself financially from bad husbands might be more timely.

The bell on the front door tinkled and Lavonne looked up and smiled at two tourists who entered carrying *I Survived Shopping in Ithaca* bags. The tourist trade accounted for most of the deli's sales. They drove down from Atlanta by the busloads to tour the quaint town and antebellum homes that Sherman had somehow forgotten to burn on his March to the Sea.

Lavonne said, "Can I help you?" Her business partner, Mona Shapiro, was on a Caribbean cruise with a group of widows from the synagogue. It was her first vacation in nearly fifteen years.

"I think we'll have lunch," the woman said, eyeing the menu board on the wall behind Lavonne. The man shook his umbrella out and put it in the stand and then took the woman's raincoat and hung it over

32

the back of a chair.

"Let me know when you're ready," Lavonne said. "The soup of the day is tomato artichoke."

Little Moses came out of the back of the store. He had cleaned himself up recently, had cut his dreadlocks and now wore his hair short. He still sported a lip ring and the tattoo of a serpent on his forearm, but all in all, his appearance was much improved over what it had been when Lavonne first met him and the rest of his Jewish reggae band, Burning Bush. The band had moved away from their Jamaican roots and was more into the blues now. They were talking about moving to New Orleans. Eadie had offered to let them stay with her in her rambling mansion in the Garden District.

"Hey, can you cover for me up front?" Lavonne said. "I've got some work I need to do in the back."

"Sure." He grinned and went up to the counter to take the tourists' order.

Lavonne took off her apron and went into the small office to work on payroll reports. It was her least favorite thing to do but she was finding that success carried its own price. She worked fifty hours a week in the store, and an additional two to four hours on the weekend helping with the catering business. She had also begun contemplating possible franchise opportunities, and now she sat up late every night in bed alone with her laptop computer, researching the possibility of further expansion. She had bought a small house over in the Historic District of Ithaca, which she shared with her Jack Russell terrier, Winston, and, sporadically, with her daughters, Louise and Ashley. Leonard had moved to Atlanta to practice law soon after Boone & Broadwell went down in flames among rumors of shady real estate deals and something unsavory to do with the partners themselves. Louise was a freshman at Tulane and Ashley had graduated early from the Barron Hall School and had left home for the University of Georgia. All in all, Lavonne lead a somewhat fulfilling, if lonely, existence.

And there were advantages to being a workaholic. Her weight, for instance. After nearly twenty years as an obese housewife, she now weighed seventy-five pounds less than she had when she was married to Leonard. Not that this had made much difference in her personal life. The truth was, she was forty-seven years old and she hadn't had a date in twenty-two years. The idea of having to hold her stomach in and shave her legs on a regular basis, not to mention the disturbing prospect of a bikini wax, was enough to make Lavonne contemplate permanent celibacy.

Still, there were times when she missed the companionship of having a man around. Then she would daydream of having someone to go to dinner with, someone who could take her to flea markets on the weekends or out to the Whistlin' Dixie Drive-In for the Friday-night double feature, someone who could appreciate her sense of humor and the fact she played a mean hand of euchre.

Lavonne had her nearly grown daughters, her successful business, her laptop computer, and Winston, and now, if she could only figure out something to do about the loneliness, her life would be just about perfect.

CHAPTER TWO

After lunch, Eadie showered and went out into the garden to do yoga and try to meditate. The rain had washed the air and left it cool and clean and damp. Sunshine filtered through the branches of the live oaks and pooled in brilliant puddles across the bricked patio and the lush green lawn. She tried to imagine herself floating on a white cloud. She tried to concentrate on her breathing, but it was no use. Her mind jumped about from subject to subject. What was it the Buddhists called it? Monkey mind? Her monkey mind was loose and it was horny as hell. There was no use denying it. The scenes Eadie was conjuring in her mind had less to do with white fluffy clouds and more to do with the Kama Sutra.

Being in love with her husband wasn't working out. Being in love with Trevor Boone, the next literary golden boy, wasn't what she had expected. It was only a matter of time before fame found him and then she would lose him completely to an adoring public who would listen with rapt attention while he gave his opinion on everything from literary symbolism to the effects of global warming on emerging weather patterns. It wasn't too hard to imagine. He would travel the country on publicity tours and he would, of course, offer to take her with him. But she wouldn't go, because what could be more depressing than watching Trevor fulfill a lifetime dream while she hadn't been able to work in over a year? When it was all she could do just to drag herself out of bed every morning? How pathetic and sad would that be?

Eadie wrenched her Monkey Mind back to the present. She tried not to think about loneliness and the delights of the flesh. On the sidewalk beyond the wrought-iron fence young mothers pushed baby strollers on their way to the park, and groups of Catholic school children in plaid uniforms straggled by on their way home from school. The distant streetcars whirred along St. Charles, clanging their warning bells at every block. Eadie closed her eyes and tried again to concentrate on her breathing. She had only recently taken up meditation and like so much else in her life, it just wasn't working out. It was too slow and sedate for Eadie, too introspective. And she didn't like the way her mind would suddenly veer off into strange dimensions, traveling down dark pathways she had long ago ceased to visit, and didn't want to revisit now.

She opened her eyes. Blinked. Dappled sunlight filled the garden. Above her the old live oaks spread their branches protectively, pushing their massive roots up through the bricked sidewalk, ancient veterans of hurricanes and floods and civil war.

She closed her eyes again and tried to concentrate on her breathing. *In, out. In, out.* But it was hard to do when hungry. She should eat something, she decided, something good, something healthy, but she wasn't sure what. Maybe some fish. Maybe a po' boy sandwich. She could walk down to the po' boy restaurant on the corner of Magazine and Valmont.

But walking down to the corner restaurant would have less to do with a po' boy sandwich, she knew, and more to do with the twenty-two-year-old art student who worked behind the counter.

His name was Richard Arcenaux, and Eadie had met him six months ago when she wandered in off the street. He called her "Ea-*die,*" putting the emphasis on the second syllable, in that soft, sexy New Orleans accent that made her feel like she was walking across the deck of a rolling ship.

Eadie sighed and opened her eyes. Monkey Mind had gotten the best of her. There was no use denying it. Somewhere in the house her phone was chirping again. She got up and went inside, finding it finally beneath a pillow on the library sofa. The house phone began to ring incessantly but Eadie ignored it, too, checking the voice mail on her cell. Trevor had called for a third time but he hadn't left a message, which meant he was definitely going to be delayed in New York.

Fine. If he wasn't here, she'd use the next best thing. She'd do whatever she had to do, given the circumstances. Meditation sure as hell wasn't working. She stuffed the cell phone back under the sofa cushions and went upstairs to find her vibrator. She had named it Milton, which probably wasn't a healthy thing, she knew, but over the years, during two trial separations from Trevor, she had grown quite fond of the little machine. She rummaged around in the bathroom drawers for a while before finally locating it behind a stack of towels in the linen closet. Since she and Trevor had reconciled and moved to New Orleans, she hadn't had much need for Milton. It lay in its little box, patient and gleaming and ready for love.

Eadie lay down in her big empty bed and thought about Richard Arcenaux. She thought about his dark eyes and his full lower lip. She closed her eyes and imagined his arms around her. She imagined kissing his mouth. *Ea-die. Do you want a po' boy?*

Too bad meditation wasn't this easy.

She had just switched Milton on when she heard a sound deep within the house. The ghosts were back. She kept her eyes closed and imagined Richard climbing the stairs, two at a time, young and strong and eager. She heard a soft sliding sound but she refused to open her eyes, afraid she might see something otherworldly shimmering in the doorway.

"Eadie. What in the hell are you doing?"

Trevor stood in the doorway, looking tall and blond and handsome. His hair had grown shaggy around his ears and there was several days' growth of beard on his face. *That's what the Vikings looked like stepping off the long boats,* Eadie thought, shivering and pressing her knees together. She turned the vibrator off and sat up on her elbows.

"What does it look like I'm doing?" she said. "I'm pleasuring myself with Milton."

"I thought I told you to get rid of that damn thing," he said.

"You can't honestly tell me you're jealous of a mechanical object," she said, but he was already striding across the room and before she could react, he had taken Milton and unceremoniously tossed it out one of the opened French doors. They heard a distant clattering sound as Milton landed on the bricked patio.

Eadie recovered quickly after that. She flung a pillow at his head, followed by a picture frame, an alarm clock, and a magazine. Each time he ducked and advanced closer to the bed, grinning.

"I've been trying to reach you for six hours," he said. "Why don't you answer your cell phone? Or the house phone, for that matter?"

She looked around, trying to figure out what else she could throw. "I thought you were calling to tell me you weren't coming home."

"Well, actually, sweetheart, I was calling to see if you wanted to go out to dinner tonight. But I can see you have other plans for this evening."

"You flatter yourself."

He grinned. "I don't think so," he said.

"I've been alone for four days, peckerhead," she said. "Shut up in this big old house while you were off doing God knows what."

"Is a Georgia Homecoming Queen allowed to call her husband a peckerhead? Because I'm thinking, no. I'm thinking that might be grounds for impeachment or crown recall or whatever it is they do to bad homecoming queens." He pulled his shirt over his head and stepped out of his shoes.

"And I don't much like what you did to Milton," Eadie said. She leaned over on her stomach to reach for another picture frame, but Trevor, taking advantage of a lull in the action, grabbed her by the feet and pulled her toward him.

"Did you miss me?" he said.

She flipped over on her back and aimed another kick at his head but he caught her feet easily and held them with one hand while he deftly pulled her yoga pants over her hips with the other. Eadie, who was ticklish, giggled.

"I'm going to take that as a yes," he said. He stood up and unbuckled his belt. Eadie, released, scrambled up against the headboard. "Don't think it's going to be that easy," she said, trying to sound bored. She wasn't fooling anyone. Looking at her husband, she could see why women threw themselves at him at cocktail parties.

"It's a good thing I got home when I did," he said, shaking his head like a doctor diagnosing a serious condition. "It looks like I got here just in time."

"Just in time for what?" she said, and aimed another kick at his head.

"Just in time for this." He grinned and grabbed her ankles and pulled her toward him. He said, "You know I can do things Milton can't."

Of course he was right. After awhile there was no denying the truth of this statement. Eadie didn't even try.

Four days before her wedding, Nita arrived home to find Jimmy Lee and Whitney in the yard playing ball with Otis, the black Labrador. Jimmy Lee was holding the ball over his head and Whitney was leaning against his chest, trying to take it from him. Otis bounced around their feet, barking. Nita was amazed at how much Whitney had grown. She was tall for twelve. Almost as tall as Jimmy Lee. A few more inches and she wouldn't have any trouble taking the ball away from him.

He saw Nita and waved, flinging the ball toward the lake. Otis dutifully went after it. Whitney glanced over her shoulder and, seeing her mother, frowned and punched Jimmy Lee in the shoulder with her fist. Nita tried not to read too much into the disappointment she saw on her daughter's face. Her relationship with Whitney had grown prickly over the past year, but surely that was normal. Nita and her own mother had never had an adversarial relationship, but Nita had read enough books on child-rearing to know that sullen teenage girls were as common as ticks on a hound dog.

Whitney thumped Jimmy Lee on the head, and he began tickling her. It was an old game of theirs. Nita climbed slowly out of the car. She had left them in charge of stringing the wires the Japanese lanterns would hang from, but she could only see one lone wire running from the porch soffit to a distant pine tree. "I thought I told y'all to get those strung up," she said, pointing.

"We're taking a break," Whitney screeched, in between her giggles.

"Don't sass your mother," Jimmy Lee said. He let go of her and walked toward Nita, smiling. A slight breeze ruffled his dark hair. He wore faded blue jeans and a T-shirt that read *Motes Construction* across the front. Whitney thumped him between his broad shoulder blades, trying to draw his attention, but he ignored her. He picked

Nita up in his arms and spun her around.

"Are you ready to take the plunge, Miss James?" He never used her married name. It was as if he wanted to forget that part of her life had ever happened. He didn't mind that she had children, he just didn't like thinking about her being married to another man.

"I guess I am, Mr. Motes," she said, kissing him lightly, thinking she must be one of the luckiest brides alive to have a husband as young and handsome as he was.

"Motes," Whitney screeched. "What kind of a stupid name is that?"

He set Nita on her feet and kissed her hungrily. Whitney shot her a murderous look and stalked past them toward the house. He was still kissing Nita when the door slammed, hard, behind them.

He looked up then. "What's wrong with her?" he said.

She put her hands on both sides of his face and gave him a little shake. "She's gotten too big for tickling."

"Does anyone ever get too big for tickling?" he said, pinching her side.

"Stop that," she said. He'd cut his hair and it lay neatly against the nape of his neck. He'd always worn it long before, shoulder length, like a pirate or a Creek warrior, and she'd liked that, but this was nice, too. "Did Lavonne call?"

"She did. She said they'd deliver the tables and chairs on Friday morning."

"I sure hope it doesn't rain."

"The Weather Channel says Saturday will be clear and sunny."

Nita looked beyond him to the yard littered with wire and tools and dog toys. A rusty patio table with four chairs and a sagging umbrella sat under a chinaberry tree. "Just remember it was your idea to have a wedding. It was your idea to have it in the backyard."

"Hey." He put his finger under her chin and lifted it gently. "It's gonna be okay. You have to have a little faith, is all."

She smiled but her throat felt tight. "I'm sorry," she said. "It's just prenuptial jitters."

"Everything will be fine. You'll see." He dropped his head to nuzzle her neck but Nita protested. She put her hand on his chest and stared at him until he stopped grinning.

"I'm happy," she said. "I'm happy and I don't want to jinx it. I don't want anything to change."

He shook his head slowly. "It's not gonna change, baby, it's only gonna get better."

She put her hand up to his cheek. "Promise?" she said softly.

He grinned lazily, tightening his arms around her. "I promise, Mrs. Motes," he said, leaning to bite her earlobe.

Lavonne finished the 941 reports and went out front to relieve Little Moses so he could take a cigarette break. The lunch crowd had thinned considerably, rain was bad for tourism, and the new girl, Maureen, had no trouble handling the few customers that remained. Lavonne took out her checklist and went down the column carefully. She had ordered the chicken and the beef for Nita's wedding barbecue, and the tables and chairs were set to be delivered on Friday. Nita was expecting around seventy-five guests and she had insisted on a simple menu and red-checked tablecloths because she had had the fancy wedding before, and look how well that turned out. Everything was on schedule and Lavonne was glad because Eadie was arriving tomorrow and she seemed to be in a hard-drinking kind of mood. God only knew how much work she'd get done once Eadie got here.

The bell on the front door rang and Lavonne looked up. "Hello," she said. "Can I help you?"

He pushed the hood of his rain jacket back

and wiped his brow, smiling apologetically. "Sorry," he said. "I don't mean to drip water all over your freshly waxed floor."

She shrugged. "That's what mops are for." He had been in before, his face looked familiar.

"It always takes me a minute to decide," he said, leaning over the counter. "Everything looks so good."

"Well, everything is good," Lavonne said. "I can vouch for that."

He grinned. He was about forty-five, Lavonne was guessing; not tall, but the kind of man who kept himself in good shape. He wore no wedding ring. "Let me have a dozen of the dinner rolls," he said. "And a loaf of the sourdough bread, sliced."

Little Moses stuck his head out of the swinging door and said, "I'll get it." She wiped down the counter while Little Moses went in the back to slice a sourdough loaf.

The man watched her work, still smiling. He had laugh lines at the corners of his eyes. Lavonne liked that. A man with laugh lines in his face couldn't be all bad. "Lavonne," he said, reading her name tag. "That doesn't sound Jewish."

"I'm not Jewish," she said. "But my partner is."

He stuck his hand across the counter. "Joe

Solomon," he said.

Lavonne shook hands with him. "Lavonne Zibolsky."

"You don't sound like a native."

"Neither do you."

He laughed and dropped his hand. "I'm from New York originally. Upstate. I got transferred down here about six months ago."

"I'm from Cleveland. Originally. But I've been here almost twenty years."

"Wow. You must like it."

"I'm getting used to it. I've learned to *mash* a button and *carry* someone to the store, if you know what I mean."

"Very impressive." He crossed his arms over his chest and looked at her as if he were trying to read something in her face. "Let me guess," he said. "You followed a husband down here and you both liked it so much you refused a transfer to Minneapolis or Chicago or Buffalo or someplace else where it snows twelve feet a year."

"I followed him," Lavonne said. "He left. I stayed."

Little Moses came out with the sliced sourdough loaf and Lavonne pointed Joe toward the register. He followed her, pulling his wallet out of his back pocket.

"I don't know how you do it," he said, as

she rang him up.

"Do what?"

"Stay so slim. If I worked here I'd weigh three hundred pounds."

Lavonne was dismayed to find herself blushing. She stuffed the loaf of bread and the rolls quickly into a bag. "I hope your family enjoys the bread," she said, handing it to him.

"My family?" He grinned, taking the bag from her and shoving it down the front of his rain jacket. "It's just me," he said.

Lavonne smiled and went back to wiping down the counter.

At the door, he turned around and looked at her. "Same time next week?" he said.

"I'll be here," she said.

He grinned and went out, the door closing softly on his heels.

Virginia had been trying for weeks to figure out how to wrangle an invitation to Nita's wedding, so it was a special bit of luck when she ran into Nita at the grocery store the Wednesday before the ceremony. She had not seen Nita in months, and Virginia almost didn't recognize her. She looked so young and fresh, not like she had looked when she was married to Charles. Then she had looked pale and worn. Virginia supposed Nita's new look probably had something to do with the young handyman she was marrying. In Virginia's day, of course, such a thing would have been scandalous, but it was a sign of the times, she supposed, that everything seemed to be changing. Even here in the Bible Belt, a woman could run off and leave her husband of sixteen years just because she wasn't *happy*. She could take up with a man thirteen years her junior and no one thought anything of it.

"Yoo-hoo, Nita!" Virginia said, smiling and waving her hand. She pushed her cart in front of Nita's, effectively blocking any escape.

Nita, startled, put down a grapefruit and smiled bravely at her ex-mother-in-law. "Virginia," she said calmly. "How are you?"

Virginia smiled, showing a line of tiny white teeth. "Oh, I'm fine," she said. Nita's eyes slid past her to the grapefruits. "And how are the children? I had hoped to see them at my wedding. Charles said something about them being . . . indisposed."

Nita looked uncomfortable. This barb had found its mark surely and swiftly, as Virginia had known it would. "Yes. About that," Nita said, glancing at Virginia and then again at the grapefruits. Color crept into her cheeks and along the line of her brow. "They had planned on coming to your wedding, of course, but then something came up. . . ." Her voice trailed off helplessly. Nita had always been a bad liar and it appeared her skills at deception had not improved over the past year. Virginia wondered how in the world she had managed to pull off whatever trickery she had used to crush Charles into submission. Any fool could read Nita's intention in her face. *But then again,* Virginia thought unpleasantly, *I didn't see an ambush coming, either.* She stood watching her ex-daughter-in-law flounder around beneath her sharp steely gaze like a moth pinned to a mounting board.

Nita cleared her throat and tried again. "I've been meaning to bring them by. They've gotten so big you'd hardly recognize them. And Logan's driving now. He just got his license." She picked up a grapefruit. "I assumed Charles would bring them by to see you on one of his custody weekends, and I've been so busy planning . . ." She stopped. Color flooded her face. "I'm back in school, you know. My days are pretty crazy."

"But of course, you've been so busy planning the wedding and all," Virginia murmured. "Didn't I hear that you were getting remarried?" This barb also found its mark.

Nita put one hand on her forehead and rubbed the worry lines that appeared there suddenly. "You know, I've been meaning to call you about that," she began hesitantly.

"Don't these look good?" Virginia said, picking up a grapefruit.

"I've gotten so busy planning the wedding and being back in school and all."

"Two for a dollar," Virginia said, sniffing the grapefruit. "Doesn't that seem a little expensive?"

"But I had you on my list to call."

"When I was a child, you could buy a whole bag of grapefruits for a dollar."

"I thought since you hadn't seen the children in a while . . ."

"Oranges, too," Virginia said.

"I thought you might like to attend the wedding," Nita said flatly.

"Oh, I'd just *love* to." Virginia put the grapefruit down and smiled her most charming smile.

Later that night, at dinner, she told Redmon about the invitation to Nita's wedding.

"Aw, honey, you're not planning on going to that are you?" Redmon said. He sat with his elbows on the table, a knife in one hand and a fork in the other, hunkered down over his plate like a hyena guarding a freshly killed wildebeest.

"Of course I'm going," Virginia snapped, trying not to watch him eat. "Why wouldn't I go?" She was curious to see the life Nita had made for herself after giving up a half-million-dollar house in the suburbs and a country club membership all in the name of *love.* Running into her in the grocery store had been a personal coup. Virginia was glad to know she still had the power to manipulate her ex-daughter-in-law into doing things she didn't want to do. Now if she could only figure out some way to manipulate her husband.

Redmon was proving more difficult to train than Virginia had originally anticipated. She had expected, after a few days, to have him well in hand, and here it was nearly a week later and he still insisted on slurping his soup and telling off-color jokes at the dinner table. He still persisted, for some unknown reason, in calling her "Queenie" and slapping her on the rear end whenever she was within striking distance.

"But Queenie," Redmon said, opening his mouth to reveal a mass of half-chewed pot roast. "I thought after what them girls done to your boy, Charles, you wouldn't want to go to that wedding."

Virginia leaned forward. "What *did* they do to him?" she asked grimly.

54

Redmon grinned and smacked his oily lips. "Now, baby doll, you know I can't tell you that. You know what happens in Montana, stays in Montana."

Virginia gritted her teeth and looked down at the carpet. It was called Elvis Red and Virginia had never seen the color in any decorator's catalog or carpet showroom. She was pretty sure Redmon must have paid thousands of dollars extra to have it specially dyed so it could look as gauche and tacky as it did.

He knew what had happened in Montana because he'd been there. But he wasn't talking. At least not now. Not only had she not been able to pry the secret of the Montana hunting trip out of him, but she'd also been unable to do anything about this monument to bad taste that they lived in. He seemed determined to keep a tight rein on their personal finances, giving her an allowance so small she could barely buy groceries, much less entertain, or redecorate the garish mansion Redmon called home. Just yesterday she had been forced to host her bridge group at the house and she had overheard Lee Anne Bales and Worland Pendergrass giggling and whispering over the gold-plated fixtures in the master bathroom with its marble floors, marble walls, and crushed velvet draperies. Not to mention the built-in, lighted cabinet in the master bedroom highlighting Redmon's collection of Elvis memorabilia, and the king-size bed that was actually suspended from the ceiling by four gold-plated chains. Virginia had glanced in the bedroom door to find Lee Anne and Worland laying on their backs on the gently swaying bed, looking up at the huge ceiling mirror and giggling like a couple of schoolgirls.

"My God, it's like a New Orleans whorehouse," Lee Anne said.

Worland snorted and put her hand over her mouth. "How desperate did Virginia have to be to marry into this," she said.

Pretty damn desperate. Virginia had stood just outside the door and felt her face burn with rage and humiliation. She could not bear to have people laugh at her. But looking around the great room with its huge stacked stone fireplace, big-screen TV, faux-wood furniture, and overstuffed Naugahyde seating group, complete with built-in beer cooler and remote control caddy, she could not blame them for laughing. She would have laughed, too, had it been anyone besides herself married to Redmon.

"All I'm saying . . ." Redmon said, grease glistening along his top lip. "All I'm saying is you might not want to show up for that wedding after what them girls did to your boy." He grinned and shook his head. "Them girls is trouble," he said.

"They don't know what trouble is," Virginia muttered, staring balefully at the Elvis Red carpet.

"What?" Redmon bellowed. *Good God,* he had hair growing out of his ears. She could see it clearly beneath the glare of the gold-plated crystal chandelier. *The Big-Ass Chandelier.* It was how Virginia referred to the monstrosity in the privacy of her own mind. It was on her long list of things that would have to go.

"Nothing," she said.

The swinging door between the dining room and the kitchen swung open and Della Smurl came out carrying a plate of biscuits. Della was the only African-American woman in Ithaca, Georgia, still willing to don a maid's outfit and do domestic work — for the right price, of course. She'd struggled to send three children to graduate school before she figured out that white folks — white folks like Virginia, anyway — were willing to pay any price just to feel like they were back in the good old days before civil rights. Before an uppity little black woman by the name of Rosa Parks rocked their world forever and brought the good old days crashing down around their ears.

Now Della made close to six figures a year, took vacations to the Bahamas, and had a retirement account she could live on for thirty years.

"I told you to make yeast rolls, not biscuits," Virginia said sharply.

Della set the platter of biscuits down, loudly, on the table in front of Redmon. He greedily filled his plate. "I don't have time to make yeast rolls," Della said belligerently. She'd wear the uniform, for the right price, but she'd be damned if she'd take the same shit she'd had to take before Rosa Parks. "You got to let it rise and beat it down and let it rise again and I don't have time for all that nonsense. Not if you want me to make a pot roast, too."

"In point of fact," Virginia said icily, "I did *not* want you to make pot roast. I wanted you to make *Boeuf Bourguignon*." She'd gone to all the trouble to put together a menu, complete with recipes, and Della hadn't followed a single one. Instead, she substituted whatever simple fare she saw fit to substitute.

Della put her hand on her ample hip, but before she could say anything, Redmon said, "I like biscuits. I like pot roast." He grinned like an idiot with his mouth full of biscuit, and winked at the black woman. She smirked at Virginia and left the room.

Virginia counted to ten. How was she supposed to bring culinary culture to this house when her husband insisted on siding with the help? When his idea of fine dining was baked possum stuffed with sweet potatoes, and turnip greens? Virginia counted to ten again, wondering how in the world Myra had stood it all those years. She stared down at the glass dining table with its gold ram's horn base surrounded by chairs upholstered in faux zebra skin, wondering what in the world she had gotten herself into.

It's not like she hadn't been warned. It's not like she'd gone into this marriage with blinders on. She had known Redmon for years, of course. He had been married to her staunchest comrade-in-arms, Myra (Virginia did not have female friends, only allies), and Virginia had pegged him correctly within ten minutes of their first meeting — he was socially uncouth, and as loud and unsophisticated in his dress and manners as only a nouveau riche redneck can be. Still, when Myra was killed in a tragic tennis accident, and Virginia's own fortunes took a tumble thanks to a portfolio overly invested in growth stocks and growth mutual funds, not to mention the demise of Boone & Broadwell, she had begun to look differently at Redmon. He *was* rumored to be one of the wealthiest men in Georgia. And she *had* managed, after several years of steady, patient work, to civilize the Judge.

But she had underestimated Redmon. She saw this now. Behind his Gomer Pyle exterior there lurked the wily, stubborn nature of a street-smart hillbilly — the kind of man her father used to call "smart as an outhouse rat." And to make matters worse, it seemed Redmon had been carrying a secret torch for Virginia for nearly thirty years, and not only insisted on actually consummating their marriage, but insisted on consummating it nightly.

Virginia spent a good part of her time these days trying to avoid her marriage bed and cursing the chemist who had discovered Viagra.

"We're going to that wedding," Virginia said curtly.

Redmon chewed steadily and watched her with a crafty expression on his big red face. "What you got up your sleeve, Queenie?" he said. "What's going on in that pretty little head of yours?"

"I don't know what you mean," she said stiffly, avoiding his gaze. She raised her voice and said, "Della, more tea."

There was no sound but for the steady *clomping* of Redmon's bicuspids chewing through a rather large piece of pot roast.

"Della," she said sharply.

Nothing.

"Della, I know you hear me."

The door swung open violently and Della came back in carrying a pitcher of sweet tea. "I don't know why some folks can't eat in the kitchen," she grumbled. "I don't know why some folks can't think of other folks and their bad feet every once in a while."

Redmon, of course, fell for it. "You want us to eat in the kitchen, Della?" he said. "We can if it's easier on you." Della put the pitcher down and went out, still grumbling.

Virginia stared at Redmon. She insisted on eating dinner in the formal dining room every evening. She was trying to set a standard. She was attempting to entice Redmon into leaving his Alabama hog-farm roots behind him, and if enticement didn't work she was determined to drag him kicking and screaming into the realm of good breeding and good taste. She was determined to overcome his penchant for gold-plated fixtures and expensive, but tasteless, furnishings, and the first thing to go, she

61

decided savagely, would be the Elvis Red carpet.

What was it Oscar Wilde had said on his deathbed, looking at the room's gaudy wallpaper? *One of us will have to go.* That was pretty much the way Virginia felt about the red carpet. That was pretty much the way Virginia felt about her whole damn marriage.

Redmon finished his meal, belched, and pushed himself away from the table, rubbing his big round belly with both hands. "Well, Queenie, what's it to be tonight? The Cheerleader and the Coach? The Naughty Secretary and the Boss? The French Maid and the Millionaire?"

Virginia thought she heard Della snort in the kitchen. "Not tonight, I have a headache," she said.

"You had a headache last night," Redmon said, standing up from the table.

"I really need to see a doctor about these migraines," Virginia said, putting her hand over her eyes and watching his big, booted feet cross the red carpet toward her.

"I know just the thing for migraines," he said in her ear, leaning down to kiss her. She turned her face to give him her cheek but he was wise to that move, and swiveled his head around, clamping his mouth over hers.

She pushed him away with both hands, standing up so quickly her faux zebra chair nearly toppled over.

He grinned in that particularly juvenile way men have when they are trying to convince an unwilling woman. "It's your turn to decide, Queenie," he said slapping her on the bottom. "But if you don't, I will!"

"What about your heart?"

"What about it?" he said.

"Do you really think the exertion would be good for you?" she said, looking around desperately. "So soon after a big meal?"

"You let me worry about my heart," he said, slapping her again on the rear end. "What's it to be, Queenie?"

"Oh, all right," she snapped. "How about the Naughty Schoolboy and the School-teacher?" She said it half in jest but his eyes got round and a spot of pink appeared on both cheeks.

He lowered his voice and said earnestly, "Will you spank me in front of the whole class, Teacher?"

"Oh, good God," she said, but he had already grabbed her hand and was pulling her toward the bedroom door.

CHAPTER THREE

Lavonne picked Eadie up at the airport on Wednesday evening and they stopped just south of Atlanta for dinner. Eadie seemed restless and quiet, like she had something on her mind but didn't want to talk about it. Lavonne had known her long enough to know that it was no good pushing her; Eadie would talk when she was ready.

They went to bed early, and when Lavonne got home from work the next day, Eadie was standing in the kitchen holding a metal cocktail shaker. Something that smelled wonderful bubbled in the pot on the stove behind her.

"What are you making?" Lavonne said, lifting the lid.

"Jambalaya. I learned to make it in New Orleans. It's all I know how to cook." Eadie looked better than she had the night before, more rested and less somber. She was wearing a pair of corduroy jeans and a V-necked sweater that showed off her good figure to full advantage. Her feet were bare.

Lavonne said, "How come you're addicted to Mondo Logs and you still look like that?"

Eadie grinned. "Look who's talking," she said. "Sit your skinny ass down at the bar and I'll pour you a drink."

Lavonne sat down. "What are we having?"

Eadie flourished the shaker like a Japanese hibachi chef wielding a Hiromoto knife. "Pomegranate martinis." She took two frosted martini glasses out of the freezer and sat them on the counter in front of Lavonne, filling each with the pale-pink liquid. "Cheers," she said, handing a glass to Lavonne.

"Damn, that's good," Lavonne said, sipping. "Where'd you get the shaker?"

"I brought it from home."

"What does that say about you, Eadie, that you travel with your own martini shaker?"

Eadie sipped her drink. "It says I like the ritual of cocktail hour. I like everything about it, the funny little glasses, the gleaming metal shaker, the routine of drinking at the same time every day. Cocktail hour is a holdover from our parents' generation. Why did we ever give it up?"

"Our generation had drugs. We didn't need martinis."

"True." Eadie put her drink down and went over to the pot to stir the jambalaya. "I called Nita. She's coming over for dinner. She made me promise this wasn't some crazy ploy to give her a bachelorette party, but I told her it was just you and me."

"And she agreed to come? Silly girl. Quick, let's call some strippers."

Eadie put the lid on the pot and turned around. "She sounds like she needs a night out. Don't you two see much of each other anymore?" She leaned against the stove with one arm draped across her stomach and the other one holding her drink.

"Not really." Lavonne sipped her martini. "I hate to say it, on account of you getting a big head and all, but it's not the same since you left town."

Eadie colored slightly. She smiled. "Well, we'll have to make up for lost time," she said.

The timer went off and Eadie took the rice off the heat and stuck a loaf of French bread into the oven. Lavonne watched her work, feeling lazy and relaxed. The vodka had gone straight to her brain and she had a nice buzz going. "Are you sure you don't need any help?" she said to Eadie.

"Nope." Eadie took the top off the shaker and poured them both another drink. The buzzing in Lavonne's head got louder. "Oh hell, that's my cell phone," Eadie said, putting the shaker down. "It's probably Trevor. I'll be right back." She rushed out of the room and Lavonne could hear her a minute later in Louise's room. "Are you going to call me every hour?" she said, and Lavonne got up to turn on the radio so she wouldn't have to hear the whole conversation. The house was small and the ceilings were high so sound carried.

Winston came through the door wagging his tail slowly and Lavonne leaned down to scratch his ears. "So there you are, you lazy good for nothing," she said fondly. He whined and grinned up at her and she went to the door to let him out. Eadie was still on the phone and Lavonne sat back down at the counter to wait. It was true what she had said about Nita; they rarely saw each other these days. You would think, in a town as small as Ithaca, that they might run into each other occasionally, but both had busy and very different lives. They had once been neighbors who saw each other practically every day, but even then it had been Eadie who had brought them all together. She was the glue that had kept their friendship intact.

Lavonne lifted the metal shaker and poured herself another drink. On the radio,

Van Morrison sang his ode to brown-eyed girls. Lavonne sipped her drink and thought about all the years she had known Eadie Boone. *Twenty years.* Their friendship had lasted longer than most marriages, almost as long as her ill-fated marriage to Leonard Zibolsky.

In the back bedroom, Eadie shouted, "Don't be such an asshole, Trevor."

Lavonne had met Eadie and Trevor Boone soon after she and Leonard moved to Ithaca from Cleveland. It was at a party at the Boone mansion, and Eadie was standing on a table singing the Georgia fight song. Trevor was trying to convince her to climb down, but he was laughing, too, and looking at Eadie like she was the only girl in the world for him. They were two of the best-looking people Lavonne had ever seen.

Eadie lost no time introducing herself. "Hey," she said. "Don't drink that shit." She threw Lavonne's glass of Chablis over her shoulder and handed her a margarita.

Lavonne knew immediately that they would be friends.

Leonard tolerated the friendship for as long as he could, which turned out to be about three weeks. Lavonne had been a quiet, steady girl in high school and college who concentrated on keeping her grade point average as close to 4.0 as possible. But Eadie Boone changed all that. Under Eadie's tutelage Lavonne became the crazy, irresponsible girl she'd never dared to be before. They were like Catholic schoolgirls on a weekend binge. They went to endless parties, took Trevor's credit card and stayed at the Ritz Carlton in Atlanta, went on wild beach trips, and out to Bad Bob's to drink tequila and dance with peanut farmers and cowboys. It didn't take long for news of their exploits to reach Leonard.

"Y'all are going to ruin your reputations," Leonard said one night at dinner. He'd only been in Ithaca a few weeks but already he used "y'all" like he'd used it all his life. Leonard had lost no time going native, standing in front of the bathroom mirror and practicing his Southern accent, wearing loafers without socks and madras plaid shorts to numerous parties.

"This isn't high school, Leonard."

"But it is a small town. A small town I have to make a living in. What you and Eadie do reflects poorly on the firm."

"You have to be kidding me."

"No, Lavonne, I am not kidding you." He was chubby and balding and when he got angry the bald spot on the back of his head glowed under the overhead lights. "You and

Eadie seem to think you can run wild with no repercussions. You don't see Nita Broadwell acting that way. She doesn't jump naked into swimming pools or streak across the Wal-Mart parking lot."

"That was Eadie. I never take my clothes off."

"Nita Broadwell does everything Charles tells her to do."

"Yeah, well, Nita needs to get a life. Charles is an asshole."

Leonard looked offended. "He's my law partner," he said, his bald spot pulsing. "And Nita Broadwell is a good Southern wife."

She reached out and flicked his nose like she was killing a mosquito.

"Well, Leonard, if you wanted a good Southern wife, maybe you should have married one."

She had been angry then, but Lavonne chuckled now, remembering. Leonard's new trophy wife, Christy, was Southern. She was from Soddy Daisy, Tennessee, and called herself *Creesty.*

"What are you laughing at?" Eadie said, coming back into the kitchen.

"Nothing. Can you make up another shaker of those martinis?"

"Is the pope Catholic?" Eadie said. "Does

a fifty-pound sack of flour make a big biscuit?"

By the time Nita showed up thirty minutes later, they had finished off their second shaker and were giggling about the time they sent a Stripagram to Worland Pendergrass's husband, Connelly, during the middle of a big dinner party.

"Nita!" Eadie said, when she saw her standing in the doorway. "Come over here, girl, and give me a hug."

"Y'all aren't drinking are you?" Nita said, taking off her coat and laying it over the back of one of the chairs. She hugged Eadie and then Lavonne.

"Of course we're drinking," Lavonne said. "Join us." She patted the stool next to her and Nita sat down at the counter. Eadie stubbed her cigarette out in an ashtray and got up to make some more drinks.

"Where'd you get the cigarettes?"

Lavonne blew a couple of smoke rings at the ceiling. "Ashley's room. We found them in the bottom drawer of her dresser next to a box of diet pills that she also told me she didn't use."

Nita giggled. "Y'all are terrible," she said.

Eadie danced around the kitchen, shaking her hips to the rhythm of the cocktail shaker like a hyperactive Carmen Miranda, like

71

Charo on speed. She opened the freezer and took out three freshly chilled glasses and poured martinis all around.

"This'll put hair on your chest," Eadie said.

"Nectar of the gods," Lavonne said.

"Is something burning?" Nita asked, sniffing.

Eadie looked at Lavonne. "Oh shit," she said. "The bread." She threw on a couple of mitts and flung open the oven door. A thick cloud of black smoke rolled out and Eadie reached in and retrieved the loaf of bread that now looked like a long narrow charcoal briquette. She carried it out onto the back deck, smoke billowing in her wake, and set the baking sheet down on the railing. Lavonne followed her out. They both stood looking down at the black lump of burned bread.

"Oops," Eadie said.

"Martha Stewart you're not," Lavonne said.

"That's the problem with martinis. You lose track of time. It's like being caught in a time werp."

"Did you just say a time *werp?* Have another martini, Eadie."

Eadie put her arm around Lavonne's shoulder. She pointed at the brick of burned bread. "Who's hungry?" she said.

Nita stood in the doorway and watched them laugh. She hoped it wouldn't take long for the martini to work its magic. She hoped it wouldn't take long to feel whatever it was they were feeling.

Eadie put her other arm around Nita and they went back into the house. Lavonne and Nita sat down at the counter. "I haven't laughed that hard in a long time," Lavonne said. "I think I might have pulled something."

Eadie took some bowls down from the cupboard. "Who wants jambalaya?" she said.

Later, after they had finished eating, Nita got up to stack the bowls and silverware in the dishwasher.

"Leave it, Nita," Lavonne said, lighting up another cigarette. "We'll clean up in the morning."

"Pass me one of those cancer sticks," Eadie said.

Nita sat back down at the bar. She was working on her third martini now and she was feeling relaxed and happy. She giggled. "I definitely won't be driving home tonight. I'll have to call Jimmy Lee to come get me," she said.

"Just spend the night here," Lavonne said.

"Yeah," Eadie said. "Let's have a slumber party."

Jimmy Lee wouldn't like that one little bit. He wouldn't tell her *no,* but he wouldn't be very happy about it, either. "I've got class in the morning," Nita said. "I shouldn't even be staying up this late when I have to get up at seven o'clock."

"Oh come on, Nita, live a little."

"Yeah," Eadie said. "It's bad luck for the groom to see you before the wedding."

Nita didn't like to think about this. She didn't like to hear *bad luck* and *wedding* spoken in the same sentence. She was jittery enough as it was. She sipped her drink and said to Lavonne, hoping to change the subject, "Were you able to find those little sweet peppers we talked about?"

"Don't change the subject," Lavonne said.

"What are you studying at school?" Eadie said. "What are you hoping to be when you grow up?"

"I'm not sure yet. I'm trying to decide whether to major in women's studies or elementary ed."

"I can see you as a teacher," Eadie said. "You're always so patient. I'd rather poke sticks in my eyes than work with a bunch of kids all day, but you'd be good at it."

"Is that meant to be a compliment or an

insult?" Lavonne said.

"I like kids," Nita said. "I volunteer at the school every chance I get. I substitute teach when I can."

"What was the name of that little girl you practically adopted back when your kids were small?"

"Angel," Nita said. "Angel Phipps."

"Hey, I remember Angel," Eadie said. "She kind of reminded me of myself at that age. She's the one you bought clothes and books and toys for. The one you had over for dinner all the time."

Lavonne said, "The one who let the air out of Charles's tires. The one who played street hockey with his golf clubs and put rocks in his shoes."

Eadie grinned. "She didn't much like him, did she?"

"She was a sweet child," Nita said.

"Hell, Nita, you'd say that about little Charlie Manson. You'd think little Jackie the Ripper was precious. You think everyone is sweet."

Nita colored slightly and shook her head. "No I don't," she said.

Lavonne said, "Little Jackie the Ripper?"

Eadie smiled lazily and twirled her hair around one finger. "How're your kids doing?" she said to Nita.

"They're fine," Nita said. "Logan just got his license and he drives Whitney to school for me every morning. He likes public school so much better than he ever liked Barron Hall. He seems a lot more comfortable there." She looked apologetically at Lavonne, whose daughter had graduated early from Barron Hall and gone off to college just a few weeks ago.

Lavonne shrugged. "Hey, private school isn't for everyone," she said.

"How about Whitney?"

Nita frowned, looking down at the pale-pink liquid in the bottom of her glass. "I'm not sure if Whitney is happier or not. Nothing much seems to please her these days."

"Don't worry about that," Lavonne said. "She's an adolescent girl. It's her job to be surly and ungrateful. Trust me, I know. I've raised two daughters."

"I was terrible to my mother," Eadie said, finishing off her drink.

"Really?" Nita said, feeling hopeful. She had always felt it was her duty to make her children happy, it was one of the primary reasons she had left Charles, and Whitney's morose behavior left her with a sense of her own failure as a parent. She and her own mother, Loretta, had always been close. Nita could not remember ever fighting with

Loretta the way Whitney fought with her.

"Lavonne says you're writing a paper that might get published."

Nita smiled shyly, happy to talk about something besides her daughter. "It's for my Women's Roles in the Post-Depression America class. I've been interviewing women who worked as domestic servants in the South prior to the civil rights movement. My professor thinks it might be good enough for publication."

Eadie put her arm around Nita. "I'm so proud of you," she said. "See how everything's worked out for the best? A year and a half ago you were still married to that asshole, Charles Broadwell, and now you've taken control of your life and gone back to school and you're getting ready to marry the man of your dreams." She got up and poured another round of drinks. Nita wished she could feel as optimistic as Eadie did. She didn't tell them how the women's sad stories had affected her in a way that went deeper than the usual relationship between an interviewer and interviewee.

"What did you decide to do about your honeymoon?" Lavonne asked.

Nita shook her head. "We're not taking one. At least not now. I've got school and there's no one to leave the children with, so

I think we're going to take one in the summer, when the kids are on vacation with Charles." She sipped her drink and then put it back down. "Not everyone takes a honeymoon. It doesn't mean anything. Virginia didn't take one."

Eadie rolled her eyes. "Hey, I'm having a good time here," she said. "Let's try not to spoil my buzz by talking about Virginia." She looked steadily at Nita. Nita pretended to find something floating in her glass. Eadie said, "Please don't tell me you still talk to that old witch."

Nita tapped the edge of her glass nervously. She didn't tell them how she'd gotten a call yesterday about a woman named Leota Quarles, who had supposedly worked for Virginia's family back when Virginia was a girl. Nita was still trying to figure out whether or not to take the interview. "I ran into her in the grocery store," she said, waving her hand vaguely.

"Well that was a special bit of bad luck for you," Lavonne said. "But remember, you don't owe her anything. She's your *ex*-mother-in-law."

"That's right," Eadie said. "Count your blessings."

"And Jimmy Lee's mother is dead so you won't have a new mother-in-law."

"There you go," Eadie said. "Count another blessing."

"Not everybody has bad mothers-in-law," Nita said. She looked at the calendar above the phone. She cleared her throat. "Sometimes people change," she said in a small defiant voice.

Eadie and Lavonne looked at each other. The clock ticked steadily on the wall. A delivery truck rumbled down the street, its headlights casting geometric shadows against Lavonne's plantation shutters. "Is there something you want to tell us, Nita?" Eadie said, looking at her curiously.

Nita cleared her throat again. "How's Trevor?" she said.

Eadie glanced at Lavonne and then back at Nita. "He's fine. He said to give you a big hug and tell you congratulations."

"He's so sweet." A delicate blue vein threaded its way up Nita's temple. She touched it lightly with her fingers and then dropped her hand back down on the counter. "I'm just so proud of him, about the book and all. I can't wait to read it."

A muscle moved in Eadie's cheek. "Let me guess," she said flatly. "You invited Virginia to the wedding."

Nita flushed and pushed her hair out of her face. "Look, y'all, she's the children's grandmother," she said stubbornly. She fanned her fingers out and flattened them on the counter on either side of her glass. "I believe in forgiveness and redemption. I believe in giving people a second chance. Virginia's not the same person she was when I was married to Charles."

"Really?" Eadie said, raising one eyebrow. "Was there an exorcism while I was away? Did someone call a priest while I was in New Orleans?"

Lavonne, who had sat quietly through all this, said, "Actually, Nita may have a point. Regardless of what Virginia may have done in the past, regardless of how underhanded, selfish, immoral, and unethical she may have been, Nita's forgiveness of her sets Nita on the path to psychological wholeness and redemption."

"Is that the pomegranate martinis talking, Lavonne, or is that you?"

"Mix up another shaker and I'll let you know."

"I shouldn't drink any more," Nita said. "I should call Jimmy Lee to come get me. He'll be worried."

"Forgiveness is overrated," Eadie said. She lifted her drink, took a long pull, and then set the glass down carefully on the counter. "Revenge. Now there's a concept you can sink your teeth into, there's a concept you can build your whole damn life around." She looked at Lavonne for confirmation.

"Put a scooch less pomegranate in this batch," Lavonne said. "I like to taste my vodka."

Eadie made up a new batch and poured another round of drinks. "I really should get going," Nita said. "I've got a lot to do tomorrow."

Eadie propped her chin on her hand. She waved her finger back and forth in front of Nita's nose. "Just say the word, Nita, and I'll call Virginia and uninvite her from the wedding."

Lavonne sipped her drink. "You don't owe her a thing," she said.

"I've thought about this and I think it's the right thing to do." Nita frowned and shook her head. "It's like starting over, you know. Rebuilding fences."

"Fences?" Eadie said. "Hell, you'll need to build a goddamn fortress if you're dealing with Virginia."

"Build a siege engine," Lavonne said.

"A trebuchet," Eadie said. "Or better yet, an underground bunker."

Nita giggled. She pulled her cell phone out of her purse to call Jimmy Lee. "Y'all are overacting," she said. "Virginia's not that bad."

Virginia awoke on Friday morning to find Redmon gone. This was a rare occurrence; they normally breakfasted together, and she found herself wondering if he might have tired of her already. Far from depressing her, this thought gave her a little hopeful trembling sensation in the pit of her stomach. But when she went into the kitchen, she found a note beneath the sugar jar: "Queenie, had to go up to Atlanta. I'll bring you something nice. Love Red." Virginia shuddered to think what "something nice" might be. The last gift he gave her had been a leopard-print push-up bra and matching thong, the kind of thing Jane might have worn if she was trying to coax Tarzan into a new zebra-skin sofa for the tree house.

Virginia poured herself a cup of coffee and sat down at the kitchen table. Behind her the coffeepot gurgled and steamed. She sipped her coffee and tried not to think about last night. She supposed the slight tinge of self-loathing and nausea she was feeling was probably no different from what a Saigon brothel girl must feel every morning of her life. Her marriage to the Judge had been no different, although with him sex had been all about power; and with Redmon it was all about his admiration of her. She supposed, in some distant, remote, unexplored crevice of her heart, she felt flattered. It wasn't love, but it wasn't exactly disgust, either. At least, not entirely.

Bright sunlight fell through the long windows, and beyond the lawn a dark rim of trees rose against a slate blue sky. She glanced at the newspaper that Redmon had left open on the table. After a while, fortified by her second cup of coffee and unable to stop herself, she picked up the paper and opened it to the editorial page. It was a long-standing habit, one of which, although painful, Virginia had never been able to break herself. The woman's photograph, small and gray, hung from the upper-left corner of the editorial page. Her byline read "Grace Pearson, Staff Writer." She seemed to gaze out at Virginia with the scornful, knowing expression of one who smells something foul, and knows it emanates from Virginia's direction. How anyone could name a six-foot, overeducated, liberal-minded Amazon *Grace* was beyond Virginia's comprehension.

Grace Pearson was a local girl whose parents had had the misfortune and short-sightedness to send to Wellesley. She had

83

rewarded them by returning to her hometown to work as a political writer for the local newspaper, where she churned out truckloads of liberal propaganda. She and Virginia had been enemies for years.

One of Pearson's earliest editorial targets had been Judge Broadwell. She had written an article about the strict sentencing of juveniles and African Americans that occurred in his courtroom. In the article she referred to him as "the Hanging Judge." On reading this, he had gone into an apoplectic fit so severe Virginia had thought he was having a stroke. After that, he took to calling Pearson a femi-Nazi obstructionist and would read her editorials aloud every afternoon over cocktails and rant and rave like a lunatic.

After he died, Pearson took on his son. Charles had been named president of the Bar Association and was just beginning what he hoped would be a long and illustrious career that might end in the governor's mansion or, who knew, maybe even in the U.S. Senate. As president of the Bar Association, he had made it his mission to try and bridge the deep divide that existed between the local legal and medical professions. With that in mind, he had gone out to the Ithaca County Hospital to observe doctors in action, the idea being that direct observation of the daily life-and-death decisions made in the operating room might lead to more understanding on the part of the legal profession for their medical colleagues. The walk-a-mile-in-my-shoes theory. Unfortunately for all concerned, Dr. Willis Guffey had ruined this opportunity for conciliation by choosing this very day to operate on the wrong knee of a young black athlete by the name of Dicie Meeks. This blunder was made worse by the arrogant Dr. Guffey, who, on being informed of his mistake at the first slice of the scalpel by the operating room nurse, quickly cursed her into horrified silence and continued cutting, bellowing from time to time, "Goddamn it! I don't see a thing wrong with this knee. Cartilage is fine. What in the hell is wrong with these people? Wasting my time like this! There's not a goddamn thing wrong with this knee!"

Charles did what he could to hush the matter up, using his position and considerable influence to ensure that no local lawyer agreed to take the Meeks case. But Meeks's parents went to Grace Pearson, and when the story broke, the scandal it caused reached all the way to the capital and beyond, thus forever squashing Charles

Broadwell's plans for a political career.

Virginia shook out the paper and raised it to eye level. Despite her determination not to, she began to read. Pearson's column today was on the inequality of women in the workforce. The whole time she read, Virginia kept her top lip curled in a scornful grimace.

Having survived the treacheries of a man's world, Virginia had little compassion for the less determined members of her own sex. She had never had a close female friendship, she gave her money to preachers who preached against the independence of women, voted against legislation that promoted sexual equality, and was a staunch member of the Republican Party. Indeed, it was during her stint as president of the local Republican Women's Club that her secret dislike of Grace Pearson had flared into open warfare. Virginia believed that a lady should never disgrace herself by allowing her name in print, but angered by one of Pearson's columns, and emboldened by the example set by her own personal hero, Phyllis Schlafly, Virginia had responded in a quarter-page letter to the editor. She had refuted Pearson's liberal viewpoint with an argument no sane, feminine, well-bred Christian woman could possibly deny as truth. Rather than retiring from the field in shame, Grace Pearson had mounted her own counter-attack, one that began with the bold-faced, italicized words, *My Dear Madame President.*

Realizing she could never win, Virginia had eventually tired of the game, refusing to respond openly to any of Pearson's jibes. Instead, during Bill Clinton's tumultuous years, she had taken to sending Pearson political cartoons that portrayed Clinton's relationships with Monica Lewinsky and Paula Jones in a less than favorable light. Since George Bush ascended the throne, Pearson had reciprocated, sending Virginia political cartoons and pages from a calendar that parodied the president's speeches. The one she received last week had read, "We've got to make sure there is more affordable homes," and the one yesterday read, "God loves you, and I love you. And you can count on both of us as a powerful message that people who wonder about their future can hear." Virginia saw nothing wrong with the last one. She thought it was rather sweet.

She closed the newspaper defiantly and rose and went over to the trash compactor to throw it away. In the overall scheme of things, Grace Pearson was just a minor irritation. Virginia had more important things to think about. Tomorrow was Nita's wedding day, and Virginia had to decide what she was going to wear and how she was going to conduct herself. She had a lot of plotting and planning to do if she was ever going to ferret out what Nita had done to Charles to make him agree to that ridiculous divorce settlement without so much as a whimper. Once she figured that out, then she'd know how to even the score.

With any luck, and a good deal of effort, she'd know the truth tomorrow.

CHAPTER FOUR

The day of the wedding dawned bright and sunny. There was frost on the grass, but by nine o'clock it had warmed up to close to sixty-eight degrees. Lavonne and Eadie showed up a little early to help set up the buffet, but by twelve-thirty Nita was still running around the yard dressed in sweatpants with her hair done up in big rollers. The ceremony was set to begin at two o'clock, followed by a buffet and live music.

"Shouldn't you be getting dressed?" Lavonne said, when she saw her. "Shouldn't you be resting?"

"I should be doing a lot of things," Nita said, looking like she might cry. "I told Jimmy Lee and the kids to get those lanterns strung and all the dog toys put up and they're just now getting around to it. I told them yesterday to get this yard cleaned up."

Eadie put her arm around Nita. "Now calm down," she said. "Everything's going to be fine. You should be enjoying this. I mean, this is the day you've looked forward to your whole life."

Nita snapped, "Why does everyone keep saying that? How does everyone know what I look forward to? For all y'all know I might have looked forward to being the president of the United States."

Eadie raised one eyebrow and looked at Lavonne, who frowned and shook her head slightly. Nita dropped her face in her hands. "I'm sorry," she said. "It's just nerves, is all."

Nita's mother, Loretta, saw them and came over to say hello. "She's nervous as a long-tailed cat in a room full of rocking chairs," she said, nodding at Nita. "She's making us all jumpy." Loretta was an upright little woman who hailed originally from a little farming town just east of Ithaca. She had a sweet face and a bad temper, and around town she was known as a good person not to mess with. She and Nita were about as much alike as a pit bull and a poodle.

Lavonne grinned. "You got your hair done, Loretta."

"My nails, too," she said, holding up ten coral-colored fingers that matched her dress perfectly. "It ain't every day your only daughter gets married, and to the right man this time, too. Praise the Lord."

"I'll drink to that," Eadie said.

"Well, from the looks of you girls, I'd say you been doing just that. You look a little wet around the gills, if you know what I mean."

"There's no fooling you, Loretta."

Loretta grinned. Her blue-black hair shone in the sunlight. She put her arm around Nita and kissed her on the cheek. "Come on, baby doll," she said. "Let's get you dressed for your wedding."

"I'll be right in, Mama. I've got to check on a few things first."

Loretta put her hand on her hip. Her coral dress fluttered in the breeze. "Check on what?"

"Check on whether or not Jimmy Lee got the rest of those lanterns hung."

Loretta waved her hand and stuck her chin out. "I'll take care of all that," she said. "You leave that to me." She sailed off across the yard like a bantam rooster attempting flight, her coral dress fluttering about her shoulders and her blue-black hair glistening in the sunlight.

Nita sighed, watching her go. "Whatever you do," she said to Lavonne and Eadie.

"Don't tell her I invited Virginia to the wedding."

Loretta had disliked Virginia for nearly forty years. She had tolerated her when Nita was married to Charles, but now that the divorce was final, she was under no further obligation to be nice.

"Don't worry, I won't," Eadie said.

"We're not crazy," Lavonne said.

"I'm hoping Virginia won't show," Nita said despondently.

"There's no reason why she should."

"She probably just wanted to hear you ask her," Eadie said. "You know how she is. Everything's a game to Virginia."

Nita sighed again but didn't say anything. They watched Loretta across the yard, giving directions to Nita's tall, stoop-shouldered daddy, Eustis, who followed her around with a box of lanterns in his arms. "I told her to get Jimmy Lee to hang the lanterns," Nita said, frowning.

"How's your daddy doing?" Eadie asked.

"He's fine. Whatever he's got, it isn't Parkinson's but something a little milder. It doesn't slow him down much. Mama, of course, thinks it's all in his head. She begins every day with, 'Are you going to shake today, Eustis? It's up to you. Just make up your mind.' "

"Loretta missed her calling," Lavonne said. "She should have been a nurse."

"The funny thing is, when she's around, Daddy doesn't shake much."

"A nurse or maybe a hypnotist," Lavonne said.

Eadie lifted one arm and pointed behind them. "Oh my God," she said, "is that Whitney?"

She was crossing the yard, dressed in a long flowing skirt and a pair of high-heeled boots. Nita looked at her daughter and blushed with pleasure, nodding her head slightly.

"She's gotten so tall," Eadie said. "She's gotten so lovely."

"They grow up fast," Lavonne said.

"Whitney," Nita called. "Come say hello to Lavonne and Eadie."

Whitney scowled at her, hesitating. She could ignore her mother easily, but ignoring other adults was a bit trickier. She put her head down and plodded toward them. Nita tried to put her arm around her daughter's shoulders but Whitney stepped aside with a smooth practiced movement. "Hello, Mrs. Boone," she said, smiling. "Hello, Mrs. Zibolsky."

"My God," Eadie said, taking both Whitney's hands and looking her over from head to foot. "You look like a supermodel. Why are you wasting your time in this little backwoods place? You should be in New York."

Whitney gave her mother an icy smile. "Funny you should say that," she said.

No one spoke. Nita looked across the yard to where Loretta stood shouting orders like Napoleon on the eve of Waterloo. Otis had managed to crawl under the fence and escape, running around the yard and barking at Little Moses and Maureen as they tried to set the tables.

"Stupid dog," Whitney said. "I'll put him in the house."

They watched her walk away and Eadie said, "Did I say something wrong?"

Nita shook her head sadly. "Whitney was shopping with some friends in New York and some guy came up to her and gave her a card for some modeling agency. Ever since then she's been after me to let her move to New York and try to make it as a model."

"Oh, right," Lavonne said. "Like you're going to let a twelve-year-old move to New York."

"That's just crazy," Eadie said.

"So y'all are in agreement with me?" Nita said, her eyes shifting from one to the other. "You think I did the right thing saying no?"

Their response was thunderous and unanimous. Nita sighed, watching Whitney corral Otis and drag him by his collar toward the house. "She hates me for it."

"She'll get over it," Eadie said. Her own mother had never said no to her. She'd been like a big kid herself, forcing Eadie to act like the parent, a role she'd always resented and spent the second half of her life trying to forget. Eadie supposed it was one of the reasons she had decided not to have children herself.

"They go through these phases," Lavonne said. "But they outgrow them. They go off to college and when they come home they've learned enough about life to know that you were right about a lot of things. They've learned that their parents aren't so stupid after all. They get a lot easier to talk to when they've learned that little lesson."

Jimmy Lee had come out on the back porch to look for Nita. When he saw them standing there, he waved and shouted, "There's trouble waiting to happen."

Eadie shouted back, "Well you should know what it looks like by now."

He grinned as he walked toward them, dressed in a pair of khakis and a blue-striped dress shirt. Eadie thought how any bride alive would give her left nipple to stand beside Jimmy Lee at the altar. Lavonne thought how love was fleeting but financial stability was forever. She hoped Nita had made him sign a prenup.

Nita thought how life was unpredictable, and she hoped the happiness and love she and Jimmy Lee had shared over the past year and a half would sustain them through the treacherous waters of matrimony she knew lay just ahead.

Somewhere around one o'clock the yard began to look like a place where a wedding might actually occur, and Nita went into the house to dress. Her mother insisted on helping her, although Nita would have preferred that she had not. Loretta's brisk, forthright manner, far from calming Nita's nerves, made her feel like she was being poked and prodded everywhere with hot needles. She waited until Loretta took a breath, and then Nita went down the guest list, reminding Loretta she expected her to be on her best behavior.

Loretta frowned, and raised her little chin in the air. She put one hand on her hip. "What's that supposed to mean?" she said. "My best behavior."

"Well, Mama, it means I've invited some people you might not appreciate seeing but

I still want you to be nice."

"Juanita Sue," Loretta said. "I am always *nice.*"

"People like Clarissa Derryberry," Nita said. "And that poor little boy of hers."

"Oh good Lord," Loretta said.

Clarissa Swaney Derryberry was a wealthy young widow who was known around town as the Pest Control Heiress. She was the daughter of Curtis Swaney, who had had the foresight to look into the future and see the proliferation of DEET-resistant strains of ants, fleas, ticks, aphids, centipedes, palmetto bugs, and termites. He had started his pest control company, Bugs Be Gone, in the sixties, and forty years later it had grown into a profitable business employing ten full-time sprayers and a bookkeeper, all due in no small part to Curtis's secret and highly carcinogenic blend of various illegal pesticides. Curtis and his wife had produced only one sickly child, Clarissa, who married one of Curtis's senior sprayers, a rascally redneck known around town as "that-fat-ass-Harry-Derryberry." Harry and Clarissa had one child, a boy named Harry Junior who had Tourette's. Harry Junior was prone to nervous tics and episodes where he would fling one hand into the air like an SS officer giving a Nazi salute and yell "Whoop!" at periodic intervals.

"I volunteer down at the library with Clarissa and I want you to be nice to her," Nita said, looking at her mother nervously in the mirror.

Loretta pushed the final pins into Nita's upswept hair. She put her fingers under Nita's chin and turned her head back and forth, appraising her handiwork. "I've got no problem with Clarissa as long as she doesn't make a spectacle of herself. After all, this is your wedding."

That-fat-ass-Harry-Derryberry died soon after Harry Junior was born — of some rare but lethal form of leukemia — leaving Clarissa a wealthy young widow. She took her role as an heiress seriously. She had grown up watching *Dynasty* and assorted daytime soaps and she believed there was a certain dress code every young heiress should adhere to. No matter what the occasion, no matter what time of year it was, no matter how hot or humid it might be, Clarissa Derryberry went everywhere dressed in a blazer and a scarf. In addition to her eccentric dress, Clarissa was a hypochondriac with enough money to indulge a series of modern but obscure ailments. Over the years she had been treated for fibromyalgia, hormonal imbalance, chronic fatigue syndrome, chemical sensitivity, allergies, yeast overgrowth, and restless leg syndrome. Only recently she had discovered she had an extra bone in her foot and now went everywhere in a wheelchair pushed by Harry Junior, attired in her usual blazer and scarf.

Loretta helped Nita slide her wedding dress over her head and said, "As long as Clarissa keeps her medical complaints to herself, me and her'll get along fine."

Loretta had had a double mastectomy some years back and she had little sympathy for other people's minor medical maladies. The news that she had "the cancer" had been delivered by a cheerful, fresh-faced young doctor who made Doogie Howser look like a retiree. "We can put you through six rounds of chemo and radiation, but I can't promise you much more than three to five years of survival, tops," the young doctor had said cheerfully, checking his watch. He had a golf game scheduled for two o'clock. Fourteen years later he dropped dead of a massive coronary at the age of forty-eight. Loretta sat on the front row at his funeral and tried not to smirk.

Having survived cancer through sheer obstinacy and her own tenacious refusal to obey male authority figures, Loretta had little sympathy for whiners, slackers, hypochondriacs, and women who couldn't get through their stressful days of bridge, shopping, and lunches at the club without the help of Xanax or Prozac. Other than that, she was real supportive.

"I know Clarissa can be a little irritating," Nita began. She thought, *If Virginia Redmon shows up, Clarissa Derryberry will be the least of your worries.* Nita could only hope that Virginia would have the good sense and moral restraint to stay home. "But she means well. I think she's just lonely is all." Nita frowned, looking down at her dress and hoping it wasn't too plain. It was a cream-colored silk with a tight, V-neck bodice and narrow skirt that fell to her feet. It looked a little young, Nita realized now, like something a barefoot girl might wear to a May Day dance. Why hadn't she realized this before? Why hadn't anyone told her the dress looked too virginal and sweet for a forty-year-old woman to wear, much less be married in? Why hadn't . . . She looked up suddenly, realizing the silence in the room had grown heavy.

Her mother stood in the doorway, leaning against her father, who had tears in his eyes. Whitney stood just behind them, peeking around his shoulder. "Oh, Mommy," she said. "You look so pretty."

"Do I?" Nita said, in genuine surprise, turning to check her appearance in the mirror. She had worn her hair up, with a gardenia tucked behind one ear.

"Just like a princess," Whitney said, coming into the room and looking less like a surly teenaged Lolita and more like the wide-eyed child who used to play in Nita's jewelry box. Nita leaned to kiss her, and Whitney put her arms around her and kissed her back.

"Just look at our little girl, Daddy," Loretta said in a quavering voice. "All grown up and ready to go out into the big old world."

"Mama, I've been out in the big old world for almost twenty years now," Nita said. "I'm getting married, not moving to Alaska."

"Well, he's a good man and you have my blessing," Eustis said, trying his best to stand up straight and not shake.

"Who's a good man?" Jimmy Lee said, behind them. He saw Nita and stopped, staring like a man in the midst of a religious experience. "Damn," he said finally.

"Okay, Whitney, let's go on outside and see if the guitar player's all set up to play the wedding march." Loretta, all business again, motioned for her granddaughter to follow her outside.

Nita blushed at Jimmy Lee's expression. "I told you, Mama, there will be no wedding march," she said. "He's singing 'Till There Was You.' "

Loretta shrugged. "Whatever," she said. "It's your wedding," she said. "If you want to hippie it up, go right ahead. No one's stopping you."

Jimmy Lee chuckled as he strolled into the room. He had put on a tie and a blue blazer that showed off his shoulders to full advantage. "Funny, I never took you for a hippie girl," he said.

Nita put her hand against his chest to stop him. "It's bad luck for the groom to see the bride before the service," she said.

"Oh, come on, honey. That's just an old wives' tale." He reached out and pulled her roughly into his arms.

"I mean it," she said.

"So what did you and the Way Crazies talk about out there in the yard?" It was his nickname for Lavonne and Eadie.

"Don't call them that."

He leaned and kissed her neck. "Those girls are dangerous," he said, ducking roguishly as she pretended to slap him.

Nita dropped her hand and smoothed his tie against his chest. "I could learn a lot from those girls. I wish I was more like them."

"I'm glad you're not." He kissed her and playfully bit the lobe of her ear. "You're perfect just the way you are."

Nita kissed him and then grabbed his nonexistent love handles. She gave him a little shake. "You never know," she said. "I just might surprise you one day."

The ceremony was simple and sweet, presided over by the Methodist minister from the church Nita's parents attended. They stood under a canopy that had been entwined with ivy and white lilies. Whitney and Logan served as bridesmaid and best man. Afterward, Jimmy Lee and some of his friends from high school entertained them with some garage band standards, including music from the Kinks, the Ramones, and the Beastie Boys.

Lavonne and Eadie sat at a table near the band sipping bottles of spring water. "How pathetic are we?" Eadie asked, raising her bottle.

"Look, we're getting too old to drink like we've been doing. My liver can't take it anymore."

"Speak for yourself," Eadie said.

Loretta and Eustis James shuffled by, two-stepping to "You Really Got Me."

"Show them how it's done, Loretta," Eadie hooted, holding her bottle high.

Loretta stopped to catch her breath. "Y'all need to get up off your asses and shake a hoof," she said. "Ain't nothing better for a hangover than a little exercise."

"I assume that's the voice of experience talking, Loretta." Lavonne sipped her water. "Is she hard to keep up with, Eustis?"

"Naw," he said. "Her bark's worse than her bite."

Across the yard, Clarissa Derryberry had arrived and was being pushed across the lawn in her wheelchair by a whooping Harry Junior.

"There's that goddamned blazer again," Eadie said.

"Someone said they saw her at Disneyworld in July," Lavonne said, "being wheeled through the park in a blazer and a scarf."

"Got more money than she's got sense," Loretta said, motioning to Eustis that it was time to get back to dancing. "You girls need to get up on your feet and plow some new ground."

Lavonne looked blank, but Eadie said, "You got any other words of wisdom for us, Loretta?"

"Never play leapfrog with a unicorn," she

104

said, as she and Eustis trundled off.

Sunlight fell from a bright blue sky. In the distance, the river glistened, moving slowly between banks of cedar and willow and pine. Lavonne stretched her legs and stood up. "I better go check on the buffet line," she said. "Do you want me to bring you a plate?"

Eadie wrinkled her nose. "I can't think about eating right now," she said. "But bring me a glass of red wine."

"You're kidding."

"Do I look like I'm kidding?"

Lavonne shrugged. "It's your liver," she said.

After a while, Jimmy Lee let another friend take over on the drums so he could dance with his bride. Anyone looking at them would have thought they were like any other happy young couple just starting out. No one would have guessed that Nita was thirteen years older than Jimmy Lee or that she had teenage children. She looked so young and pretty dancing in her husband's arms. The band was playing, "When a Man Loves a Woman," and looking up into his handsome face, Nita felt like she might be living a dream. She remembered the dark days of her marriage to Charles Broadwell, shut up in his big old house in River Oaks, feeling like she was being slowly entombed and counting the days until her children would be grown and flown away to freedom.

Married to Charles, Nita had had every material comfort she could want, but she hadn't been able to imagine happiness. She hadn't been able to imagine a future with a man like Jimmy Lee Motes.

He kissed her gently. "I love you, Nita."

"I love you, too."

"And I'm sorry about not being able to afford a proper honeymoon." The money in the bank was Nita's and Jimmy Lee wouldn't touch it. He had too much pride for that.

"You know I don't care about any of that stuff."

He frowned, looking past her shoulder. "But, honey, I promise. Things are going to get better." Lately, he'd been ordering tapes off the Internet on how to make a million dollars in real estate with no money down. He stayed up long after she'd gone to bed and drove off to work every morning with the tapes blaring in his truck. "I've got plans for our future," he said.

"I don't care about any of that, Jimmy." Every time a new tape arrived, Nita got a queer feeling in the pit of her stomach. Like someone had punched her or left her stranded at the top of a tall swaying ladder. She said, "I'm happy just the way we are."

"I want to be able to give you things. I want to be able to provide for my family."

Nita shivered. Somewhere off in the cold dark woods beyond the river, tragedy waited. She could smell it. No matter how hard she tried, she couldn't seem to convince Jimmy Lee that she didn't need a big house and diamond jewelry and exotic vacations. She had had all that before and it hadn't meant a thing. All she needed was him.

The sun disappeared behind a bank of high-flying clouds. Nita was suddenly cold. Goose bumps rose on her arms. As if to confirm her premonition of disaster, a car turned slowly into the sandy drive.

Virginia Redmon had arrived.

"Katy bar the door," Loretta said, appearing suddenly at Nita's elbow. "Look who just showed up."

"Now, Mama," Nita said.

"The nerve of that woman, showing up to crash your wedding."

"She's not crashing my wedding." Nita smoothed the bodice of her wedding gown. "I invited her."

Loretta stared at her in disbelief. "Are you crazy?" she said finally. "Honey, have you lost your marbles?"

Nita walked away from her, across the lawn toward the big table where Eadie, Lavonne, and Grace Pearson sat nursing their drinks. Loretta trailed behind her like a sturgeon caught on a trotline, and Jimmy Lee brought up the rear. Nita was hoping that being around other people might keep her mother quiet, but the odds of that happening were, she knew, pretty slim.

Eadie, Lavonne, and Grace were talking about this year's Kudzu Ball. "That's just about the best fun I ever had," Lavonne said. "If it was any more fun, it couldn't be legal."

"Tell me about it," Grace said.

"Y'all try not to rub it in because I missed it," Eadie said.

The Kudzu Ball was held every year in the Wal-Mart parking lot. It was a parody of the high-browed Ithaca Cotillion Ball that was thrown every year by the cream of Ithaca society. Mothers worked behind the scenes for years to get their daughters presented at the Ithaca Cotillion, but Kudzu debutantes could present themselves. Anyone could be a debutante. The only prerequisite was that you had to be female (or look female — there was a growing contingency of female impersonators who showed up every year from places like Atlanta or Birmingham or Charlotte), you had to wear the tackiest ball gown you could find, and you had to wear some kind of headgear made from kudzu vine. Whether or not to use an alias was entirely up to the individual debutante. Lavonne had gone to the ball two years straight as Ima Badass, and Eadie had gone that first year as Aneeda Mann. She had missed this year's throw-down because she'd been in New York with Trevor while he met with his agent and strategized about becoming the next John Grisham.

"I'll never miss another Kudzu Ball for as long as I live," Eadie said, stubbornly shaking her head.

Grace said, "Yeah, we missed you. I guess you heard they crowned Rosebud queen." She was wearing a long, red, flowered dress, a jeans jacket, and a pair of chunky-heeled shoes. It was one of the few times anyone had ever seen her in a dress.

"Yeah, I heard," Eadie said. "Rosebud's the perfect Kudzu Queen."

Rosebud Smoot was one of only three female attorneys in town, and she made her living defending the ex-wives of lawyers, doctors, and corporate executives who couldn't find legal representation among the closed, old-boy network that was Ithaca, Georgia.

"I can promise you this, girls," Eadie said, lifting her wineglass. "I'll never miss another Kudzu Ball. Ever. Fuck New York. Fuck Trevor Boone and his big-ass book deals."

"Hey, that's my lawyer you're talking about," Grace said. Trevor had represented her years ago in a libel suit filed by an overzealous county commissioner, and they'd been good friends ever since. "And speaking of my lawyer, where is he?" Grace grinned her lopsided grin and there was something in her expression that reminded Eadie of Trevor. She felt suddenly lonesome for him. She hadn't asked him to come, but she should have.

"He stayed in New Orleans. He's trying to finish his second novel before the first one comes out and he has to travel." She smiled at Nita who had moved up to the table with her husband on one side of her and her mother on the other. Loretta looked stressed out. She kept glancing over her shoulder toward the makeshift parking lot. "Well, here's the wedding party now," Eadie said.

"So old Trevor couldn't make it?" Jimmy Lee said to Eadie.

"No, old Trevor couldn't come. Although he says to tell you and Nita that he's sorry he missed your wedding and he wishes you the best of luck in your future matrimonial endeavors."

"That sounds like something a writer would say."

"Hey, Loretta," Grace said.

Loretta, who'd been craning her neck to check out the parking lot, stopped and swung around. "Well, hey, yourself," she said. She came around the table to give Grace a hug. She had grown up with Grace's parents in Vienna, pronounced Vi-anna, a little farming town east of Ithaca. "How's your mama and daddy?" she asked. "I don't get back to see them much anymore."

"They're good. Daddy still jumps when Mama hollers frog, but other than that they're fine." Grace spoke two languages: Wellesley English and pine-barren redneck.

"What'd y'all think of the ceremony?" Nita said.

"Don't change the subject," Loretta said darkly, looking at her daughter. Now that the pleasantries were over, Loretta was ready to get back to lambasting Nita for her decision to invite Virginia. "What in the world made you ask her?"

"Mama, she is the children's grand-mother." Ever since she found out about Virginia marrying Redmon, Nita had felt kind of sorry for her. She had felt kind of guilty about keeping the children from Virginia over the past eighteen months.

"Now, Mama James, don't get excited over something silly," Jimmy Lee said. He couldn't bear to hear Nita criticized in any way, shape, or form. "Nita's just doing what she thinks is right."

"Who said you could call me Mama James? My name's Loretta, son."

"Oh my God, is Virginia here?" Lavonne said, scanning the crowd.

"Did the Bride of Satan show up after all?" Eadie said.

Loretta looked suspiciously from one to the other. "Did y'all know about this?"

"It's my wedding," Nita said stubbornly, and Jimmy Lee put his arm around her. "I can invite who I want."

Behind them, Harry Junior threw his hand in the air and yelled "Whoop!"

"What in the hell was that?" Loretta said darkly, looking around.

"It's nothing," Nita said quickly. She smiled at Harry Junior, who'd just sat down at a picnic table with a big plate of food. His mother sat in her wheelchair behind him surrounded by a group of spellbound women. She had her bad foot propped up on the table bench and was holding forth on the dangers of ingrown toenails, gangrene, and amputation.

Loretta shook her head ominously and stared at her daughter. "Juanita Sue, you're tied to the train tracks and you don't know there's a train coming."

Jimmy Lee snorted and bit his lower lip. He'd always thought Loretta could make it on the comedy circuit.

Lavonne said, "Hey, Loretta, can I get you a plate?"

Grace said, "The barbecue brisket is really good."

Eadie said, "If you kick her ass, Loretta, I want to be there to see it."

Nita stared nervously at Virginia's big Mercedes. So far no one had climbed out. Maybe Virginia had forgotten today was the wedding. Maybe she had just stopped by to drop off a gift and would leave now that she realized.

"Whoop!" Harry Junior said.

"That boy's getting on my last nerve," Loretta said, eyeing him grimly.

"Mama, he can't help it." Nita pinched Jimmy Lee, who was still giggling. "Why don't you try and relax?" she said to her mother. "Why don't you try and have a little fun?"

Loretta stared balefully at Virginia's car. A slight breeze ruffled her black hair, making it stand up above her forehead like concertina wire. "You'll think fun," she growled, "when you're standing there helpless as a mute in handcuffs."

Jimmy Lee snorted again and put his head down. Nita shoved him in the ribs with her elbow. "Why don't you go get Daddy and y'all have another dance?" she said, trying to draw her mother's attention away from the parking lot. "Or get a plate and maybe sit down for some dinner."

"Who catered this throw-down anyway?" Grace said.

"Someone with a great deal of class and good taste," Lavonne said.

"Whoop!" Harry Junior said.

Loretta spun around suddenly. "Hon, would you like a cough drop?" she said, leaning across the picnic table with her hands resting heavily on the checkered surface. "I've got some cherry red ones that should fix you right up."

Harry Junior's eyes got wide. "Sure," he said.

The Ramones sang "We're a Happy Family." Jimmy Lee coughed and looked at the sky. He chewed his lip and stared at his feet. Nita looked at him and shook her head. She smiled, feeling the tension rise up out of her neck and shoulders. The sun peeked from behind the clouds and shone brightly on the slow-moving waters of the Black Warrior River. Nita felt hopeful for the first time in a long time. Her children were happy. Her family was safe. Her husband was handsome and tenderhearted, and they were in love.

No one could ruin that.

Virginia climbed slowly out of the car, putting on her best game face. The wedding was every bit as tacky as she had expected, complete with rock-and-roll band, a crowd of people she barely recognized, and what looked like picnic tables scattered around the yard. It was being catered, of course, by Lavonne Zibolsky and her partner, that Shapiro woman.

She adjusted her skirt and took a deep breath, wondering if she really wanted to put herself through this ordeal. But then she remembered the way her son had let himself be humiliated in front of the entire town by a little scrap of a girl who Virginia hadn't even wanted him to marry in the first place. When she remembered this, she was steadfast in her resolve for vengeance.

She checked her hair in the window glass. She was probably overdressed for this sorry function. Already, her Jimmy Choo heels were caked in a half-inch of mud. At least she hoped it was mud, and not something worse. She smoothed her hair and put her shoulders back. She would prevail, even here, stuck at a wedding she didn't want to attend, in the middle of a mosquito-infested swamp with a bunch of college professors, blue-collar workers, and the three women Virginia felt certain had brought her to this sorry state of affairs.

"Let's go," she said to Redmon, over her shoulder.

He patted her on the backside and took her elbow. She stiffened but let him keep the arm. "Hot damn," he said, watching the wedding revelers. "Nothing I like better than a good throw-down."

Virginia tried walking on her toes so her heels wouldn't get sucked into the sandy soil. Redmon clung to her arm, trying to steady her. "We're not staying long," she warned him. Just long enough for her to gather the information she needed. Just long enough to figure out where to strike.

"Aw, come on, Queenie," he pleaded. "Let's have a good time. You know I was born under a honky-tonk moon."

Virginia muttered, "Under a trailer, more likely."

"What?"

"Nothing."

"Come on, honey, let's dance," Redmon said. "Let's shake it up a little bit."

"I'm not dancing to this so-called *music,*" Virginia said in disgust. They stood at the edge of the yard, watching the dancers cavort to "I Wanna Be Sedated."

"Aw, come on, honey, loosen up. You're tight as a wood tick on a dog's tail."

Virginia was spared the necessity of a reply by the sudden appearance of Loretta James, standing in front of them like an enraged little terrier.

Virginia put on her best smile. Her eyes swept over the little woman. "My, Loretta, what a lovely dress," she said.

Loretta wasn't having any of it. "How come you're here, Virginia?" she said.

"I just came by to offer my congratulations to the happy couple. I just came by to see if there was anything I could do to help out."

Loretta's eyes were gray and sharp as pencil points. "Well, aren't you sweet?" she said. "You're just about as sweet and handy as a Braille Bible to a blind preacher."

Virginia smiled but looked puzzled. "What exactly is that supposed to mean?" she said.

Redmon, who obviously understood what it meant, snorted. "Hey, Loretta," he said. "Do you want to dance?"

Virginia paid her respects to the newlyweds, smiling and clenching her teeth so hard her jaw ached for days. There was not much information she could pry out of Nita, at least not while her young bridegroom stood glued to her side like an overprotective bodyguard. He was polite to Virginia but she could sense his dislike, and didn't really blame him for it. He was intelligent enough to recognize an enemy when he saw one, which was more than Nita seemed capable of doing.

Virginia wandered over to the buffet table. Out in the yard, Redmon two-stepped with Loretta James to his request, "Kansas City." She saw Eadie Boone leaning against a pecan tree, sipping her drink while she watched the dancers. Virginia was not surprised to see her here. She had expected Eadie to come in but she had hoped she'd bring Trevor with her. Virginia got up on her tiptoes and scanned the crowd. No Trevor. She spotted Grace Pearson over by the buffet table. *Now who in the world invited her?* she wondered. The woman was wearing a jeans jacket and looked like she might be headed for a hoedown, not a wedding. Virginia did not understand why women who attended schools like Wellesley could be so clueless when it came to fashion. She felt a twinge of sympathy for Ms. Pearson's mother, who had probably tried to raise her to be a good Southern girl with an appreciation of good grooming and polite society, and then made the mistake of sending her up North to be educated. When she saw women like Grace Pearson, Virginia was glad she had not raised a daughter of her own.

She picked up a glass of white wine and strolled over to visit with Eadie. She had gotten halfway across the lawn when Grace Pearson swung around suddenly and headed toward her. Virginia, dismayed and realizing she could not, at this stage, turn and run for cover, rearranged her face into a blank, pleasant expression.

"Ms. Pearson," Virginia said, smiling grimly.

The big woman nodded her head curtly. "Madame President," she said.

Really, Virginia would like to smack her. She'd like to wrap her fingers in that mop of red hair, pull her face down to eye level, and slap her repeatedly. They squared off in the middle of the yard, eyeing each other warily. Eadie, watching from the sidelines, thought they were a perfectly matched set, which was odd given the disparity in their physical sizes.

Virginia broke away first. "Excuse me. I think I see someone I know," she said in a cold, tinny voice.

"Always a pleasure," Grace said, moving off.

Virginia continued on toward Eadie, who saw her coming and ducked her head, turning one shoulder slightly. Virginia pretended she didn't see this.

"Yoohoo! Eadie!" she called gaily. "How *are* you?"

"Hello, Virginia." Eadie looked tired. Something around the eyes, Virginia noticed with satisfaction, a puffiness that promised to get worse with age.

"Did you not bring your gorgeous husband with you?"

"My gorgeous husband is at home," Eadie said flatly. "In New Orleans. He couldn't make it."

"You tell him we're just so *proud* of him, with the book and all. He's our very own celebrity author." No one had ever been able to figure out how Eadie had managed to bag and hang on to the most eligible bachelor in Ithaca. Sure, she was beautiful, but there were lots of beautiful girls around, and every one of them had a better pedigree than Eadie Wilkens, who had grown up in a trailer on the wrong side of town. Virginia looked her over carefully, trying to figure out Eadie's secret.

"It's just so exciting," Virginia murmured, sipping her drink. "Just think, to have had a famous writer living in our midst all these years and not even know it."

"Yeah, well, you never know how things will turn out," Eadie said. She had one arm crossed over her stomach and the elbow of the other arm, the one holding her wineglass, rested lightly on it.

"Did you not?" Virginia said, looking at her curiously. "Did you not know how things would work out?"

Eadie cut her eyes at the older woman, trying to decide what she meant by this. For some reason it sounded vaguely insulting, and knowing Virginia, it was probably meant to be. Eadie sipped her wine and wished she had something stronger to drink. She wished she'd thought to make up a shaker of vodka martinis to bring with her. Or hell, she thought, glancing at Virginia, maybe even two shakers.

Virginia crossed one little foot in front of the other. "If you could have looked into a crystal ball as a child," she said dreamily, "wouldn't you have been surprised to see the way things turned out? Just like a fairy tale."

Eadie always did her best not to let Virginia rattle her, but today she felt strangely vulnerable. As if to make matters worse, Lee Anne Bales strolled by and Eadie turned her head, hoping Lee Anne hadn't seen her. Eadie had hated her since high school. She and Lee Anne were in the same home ec class, and Lee Anne was the one who had started the petition to have Eadie expelled from school after she managed to sew her finger to her apron and set fire to the simulated kitchen with her version of Tuna Surprise. The fire had only destroyed half the classroom, but it had done enough damage to cause cancellation of the Home Economics Cook Off, an annual tradition where the home ec girls donned homemade aprons and cooked and served meals to members of the Ithaca High football team. Being denied this opportunity to show off their educations hit the home ec girls hard. They got up a petition, signed by everyone but Nita, and Eadie was deemed an example of womanhood gone wrong, everything the home economics curriculum was trying desperately to stamp out, and she was suspended from school for three days. After that, Eadie got her revenge by thumbing her nose at Ithaca every chance she got, not the least of which was marrying Trevor Boone.

Virginia watched Lee Anne disappear in the crowd. "It's gotten so no one will ever recognize a real bosom," she said archly, "with all the false ones there are in the world today." She looked down smugly at her own petite, well-rounded figure and then glanced at Eadie's chest. "Of course, you and I don't have to worry about false bosoms. We can be happy with what the good Lord gave us." She was trying to draw Eadie in, and Eadie wondered why.

"Look, Virginia, I didn't marry Trevor for his money, if that's what you're implying. I didn't marry him because I thought he'd be famous some day."

Virginia did her best to look horrified. "Oh dear, I've said the wrong thing," she said, putting her fingers to her mouth. "Of course, I never *meant* to imply you married for money."

Eadie lifted her drink and said, "Talk about the pot calling the kettle black."

Virginia decided to ignore this remark.

She smoothed the front of her suit jacket and scanned the crowd. After a minute she smiled and said, "Anyone who's ever met Trevor could see why you married him."

Eadie wondered what the woman was getting at. It was apparent she had some kind of agenda. Eadie sipped her wine, thinking about that time in the principal's office after the home ec fiasco when Lee Anne had broken down and cried and the principal had instantly sided with her. It was the thing Southern girls did when dealing with irate male authority figures. They broke down and cried and tried to look as small and helpless as possible. If Eadie had used the same tactic, she might have received nothing more than a slap on the wrist. But she had never been able to bring herself to grovel. Her stubborn, dry-eyed, stoicism had earned her the three-day suspension.

Virginia watched Nita and Jimmy Lee dance by, doing some kind of modified two-step. Nita had her head thrown back and was laughing loudly. Virginia said, "I do hope Nita will be happy. I do hope *this* marriage will work out for her."

Eadie glanced at the older woman but her face seemed calm. Virginia's voice seemed a little sharp but her manner was composed and sincere. Eadie figured given other circumstances, Virginia might have been one of the greatest stage actresses of the twentieth century. She might have been a cold war spy capable of withstanding torture or sophisticated lie detector tests. "Speaking of marriage," Eadie said, "how's Redmon?"

Virginia's face shifted slightly, a ripple occurred just beneath the veneer of calm composure. But when she looked at Eadie, Virginia's eyes were smooth and blue as colored glass. "Isn't it wonderful," she said brightly, "to have finally found your true soul mate?"

She was good. Eadie would give her that. A mist seemed to have formed over Virginia's eyes, a trembling veil of unshed tears. Eadie looked away. Any expression of strong sentiment made her uncomfortable. Eadie never cried. If she had given way to tears during her wretched childhood, she would have cried herself blind by now.

Virginia sniffed and ran one well-manicured finger lightly beneath her damp eyes. She waved at someone she knew across the yard. "But of course you already know about soul mates," she said to Eadie, "married to Trevor and all. I mean, the Boone boys just *ooze* charm."

Eadie clutched her drink and looked at Virginia curiously. "Boone boys?" she said.

It was Virginia's turn to flush. "Trevor's father, Hampton, was a handsome man, too. But you probably don't remember him." She turned slightly to look at the assembled wedding guests. Eadie was quiet for a moment, considering this. Her wine was almost gone and when the drink was finished, she decided, this conversation was, too. "How's Charles?" she asked, trying to change the subject.

Virginia took her time answering. She sipped her drink. Her cheeks turned a slight shade of pink. "Why, Charles is fine," she said finally. "He's been dating a girl from Valdosta. An accountant. She's got a small child, a boy I think, about ten years old. I don't know if anything will come of it, of course. But I hope it will. Charles was always so good with children."

Eadie shuddered. She thought, *Poor kid.* She thought, *Poor lady accountant.*

"We're thinking about going skiing in March and he's talking about bringing the accountant and her son. Out west somewhere. Maybe Park City. Maybe Crested Butte."

Eadie finished her drink.

"Of course Charles hasn't been out West since that last hunting trip. The one they all took last year. Does Trevor ever mention that trip?"

"Never."

"I guess he wouldn't since he came back early." Virginia looked down at her glass. "Since he came back before all the fun and games started. Those bad boys, those little rascals." She smiled indulgently, like she was describing a slumber party for ten-year-olds.

Eadie yawned and pushed herself upright. "Well, Virginia, it's been nice talking to you. I think I'll go see if Lavonne needs a hand."

"Of course Trevor was there for all the other trips. It was a tradition started by the Judge, you know. A trip where men get to do manly things and leave all the cares and worries of work behind them. I always encouraged the Judge to go. He was in such a good mood when he got home! Still, I have often wondered what men get up to when they're playing at being boys. I always wanted to be a fly on the wall." She put her hand over her mouth and giggled conspiratorially, her face becoming pink and child-like. "I've often wondered what shenanigans they got up to. Haven't you always wondered, Eadie? Haven't you always wanted to go along? Haven't you always wished . . ."

"Look, Virginia, if you want to know what happened, why don't you just ask your new husband. He was there."

Virginia stiffened. A cloud passed suddenly over the sun, darkening the yard and bringing with it a cool breeze off the water. "Yes, I know that," she said shortly. "I know he was there."

Eadie noted Virginia's discomfort. She grinned suddenly. "I thought soul mates told each other everything," she said.

Virginia stared at her steadily for several seconds, her face becoming less soft and childlike and more like a slab of granite. She poured the rest of her drink out on the ground. "Oh, I'll find out what happened," she said briskly, squaring her little shoulders. "You can bet on it."

Eadie shrugged. "Good luck with that," she said. She turned, and moved off through the crowd.

Virginia watched her go, a tense expression on her face. Her eyes flattened out over the crowd of revelers and then grew sharp as pitchfork prongs as they settled on the hapless Redmon, who, unaware of his wife's piercing gaze, trundled by with Loretta James wrapped in his arms.

Virginia saw her grandson later, standing at the edge of the crowd, watching the band play. Public school had obviously not been good for Logan. He was dressed all in black — black pants, black T-shirt, a black leather jacket, and his hair was dyed a deep purple color. He was with a lovely girl, a breathtakingly beautiful girl, who reminded Virginia of herself as a young woman. Startled, she realized it was her granddaughter, Whitney, who, over the nine months since Virginia saw her last, had metamorphosed from a chubby adolescent into a slim-waisted swan. It was too late for Logan, of course, but Whitney showed signs of promise. Virginia imagined herself taking the girl under her wing. She imagined tea parties and shopping trips to Atlanta. Virginia had always thought she would make a better mother to a daughter than she had made to a son. If only fate had worked to her advantage. She pulled herself up straight, and watched the girl, her lips pursed. With the right guidance Whitney might yet make something of herself. Her eyes narrowed. Her breathing slowed. She stared at her granddaughter, feeling a slight tremor of excitement.

Virginia had suddenly realized what shape her revenge would take.

CHAPTER FIVE

The day after the wedding Eadie woke up early, borrowed Lavonne's car, and drove out to the office supply store at the mall. She bought herself a sketchbook and some charcoal pencils and then she dropped the car off at Lavonne's and walked down to the River Park and sat and sketched families throwing Frisbees, families picnicking in the sun and Rollerblading along the concrete sidewalks. She hadn't worked in nearly eighteen months but today it just poured out of her. She filled page after page of the sketchbook.

Around twelve-thirty, Lavonne called. "Hey, where are you?" she said, still sounding sleepy.

"I'm down at the River Park, sketching."

"Sketching? Really? Stay right there. I'll go by the store and pick up a couple of double lattes and some cream cheese muffins and meet you there." Lavonne was happy to have the day off. The deli was closed on Sundays and Mondays. Usually she just sat around working on her laptop, but Eadie was flying back to New Orleans tomorrow so Lavonne was glad to spend the day with her.

Eadie put her cell phone down and thumbed slowly through the sketchbook, amazed at the work she had done. It was as if something inside her had suddenly let down like rainwater through a clogged gutter. Eadie didn't believe in therapy but she could imagine a therapist making much of her sudden flow of creativity. She could imagine a guy who looked like Freud saying, *Go back to your hometown and find out why it is the source of your unhappiness. Find out why you feel disconnected and disjointed when you are away from it.*

Far out on the river a barge passed, its metal decks gleaming in the sun. Swallows darted in the deep blue sky. Eadie thumbed through the sketchbook and tried not to think about Trevor.

Driving through the outskirts of Ithaca a few days ago, she had felt the baggage of her childhood settle through her like sediment. It had stunned her to feel that old familiar feeling of dread returning. She had made Lavonne turn right on Tuckertown

131

Road and drive slowly through the Shangri-La Trailer Park, past the lot where the Wilkenses' trailer had stood, past the sandy creek bank where Eadie had sat as a child and dreamed of a life better than the one she had.

Trevor was responsible for all this somehow. She wasn't quite sure how, but it was easier to blame him than it was to crash through all the barricades she had long ago erected inside herself. He was the one who'd insisted they could go away and start over again. It had been easy for him. He'd had every opportunity: money, looks, family connections, a safe and happy childhood. Talent. It was hard loving someone so damn perfect.

Eadie saw Lavonne's car pull into the parking lot and a few minutes later, Lavonne was crossing the lawn, carrying the double lattes in a cardboard tray with one hand, and the bag of cream cheese muffins in the other.

"Hey, look at you," Lavonne said, sitting down on the bench. "You're working again."

Eadie closed her sketchbook. A slight sheen of perspiration glistened across her forehead. She looked tired but happy. "It just came over me," she said, reaching for one of the lattes. "I got up this morning and knew I had to work." She took the plastic lid off the coffee and sipped carefully. "I think it has something to do with this place," she said, looking around the crowded park.

"I know, isn't it great? They finished it right after you moved to New Orleans."

"No. I don't mean the park. I mean Ithaca. I mean running into Virginia and Lee Anne Bales at the wedding. It has something to do with conflict. I need conflict to work."

"What," Lavonne said, opening the sack of muffins, "you don't get enough conflict married to Trevor?" She offered one to Eadie.

Eadie shook her head sadly. "We don't fight like we used to," she said. "He's always working. And when he's working, he's happy."

Lavonne chewed slowly and stared at her for several minutes. "You poor thing," she said. "Your husband's happy and you don't fight anymore. How do you stand it?"

Eadie made a wry face and sipped her coffee. "It's hard to explain," she said. "It's complicated."

She had met him her freshman year at the University of Georgia, where he was a second-year law student. They were from the same small town but Trevor was six years older and he came from money and the land-owning aristocracy. Eadie came from people who had only recently embraced the joys of indoor plumbing, people whose idea of moving up was a double-wide trailer instead of a single-wide.

Their attraction for each other smoldered for a few weeks and then erupted into a blazing love affair, more like a wildfire than a controlled burn. She met him in September and by Thanksgiving he had proposed. Eadie was aware that everyone in Ithaca thought she married him for his money, but the truth was, this never occurred to her. She married him because she had never met anyone like him. Until Trevor Boone, she had never met anyone she felt had the stamina, courage, and strength of character to survive loving her. Not to mention his all-American good looks and the fact that he was an absolute pervert in bed. Eadie was crazy about him and would have married him if he'd been penniless. The family name and money was just a bonus.

His mother, horrified, put her foot down but it did no good. The wedding was held at a small Episcopal chapel near the UGA campus, and Maureen Boone attended because she could not bear for the rest of Ithaca to gossip about Boone family squabbles. She could not air the family linen in public. Still, she could, and did, sit in the front pew sobbing so loudly the priest had to raise his voice to be heard. When this didn't work, she fainted. Eadie, looking over at her prone mother-in-law, thought grimly, *So that's how it's going to be.* Trevor, accustomed to his mother's histrionics, smiled calmly at the rector, and in a deep voice said, "Proceed."

"There's a solution to your problem," Lavonne said. "It's called therapy."

"Therapy's for whiners and weaklings," Eadie said. "Therapy's for poor slobs who don't know how to make a good vodka martini."

A slight breeze blew across the river, bringing with it the scent of fish. Over by the picnic pavilion a young man took out a guitar and began to play. Lavonne pulled another muffin out of the bag. She chewed thoughtfully and watched the sunlight playing along the surface of the river. "I guess I'm just caught up in the irony of your situation," she said to Eadie. "It's what you always wanted. To get away from Ithaca. To make Trevor be faithful to you and his art." She looked at Eadie. "And he has been faithful, right?"

"Yes."

"So what's the problem?"

Eadie tapped the rim of her latte with her fingernails. "Like I said, be careful what you wish for."

Lavonne squinted her eyes and looked at the sky. A kite floated motionless, its tail curling in the breeze. "It's not as if Trevor's being inattentive," she said. "He's called a dozen times since you've been here."

Eadie shrugged. "I think he's nervous. He knows I'm bored. He's afraid I'll relapse."

"He's afraid you'll sleep with someone else?"

"No. He knows I won't do that." Eadie repressed a sudden, graphic image of the young po'boy sandwich maker stretched out, naked, in her bed. She sighed. "The only thing he's going to catch me in bed with these days is my vibrator." She told Lavonne about the unfortunate incident involving Milton.

Lavonne dropped her jaw in amazement. She put her head back and laughed. "Oh my God, are you telling me your husband caught you using your vibrator? How humiliating."

"Right," Eadie said. "Like your husband never caught *you.*"

"Eadie, I don't even have a vibrator."

She twisted her head and looked at Lavonne in astonishment. "What? You were married to Leonard Zibolsky for twenty-one years and you don't have a vibrator? No offense, Lavonne, but I *know* Leonard."

Lavonne didn't look offended. Leonard was pretty much universally unappealing to women. "Celibacy is an underrated virtue," she said.

"Are you crazy? That's not healthy. When was the last time you had sex?"

Lavonne didn't like being reminded of the barrenness of her so-called sex life. "I don't know," she said. "Big hair was in. Princess Di was still in love with Charles."

Eadie didn't think this was funny. She sipped her coffee and looked at Lavonne the way she might look at a crippled dog that had been run down in the street. After a while she said, "Okay, we're going to fix this problem."

"What problem?" Lavonne said nervously. "There is no problem."

But Eadie was on a mission. There was no stopping her now. "I was going to order a replacement for Milton anyway," she said. "They've come out with a new and improved version. The Love Monkey II. When we get back to your place, we'll get on the Internet and order two, one for you and one for me."

"Are you crazy?" Lavonne said. "I can't have the postman delivering a package to my door with a return address that reads Love Monkey II."

"It comes in a plain brown wrapper," Eadie said. "Everything from Fleshy Delights comes in a plain brown wrapper."

"Fleshy Delights?"

"It's an Internet sex shop where you can order sex toys and marital aids. You know. Vibrating panties, flavored skin lotions, strap-ons, handcuffs."

"There's a whole portion of your life I don't want to know anything about."

"Don't worry. I'll show you how to use it."

Lavonne groaned and put her head in her hands. After a minute she tried again. "Look, Eadie," she said evenly. "I appreciate your concern over my sex life, but you don't need to worry about it. I'm doing just fine, even without the Love Monkey II. I'm older than you are. I'm forty-seven years old. I'm nearly fifty. I'm too old to be ordering stuff from a porn website."

"Don't be ridiculous. Fifty is the new thirty. Look at Goldie Hawn. Look at Meryl Streep and Susan Sarandon."

"Hey there." They both turned around. A man dressed in biking gear stood about

138

twenty feet away in the shade of a boxwood hedge. He perched on the bicycle seat with one foot resting on the bike path and the other resting on a pedal. "How're you doing?" he asked, still trying to be friendly. Men were always trying to pick Eadie up. Lavonne was used to it by now.

Eadie, obviously thinking the same thing, stretched her legs out in front of her. She yawned and put her fingers over her mouth. "Do I know you?" she said.

"Hey, Lavonne," he said, taking off his helmet and his sunglasses.

"Joe," she said, sitting upright. "I didn't recognize you." A sudden unpleasant realization came to her. She wondered how much of their conversation he had overheard.

He swung his leg over the bike and walked it toward them. It made little clicking sounds, like a cricket stuck in a closet, like a time bomb ticking down to destruction. Lavonne handled the introductions as best she could. She felt him studying her and her face flamed. "Joe Solomon, this is Eadie Boone. Eadie, this is Joe."

Eadie looked from one to the other. She grinned slowly and stuck her hand out. "Hi, Joe," she said in a sleepy voice, giving him the full effect of her eyes. This was usually the point where the man in question fell instantly and irrevocably in love with Eadie. Lavonne tensed, waiting for this to happen.

He quickly let go of Eadie's hand. Behind his head, a box kite climbed slowly up the sky, trailing its tail like a broken limb. "I forgot the deli wasn't open today," he said, smiling at Lavonne. His eyes were green with flecks of gold around the iris.

"What?" she said.

"I went by the deli but it was closed. I needed a cream cheese muffin fix."

Lavonne held up the sack. "You're in luck," she said. He seemed pretty relaxed. Maybe he hadn't heard anything after all.

"You're kidding me," he said, looking down into the bag. "You mean you read my mind?"

"She's a mind reader," Eadie said. "Ask her what I'm thinking right now."

"There's only one left," he said.

"Go ahead, take it. There's plenty more where that came from."

He grinned and took the sack from her. He zipped it into a small pouch on the back of his seat. "I'll eat it later," he said.

"That's a nice bike," Lavonne said.

"Thanks. I built it."

"Really?"

"It's a prototype. It's a carbon composite

that's lighter than titanium. Do you ride?"

"No." *Conversation 101. Avoid dead-end statements if at all possible.*

"She's thinking about learning to ride," Eadie said innocently.

"Really?" Other than his first glance at Eadie, he hadn't looked at her at all. He wiped his forehead with the back of one of his racing gloves. His biking shorts left little to the imagination. "Do you have a bike?" he asked Lavonne.

"She's thinking about ordering one off the Internet," Eadie said coolly. "We were just talking about that."

"You need to do it, Lavonne," he said, putting his helmet back on. "Then we could ride together."

Eadie lifted one eyebrow and looked at her. "Did you hear that, Lavonne? Then you could ride together."

Lavonne ignored her. She glanced at Joe, trying to think of something clever to say. Something smart and flirtatious. "Wednesday is half-price cookie day," she said. It was the best she could do, given the circumstances.

"Really? Half-price cookie day? I guess I'll have to check that out." He put his foot on the pedal. "Nice to meet you, Eadie."

" 'Bye, Joe," Eadie said.

141

"I'll see you Wednesday," he said to Lavonne.

"Okay."

He pedaled a few paces and then stopped, looking back over his shoulder. "Fleshy Delights doesn't sound like much of a bike site," he said. "You might want to try Biker's World." He grinned.

Lavonne tried to hold his gaze, but could not, naturally. "I'll remember that," she said. She looked at her feet, listening to the clicking of his bike getting farther and farther away.

"Damn," Eadie said. "He's cute."

The week following her wedding, Nita went out to the Suck Creek Retirement Home to visit Leota Quarles. She had found Leota quite by accident, several months after she began her women in servitude project. Caught up in the excitement of trying to finish the paper, Nita had almost decided not to visit Leota. But then one of the other ladies had said, "Oh, you have to talk to Miz Quarles. Her people come from over on the island and she worked for your mama-in-law's people, the Kellys. Miz Broadwell was a Kelly before she was a Broadwell." It had taken Nita a minute to realize she was talking about Virginia. Her curiosity aroused, she had decided to keep the appointment with Leota Quarles. Virginia had never said much about her childhood. It was hard to imagine her as anything other than a strong-willed, self-assured woman. It was hard to imagine her as anything other than an adult, hatched from an egg, fully formed, like a Greek goddess of old, or some alien life-form.

The home was crowded today with visitors. Nita smiled at the young nurse who showed her into Leota's room. The old woman was sitting in a rocking chair, facing a window that looked out over the parking lot. Leota was ninety-four years old and she was hard of hearing.

"Look, Miss Leota, you have a visitor," the young nurse said. The elderly woman continued to gaze out the window, a pensive look on her face. Nita smiled at the nurse who went out, closing the door behind her. Nita took out her notepad and tape recorder, and pulled a chair closer to the window. She touched Leota's arm and the old woman turned her head and smiled, showing a set of large white dentures.

"Are you Miz Broadwell?" she said.

"Yes." Nita smiled apologetically. "I hope I didn't startle you." The room smelled of disinfectant and mothballs. "We talked a

143

little bit on the phone, Mrs. Quarles, about Virginia Broadwell. Do you remember?"

"Virginia Kelly?"

"Yes. Virginia Kelly."

"Of course I remember." Leota looked out the window. A high-flying jet left a thin vapor trail across the blue sky. Nita had learned from interviewing the other elderly women that it was best to just let them talk. If she asked too many questions, their minds might wander and they might drop off to sleep. Talking to them was like panning for gold: you had to sift through a lot of dirt and rough stones to get to those gleaming bits of information, but what you came up with was pure gold.

After a while Leota cleared her throat and began.

"Miss Virginia always was a pretty girl. She had long gold ringlets and big blue eyes. She had a bad temper but her papa thought it was cute, I guess, because he seemed to encourage her. Her mama couldn't do nothing with her. She'd walk around the island carrying a peach switch like she was carrying a riding crop and anybody that crossed her got the stinging end of that switch, I tell you. She was something. Tiny as a china doll and just as pretty. Spoiled and pampered her whole life, I guess, on account of the fact she come so

late in her mama and papa's life."

Leota smiled and closed her eyes. Her lids were nearly transparent, heavily veined and wrinkled like damp parchment. They fluttered for a moment and then flew open again.

"When she was real small, before she went to school, she'd play with all the little colored children on the other end of the island. She was the Queen Bee, that's what her papa called her and it stuck, and she'd boss everybody around and make them do whatever she said. The colored folk were left over from the olden times, from slave days, back when the island had been a cotton plantation and the Kellys owned everybody. Back then there was a natural bridge from the mainland, it weren't really an island but more like a fist at the end of a long arm stretching out into the river. And the old Kelly house was a showplace, they say. But then the earthquake happened, right before the silver war, and the river swallowed up the land bridge and after that you had to take a rowboat over. All that was long after the first Kellys come down and settled the island, long after the Old People had gone."

Nita looked puzzled. She wrote down "Old People" and put a question mark next to it.

"We had no electricity back then, back

before the PWA workers brought it to the island. Nineteen forty-two it was, not too long before the war ended. Miss Virginia was just a little girl then, about seven years old, but she'd started school in town and was ashamed we didn't have electricity or plumbing on the island. The kids at school used to tease her about that — about no lights or indoor plumbing and us all using outhouses still. She'd come home crying about us being a bunch of ignorant swamp hicks and I'd have to lay her down in her little bed and put cold washcloths on her head to quiet her down."

The old woman put her head back against the rocking chair. Her slippered feet tapped the floor softly as she rocked.

"If you stand on the shore and look, there's this hump in the middle of the island. That's the Big Ridge. That's left over from the Old People, and my grandmother and the other grandmothers would tell us not to play up there when we was kids. They said the Hungry Spirits would get you."

She laughed, seeing Nita's face.

"A Hungry Spirit is kind of like a ghost."

Nita got up and went to the bureau and poured them both a glass of water. Then she sat back down, handing a glass to Leota.

The old woman smiled and sipped her water, and then set the glass down on the

146

small table beside the bed. She stretched her hands along the arms of the rocking chair, her filmy eyes fixed on the shimmering green fields beyond the parking lot.

"The Quarles were always house servants. Our cabin was up close to the Big House. All the rest were field hands and their cabins were at the other end of the island, past the Big Ridge and closest to the fields. The land was rich, on account of the river, and we grew cotton and corn and potatoes. But once every twenty years or so the river would rise and flood us out and then everything would be ruined. Then the starving times would come. In the old days, the colored folk would go to the beach and hail the passing steamboats for food. That's why all the houses are built up on stilts, even the Big House. 'Cause of the floods."

Nita was quiet a moment, imagining how it must have been. Somehow she'd pictured a more aristocratic background for Virginia. Her mother-in-law had always been careful to imply, without actually coming right out and saying it, that the Kellys were gentry. "Were Virginia's parents educated?"

Leota clasped the neckline of her flowered robe with an arthritic hand and pulled it tighter around her throat.

"Maybe at one time the Kellys were sent off

147

to school, but after the silver war they fell on hard times just like everybody else. The war and the floods took a toll on the Kellys. The Grandpapa Kelly rode away on his fine-blooded horse with his little servant boy, but after the war he come back without the boy or the horse or his right arm. The Big House was in ruins then. Some renegades from Sherman's army had camped out on the island and built a campfire right in the middle of the dining room floor. They took whatever they could carry away in a rowboat and burned most of the rest."

She blinked her eyes several times. Her face relaxed into a dreamy, faraway expression.

"After that the Kellys were dirt poor just like everybody else. Old Jennings Kelly, Miss Virginia's papa, worked for the railroad. Her mama's people come from somewhere over by Moultrie. They were small farmers."

Her head drooped. She lifted it again, fighting sleep.

"Everybody always said Miss Virginia was born with a silver spoon in her mouth, but Miz Kelly said she didn't know how that came to be since the Kellys had been living on tin for generations. Old Mr. Kelly said Virginia was a throwback to better times. He named her after his grandmother Virginia, whose people had

been big landowners over by Valdosta before the silver war."

Leota's head dropped on her chest. She began to snore softly.

Nita turned off the tape recorder and quietly gathered her purse.

CHAPTER SIX

After weeks of trying, Virginia finally discovered what made Redmon weak in the knees.
Herself, dressed as a debutante and wearing
a sequined tiara. She had been cleaning out
her closet a few days after Nita's wedding
and had stumbled on the box, yellowed with
age, by accident. Unable to help herself, she
had opened it and put on the dress to see if
it still fit. It did. Perfectly. She turned to
find Redmon standing in the doorway looking much the way a steer in the slaughter-
house must look as the stun gun is dropped
between its eyes. It seems Redmon had
always had a thing for Homecoming
Queens, and Virginia, dressed in her gown
and tiara, was close enough to the real thing
to get his heart rate up. If she had known
how easy it would be, she could have forgone the French maid outfit, the cheerlead-
ing costume, and all the other humiliating
getups she wore trying to pry the truth

about the hunting trip out of him. One look at her dressed as a debutante and Redmon told her everything she needed to know.

She lost no time calling Charles. He was sitting on the balcony of his condominium watching the river and trying not to think about Nita and Jimmy Lee on their honeymoon. The caller ID showed the call was from his mother, and for a moment, he was tempted not to take it. But if he didn't answer she would continue to call, or worse, show up in person. He sighed. "Hello," he said despondently.

"Charles, this is Mother." Her voice shook. There was a sound in her head like an engine at full throttle. Virginia prided herself on her ability to control her temper, but today there was no containing her rage.

"Yes?" Charles sounded nervous.

"I went to the wedding. It was every bit as tacky as I expected it to be. I didn't see a soul we know except for Lee Anne Bales and the Zibolsky woman, of course. And Eadie Boone."

"Did Nita look happy?"

"Yes," she said. "Ecstatic."

"Oh," he said flatly.

"That ship has sailed, Charles," she said sharply. "The sooner you realize this the better you'll be." Charles was quiet. Goaded by his silence, she said, "You've got to get on with your life. By the way, did you ask that accountant, oh what's her name, to go skiing with us?"

"Mother, I'm not going skiing," he said. And he sure as hell wasn't asking Kerry Covington with her thick ankles and attention deficit disordered son to go with him. His mother had fixed up a blind date with Kerry through one of her garden club acquaintances, and Charles had been to dinner with her twice. She was a large, solid woman with a pretty face. Charles liked her okay, but he had no intention of dating her again. She wasn't his type. She wasn't Nita.

"If you sit around and mope the gossips will never stop talking." Virginia knew very well how gossip worked. She had spread her fair share of rumors over the years. "You've got to get back out there and date and remarry, too. You're still a young man, relatively speaking. Find a pretty young girl and settle down and start another family, although on your income I don't know if you'll be able to afford another family."

"Mother, I have to go now."

"And don't think I don't know about what happened in Montana. Redmon told me everything."

Charles gripped the phone. "Well, good

152

for Redmon," he said. Redmon had been one of Boone & Broadwell's biggest clients before the hunting trip. Now he hardly gave Charles the time of day. After the dissolution of the law firm, Charles had been forced into a cramped, dusty little two-attorney storefront close to the Courthouse. You would have thought Redmon would throw some business his way now that he'd married Virginia, but so far he'd done nothing except refer a contractor who'd been arrested for DUI.

Virginia was wound up now. "The very idea that a son of mine would let himself be hoodwinked by a group of *housewives,* would let himself be made a laughingstock in front of the whole town by his dim-witted little wife . . ."

"She's not dim-witted."

"By his *unsophisticated* little wife. Charles, your father must be spinning in his grave!"

"Whatever," Charles said bleakly.

"How could you let them blackmail you over something as stupid and inane as photographs and videos?"

"Photographs and videos of us partying with female impersonators. Those are men, Mother," he said tersely, "dressed up like women."

"Yes, I know what they are," she snapped.

"But how could you let them blackmail you into bringing the whole firm down? Into letting Nita walk away with $600,000 in assets?"

"It was a partnership, Mother!" Charles could feel a pulse in his temple, steady and relentless as a ball-peen hammer. "I couldn't keep the firm afloat by myself! I couldn't keep it all together when one of my partners decided to bail and move to New Orleans, and the other was videotaped dressed up like Cher, singing 'Do you believe in life after love'." His left arm tingled and there was a tightness in his chest that probably wasn't a good thing. He didn't tell his mother what they had videotaped him doing.

Virginia appeared not to have heard a word he said. "Why didn't anyone put a stop to this? Where was I when this travesty was going on?"

Charles forced himself to calm down. He breathed deeply for several seconds. He counted to ten. When he spoke again, his voice was cold but steady. "As I recall, you were down in the Bahamas with Myra Redmon. You know. Your new husband's recently deceased wife. You do remember her, don't you, Mother?"

She didn't like his tone. There was something in his voice, some threat of impropriety that she found offensive. After all, Myra had been dead six months and Redmon had been open game, untagged and roaming free, when she bagged him. *And don't tell me Myra wouldn't have done the same thing if she'd been in my shoes,* Virginia thought savagely. "Why didn't you stand up to them?" she said. "Why didn't you take them to court?"

"I had my career to think about, Mother! I had my reputation to worry about."

"What career? What reputation?" Virginia said. "You advertise on cable access TV and you represent personal injury clients. Why cling to any hope of a good reputation?"

Charles hung up on her. Virginia clicked off. She thought about calling him back but she knew he wouldn't answer. It was clear she wouldn't get any help from Charles in avenging the family honor.

There were some things a mother just had to do herself.

Virginia was there the day Myra Redmon was killed, so tragically and unexpectedly, on the tennis court. It was an accident, of course, and as Myra didn't actually die until thirty-six hours after the event — a doubles match with Virginia and Lee Anne Bales pitted against Myra and her new and rather nervous partner — it was not determined until some time later that her death was actually attributable to tennis.

The whole tennis team was down at Amelia Island, on their annual trip, staying in Susan Barrows's condo. The condo was on the Plantation, had a private pool, next to a private tennis court, tucked into a veritable Garden of Eden, and was the primary reason Susan had been asked to join the team. The pool and the tennis court were screened from the rest of the sprawling complex by a curtain of bamboo, live oak, and yaupon and, with the exception of the few tourists who stumbled upon them by accident, the Ithaca Belles pretty much had the place to themselves.

Virginia and Myra were the co-captains and ran the team like they had run the Ithaca Garden Club, the Junior League, the Ithaca Cotillion Board, the Daughters of the Confederacy, and every other social organization worth belonging to in town — like a South American dictatorship. They had started out playing tennis with contemporaries thirty years ago, but Myra and Virginia liked to win, and as the years rolled by they began filling their roster with younger, more athletic girls. They cut players who weren't pulling their weight, held tryouts to fill open positions, and regularly won the BMW Southeastern over-thirty-five championship. Their elitism paid off. A slot on the Ithaca Belles tennis team became a coveted position of honor among the up-and-coming young housewives and stay-at-home moms, a competitive place to channel their energies now that they had given up boardrooms and six-figure-income careers.

But there was a price to pay, bringing all these younger women on board. Virginia grumbled about it often. It seemed each succeeding wave of fresh-faced recruits brought with them a growing, unsettling form of social anarchy. Far from being sedate and reserved in their manners and habits, they liked to spend freely and competitively, outdoing each other on Range Rovers and Hummers, big houses and vacation properties, liked to take frequent shopping trips to New York or Destin, liked to drink too much at cocktail parties, make fools of themselves at country club dances, liked to sleep with one another's husbands.

In short, they liked to enjoy themselves in a manner that Virginia found both uncouth and morally irresponsible. And Myra, far from remaining a staunch ally, seemed to be gradually going over to the enemy herself. Which made the circumstances surrounding her tennis accident and subsequent death all the more ironic, Virginia thought later, replaying the incident in her head.

The day before they were scheduled to leave the island, they had spent the morning drinking and driving two golf carts around the Plantation. Paige Finley had made several batches of frozen margaritas using her mother's tried-and-true recipe, which Virginia had to admit was awfully good. You couldn't even taste the tequila. They had filled two large thermoses with the stuff and drove around the Plantation giggling and sipping the potent green liquid out of champagne glasses like a bunch of bridesmaids gone bad. Virginia and Myra were the designated drivers, although it soon became apparent that Myra was doing her fair share of sipping, and when Virginia stopped at a stop sign, Myra slammed her cart into the rear of Virginia's cart, nearly severing Worland Pendergrass's leg in the process. Everyone, except Virginia, thought this was extremely funny.

Myra, still clutching her champagne glass, said, "Oops!" She looked at Virginia's golf cart and said, "Goddamn! Where'd that come from." She said, "I thought I was hit-

ting the brake but I must have hit the gas!"
She began to giggle and drained her glass,
and the injured Worland, anesthetized by
tequila, snorted and rolled off the back of
the cart onto the pavement. Not to be
outdone, Susan Barrows laughed until she
lost control of her bladder, and then told
everybody about it.

Later, they went back to the pool to get
some sun. They had the place to themselves.
Everyone stripped down to their swimsuits
and either cavorted in the pool or sprawled
in lounge chairs along the deck. Virginia sat
in the shade and filled out the round-robin
schedule on the off chance someone might
actually want to play tennis. Lee Anne Bales
and Paige Finley prank-called the strapping
young bartender who had waited on them
the previous night. Myra snored in the sun.
Laura Teague, on a dare from Susan and
Worland, pulled down her bathing suit and
flashed her boobs at a group of stunned
Japanese businessmen who sped by in a
crowded golf cart.

Virginia felt like a Girl Scout leader trying
to maintain control of an unruly troop. She
rose suddenly and announced the court as-
signments, looking severely at Lee Anne and
Myra, who rose reluctantly and went into
the dressing room to change into their ten-

nis clothes. Myra's new partner, Molly Ditri, jumped up obediently and went to change. She was a newcomer to Ithaca, a thirty-five-year-old Yankee who tried, unsuccessfully, to soften this by saying she was from the Midwest. She was married to an anesthesiologist and was apprehensive and shocked to find herself not only on the best tennis team in Ithaca, Georgia, but actually playing as Myra Redmon's partner. She had played college tennis for Michigan State and had a ninety-mile-per-hour serve, but she was still intimidated about playing with Myra and would constantly apologize when she missed a volley at the net or hit an overhead long, a trait that infuriated the competitive Myra.

"Stop apologizing and do your job," Myra would growl, and Molly, mortified, would dip her head and thump her fist on her racket, determined to do better.

But today, after a good nap and several pitchers of frozen margaritas, Myra was in a good mood. She could have cared less if Molly double-faulted on her serve or hit a passing shot wide. They lined up on the court, Virginia and Lee Anne on one side and Myra and Molly on the other. The sun was almost directly overhead but the trees arching over the court provided a cool shade. Virginia served first, and she and Lee Anne won the first game. They were switching courts when Paige pulled up in one of the golf carts with a new supply of frozen margaritas. The women in the pool hooted and lifted their champagne glasses.

Virginia said, "Oh good God."

Myra said, "Bring that pitcher over here and pour me another glass."

Paige did as she was told. They stood in the shade taking a breather, Virginia and Molly sipping their bottled water while Myra and Lee Anne gulped frozen margaritas.

"You know," Virginia said, looking sternly at Myra, "we're supposed to be getting ready for BMW. That's the whole reason we're down here."

Myra said, "Hey y'all, after we finish this pitcher, let's go skinny dipping in the pool."

Lee Anne giggled. Virginia handed the balls to Molly and walked out onto the court.

Molly had drunk enough frozen margaritas earlier to take the edge off her nervousness, but not enough to make her totally relaxed. Like all college players, she had a blinding serve but it was erratic and prone to miss the service court entirely. Since joining the Ithaca Belles, to keep from double-faulting and incurring the wrath of her partner, she had taken to hitting the second serve soft if she hit the first one out. To a girl who had once, briefly, considered going pro, this was a humiliating state to find herself in. But it couldn't be helped. Molly looked at Myra, bent over at the net with her long slim legs tensed and her tennis panties clearly visible, and prayed her first serve would go in.

It went wide.

Myra, under the influence of tequila, looked at Molly over her shoulder and grinned. "Come on, partner," she said, slurring her words only slightly. "You can do it. Come on, girl. Hit that ball like you used to hit it in college."

It was all the encouragement Molly needed. She threw the ball high, rose up on her toes, and drilled a ninety-five-mile-an-hour serve directly into her partner's backside.

There was a moment of stunned silence. Molly dropped her racket on the court and covered her mouth with both hands. The girls in the pool, who had seen the whole thing, watched in slack-jawed astonishment. It was Lee Anne who broke first, slumping to her knees, her racket clattering against the court. She hooted and screamed, and rolled onto her back, kicking her legs in the air. The girls in the pool followed suit, and eventually Myra, tears of laughter and pain streaming down her face, pulled her panties down to reveal the perfect imprint of a tennis ball. Even Virginia giggled then. They were still laughing that night at dinner, getting Myra to show them her "tennis tattoo," still giggling and slapping each other on the arms on the long drive home. They were still chortling that night around their dinner tables, as they told their husbands and children, still smiling as they dropped off to sleep, while the fateful blood clot formed by Molly's blinding serve made its way slowly but inexorably from Myra's ass, through her femoral artery, and into her heart. Redmon awakened next to his wife the following morning to find her stone cold dead, a peaceful smile on her lips.

Having killed her tennis partner, Molly Ditri did the only thing she could do: she left town in the middle of the night, leaving her husband to arrange the packing of the furnishings and the sale of the big house. He followed her six months later to the suburbs of Chicago where she had settled in anonymity, hoping to leave her tragic past behind her.

She never picked up a tennis racket again.

CHAPTER SEVEN

When Eadie got home from Nita's wedding, Trevor was glad to see her. He had made scallops Creole with rice and they ate in front of a roaring fire in the dark, cavernous library. After dinner they laid down on the sofa and got reacquainted in ways that went beyond what might have been expected of a couple that had been married for twenty-two years. The following morning they got up at noon, packed a hamper full of sandwiches and martinis, and went for a picnic at Lafayette Cemetery #1. It was a beautiful day, cool and sunny. A damp fishy breeze blew steadily from the sea. The gravestones and walls of the old mausoleums were covered in lichen and mildew, and around the graveled paths the St. Augustine grass grew in thick, springy clumps. They found a secluded spot in one of the back corners, between the brick wall and the tomb of Angelique Wirz who died in 1826 at the age of twenty-one. Trevor spread the blanket and they lay down, their martini glasses resting on their stomachs, gazing up at the azure sky through the thick twisted canopy of live oak.

Eadie closed her eyes. After a while Trevor rolled over on his side and propped himself up on one elbow, setting his drink on the ground in front of him. He picked a handful of coarse grass and dropped it, blade by blade, onto Eadie's face.

"Stop it," she said, waving her hand in front of her nose like she was swatting a persistent fly. "I'm trying to sleep. I'm tired."

"I'll bet you are," he said. "After last night. After this morning."

She opened one eye and regarded him lazily. She yawned and patted her mouth. "Jet lag," she said.

"Jet lag, my ass," he said, and leaned to bite her belly.

She yelped and sat up, spilling her drink. "Now look what you made me do," she said.

"Here, I'll make you another one." He took her glass and sat up, pulling a metal cocktail shaker out of the hamper. He topped off both drinks, and they lay down again on their sides, facing each other.

"In all the get reacquainted frenzy last

night, I forgot to ask you." He grinned and she did, too. "What's new in the old home-town?"

She ran her finger lightly around the rim of her glass trying to make it sing. "Not a damn thing," she said.

"Did you see any of your old boyfriends?"

"What old boyfriends? I don't have any old boyfriends from Ithaca."

"You have one," he said.

She snorted and lifted her glass, arching one eyebrow. "Some boyfriend," she said.

He groaned and rolled over on his back. "Come on, honey, don't bust my balls. I know you love me. I know you missed me."

She leaned over, giving him the full effect of her almond-shaped green eyes. "Yeah?" she said. "What makes you so special?"

He rolled over on top of her and nuzzled his face roughly against her neck. "You know very well what makes me so special."

She poked him in the ribs but he wasn't ticklish. "Get off me, peckerhead."

"That's not what you said last night."

"Very funny."

It didn't last, of course. He was attentive for two whole weeks but on a rainy Tuesday evening she heard him rise, long after he as-sumed she had gone to sleep, and walk quietly out of the bedroom and down the stairs. After a while she rose and followed him.

He sat at his desk in the library, his face lit by the neon screen of his laptop. A fire crackled in the grate. Outside the long windows, a steady rain fell, drumming against the roof and rattling the glass.

"What're you doing?" she said.

He jumped and swung around, ducking his head slightly. "Goddamn it, Eadie, you almost gave me a heart attack. Don't creep up behind me like that."

"Sorry."

"Why were you turning the lights on and off in the kitchen?"

"I wasn't in the kitchen."

He frowned. "Then who was?"

"I told you the house was haunted."

He sighed and ran his hand over his face. Then he clasped his hands behind his head and leaned back in his chair. "Look, if you don't want to live here, that's fine. You don't have to make up stories just to get me to sell the house."

She went over to the bar to pour herself a whiskey. She stood for a moment with her back to him, listening to the rain. "Do you have any idea how insulting it is to find you skulking around the house at all hours of the night, hiding so you can work?" she said, turning around to face him.

He watched her steadily, his elbows spread out on either side of his head like wings. He said, "Do you know how guilty it makes me feel, that I can work and you can't?"

"Now you know how I've felt for most of our marriage."

"Then you should be more sympathetic."

"I could work and you couldn't." She smiled arrogantly and lifted her drink. "As I recall, you drowned your frustration by chasing tail."

"Just like you drown yours in sleep and Mondo Logs."

She threw the glass at him. It crashed against the far wall and fell against the floor, shattering. He watched her coldly. "Sooner or later," he said. "I'll get too old to duck."

She went back upstairs. A little while later, he followed her. *My Fair Lady,* the late-show movie, was playing on Channel 9. Eadie was lying in bed with a box of Mondo Logs resting on her stomach. She rummaged around in the box, the empty papers rustling like leaves along a deserted street. He stood in the doorway with his shoulder pressed against the jamb, his arms hanging down against his sides.

"You'd be happier if you were working," he said.

"No shit, Trevor. You're a genius at stating the obvious."

He sighed and ran his fingers through his hair. Outside the window the rain fell in sheets.

"I worked the whole time I was in Ithaca," she said.

"So what are you saying?"

"I'm saying I can't work here."

"Look, I love New Orleans," he said, pushing himself off the jamb. "Don't blame the city just because you've got artist's block."

"I'm not blaming anything," she said. "I'm just telling it like it is."

"You're showing the classic symptoms," he said.

"The classic symptoms for what?"

"For depression."

"Fuck off, Trevor."

"You sleep all day, some days you don't even get dressed. I want to help you, Eadie," he said. "But I don't know what to do."

"Stay here," Eadie said. "Don't go to New York."

"Goddamn it, Eadie, that's so unfair."

"I need you here."

"You *need.* That's the problem, Eadie. You need too much. You're like a goddamn succubus. I can't give you everything you need and have anything left for me."

He went to the closet and took down his suitcase. Eliza Doolittle was learning to say, *The rain in Spain falls mainly on the plain.* Trevor put the suitcase on the end of the bed and opened it. Then he went to the dresser and began to take out stacks of clothing. He tossed them into the case without looking.

"I thought you weren't leaving until Thursday," Eadie said.

"I've got to get some work done. I've got a second novel to write, Eadie. I've got deadlines and pressures. If I can't write here, I'll write in New York."

She kicked suddenly and pushed the suitcase off the bed onto the floor. He picked it up and flung it onto a chair and began to repack.

"Don't bother going to New York," she said evenly. "I'll leave. You can stay here and I'll go."

Trevor slammed the suitcase lid closed. He went into the closet and came out with a couple of dress shirts and a tweed sports jacket. They were still on hangers and he zipped them into a garment bag and laid it over the chair. He stood looking at her, his face shadowed by the green glow of the TV screen. "I love you, honey," he said. "And I want to help you. But I can't do anything if you won't try."

"Unpack that suitcase," Eadie said. "You're not going anywhere."

"Sally Potter gave me the name of a good therapist." He took his wallet out of his back pocket, opened it, and began to rifle around inside. "She gave me his card."

Eadie's mouth sagged. Her face flushed on one side like she'd been slapped by an unseen hand. "Tell me you haven't been talking about me with Sally Potter," she said. They'd served together on a committee to raise money for Audubon Park. Eadie hated the woman.

"Sally's been on Prozac for about a year now. She says it's made all the difference. She says some women have trouble with their endorphin levels as they age."

"Tell me you haven't been talking about me with goddamn Sally Potter." She was so mad she began to cry, which surprised even Eadie. She'd never been the kind of woman who cried, especially during heated arguments with her husband. Crying seemed like the coward's way out.

"Honey, you need endorphins. You need serotonin." He took a step toward her but she put her hand up to stop him. He swung the garment bag up on his shoulder.

"I don't need a therapist," she shouted.

He picked up the suitcase. "Sleep won't work," he said sadly. "Mondo Logs won't work."

She grabbed pillows off the bed and began to fling them at him as he walked out of the room. They bounced off his head like pellets fired from a shooting gallery gun at a row of moving ducks. Over the years, she'd become a pretty good shot. "If you leave now, we're through," she sobbed. She wasn't even sure why she had said that. She floated around on the ceiling looking down at the violent crazy woman below her. She thought, *Who is that woman?* She thought, *Maybe I should get my hormones checked.* She said, "If you walk out of this room, our marriage is over."

She'd run out of pillows to fling. "I'll call you tomorrow," he said. He closed the door softly behind him. She was reminded of all those times, years ago, when her lonely mother had brought home a steady procession of worthless men who never seemed to stay longer than a few days. Eadie would awake some mornings to the sound of her mother sobbing quietly in the tiny bedroom of the trailer and she would know that the latest Romeo had gone, stealing away in the dark hours just before dawn.

172

She lay back down in the middle of the big empty bed. Downstairs she heard Trevor's car pull out of the drive but she wouldn't go to the window to look. She wouldn't stand there and watch him drive away. She thought of all the men who had paraded through her sad mother's dreary life. Eadie hadn't had a parade of men.

She had only had one.

On a Wednesday in late February, Joe Solomon showed up for half-price cookie day. Lavonne was in the office working on some inventory reports when Little Moses stuck his head in the door. "Hey, you've got company," he said, grinning. "A gentleman caller."

"A gentleman caller?" Lavonne said. "What in the hell is that?"

Little Moses lowered his chin and pursed his lips. "Come out front and I'll show you," he said.

Joe Solomon was standing over by the display case she had set up showcasing some of their bottled products. She hadn't seen him since that day in the park after Nita's wedding. When he saw her he grinned and lifted a slim bottle. "Grandma Ada's Kosher Barbecue Sauce," he said. "Now this I have to try." He was dressed in a blue oxford

173

cloth shirt and a pair of khaki slacks. His eyes, she noticed, were less green today and more of a slate-blue color. She wondered where he'd been the last couple of weeks.

"I'll make you up a gift basket if you like. We've got several kosher products you might enjoy. We make them from my partner's old family recipes."

Joe walked slowly toward the counter still holding the bottle. "I'll take a basket and I'd like one sent to my mother, too, in Buffalo."

"We can do that," Lavonne said, trying not to seem too friendly. She figured if he hadn't been in since that day in the park, he probably wasn't that interested in her. She'd probably imagined the whole thing. She stared steadily at Little Moses who was wiping down the top of the glass case as if he was the only one in the room, as if he wasn't listening to every word of their conversation.

"Oh," Little Moses said, feeling the weight of her eyes. He grinned. "Let me get those baskets for you."

"That would be nice," Lavonne said.

"It'll take just a minute," Little Moses said, putting down the cloth. "I'll have to go in the back to make them up."

"Yes I know that."

He stood there grinning and wiping his hands on his apron. Lavonne made a slight movement with her head toward the kitchen door. Joe pretended to read the ingredients label on the back of the bottle. Little Moses thrust his arm suddenly across the counter. "Moses Shapiro," he said to Joe.

"Joe Solomon," he said, taking his hand firmly. He set the bottle down on the counter.

Little Moses cocked one eyebrow at Lavonne as he went out. "You kids be good," he said. "I'll be right back."

"He's a cheerful fellow," Joe said as the door swung shut on his heels.

"Yes, isn't he." Lavonne picked up the cloth Little Moses had dropped and began to clean the glass. Now that they were alone in the room, she felt self-conscious, aware of the fact that he was watching her work with a curious expression on his face.

"You missed a spot," he said, pointing at the glass, and she couldn't tell if he was teasing her or if he was disappointed.

"Thanks," she said. She was aware of the awkward silence that seemed to rise and flatten out between them like a bad odor. She barely knew the man. Why should she care that he hadn't come by to see her since that disastrous day in the park? She wished she was one of those women who could ramble on about nothing in particular, the kind who could make outrageous comments to men without feeling self-conscious or awkward. It didn't help that Joe Solomon looked so damn attractive, standing there in his blue shirt with his light brown hair and eyes the soft gray color of rain.

He cleared his throat. "So what's the deal with half-price cookie day?" he said gruffly, leaning his elbows on the top of the glass so Lavonne would have to stop wiping.

She stepped away from the counter and folded the cloth in a neat square, stuffing it down in the pocket of her apron. "Buy a dozen and get the second dozen at half price."

"Oh yeah? What's good?"

She leaned over and tapped the glass in a professional manner. "The May Days are good," she said. "But if you like chocolate, the Chocolate Walnut cookies are to die for."

"I'll have a dozen of each," he said. Again, that tone in his voice, not friendly, but brisk and stilted.

It probably has something to do with that day in the park, she thought, leaning over to pick up the cookie trays. It probably has something to do with Fleshy Delights. As she stood up, she accidentally knocked the tray against the case and two of the cookies slid off onto the floor. She swung around, catching her apron pocket on the edge of the counter. It ripped open along one seam. "Shit," Lavonne said.

The kitchen door swung open and Little Moses came out carrying two gift baskets. He set them down on the counter with a flourish and Lavonne said to him, not looking at Joe, "Okay, he wants two dozen cookies, too. Can you ring him up?" Her voice was curt and businesslike.

Little Moses glanced from one to the other. "Sure," he said.

Lavonne took off her apron and fled to the back office. The door was open a crack and she heard them talking in low voices while Little Moses rang him up. *What in the hell is wrong with me?* she thought glumly. *I've probably just offended a paying customer.* A few minutes later she heard the bell on the door tinkle as he went out.

She put her elbow on the desk and covered her eyes with one hand. She could hear Little Moses's footsteps as he headed for the office but then the bell tinkled again, as another customer came in, and he went back up front. *Maybe I should take a class,* she thought despondently. *Maybe I should read a book on how to talk to men I find at-*

tractive. Or, hell, maybe I should just get Eadie to teach me. She heard Little Moses's footsteps again in the hallway. A moment later he knocked lightly on the door. She dropped her hand and looked up.

Joe Solomon stood in the doorway. "I'm not very good at this," he said.

"Good at what?"

"At asking people out. At dating. It's not something I do a lot of."

"And I'm a regular Mata Hari, as you can tell."

He grinned. "Mata Hari," he said. "I like that."

"My friend Eadie says flirting is nothing more than the ability to give a candy-coated insult, and that I should be good at it, given my sarcastic wit."

"I can imagine your friend Eadie saying that."

"You met her at the park. The pretty one with the long legs. Remember?"

"I remember," he said. He shrugged and leaned one shoulder against the jamb. "She's not really my type. I go for the pretty, awkward girls with the sarcastic wit."

"Oh, thank you very much." She smiled and drummed her fingers on the desk, enjoying this.

"So is it a date then?" He pushed himself

off the jamb. It occurred to her he was as nervous as she was. "Friday night. Dinner. I'll pick you up at seven?"

"Sure," she said. "Why not."

He turned to go but then stuck his head back in the door. "By the way," he said. "I've been in Chicago. Visiting my daughter. In case you were wondering."

After he left, she sat there feeling like she had grabbed hold of a high-voltage wire. Her feet vibrated. Her hands shook. It occurred to her that she hadn't had a date in twenty-two years, if she didn't count the three years she was engaged to Leonard. Things had certainly changed since then. Twenty-two years ago a first date ended with a kiss and a handshake, *if* you liked each other. Now it seemed that pretty much anything goes.

She stopped at the grocery store on the way home and picked up a *Cosmopolitan* magazine trying to get a few tips on the modern dating scene. After dinner, she fixed herself a vodka martini and got halfway through the article "How to Please Your Man in Bed," when she realized she wasn't going to be able to do this. Any of this. All the Kegel exercises in the world wouldn't fix a leaky bladder. Not to mention the fact that no one had seen her naked since 1982.

She sighed and tossed the magazine over the edge of the bed. It would probably be less humiliating for them both if she just called him and told him she couldn't make it Friday night, something had come up. But that seemed rather cowardly. The truth of the matter was, she was looking forward to the date. She still felt a little like she had this afternoon in the office, like she was harnessed to some kind of electrical current that was sending vibrating waves of energy through her body.

Not an unpleasant feeling, really.

CHAPTER EIGHT

Now that she had finally gained the upper hand over Redmon, Virginia set about planning her revenge with all the cunning and strategy of which she was capable. Gaining her granddaughter's affections was turning out to be easier than she had imagined. She made arrangements with Charles to pick up Whitney from school on his visitation days, and took the girl out to dinner on those days when Charles was working late. She took Whitney shopping every chance she got and made arrangements with Nita to take her granddaughter and some of her friends to Atlanta next month for an overnight visit. Virginia was careful to consult Nita in all things, implying that she and Nita were allies protecting a lovable but naive teenager. When she was with Whitney, however, it was a different story. Then she was all sympathy and unconditional approval.

Like most teenage girls, Whitney harbored

an intense feeling of resentment toward her mother, a feeling she was only too happy to share with Virginia. Nita was a "control freak," she was unfair and unforgiving, she wanted to force Whitney into being someone she was not. Nita was forty, her life was nearly over anyway, and she was determined that Whitney's life would be as drab and boring as hers was. The revelations were endless and dramatic, accompanied by groans and gnashing of teeth and much rolling of her eyes. Virginia had only to listen and cluck her tongue in sympathy. She had only to tell Whitney that she, too, had dreamed of fame and glory as a young girl, but had been thwarted at every turn. Whitney sighed and nodded her head in acknowledgment of Virginia's struggles. The trap was set.

She took Redmon out to the island three times in the weeks following Nita's wedding. The first time, they spent several hours exploring the old Kelly place, which was in ruins now and covered in creeping vines. The kitchen wing had fallen down years ago and the windows across the front had all been broken so the rain had poured in and made a mess of the pine floors. There were still bits and pieces of furniture scattered throughout the rooms. Virginia's grandmother's grand piano stood in one corner, a nesting place for rats and swallows, its keys yellowed and blistered with age. In the dining room, someone had dragged in an old mattress. It showed recent signs of occupancy. Teenagers used the island as a place to hold parties and bonfires in the summer months, swimming across the narrow river or paddling over on rafts.

"It must have been a showplace, Queenie," Redmon said, looking up at the vine-covered monstrosity.

"It was," Virginia said. She had a daguerreotype taken not long before the War Between the States that showed the house in its prewar glory. It had, indeed, been a showplace.

"It would take more money than it's worth to fix it up though."

"Oh, I'm not talking about fixing it up," she said quickly. They stepped outside onto the porch. "We would have to bulldoze this old place. I'm talking about the property itself," she said, lifting her arms and indicating the heavy forest, thick with sweet gum and cottonwood and wild pecan. "I'm talking about the island," she said pointing at the tall trees where brightly colored birds chattered like monkeys. Out in the slow-moving river a herd of turtles sunned themselves on a cypress stump. Great herons fished in the shallow coves along the beach. "I'm talking about two hundred twenty acres of prime lakefront property."

She had done her homework well. She had laid the groundwork as carefully and steadily as a mason building a foundation out of handmade brick. She had started in at dinner, several days ago, softening him up with tales of retirees who were flocking to the South in droves, noting various television shows that highlighted vacation home properties, lying awake in bed and whispering about aging baby boomers who thirsted for second homes the way de Soto had thirsted for gold.

The first time she took him out to the island, he had done nothing but criticize, noting the island's remote wildness, the difficulty of providing adequate utilities to the home sites, the expense of building an access bridge. She had taken him out in the boat and shown him the old land bridge that still existed, although submerged several feet below the surface of the water. "Perhaps it wouldn't be as difficult to build a bridge as you might think?" she had suggested. The second time they went out, he had already worked out solutions to the problems of access and utilities in his mind.

Now he rambled on about the costs of development; they would be astronomical. It would involve huge loans and risky leveraging. "Of course I don't know anything about business, dear," Virginia had said, her eyes wide and angelic. "But would the fact that I own the property outright help with the leveraging?"

By the third visit, Redmon strode along the remains of the sandy road that ran the length of the island explaining where the utility lines would go, pointing out natural features that would need to be kept and walking off the potential lot lines himself. He figured, with careful planning, they might be able to carve three hundred home sites as well as a clubhouse and, who knew, maybe even a nine-hole golf course out of the property. Virginia followed behind him, saying things like, "Oh, I never thought of that," or, "Oh, I wish I had a head for business like you do," and once, her little hand resting on her cheek, "Of course I don't know anything about the development game, but do you think we could get Arnold Palmer to do the golf course?"

They reached the top of the Big Ridge and stepped out from beneath the tall trees into a clearing. Below them the fields, fallow now for years and covered in groves of

Johnson grass and honeysuckle and wild chinaberry, hugged the river like a ragged crust. In the narrow coves, catfish as big as feed sacks rolled on their bellies like whales.

"Plantation Island," Redmon said, standing with one leg cocked, his weight on the other, and his belly swaying over his belt like a sack of potatoes. He frowned. "Naw, that ain't it. Something Plantation. We need Plantation in the name because it sounds classy. Yankees like that shit."

"My grandmother was a Culpepper," Virginia said softly.

"Yeah," Redmon said, squinting his eyes. "Something Plantation. And we need one of those sayings that go along with it. You know, like 'Wheaties, Breakfast of Champions.' Or 'Nike, Just Do It.' "

"You mean a slogan?"

"We need a slogan to go along with it." He looked up into the trees, narrowing his eyes like he was trying to read something on a road sign.

"Southern graciousness. Down-home friendliness," Virginia said.

"Something that makes people want to visit and settle down." Redmon puffed out his cheeks and sucked in his lips, looking like a man trying to pass a rather large kidney stone. "Something they might read on a billboard or in an ad in the *Wall Street Journal.* Something that makes them want to come on down here and visit, and hell, maybe even stay." Redmon scratched his head. He looked up at the blue sky. Then he looked down at the slow-moving river. "I've got it!" he said suddenly, his face relaxing into a wide grin. He put his hands up in front of her like a movie director trying to describe a scene to a dim-witted actress. "Culpepper Plantation," he said. "Southern graciousness. Down-home friendliness."

"Oh my," Virginia murmured. "Now that is clever."

"I tell you, Queenie, I think we can make a go of this."

Virginia put her soft little hand on his chest. Her eyes were as wide and blue as saucers. "Do you think so?" she said.

"Oh, hell yes. Sometimes, when an idea comes to me, I just know if it's right. I just know if it's going to work or not. It's a feeling I get right here," he said, touching his sternum. He picked her up in his arms and then put her down again, slapping her so hard on the rear end that she squealed. He kissed her before she could protest and then stood looking down at the river. Gradually, his expression changed. He chewed his

187

lower lip in a manner she had come to recognize as worry. "Only thing is, I don't know who I'll bring in with me to do the work. Hell, I can't get nobody around here to do it. Not after that last shopping center deal and all those crybaby subs who lost their shirts. I might have to go all the way to Atlanta to get a contractor."

Virginia didn't miss a beat. "How about Nita's new husband?" she asked sweetly.

Nita had spent most of her honeymoon finishing up her paper on domestic servants. She had told her professor that she'd get a rough draft to him before Christmas but with all the excitement over the upcoming wedding that hadn't happened. She had dutifully warned Jimmy Lee about her need to work and he'd agreed that was okay with him, but once the honeymoon came and she went around all day with her nose stuck in her notes, he wasn't happy. Their little cabin took on a dismal atmosphere. The children were staying with Charles for that week and Jimmy Lee had told his customers he couldn't work on account of his responsibilities as a new bridegroom. He spent most of his time out on the river in his boat.

Nita tried not to feel guilty. Guilt was one

of those things she had decided to give up when she ended her marriage to Charles Broadwell. She had told Jimmy Lee when she went back to school that this was important to her. She had warned him it would be best to postpone the wedding until summer but he had seemed anxious to slip a ring on her finger as quickly as he could. The fact he had disregarded her warnings was his fault, not hers.

Still, it was hard watching him trudge off toward the boat every morning with his fishing tackle under his arm and a look of lonely depression on his face. "We'll go somewhere for spring break, honey," she'd call to him from the screened porch. "I promise."

But here it was almost the end of February and she'd finished her paper and turned it in for review, and she was still no closer to freeing up time to spend with her new husband. She was taking fifteen hours this semester and was substitute teaching at the local public schools from time to time, still trying to decide whether she wanted to take her degree in women's studies or elementary ed. And then there was the little matter of Leota Quarles. It made no sense, really, to visit the old woman. It was too late to include her in the paper, and there was no reason to be driving out to the nursing

189

home to interview her about the Kelly family. No reason except that Nita was beginning to find herself deeply and irrevocably fascinated by the story of Virginia Kelly's childhood. She had to admit, now that Virginia was no longer her mother-in-law, there was something about her that drew Nita in. And there was a big question Nita had always wanted answered. She had always wondered what it was that made a woman like Virginia act the way she did.

Virginia was like one of those destructive icebergs that cruise the North Sea in January. What you saw was only the bright shining tip, while underneath the surface something dark and cold and deadly loomed. Something that made your spine shiver. Something you couldn't outrun no matter how hard you tried.

On this warm Thursday afternoon in late February, Nita stood on her back steps and thought about her ex-mother-in-law. She thought about how much time Virginia was spending with Whitney these days and she felt suddenly ashamed of her distrust of the older woman. Maybe she had misjudged Virginia all these years. True, it would have been nice if she had been as conscientious a grandmother when the children were small. It would have been nice to have an occasional babysitter or even a grandmother who showed up for soccer games or school performances. But Nita was willing to accept the notion that people can change. She was willing to give Virginia the benefit of the doubt.

She stood on the back steps and called to Jimmy Lee. He was at the corner of the yard closest to the river, building a garden shed to house the lawn mower and the gardening tools he hoped Nita would soon learn to use. "Jimmy, I'll be back in a couple of hours," she said, cupping her hands around her mouth.

He stood up and looked at her. He was dressed in a pair of faded jeans and a Southern Culture on the Skids T-shirt. "Where are you going?" he said irritably. He was in between carpentry jobs, February and March were typically his slow months, and this could explain his foul mood. Or partially explain it, anyway.

"I'm going out to the nursing home to interview someone."

He wiped his brow with the back of one hand. "Why do you have to go out to the goddamn nursing home today?" He stood there looking sweaty and dejected.

"I've got a paper to finish. I told you that." She blushed and looked at her feet. Lying

191

wasn't something that came naturally to Nita.

He leaned over the sawhorses and went back to work, measuring a piece of plywood. "I can pick something up for dinner on the way home," she said hopefully. She didn't have to cook tonight. Whitney was spending the weekend with Virginia and Charles had taken Logan on a desperate, last-ditch effort at father-son bonding trip to Atlanta.

Jimmy Lee snapped his metallic measuring tape like he was cracking a bullwhip. He slid his pencil into his back pocket. Nita tried again. "What would you like for dinner?"

He stood up. "What difference does it make what I want?" he said bleakly. He wore a Dale Earnhardt cap turned around backward. Standing there with his shoulders slumped and his face set in lines of disappointment and self-pity, Nita didn't like to think about how much he reminded her of Charles.

"How about barbecue?"

He swung around and headed for a pile of lumber at the edge of the yard. "Suit yourself," he shouted over his shoulder. "You will anyway."

On the way out to the nursing home, Nita thought about what had happened. Wasn't it just like a man to promise one thing and then change his mind once an agreement had been reached? Hadn't Charles done the same thing when he promised to love, honor, and obey her all the days of his life? Or had he promised to obey? Nita frowned, trying to remember. Well, it didn't matter. She had promised to obey and look what that got her. Sixteen years of misery. That was the first thing she had changed in her wedding vow to Jimmy Lee. She had the minister take out obey and instead they had both agreed to love and honor each other. This had seemed a reasonable and achievable goal.

Nita had spent her whole life obeying someone — her parents, her teachers, Reverend Reeves, her Girl Scout leader, her boss down at the Dairy King. Her ex-husband. Going back to college was something *she* had wanted to do. No one had told her to do it. It was something she had wanted for herself. She enjoyed school. She enjoyed learning. And she liked substitute teaching, too. She liked walking into a classroom and seeing all those bright, eager young faces looking up at her. She had spent sixteen years as a stay-at-home wife and mother, and now she had a life of her own and she liked it that way. She had thought Jimmy Lee understood this. He had promised her he did.

Well, he would just have to live up to his promise. She wasn't going to change who she was to suit someone else. She had tried that before and it had nearly driven her to a nervous breakdown.

She turned right at Bennie Lane and drove slowly past the Ithaca Middle School. The marquee out front read "Fruitcake Sale! Do Your Part! Buy a Fruitcake!" The school looked bleak and deserted. A small group of skateboarders stood around the flagpole smoking cigarettes and slapping their boards with their feet. Nita lifted her hand and waved as she drove past. They waved back.

She had been volunteering at the school last week when she ran into Angel Phipps. Nita was out in the hallway hanging "Abstinence Works — Just Say No" posters on the wall, when fourteen-year-old Angel walked by with her one-year-old daughter, Precious Memory, on her hip.

"Hey, Miz Broadwell," Angel said.

"Well, hello, Angel," Nita said, hugging her and the baby. Angel switched Precious to the other hip. The baby stared blankly at Nita. Her nose ran steadily. "I didn't know you and your family had moved back to town. Are you still in school?"

"Yes'm. I'm finishing up the eighth grade. I sat out after Precious Memory came but then I went back this year. If she ain't working, Mama watches her when I'm in school."

"I'm glad," Nita said. "An education is important. I'm back in school myself."

Angel blinked. "Are you, Miz Broadwell?" She sounded so surprised that Nita laughed. Angel said, "GED?"

"No, college." She put her hand up and touched the baby's face lightly with her fingers. Precious Memory stared vacantly. She lifted a chubby hand and stuck one finger in her nose. "Listen, I've got some old baby things of Whitney's I'd love to give you. A stroller, car seat, high chair, some clothes and toys." It was a lie, of course. She'd given those things away years ago. She'd have to stop by the church thrift store on the way home but she didn't want Angel to know that. "I've been meaning to have a garage sale but I really don't have the time. It'd be a lot easier if I could just find someone to give the stuff to. Do you think you can help me out, Angel?"

"Sure, Miz Broadwell, I can help you out." She obviously hadn't heard about Nita remarrying.

"Okay, give me your phone number." Nita

took her cell phone out of her pocket and punched the number into memory. "I'll call you," she said to Angel as she moved off.

"Okay. See you later." Precious Memory watched her solemnly over Angel's shoulder as they walked away, her fat finger still lodged in her nose.

Nita watched them go and thought about Angel Phipps as she had been years ago, a bright kindergartner with a gap-toothed smile and domineering spirit. In those days Nita had volunteered at the elementary school, helping the children learn to read. The first day of class, Nita had herded a group of timid five-year-olds out into the hall for a drink of water from the fountain. They all lined up obediently behind Angel who pushed herself roughly to the front of the group. She took her time at the fountain, making loud slurping noises and rolling her eyes at the others.

Finally, Bobby Barfield touched her timidly on the shoulder. "Are you finished?" he asked politely.

"Get off me motherfucker," Angel said.

After the others had filed back into the classroom, Nita kept Angel outside for a little talk. She gently explained that it was wrong to use bad language, especially at school. Angel nodded as if she understood perfectly, but later, during nap time, when they were stretched out on the floor on their little mats, Angel told Willie Connor to move his fat ass before she kicked him in his man-jewels.

"What?" the frightened Willie said.

"You heard me asshole," Angel said.

Later, Nita sat with her on the little bench outside the principal's office, waiting for Angel's mother to show up. She heard her coming before she saw her, a huge woman wearing cut-off shorts and slippers that slapped against the floor like cannon fire. Her hair was loose around her shoulders and she had a mouth full of yellow teeth and a mole on her left cheek that sprouted black curly hairs. Nita sent Ophelia Phipps on into the principal's office and a few minutes later they heard her shouting behind the closed door, "Goddamn it to hell, I've told that girl not to use bad language at school but she's so fuckin' stubborn you can't tell her a motherfuckin' thing. What the fuck's a mother to do with a kid like that?"

Soon after that, Angel's father got a job in a machine shop over close to Tifton and the family moved. Nita lost track of Angel. But one hot July morning several years later, Nita got a panicked call from Ophelia

Phipps. It seemed her husband, Edgar, had dropped dead at work and Ophelia was in a panic to get over there and pick up his paycheck so she could cash it before the bank found out he was dead. Nita didn't question the logic, or the legality, of this situation, but simply drove over to Tifton to get Ophelia, drove her out to the Battle Smoove Machine Shop so she could go through the dead man's pockets, and then waited in the car while Ophelia went into the Wal-Mart and successfully cashed the check.

Six months later, Nita ran into Ophelia's sister out at the Wal-Mart and she told Nita how Ophelia had killed Edgar for the insurance money and because she suspected him of being Precious Memory's daddy. "She was real smart about it," the sister bragged, looking around slyly. "She loaded his oatmeal up with maple syrup and antifreeze and fixed it so he'd die at work where no questions was asked."

The sister reeked of Jack Daniel's, so Nita couldn't be sure any of this was true, but she had hoped, for Angel's sake, it was. Some people just needed killing.

Leota Quarles was sitting up in bed when Nita entered the room and the nurse said,

"Oh, Mrs. Broadwell, I mean Mrs. Motes, I tried to call you and tell you Miz Quarles isn't feeling well today."

"I'm sorry," Nita said, going around to the other side of the bed. She patted Leota's arm. "I bet you don't feel up to visitors today."

Leota smiled gamely. "Well, honey, I always look forward to your visits. You know that."

"I've given her something to make her sleep," the nurse said.

"Maybe just a few minutes?" Nita asked.

"Just a few minutes," Leota said, looking at the nurse stubbornly.

"All right," the nurse said. She tucked Leota's blanket around her chest. "But you need to get some rest," she said. She turned off the overhead light as she went out, leaving only the bedside lamp glowing.

Nita took out her notebook and began to read back over what she'd transcribed from last time. Leota's eyes fluttered. "Oh yes," she said, pulling her hands out of the blanket and folding them over her chest. "I remember now."

"Seems over on the island Miss Virginia was the Queen Bee, but to the town kids she was just a hick. Most of them weren't much better. Their daddies were just cotton mill workers or

farmers, but they all looked down on Miss Virginia and made fun of her on account of the fact she lived on an island in the middle of the river with a bunch of colored people and her house didn't even have electricity or indoor plumbing until 1942."

Leota put her hand over her mouth and coughed for several minutes. She looked apologetically at Nita, and then settled down again.

"Miss Virginia could give as good as she got when it came to the boys. She told Clifford Barrows that he had no right to make fun of her on account of the fact his daddy was the town drunk who spent most of his Friday nights drinking down in Colored Town. And later, in high school, when they were studying business law and Lamar Terrell raised his hand and asked what L-t-d at the end of a company name stood for, Miss Virginia said, without skipping a beat, It stands for Lamar Terrell, Dummy."

Leota giggled. The medication the nurse had given her appeared to be working.

"Miss Virginia could handle the boys, but the girls were a different matter. It didn't matter that Miss Virginia was pretty and wore big bows in her hair and clothes just as nice and clean as anybody else. The other girls went around the school yard, arm in arm, giggling

200

behind their hands and rolling their eyes at Miss Virginia's handmade dresses and letting her know, in that sly, cruel way that girls have, that she was an outsider. They had slumber parties and birthday parties and they only invited Virginia because their mothers, who remembered the tales of the Kellys' good days, made them."

Her eyes fluttered for a moment. Leota stirred, rousing herself.

"Everyone invited her to their parties except for Mary Lee Hamilton. She and her older sister, Maureen, were two of the prettiest girls in town. Their daddy owned the Chrysler dealership and they wore department store clothes and lived in a big columned house in the good part of town. Every year Mary Lee would have a Halloween party and every year Miss Virginia wasn't invited. Mary Lee Hamilton would come to school and pass out invitations to the girls she wanted at her party. I'd see Miss Virginia coming back across the river in the rowboat with her daddy and her little shoulders would be shaking but her head would be up. Miss Virginia never was one to let others see her cry. She was too proud for that. She'd come in the back door and walk through the big hall with her head held high and later on I'd go into her bedroom and she'd be laying on the bed with a pillow over her head and

201

her little shoulders would be shaking with her sobs. I'd stroke her back until she was quiet. Later on, she'd gnash her teeth and beat the pillow with her tiny fists and I'd think to myself, Lord, Lord, I wouldn't ever want to make her so mad at me, I wouldn't want to be that Mary Lee Hamilton or any of those snotty town kids for all the tea in China."

The old woman's lids fluttered down over her eyes. In a few minutes, she was snoring softly. Nita quietly closed her notebook and gathered her things, and then turned off the bedside lamp as she went out.

CHAPTER NINE

Two days after Trevor left, Eadie awoke to the quiet of an empty house. She had been dreaming about her dead mother. Reba had been trying to tell her something but Eadie couldn't remember what it was. She struggled up out of her Ambien-induced sleep and looked around the room. Pale sunlight slanted through the blinds. Dirty dishes were stacked on the floor and on the dresser an opened jar of peanut butter stood with a knife stuck in it. *Now how did that get there?* she thought dully. The room was cold. Her breath fogged the air around her face and she put her hand on her cheek and felt something sticky. She pulled her hand away and smelled her fingers tentatively. *Peanut butter.*

She had no recollection of going down-stairs to make herself a sandwich. Or of anything else she'd eaten, although from the looks of the stacked dishes, it had been quite a feast. Her head felt swollen. She felt like she used to feel after a particularly vigorous drinking binge; groggy and thick-headed.

She took a long, hot shower and when she got out she felt better. She checked her cell and the house phone. Trevor hadn't called. She turned on the TV for company and cleaned up the bedroom and made the bed. It was almost eleven o'clock.

She went downstairs and made some lunch and took it out into the garden to eat. Sunlight slashed through the overhanging trees and fell across the mossy bricks and the glossy leaves of the banana plants. Eadie sat in a lounge chair in a pool of sunlight, wrapped in a blanket, trying to warm her-self. The garden fountain splashed and frothed in its mossy basin. Traffic passed lazily in the street. After a while, she began to feel drowsy. She had already slept twelve hours but it didn't matter. Sleep was like a drug. It was better than work or chocolate Mondo Logs. It was better than sex.

She remembered a time not long after they moved into the house when they had quarreled and Trevor had left in the middle of the night with his suitcase. The doorbell rang the following morning and she rose, bleary-eyed and groggy from lack of sleep and went to the door, thinking it was one of the workmen come to fix the kitchen stove. It was Trevor, holding a bouquet of lilies, his suitcase resting at his feet.

By noon, she realized he was not going to call. By two o'clock she had made up her mind what she must do, and wrapping the blanket tightly around her shoulders, she rose and went into the house to make her flight reservations.

She left the house at noon on Friday, taking a taxi to the airport. The sky was gray and blustery, and the overpasses were slick with rain. Streetlamps stretched into the distance like a necklace of pearls. Beneath the leaden sky, the lights of Metairie glowed in the distance.

She arrived at LaGuardia a little after six o'clock, and took a taxi to the Crown Park Hotel. Leaving her bags at the front desk, she asked the concierge to ring Trevor Boone's room.

"I'm sorry, Mr. Boone cannot be disturbed," he replied.

"I'm his wife."

He smiled smoothly. "In that case, Mr. Boone is in the bar," he said, pointing toward a set of ornate doors across the lobby.

The bar was filled with the usual assortment of tourists and after-five office workers. Eadie saw him immediately, sitting at a corner table with two men and two women. He had his back to her but as she approached, one of the women said something, and he swiveled his head around. Seeing her, he stood up.

"Eadie," he said. He was glad to see her. He smiled so deeply his dimple showed.

"Trevor." She was still a little embarrassed about her crying jag the other night. She had never cried in front of him before. She had never showed any sign of weakness in front of him.

He leaned over and kissed her, lightly, on the mouth. He looked tired, she could see it now around his eyes, a slight yellow puckering of the skin. "I wasn't expecting you," he said.

"Obviously," she said, looking at the women.

He wasn't drunk, just tipsy enough to fumble the introductions. The two men at the table stayed seated. Eadie looked from one to the other, nodding her head curtly. Say what you like about Southern men, at least they had good manners. They might be child molesters or wife beaters but they knew to stand up when a woman entered

206

the room. One of the men was a television producer and the other was an editor at Trevor's publishing house. The two women were introduced as "friends." One of them was strikingly beautiful, with a dark exotic face. She put her hand possessively on Trevor's arm as he sat down and slid around in the booth, making room for Eadie. "I won't stay long," Eadie said, sitting down. "I have a nine o'clock flight to catch."

"What do you mean?" Trevor said, moving his arm away from the woman. "You just got here. Where are you going?"

"I came because I had something to tell you. Something I didn't want to tell you over the phone."

Trevor glanced nervously around the bar. "Do you want to go upstairs?" he said, in a low voice.

"I don't have time."

"We can move to another table," he said, indicating a dark corner of the bar. "Someplace where we can have a little privacy."

"It doesn't matter."

Trevor looked at her like he was trying to read her mind. He seemed nervous, although Eadie couldn't tell if it was because she'd caught him with the dark beauty, or because he was afraid of what she might say. "Do you want a drink?" he said, looking past her at the waitress who had appeared at the table.

"I'll have a cranberry vodka martini," Eadie said.

"Don't you mean a mint julep?" the dark woman said to her companion, sipping her drink. The companion giggled. Eadie eyed them steadily.

"My wife's an artist," Trevor said to the men, trying to draw her attention away from the women. He put his arm around her but Eadie sat stiffly at the table, refusing to relax.

"Cool," the book editor said. "An artist." He was the younger of the two, a slightly balding thirty-year-old named Mike.

"Southern artist?" the woman said, slanting her eyes at Mike. "Isn't that an oxymoron?"

"Kind of like well-mannered Yankee," Eadie said.

"Smart redneck," the woman shot back.

"Sexy Jew," Eadie said.

Trevor sighed. "Okay girls," he said. "That's enough."

Everyone at the table got real quiet. Eadie was embarrassed by her last outburst. She didn't normally like to cast aspersions on minorities or ethnic groups, but the woman had goaded her, not to mention the fact that she obviously coveted Eadie's husband. Still, Eadie had promised herself on the plane ride up here that she would get a handle on her rage and feelings of insecurity. She had agreed to make some changes in her life, starting now. Mike and the TV producer, Sam, launched into a discussion on the movies of Quentin Tarantino. It was obvious this conversation had been going on for a while. The two women looked around the bar, bored. Trevor leaned over and kissed Eadie, trying to start over again. "I've missed you," he said quietly. He tapped two fingers gently on the inside of her wrist.

"Really? Is that why you didn't call me?"

"You didn't call me, either."

"I guess it's a draw then." The waitress brought her drink. Eadie sipped her martini and avoided Trevor's eyes. Behind his shoulder the two women were arguing over a *Sex and the City* episode. "I'm going back to Ithaca to try and figure some shit out," she said to Trevor.

He slid his arm off her shoulders and put his hands on the table. At the bar, two men laughed loudly, looking at Eadie. Trevor picked up his glass, chewed a sliver of ice, and then set the glass down again. "Are you leaving me?" he asked finally.

"No. I'm leaving a big empty house."

"Eadie, it won't always be like this."

"It's like this now," she said.

He laced his fingers around the glass. "Let me talk to my agent," he said. "Let me see if I can rearrange my schedule."

"No," she said. "That's not what I want." She worked on her drink a little while and then set it back down on the table. "You were right when you called me a succubus. When you said I wanted too much from you."

Trevor groaned. He put his head back and bumped it repeatedly against the booth partition. When he had finished, he looked at her again and smiled sadly. "Sometimes I'm an idiot, honey. You should know that after twenty-two years of marriage."

"For true." It was one of the things she had learned to say living in New Orleans. Eadie sipped her drink. She wasn't going to make this easy for him. "But every so often you're right, and you were right this time. Whatever it is I need, you can't give it to me. I need to figure it out for myself."

Trevor slid his hands off the table and dropped them into his lap. He looked tired and dejected. He'd been in love with Eadie long enough to know that once she set her mind to something, there was no talking her out of it.

"Where are you going to stay?" he asked.

"With Lavonne."

"And this is only temporary?"

"Yes," she said. She finished her drink. Mike droned on about symbolism and violence in American culture. The dark-haired woman said, "Carrie should have known Mr. Big wasn't in it for the long haul. He had noncommitment written all over him." Faintly, in the background, Paul Simon sang about going to Graceland.

"At least let me take you to the airport."

"No, you stay here with your friends." She kissed him and stood up. Mike stopped talking. "It was nice to meet y'all," Eadie said, nodding at everyone but the dark-haired woman. She was turning over a new leaf but that didn't mean she had to be a hypocrite. She kissed Trevor again and slung her purse over her shoulder. "I'll call you when I get there."

"Eadie," he said.

She bent down and put her hand over his mouth. "I'll call you when I get there and we'll talk about when we can see each other again. Maybe I'll meet you in New York or London. This isn't a separation, Trevor. It's something I have to do until I can figure out what I need."

She glanced behind her as she reached the doorway. He was still watching her from the shadowed booth. He lifted two fingers and gave her a sad little wave. She waved back, and then went out, the heavy door closing with a soft sucking sound on her heels.

Joe showed up ten minutes early for their first date but Lavonne was ready. She opened the front door to find him standing on her porch holding a bouquet of orchids.

"Jesus," he said, sweating into his collar. "This is worse than my first prom. I can feel my face breaking out."

"I'll worry if your voice starts to squeak," Lavonne said.

They went out to dinner at The Pink House Restaurant and then to a movie. Later they went back to Lavonne's house to sit out on the deck and drink Coronas out of icy bottles.

"So you went back up north recently?" Lavonne asked. "How was that?"

"Look, there's Orion," he said, pointing at the sky. "I picked my daughter up in Chicago and then drove to my mother's place in upstate New York." He had an eleven-year-old daughter named Katie from his prior marriage. Over dinner, Lavonne had discovered that he'd been married to the same woman for fifteen years, divorced about five years, and saw his daughter several times a month, as well as a month every summer and every other Christmas vacation. His ex-wife had remarried soon after the divorce and moved with her new husband and his three kids to Chicago. Joe had allowed the move, even though it meant less parenting time for him, because he thought it was better for Katie to be in a family environment. That's the kind of father he was.

"Isn't that Taurus?" Lavonne asked, pointing at the glittering constellation. She'd spent a week at Lutheran Camp when she was a girl and had never forgotten how to read a night sky.

"Wow," he said, sipping his beer and looking at her appreciatively. "You must have been a Girl Scout."

"Nope. Camper for Christ."

"That's not something a Hebrew boy wants to hear."

She laughed and picked up her beer. The moon, wreathed in yellow clouds, hung low over the trees. One block over, the neighbor's neon Christmas lights lit up the street like the Las Vegas strip.

"I don't know if I could sleep with those things on," he said, pointing at the lights with his beer.

Lavonne wasn't sure if this was an invitation or just an observation. She cleared her throat and said, "They turn them off about eleven."

"Shouldn't they take them down now that Christmas is over?"

"This is the South. We like to leave our Christmas lights up until Easter."

He finished his beer and leaned over and kissed her lightly. "I had a great time tonight," he said.

She smiled, amazed at how easy that kiss had felt. She hadn't seen it coming and she appreciated that, she appreciated how smooth and relaxed he had made it seem. He was only three years younger, so his first-date expectations were obviously not as high as Lavonne had worried they might be. "I had a great time, too," she said.

"Hey, try not to sound so surprised."

She leaned back, trying to see his face in the shadows cast by the dimly glowing porch light. An owl swooped above the shed roof. The moon lay in slivers across the frosty lawn. "I don't get out a lot," she said. "In fact, you're my first date in a long time."

"How long?"

"Twenty-two years."

He grinned, his teeth gleaming in the

darkness. "It's a good thing I didn't know that before I came over," he said. "That's the kind of pressure that could give me hives."

Lavonne pulled on her beer and then set it back down. "How about you?"

"I don't know. About three years, I guess." He pushed one of the deck chairs out and put his feet up. "I tried dating after the divorce, but it felt weird."

"So you're not one of those guys who rushes out after the divorce trying to find a new trophy wife?"

"Oh, I wouldn't say that," he said, looking at her steadily.

Lavonne reddened and lifted her beer. She'd only dated two men her whole life; a quiet shy boy she'd bagged at Lutheran Camp named Carl Imhoff, and Leonard. Neither one had been the type to give compliments. Three weeks after she began dating him in college, Leonard, feeling chivalrous, had told her she had "small feet for a big girl." It was the best he could do.

"I didn't mean to embarrass you," he said.

She sipped her beer. "Yes, you did."

"I figured a woman like you must be used to compliments by now."

"A woman never gets used to compli-ments." She almost told him about her seventy-five-pound weight loss, but then she didn't. She kind of liked the fact that he thought she'd always been thin and attractive.

He looked like he might kiss her again but just then someone started banging on the front door. Lavonne set her beer down on the table. She turned half way around in her chair with her hand resting on her throat. "My God," she said, "who in the world can that be at this time of night?"

He was already on his feet. "Stay here," he said. "I'll find out."

Eadie had rented a car at Hartsville and drove to Ithaca, arriving a little before midnight. She had planned on surprising Lavonne. She hadn't called her, not because she was afraid she wouldn't have a place to stay, but because she was afraid Lavonne would try to talk her out of leaving Trevor. Even temporarily. Once Eadie was there on her doorstep, it would be harder for Lavonne to scold her and send her home.

She was surprised, turning down Lavonne's street, to see a strange car in the drive. She figured it might be Ashley, home from college for the weekend. Eadie parked in the street and took her suitcase out of the car. The porch light was on but the rest of the house was dark except for the kitchen. She rang the bell twice but the house was quiet. Finally, in desperation, she pounded on the door.

It swung open suddenly and she found herself face to face with a strange man. For a moment, given her current emotional state, Eadie wondered if she might have come to the wrong house. But then he said, "Eadie," and she recognized the man from the park. He stepped back to let her enter.

"Hello, Joe," she said.

Lavonne materialized suddenly in the darkness behind his shoulder. "Goddamn it, Eadie, it's a good thing I don't have a gun or you'd be dead," she said.

Eadie dropped her suitcase at her feet and stared at Lavonne who stood there fluffing her hair nervously. "What kind of greeting is that," Eadie said. She grinned slowly, looking from Lavonne to Joe and back to Lavonne again. "Am I interrupting something?"

Lavonne did her best to ignore the question. She looked at the suitcase slumped against Eadie's feet. "Are you running away from home?"

"Sort of."

Joe said, "Well, I better be going." He leaned and kissed Lavonne. "I had a great

217

time. I'll call you tomorrow."

She really didn't want him to go, but there wasn't much else she could say. Not with Eadie standing there grinning like she had caught them in an unnatural act and couldn't wait to see what happened next. "Okay."

He let go of Lavonne's hand and slid past Eadie. "There's a Harold Lloyd film festival out at the college this weekend, if you're interested."

"Oh, she's interested," Eadie said.

"Call me," Lavonne said to Joe.

They stood there looking at each other while he started his car and drove away.

"You sly dog," Eadie said.

"It's only our first date. Don't get excited."

"You know, I can get a hotel," Eadie said drily.

"Don't be ridiculous," Lavonne said. She leaned and turned on a lamp. "Why don't you come into the kitchen and I'll make us some breakfast and you can tell me what's going on."

Eadie took a present out of her suitcase and followed Lavonne into the kitchen. She laid the gift on the counter. "Forget breakfast," she said. "Let's make some vodka martinis."

"It's late, Eadie."

"Shit, Lavonne, it's Friday night. You didn't use to be such a party pooper."

"What's this?" Lavonne said, looking at the gift.

"It's your late Christmas present," Eadie said. "I wanted to deliver it in person although I don't guess you'll be needing it. At least not for a while." Eadie was trying not to feel jealous of the fact that Lavonne obviously liked Joe. A lot.

"It's not a Mondo Log is it?" Lavonne said, tearing through the paper. Inside was a black shiny box with a small horned figure etched on one corner. Lavonne squinted and saw the figure had a long forked tail and carried a pitchfork. Underneath, in red letters, it read "Love Monkey II." "You didn't," she said, lifting the lid.

"I did," Eadie said, grinning.

"It looks like an instrument of torture," Lavonne said, looking down at the gleaming apparatus in its form-fitting box.

"Oh come on. Admit it, Lavonne. You might use it."

"I might use it if I was making a movie about chicks in prison."

"Go ahead. Touch it."

"What are those little pointy things?"

"Those are pleasure nubs."

"Nubs? They look more like porcupine quills."

"Touch it."

"I don't think so."

"Touch the Monkey, Lavonne."

"No."

"Lavonne, touch the Monkey."

Lavonne touched it. "There," she said. "Are you happy now?"

"Not as happy as you'll be once you learn to use it," Eadie said, and turning, she went over to the counter to make them some drinks.

CHAPTER TEN

Having finally snared Redmon in her plans for revenge and retribution, Virginia had no intention of letting him wriggle free. There wasn't a lot of time to pull this off without a hitch, although Virginia was the only one who knew this, of course. In the weeks following their trip to the island she worked feverishly behind the scenes to ensure that the Culpepper Plantation project proceeded ahead of schedule. She made sure Redmon met with the designer, made sure the permits were pulled and all the zoning approval processes were streamlined. Under Virginia's careful tutelage the slow, methodical wheel of county government spun like a well-oiled turbine. And she did it all without ever once expressing more than a glancing interest in the project. Virginia was a genius of detached involvement. She was a master of understated micromanagement.

There were times, though, when Virginia's

impatience nearly got the best of her. There were moments, when Redmon dragged his feet over some insignificant detail, when she wanted to stamp her feet and rant and howl like a madwoman. It was at times like these that Virginia's sixty-five years of training as a Southern Lady served her well. A Southern Lady did not raise her voice or curse her husband. She did not throw crockery or kitchen knives or fireplace tools no matter how great the provocation. She was always a picture of serene and detached attractiveness, from her well-pedicured toes to her perfectly styled hair. She was a cool oasis of calm and reasonable sanity in the uncertain maelstrom of life.

There were days when it took every bit of false patience and cunning artifice that Virginia could muster.

By the first of March, her steel-jawed trap had been set, waiting only for Jimmy Lee to insert one of his hapless but expendable limbs. On a bright, sunny Tuesday morning, Virginia rose early to make Redmon's favorite breakfast: scrambled eggs, fried country ham, grits, biscuits, and red-eye gravy. Redmon followed the scent down the stairs like a bloodhound, standing in the doorway and lifting his big red nose to sniff the air.

"Goddamn, I smell ham," he said glee-fully. "What's the occasion?"

"Well, now, does there have to be an occa-sion?" Virginia said, widening her eyes coquettishly. She had made up her face and fixed her hair, and forgone her usual cotton bathrobe and slippers for a shimmering silk kimono and a pair of leopard-print mules. Normally, the mules alone would have been enough to capture Redmon's attention for some time, but at this moment he was fixed on something infinitely more appealing: fried ham. His doctor had long ago forbid-den salty foods and cured meats. Standing there in the warm, fragrant kitchen with the smell of fried pork flaring in his nostrils, Redmon was like a recovering addict stum-bling across a cache of Mexican black tar heroin.

"Goddamn, Queenie, what are you trying to do, kill me?"

She blanched and swung around to face the sizzling skillet. She thought, *Now there's an idea.* She said, "Oh, a little bit every now and then won't hurt you. Sit down. The biscuits are almost done."

He sat down and she poured him a cup of coffee and slid a thick slice of ham onto his plate. She took the skillet back to the stove to make the gravy while he loaded his plate with eggs and grits.

"Um-um," he said, chewing loudly. "If I'd known you were such a good cook, Queenie, I'd of had you down in the kitchen every morning making my breakfast."

She thought, *Fat chance of that ever happening.* She said, "Silly," grinning at him over her shoulder. She browned some flour in the skillet and then poured a little coffee in, stirring until it reached a rich brown color. The oven dinged and she took the biscuits out. "You've got that big meeting today," she said briskly. "You need a good breakfast."

Redmon chewed his ham and looked at her blankly. "What meeting?" he said.

She glanced up at him. "That meeting with Nita's husband, silly. About the Culpepper Plantation project."

He took a swig of coffee and grimaced. "How'd you know about that?"

She turned and took the skillet off the fire. "Oh, I don't know," she said, waving one hand vaguely. "You might have mentioned it at dinner." She set a plate of biscuits down on the table in front of him. "Are you ready for some gravy?"

Redmon grinned and sucked his cheek. "Does a wet dog stink?" he said.

He opened up a biscuit on his plate and

she poured gravy over it. Then she set the skillet back on the stove. "What time did you say it was?" she said. "The meeting?"

"There ain't no meeting," Redmon said. "Goddamn, Queenie, where'd you learn to make red-eye gravy like this?"

Virginia put her hand on her hip. "What do you mean there *ain't* no meeting?" she said sharply.

Redmon frowned, looking at her suspiciously. She quickly turned to the sink and began to wipe the counter down with a dishcloth, trying to catch her breath, trying to drown out the sound of jungle drums that had started up suddenly and were pounding in her head. "I'm playing golf today," Redmon said, behind her. "Got a ten o'clock tee time with that sumbitch Jack Ledford who took fifty dollars off me last week. I aim to get it back today," he said, scooping a piece of biscuit up on his fork.

Virginia waited until her breathing was even, until the pounding in her head had gone from a base drum to a snare. Then she swung around to face him, both hands stretched out on either side of her, gripping the marble counter. "Golf?" she said sweetly. "But what about that meeting? What about the Culpepper Plantation project? We need to get a contractor lined up so we can get started immediately on the foundations."

Redmon stared at her steadily, his jaw moving like a pile driver. "This is business, Queenie. You let me handle it."

Virginia relaxed her stance. "Well, of course, dear, I don't know a thing about business. Obviously, you know what you're doing. I didn't mean to imply —"

"Why do you care so much about it anyway?" Redmon said, narrowing his eyes suspiciously.

"Me? Oh I could care less," she said with a throaty little laugh. "I just thought you had everything worked out. I just thought you were ready to begin."

He sucked his teeth and looked at her irritably. "I'll be ready when I say I'm ready."

"Well, of course, dear." She put a hand up and carelessly fluffed her hair. She picked up the coffeepot and poured him another cup of coffee. "Everyone gets cold feet and I do understand not everyone's a gambler," she said casually.

He squinted at her, chewing high up in his right cheek. "I've done pretty good up to now," he said.

"Of course you have! And I understand you wouldn't want to risk it all." She shook her head and put the coffeepot down. She crossed her arms over her chest and tapped her little foot. "In fact, now that I think of it, I don't think it's something you should do at all."

"Goddamn it, I've made up my mind."

"That kind of risk, at your age."

"Hellfire, woman, I know what I'm doing!"

"Maybe we can take a cruise instead."

"I'm meeting with that pasty-faced churnhead Friday at nine o'clock!"

"More biscuits?" Virginia said brightly, lifting the plate.

She crashed the meeting of course. She couldn't help herself. Besides, she didn't trust Redmon to close the deal, and her whole plot centered on Jimmy Lee taking the bait.

She sailed into Redmon's office Friday morning carrying a box of Krispy Kreme doughnuts. Sunlight flooded the room. Jimmy Lee sat in a chair in front of Redmon's desk looking dazed and confused. Redmon leaned toward him with his elbows resting on the desk, a sly, crafty expression on his face. *If that's his business face, it's no wonder no one will do business with him,* Virginia thought savagely.

"Yoo-hoo!" she said gaily. "Oh dear, excuse me! Here I am coming to bring my husband a breakfast treat and I had forgotten all about his Big Important Meeting." She put her hand up in front of her mouth and giggled. Jimmy Lee looked relieved, which Virginia thought was a bad sign. If Redmon wasn't careful, her Big Fish would wiggle off the hook and she'd be left with nothing but the worm. A big fat red-nosed worm. "Doughnut?" she said, opening the box and pushing it toward Jimmy Lee.

"Thanks," he said, reaching inside. She smiled and offered the box to Redmon.

"We were talking business," he said gruffly, taking a doughnut.

"Oh, I know, men and their business! It's a good thing the business world is run by men and not silly women like me!" She giggled again and smoothed her hands over her trim little hips. Her figure really was quite stunning, and Jimmy Lee's expression told her he thought so, too. Good. That would make it easier.

Jimmy Lee cleared his throat. "I'm a little unclear why you need me," he said, looking at Redmon.

"I need a general contractor," Redmon said impatiently. "Someone to make sure the subs show up and the work gets done. Someone to . . ."

"I'm sure my husband has already explained all this," Virginia said, letting one small hand rest against her ample bosom. "He's explained it to me until I'm sure he's blue in the face, but from the little bit I can understand, this is how it goes. And do interrupt me, dear, if I get it wrong," she said, turning to Redmon who watched her with a gloomy expression. He reached a big hairy hand in the box and pulled out another doughnut. "I own the property," she said, thumping her bosom lightly with her hand and smiling at Jimmy Lee.

"You and" — she struggled for a moment, trying to remember Redmon's Christian name — "Bob . . . You and Bob will go into partnership in the Culpepper Plantation Development. You'll pay me a finder's fee, a lump sum due at the beginning of the project, and you'll cover all the initial development costs, surveying, design, roads, utilities, well, you know, all that icky stuff." She giggled apologetically and rolled her eyes. Jimmy Lee smiled and looked at his hands. "I'll retain ownership of the property but as each lot is improved, I'll release title to that lot to you at a preagreed price. A price *much* below market value, of course." She smiled at Jimmy Lee like they were coconspirators. Redmon helped himself to another doughnut.

"Once the first ten lots are developed, sold, and paid for, I'll release the remaining acres to Culpepper Plantation Development Company." She nodded her head at his stunned expression. "That's right," she said. "You two will own the entire remainder of the island, which should be worth a pretty penny by then, to do with as you please."

Jimmy Lee looked at her, openmouthed. A minute later he looked at Redmon and then back at her, swiveling his head back and forth like a spectator at the Darlington 500. "But why would you do that? Why would you give up the property so cheaply?"

She put her hand to her throat and laughed her girlish laugh. "Really, what do I want with an island in the middle of the Black Warrior River. It's not like I plan on doing anything with it. I don't need the money." She smiled at Redmon. "And it would be lovely to see the old home place restored to some of its past glory."

Jimmy Lee frowned and shook his head. "What does the bank say to all this?"

"No banks," Virginia said briskly.

"Why?"

"That's what I said," Redmon said glumly.

"Now," Virginia purred, cocking one eyebrow at Redmon. "Banks prolong the process. They can tie you up in red tape so long you're practically a grandfather before the approval is made."

"But that means we'll have to come up with the development money ourselves," Jimmy Lee said.

Redmon grunted. "You hit the nail right on the head, son," he said.

Jimmy Lee was quiet a moment, considering this. "But why me?" he asked finally. "I mean, I know you need a general contractor, but why me, exactly?"

"Well," Virginia said, letting her eyes mist. She paused a moment before continuing. "It's all about family." She stopped again and touched a fingertip to the outer edge of both eyes. After a few moments of awkward silence, she went on. "Now, of course, you're not actually family, but you are my grandchildren's stepfather. And my grandchildren are important to me. I want them to be happy. What's good for you is good for them. I want this to feel like one big happy family."

Jimmy Lee was aware that Virginia had been spending a lot of time with Whitney. Nita had remarked about it just the other day, going on and on about how she had maybe misjudged Virginia over the years, how it was never too late for people to change for the better. And it was a fact

Jimmy Lee had been racking his brain trying to figure out some way to make a better life for himself and Nita. This was the deal of a lifetime. The deal that would put him at the top of the monetary heap, for a change. He'd be able to afford a new house and a proper honeymoon for Nita, maybe a trip to Europe, or a cruise to the Bahamas. And he'd be able to afford to buy the kids the things their real daddy could give them, things like new cars or trips to Disney World or tuition to that snotty private school they used to go to. And who knows? Maybe having a husband who was a good and steady provider would make Nita change her mind about having other kids, too.

He looked at Redmon. "How much?" he said.

Redmon never skipped a beat. "Five hundred thousand," he said. "Each."

Jimmy Lee put his head back and hooted. He laughed and looked at the ceiling like that was the funniest thing he'd ever heard. "I could sell my truck, my house, my boat, and all my tools and still not have a quarter of that. I guess y'all better find yourself another partner."

"Hey, no problemo," Redmon said. "Not everybody's cut out for the high stakes game of real estate investment. It takes a smart man to know when he's skating on black ice."

Virginia looked at him like *do shut up.* She sighed and checked one of the freckles on her arm. "Of course we understand," she said. She looked out the window at the low-lying Ithaca skyline. "We wanted to give you first chance at the deal, but we have a list of other potential partners." She smiled wanly at Jimmy Lee. "Charles perhaps."

Redmon said, "Charles? Charles who?"

Virginia looked at him coolly. "He's been talking about doing some development deals," she said flatly. "He's been talking about trying some other field besides the law."

Redmon snorted. "Your *son,* Charles? That pencil pusher couldn't split enough firewood to fry an egg, much less run a multimillion-dollar job site."

Virginia gave him a dirty look but kept her mouth shut.

Jimmy Lee sat forward with his elbows resting on the arms of the chair, his hands clasped in front of him. He wasn't laughing now. One knee vibrated nervously while he thought about things. "Let me make a few phone calls," he said finally. "Give me until the first of the week to see if I can come up with the money."

"Now, boy, don't do anything stupid," Redmon said gravely, shaking his head. "Keep your wagon between the ditches, if you know what I mean. If it don't feel right in your gut, don't do it."

Jimmy Lee coughed politely. Virginia clamped her lips together so tightly she tasted blood. She ignored Redmon, staring out the window at a flock of buzzards nesting on the Courthouse roof. When she felt her blood pressure had dipped back down into normal range, she smiled flatly at Jimmy Lee and said, "Will you let us know by Tuesday?"

"Yes, ma'am." He stood up slowly and stretched his hand across Redmon's big desk. "Sir."

Redmon took his hand. "I like you, boy," he said. "If this don't work out I maybe got some work for you over in Walnut Springs."

"Okay." Jimmy Lee nodded once at Virginia. She stepped aside so he could pass but at the last minute she said, "Oh, and one other thing." He turned around. "Let's keep this between us, for the moment. Just until we see if it's going to work out or not. We're kind of in a sticky situation what with offering the partnership to you first, and not Charles. I don't want Nita caught in the middle, if you know what I mean." She

234

smiled in what she hoped was a friendly manner.

Jimmy Lee shrugged. "Sure," he said. "I'll keep it quiet for the time being. Let me see what I can do."

Leota Quarles was still in bed when Nita arrived, although she was sitting up and smiling. She'd been sick with pneumonia the last few weeks and hadn't been able to have any visitors. The pneumonia had hung on, persisting through three rounds of antibiotic treatment before finally disappearing.

"Hey, Miz Broadwell," she said, catching sight of Nita. Nita had told Leota her name was Motes now but she had obviously forgotten.

"You're looking so much better," Nita said, putting the flowers she had brought on the nightstand beside the bed.

"Oh, thank you. Those are lovely. Lilies are my favorite."

Nita stood beside the bed, patting her arm. "Miss Leota we don't have to talk today. You go ahead and save your strength."

"Good gracious, no," the old woman said, shaking her head. "I look forward to your visits, honey. The older you get, the more time you like to spend in the past. And sometimes it's nice to have someone along with you." She motioned for Nita to sit down. After a while, she cleared her throat and began to talk.

"Her fifteenth year, everything changed. Miss Virginia got an electric sewing machine for Christmas and she began to make her own clothes, studying the glamour magazines she checked out from the public library and copying the styles she saw movie stars and debutantes wearing. Every Saturday, she went to the movies with a different boy and she'd come home with stars in her eyes and set about making whatever outfit she'd seen Bette Davis or Lauren Bacall or Ava Gardner wearing. She was still small in stature but she had a lovely figure, which her stylish clothes showed off nicely. That was also the year Mary Lee Hamilton died. She just stopped eating and then she died. She had that disease, that . . . oh, now, what do you call it?"

"Anorexia nervosa?"

"Is that what they call it? We just called it starving yourself to death. Anyway, she died in the fall and after that the other girls started being a lot nicer to Miss Virginia. They started asking her to go with them to the malt shop and the drive-in theater and downtown on Saturday afternoons. The boys had been nice to her for a while but now the girls started be-

236

ing nice, too, and just when it seemed like everything was going Miss Virginia's way, just when it seemed like the Queen Bee might be back for good, trouble found her. Trouble with a capital T. That was the year Hampton Boone came back from Vanderbilt for Christmas."

She coughed a little bit and Nita poured her a glass of water and waited while she drank it. Leota smiled and lay back with her head on a pillow.

"Hampton Boone was three years older than Miss Virginia and he'd gone to that fancy school out on the river, oh, now, what do you call that school?"

"Barron Hall?"

"Yeah, that's it. Only in those days it was a boys school, there were no girls allowed. Anyway, Hampton Boone was what you'd call movie star handsome. He was tall and blond and he'd walk down the street and the girls would practically swoon at his feet. He'd gone up to Vanderbilt with that Maureen Hamilton, Mary Lee's older sister, and everybody said they were engaged. Miss Virginia must have known who he was, but I'd never heard her speak of Hampton Boone until that Christmas he came back to visit his mama on his school vacation.

Miss Virginia'd been coming out of the malt shop with some of the other girls and Hampton was going in. He stood there holding the door and looking at her like he'd seen an angel. She told me about it later, how he stood there with the sunlight shining on his blond hair and staring at her. She'd said thank you, and tripped out with her little nose in the air, 'cause Miss Virginia was savvy when it came to boys. She knew the only way to catch one was to act like you didn't want nothing to do with him.

Anyway, Hampton Boone had never been treated like that by a female in his whole life, and he fell hard, right there in the doorway of the malt shop. He called Miss Virginia on the phone and asked her to go with him to the movies and she said no, she already had a date, and he said, break it. Just like that. Later on, he showed up at the movie theater where Miss Virginia and her date were, and he had a bouquet of yellow roses, and when Miss Virginia came out with her date he handed them to her. She said why didn't he give them to Maureen Hamilton since they were en-gaged, and he said he wasn't engaged to nobody, least of all Maureen Hamilton. She was with Bob Parsons and she said, Bob, take me home now, and Hampton Boone said, I'm taking you home, and she said, Not on your life. He looked at Bob and said, I'm taking her home, and Bob said, Sure, Hamp, whatever you want."

All the way home Nita thought about Virginia's sad childhood. She could almost picture the childish Virginia, disparaged and cruelly treated by the Mary Lee Hamilton's of the world, yet proud and defiant still in the face of poverty and adversity. The loneliness and isolation of the island must have been like a physical wound to someone as dignified and socially needy as Virginia was. Nita felt certain that the chains that bound her had been forged on that lonely island in the middle of the Black Warrior River, chains that Virginia had never been able to break, no matter how hard she tried to reinvent herself, no matter how many wealthy men she married. Although none of this excused Virginia's domineering nature, it did help explain it.

Nita got home early enough to make dinner, for a change. Jimmy Lee had a meeting at the bank and Logan was in his room, strumming his guitar. Whitney lay on the sofa in the den, idly flipping through TV channels.

"Wash your hands," Nita said to her. "And set the table for dinner."

Whitney groaned and covered her face

with a pillow. "Why do I always have to set the table. Why doesn't Logan ever do anything around here?"

"Logan mows the grass and takes out the trash. But if you'd like to switch jobs for a while, that's fine with me."

Whitney threw the pillow across the room and got up and lurched into the kitchen like a felon on her way to a public flogging. Nita watched her in amazement. She couldn't understand Whitney's surly behavior. Nita had always been a happy child. She came from a family who'd always loved one another and not been ashamed to show it, a family who'd done their chores without complaining. Times were lean, financially, when Nita and her two brothers were children, but Nita had not been aware of this. Her daddy was a stonemason, a working man, whose fortunes did not improve until Nita and her brothers were nearly grown. But even when times were tough Loretta and Eustis had made sure their children didn't go without. There might not have been fancy vacations to Disney World or the Grand Canyon, but Eustis had built them a sweet little camper out of plywood and canvas and they'd camped all over the Southeast, swimming in lakes so clear you could see the mussels nestled in their silty bottoms, and hiking mountain trails where Cherokee war parties had once roamed.

When Jimmy Lee got home that night he looked tired and discouraged. He'd had a lean spring so far and Nita knew he was worried about money. She was able to cover their expenses and some of the mortgage with the money Charles paid her for child support. And she paid for her college tuition with money from her own account. But she knew firsthand the terrors of self-employment — her own father had struggled for years before his masonry business showed a fat bank account — and she knew Jimmy Lee was worried about the next job coming in. They had four hundred dollars in their bank account and the mortgage was due in three weeks. Well, it couldn't be helped. Nita would transfer some of the money in her account into their joint account, although how she would do it without hurting his pride, she wasn't sure.

"You cooked dinner," Jimmy Lee said, leaning to kiss her. He was wearing khaki slacks and the blue-striped shirt he had worn to their wedding, and looked as handsome and successful as any New York stockbroker on his way up the corporate ladder. He had dressed up for his meeting at the bank, although she could tell from his face

241

it hadn't gone well.

Nita put her hands on his shoulders and kissed him again. "Wash your hands and we'll eat," she said.

Nita filled everyone's plate and then sat down. They held hands while Jimmy Lee said the blessing.

"Hey, Jimmy, I downloaded those chords from 'Statesboro Blues' today," Logan said, opening up his napkin. He and his step-father shared a love of music.

"Cool," Jimmy Lee said. "Did you learn them yet?"

"I've got the first part figured out but the instrumental is pretty complicated." Logan had recently dyed his hair a deep shade of red. Beneath the overhead light, his lip ring glistened wetly.

"Yeah, I know," Jimmy Lee said. "Dickey Betts is God."

Whitney sniffed her plate and said, "What exactly is this stuff?"

Jimmy Lee chewed steadily, looking at her. He clutched his fork and rested his chin on the top of his hand. "You're welcome to help out with the cooking if you don't like the menu. Feel free to do some work around the house if you don't feel we're living up to your high standards."

"It's a chicken and rice casserole," Nita

242

said, frowning at Jimmy Lee. He scowled and looked at his plate. There was a lot of tension between him and Whitney lately.

"Grandmother has a cook," Whitney said, trailing her fork around her plate but not putting anything in her mouth.

"Well, bully for grandmother," Jimmy Lee said.

"Pass the biscuits," Nita said to Logan.

"If I was married to one of the richest men in Georgia, I guess I'd have a cook, too," Jimmy Lee said bitterly.

"Well, technically, you have a cook," Nita reminded him, pointing to the chicken casserole. She wished he'd figure out some way to knock the chip off his shoulder.

"I like it, Mom," Logan said, spooning out a second helping of casserole. "It's good."

Nita smiled at him. "Thanks, honey," she said.

Whitney put her hand on her hip and looked at her mother. "Is that true?" she said. "Is Grandmother married to one of the richest men in Georgia?"

Later, helping her clean up after dinner, Jimmy Lee came up behind her at the sink and put his arms around her, nuzzling her ear. "Sorry about being an asshole," he said.

She turned her head and kissed him.

"Were you being an asshole?" she said. "I didn't notice."

"It was really good," he said. "The casserole."

"Thanks." She pulled her rubber gloves off and then turned around and slid her hands into his back pockets. "Look," she said in a quiet voice. "It's going to take some adjusting. But it'll work out."

He frowned and smoothed her hair off her face. "It's just that, sometimes I feel like she's criticizing me."

"She's twelve years old. She criticizes everybody."

"I can't give her the things her father can give her. The things her grandmother can give her."

Nita laughed. "No one's asking you to," she said. "You're the one putting pressure on yourself. I told you. Material things are just things. They're not important. None of that matters."

Jimmy Lee humped his shoulders and stared out the window. "It matters to me," he said.

She kissed him and then turned again to the sink, leaving it at that. Between going to school, working on her paper, and trying to keep the family together, she was too tired to argue. She picked up the rubber gloves.

He reached around her, and took the sponge and the gloves away from her.

"Go sit down, Mrs. Motes," he said. "I'll finish this."

Later he came into the bedroom where Nita was working on her paper. She had given it to Professor Limerick, who had edited it and given it back to her for revision. He had agreed to meet with her tomorrow morning to review it one more time before she submitted it to the *Journal of Southern Historical Perspective.* She had worked on the paper feverishly over the past few days. Laundry piled up in the laundry room. Dishes stacked up on the kitchen counter. Beds went unmade.

Jimmy Lee closed the door softly behind him. "We need to talk," he said.

He never discussed money with her. What else could make him sound so serious? The only thing she could think of was that he meant to criticize her housekeeping ability. Or lack thereof. He stood quietly for a few minutes, running his fingers through his dark hair. Down the hall she could hear Logan playing video games in the den.

"Look," she said. "I know I'm a little behind with the housework. But I'm trying to get this paper finished, and once it is, we'll get back on a regular routine. I promise."

"No, no, it's not that," he said.

She sat on the bed with one leg drawn up beneath her. She closed her laptop and dropped both hands into her lap, waiting.

"I have an opportunity to go into business with someone," he said, picking his words carefully. "On a development project out on the river. It's the kind of thing where I really think I can make some money, some good money." His voice shook with excitement, or nervousness, she wasn't sure which. Maybe both. "I haven't done any development deals, of course, so it's a stretch for me, but I really think I can do it." He looked at her. There was color in his cheeks and along the dark ridge of jaw just above his throat. "Honey, it's the opportunity I've been waiting for. I know it in my heart."

Nita shrugged, relieved that this wasn't about her bad housekeeping. "Well, if you think it's what you want to do, then go for it."

His eyes widened. "Do you mean it?"

"Of course."

He slid his hands into his front pockets. He bumped the toe of his boot against the leg of the dresser. "There's only one problem."

"Oh?" She had already opened her laptop and pulled up the screen.

"I need money."

She reread the last paragraph again, and decided it wasn't right. "Talk to the bank," she said.

"I did. They say I don't have enough collateral."

She pushed the laptop away and looked at him. The table lamp glowed, washing the cypress-paneled walls with a warm light.

"How much?"

He told her. Down the hallway, Logan took on the entire Japanese army. The sound of machine-gun and mortar fire ricocheted down the narrow hallway. She looked down at her hands and thought, *I have college. I have this paper. He should have something.* She spread her hands in her lap. "If I put the money up for collateral, will the bank give you the loan?"

He looked worried. "Maybe," he said. "But they want to take a look at the deal first. It'd be easier if I just borrowed the money from you."

She shrugged. "Look," she said. "If it's what you want to do, just go for it."

The tension drained out of his shoulders. He sat down on the bed and put his arms around her. "I've got the prospectus," he said. She could hear a tremor in his voice. His mouth was warm against her hair. "You can read it and you'll see I'm right. It's the deal of a lifetime, honey."

She pulled away and patted his cheek playfully. "If you say so. But I don't want to read it. I don't have time. I've got to get this paper finished before I lose my mind." She nodded at the laptop.

"You won't be sorry," he said, letting her go. He stood up and put both hands on her shoulders. "I won't need the money for very long. Just until the first five or six lots sell and then I'll be able to pay you back. You can charge me interest," he said. "More than you were getting at the bank."

She tilted her head back and looked at him. "Don't be ridiculous," she said.

All the way to Professor Limerick's office the next morning, she thought about how happy Jimmy Lee had been this morning, how he'd gone around the house whistling and joking with the kids, just like when they first lived together. She had left him happily going over a plat that was spread out over the kitchen table. *Culpepper Development Company,* the plat read in one corner.

Nita didn't know any Culpeppers but she hoped whoever it was would realize Jimmy

Lee's trustworthiness, and treat him accordingly.

CHAPTER ELEVEN

In the weeks following their first date, Lavonne saw Joe nearly every day because he showed up at the Shofar So Good Deli for lunch. He'd sit at a small table over by the window and when she had a break, she'd join him. He was an engineer at Du-Pont and could pretty much set his own schedule. His father had worked for General Electric for forty-five years but Joe had worked for a half-dozen Fortune 500 companies over the past twenty years before settling down with DuPont. During that time he'd had plenty of chances to grow disillusioned with the corporate world. "I don't know," he said one afternoon to Lavonne. They were sitting at the window watching a crowd of teenage boys mill around the next-door parking lot with their skateboards. "One day you're like those guys, free and easy with your whole life in front of you, and the next day you wake up and it's twenty years later and you're stuck in a dead-end job you hate." He sipped his sweet tea and looked at the boys wistfully. Lavonne refilled his glass from the pitcher that rested on the table between them. It was one of the things she had found Northerners took to best — sweet tea. If you ordered it in a restaurant up North, people looked at you like you were crazy, but once you got a taste for it, it was like a cocaine addiction. "Sorry," he said. "I don't mean to bore you."

"You're not boring me," she said. "If you start to bore me, I'll look like this." She put her head back and closed her eyes, pretending to snore.

He grinned and went on. "My dad worked for the same company for forty-five years and I guess I thought it would be that way for me, too. When you're young and just out of college with a wife and college loans to pay back, you think a nine-to-five job in the corporate world is the best thing that could happen to you. These days, the only way to get ahead is to move around, and so you do that, even though it's the same thing wherever you go, and eventually you have a mortgage and car loans and a kid and you wake up one day and twenty years of your life is gone." He took a bite of his sandwich, pastrami on rye, and chewed slowly. "And now I'm forty-four years old and I'm competing with a bunch of twenty-something Harvard MBAs who can live on half my salary. I've survived three layoffs but the writing's on the wall, it's just a matter of time until I get the ax, and the funny thing is, I don't even care. I can't wait until the ax falls because then I'll have an excuse to start over. Is that crazy, Lavonne?"

No, it wasn't crazy. Lavonne knew exactly what he meant. She'd gone through the same thing two years ago when she realized her daughters were nearly grown, her husband had a life of his own, and she didn't know what she wanted to do with the rest of her's. It wasn't long after that that she latched on to the Shofar So Good Deli plan. "I know what you mean," she said. She played with a container of Sweet 'n Low, stacking and restacking the little packets while she thought about it. "You spend the first half of your life living up to everyone else's expectations, and then one day it hits you. You're not happy. You're not living the life you want to live. I think everyone goes through it, but everyone reacts differently. Some people buy sports cars, some get plastic surgery, some undergo a health or spiritual crisis, some start new businesses or new careers. And some start new families.

I want you to think of the number of men you know who leave twenty-year marriages and then turn around and marry a woman who looks *exactly* like the first wife, only twenty years younger. Men with grown children who turn around and start having kids again."

"You mean, they're trying to recapture their youth?"

"Maybe. Or they're trying to start over, only this time they're trying not to make the same mistakes they made the first time around. For most of us, that's all middle age is. It's letting go of what happened in the past and starting over."

He took both of her hands in his, smiling. "How'd you get to be so wise?" he said.

"Years of pain and suffering."

Little Moses came out of the back carrying several plates that he set on the pickup counter. He thumped the bell and called out, "Number twenty-six, your order is ready!" He saw Lavonne and grinned.

"Do you need some help?" she said.

"No." He shook his head and waved at her to stay where she was. It was one-thirty and the lunch crowd had thinned considerably. Lavonne put her chin in her hand and looked at Joe.

"So tell me," she said. "If you could do

anything you wanted, what would that be?"

"You mean like an occupation?" She nodded and he scratched his head and smiled, like he was afraid to tell her. She waited, her eyes fixed steadily on his face. "Okay, I know it sounds crazy, but I've always wanted to open a small bike shop. Maybe start a company that manufactures carbon composite alloy bikes similar to the one I built myself. And I've always wanted to go to France and live for a while, maybe bike around Europe. You know, the Tour de France and all that."

She smiled and lifted her glass.

He shook his head apologetically. "I know. It's crazy."

She sipped her tea and put the glass down. "No, it's not that," she said. She unstacked and restacked the Sweet 'n Lows. "I used to want to move to the south of France and write a cookbook."

He laughed. "See," he said. "We're soul mates."

She smiled, afraid to look at him in case he was kidding. The front door swung open and two tourists came in carrying shopping bags. One of the women opened her bag and the other leaned over and said, "Oh my God, those shoes are darling. I almost bought a pair but they didn't have my size and I can't wear normal shoes since my feet are so skinny." Lavonne rose to clear away Joe's empty plates.

"Here, I'll do that." He stacked the dishware and took it to the clean-up station. "Hey, are we still on for *Seinfeld* at my place?" he said, looking at her over his shoulder.

"Sure," Lavonne said. "I'll bring the beer."

By the first of April, Eadie and Lavonne had settled into a comfortable routine. Lavonne left for the deli a little before six o'clock and Eadie got up and went out to work in the shed behind the house where she had fixed up a makeshift studio. It was one of those old-fashioned one-car garages with double doors that swing out on heavy hinges. The previous owners had used it as a garden shed but Lavonne was not a gardener, and she'd had no objections to Eadie taking it over.

Eadie was amazed at how much work she'd gotten done since returning to Ithaca. She had spent her entire life involved in a life-and-death struggle with her hometown, but she had thought all of that would disappear once she moved to New Orleans to start a new life. What she had discovered, though, was that her old desire to prove herself to people who had tried to hold her down her whole life was still there. What she had found was that some things never change.

She was working in oils again. She had started out painting neo-abstractionist women from the waist up, but over the weeks her style had evolved into something more traditional, and now she found herself painting baroque cherubs who sported around the dark-hued canvases like winged gargoyles. The backgrounds were industrial, postmodernistic, and oddly disjointed behind the round rosy figures of medieval infants. There was an odd sense of the religious about the canvases, which was unusual given the fact that Eadie was an agnostic, a surreal vision of a chaotic but unseen world, like Dante's vision of Hell in *The Divine Comedy*.

"Goddamn, you need to lighten up on the vodka martinis," Lavonne said, the first time she saw the work. "This shit's scary." She was standing in front of a canvas that showed a red-cheeked cherub with wings like a bat flying over a fortress that belched fiery smoke into a metallic sky. Skeletal trees rimmed the fortress. Dead fish floated in the moat.

Eadie wiped her fingers on a rag. "Does it

disturb you?"

"Hell, yes."

"Good. Art should be disturbing."

She had seen Trevor three times since she left New Orleans; once in New York, once in San Francisco, and most recently in Atlanta. They spent their weekends together holed up in some four-star hotel, ordering room service and getting reacquainted in every way they could think of. Eadie had made him promise not to ask her about her work, and she tried not to ask him about his. She knew the prepublication reviews had been good and there was already a buzz going about his novel. The publicists were quickly lining up an extended signing tour, which meant that after May, he wouldn't be home much anyway, so it was a good thing she had decided to spend the summer with Lavonne. They kept it light, enjoying each other's company without talking too much about the past or the future or when things might get back to being normal between them again. Trevor was being patient with her but Eadie knew his patience wouldn't last forever.

Their last night together in Atlanta, they had dinner at an upscale restaurant in Buckhead. It was a beautiful balmy night in April and the dogwoods were blooming all along

Peachtree. They sat in a bricked courtyard at a linen-covered table, surrounded by eight or nine other couples sitting at linen-covered tables. Candles flickered in the soft darkness. Vivaldi played in the background.

Trevor picked up her hand and kissed her fingers. "Come with me to New York next month," he said. "I'll do my book signings and then we'll go out to the Hamptons and lay in the sun."

"I can lay in the sun down here," Eadie said. "Besides, I can't think of anything more boring than standing around listening to a bunch of fawning flatterers tell you how wonderful you are."

Trevor grinned, his teeth glimmering in the candlelight. "You never know. You might enjoy that."

"I might enjoy watching your head swell like a beach ball? I don't think so."

"My head will never swell as long as I'm married to you. You've got a tongue like an ice pick."

"You didn't complain about that last night," Eadie said, taking out her compact mirror. "I didn't hear you complaining about my tongue being too sharp then."

Trevor watched her with a bemused expression. He raised his hand. "Waiter," he said. "Check!"

"Stop it," Eadie said. "I'm not ready to go yet."

"Sorry, that sounded like an invitation to me."

"Everything sounds like an invitation to you." Eadie took out her lipstick and re-applied it carefully. She closed the compact and slid it back into her purse. "I tell you what," she said. "Let's go back to the hotel and drink a bottle of Merlot."

Trevor looked around for the waiter. He leaned forward and crossed his arms on the table. "Well, now that sounds good, honey, but I have to ask. What's in it for me?"

She put the lipstick back in her purse. She yawned and covered her mouth with her fingers. "We'll drink a bottle of wine and then, if you're really lucky, maybe I'll let you rub my feet."

Trevor grinned and shook his head. "That's not what I had in mind," he said.

"Oh well," she said. She looked around at the other dimly lit diners.

"I tell you what." He reached his hand across the table and took her wrist like he was checking for a pulse. "I'll rub something of yours if you'll rub something of mine."

Eadie giggled.

"My choice," he said.

■ ■ ■ ■

Eadie had only been back in town two weeks when she organized the first bunco meeting.

"Bunco? What in the hell is that?" Lavonne said.

"It's where you get a bunch of women together to drink and gossip and roll dice and at the end of the evening the one with the most points takes home a pot of cash."

"That sounds like something you might get arrested for. I think gambling might be illegal in the State of Georgia."

"Hell, if they arrested us, they'd have to arrest every bridge group between here and Resaca. Don't tell me those bridge ladies don't play for money."

As it turned out, Grace Pearson won the bunco pot at the first meeting and Nita won the most wins. Their second meeting was scheduled for a Thursday night in mid-April. After Lavonne left for work, Eadie went out to Sam's and bought a bunch of party food and then she stopped by the Shake Rattle 'n Roll Liquor Store and picked up several bottles of vodka. When Lavonne got home that evening, Eadie had three card tables set up on the back deck.

She'd strung some party lights shaped like margarita glasses in the trees and the citronella tiki torches were flaring. On the CD player Southern Culture on the Skids sang their ode to female frailty, "Liquored Up and Lacquered Down."

"Is that our theme song for the evening?" Lavonne asked, indicating the CD player.

"You bet," Eadie said.

"Damn, you've been busy." Lavonne stood at the kitchen bar where Eadie had set out trays of quiche bites, crab dip, cream cheese with pepper jelly, and pecan-crusted baked brie.

"It was a labor of love," Eadie said. "Martini?"

"Hell, yes." Lavonne sat down at the bar and watched Eadie shake up a batch of pomegranate martinis. "What time do the girls get here?"

Eadie took a tray of martini glasses out of the freezer and set two glasses down on the counter. "I told them to come around seven-thirty." She poured out two glasses and handed one to Lavonne. "Cheers," she said.

Lavonne sipped it and closed her eyes. "Damn, that's good." Eadie smiled at her over the rim of her glass. Lavonne set her glass down and said, "Where'd you learn to play bunco?"

"New Orleans. I used to play with a group of my neighbors."

"It's funny," Lavonne said. "I never pictured you hanging out with groups of women. You were always so adamant about not joining sororities, church groups, social clubs, the Bar Auxiliary, or the Junior League. And you never talk much about your childhood, but I kind of got the idea you were like me. A solitary kid."

Eadie shrugged. "People change," she said. Eadie never talked much about her childhood. Her father had left soon after she was born, and her mother, Reba, worked a number of jobs to put food on the table. At various times she worked as a beautician, a waitress, a maid out at the Holiday Inn, a cashier at the Piggly Wiggly, and a laborer on a construction road crew. Reba was one of those women who couldn't be happy unless she had a man around to make her miserable. After Eadie's daddy left, she brought home two more husbands until Eadie reached an age where she could put her foot down about having any more stepdaddies. The first was Luther Birdsong. He was what you called in the South "bad to drink," meaning that when he was sober he was as docile as a lamb and when he drank he was prone to episodes of violence. Eadie and Reba spent most Friday nights hiding under the bed in the little trailer watching Luther Birdsong's big feet go stomping past.

The second stepdaddy, a manic-depressive encyclopedia salesman named Frank Plumlee, was even worse. Eadie was twelve by the time Reba dragged Frank home, and already the kind of girl who could stop traffic in the street. It didn't take long for Frank to start bothering her, sitting around in his underwear in the small trailer and following her with his eyes, leaving her with the feeling he was touching her in places she didn't like to think about. When she came home from school one day to find Frank alone and half-naked in the trailer, his private parts flopped out on his thigh like a sea slug, Eadie did the first thing that came to mind. She threatened to put on her Girl Scout uniform and go downtown and tell the sheriff and his big deputy what Frank had done, unless he agreed to take the money she'd been saving and leave town immediately. In those days treatment of pedophiles, especially those who trifled with Girl Scouts, was swift and severe. Frank, being a man of above-average intelligence and a coward to boot, took the money and ran.

"You think we'll need to turn on the bug zapper?" Lavonne asked. "The mosquitoes are getting pretty bad."

"No, I think we'll be all right," Eadie said. "I've got the citronella candles burning. If you think the bugs are bad here, you should see New Orleans. They've got mosquitoes the size of hummingbirds and those Formosan termites will eat through anything."

By ten o'clock the bunco party had degenerated into a raucous affair of screaming women, clattering dice, and clinking martini glasses. Someone had turned up the CD player and the song "Put Your Teeth (on the Windowsill)" reverberated across the yard, followed shortly thereafter by "Dirt Track Date" and the ever-popular "Daddy Was a Preacher but Mama Was a Go-Go Girl." Every fourth round of dice rolling, the losing partners got up and moved to the next table, which kept things lively and also indicated who was in need of a designated driver to get home. By the twentieth round, Nita, Lavonne, Eadie, and Grace Pearson found themselves seated at the same table.

"How's Trevor?" Grace said. She and Nita were partners and so far had the most losses for the evening. Which was good, because the ones with the most losses got to go home with their money.

Eadie shrugged. "He's out in L.A. putting the final touches on his movie deal. I forgot to tell y'all. His manuscript's been optioned by Paramount."

Lavonne looked at her with a stunned expression. "How do you forget to mention something like that?" she said.

"This thing that's going on between you two," Grace said, rolling two ones. "You don't call it a trial separation. What do you call it?"

"A working vacation," Eadie said.

Over at the next table Kaki Murdock squealed "Bunco!" and clapped her hands like a cheerleader.

Eadie said, "No way. Y'all are cheating. That's five buncos tonight. There's odds against that happening." She looked at Lavonne for confirmation of this mathematical precept.

Lavonne, a former accountant, lifted her drink and said solemnly, "The law of probability makes that a definite improbability."

"See," Eadie said.

"You're just jealous 'cause I'm winning and you're not," Kaki said. She flipped Eadie the bird and wrote down her score. "Rolling twos," she shouted.

Eadie picked up the dice at her table and

rolled. "Speaking of husbands, Grace, whatever happened to yours? You didn't chop him up into little pieces and hide him under the floorboards, did you?"

"Who, Larry?"

Eadie stopped rolling and looked at her. "Yes, Larry. How many husbands did you have?"

Grace shrugged her wide shoulders. "He moved up to Atlanta about twenty years ago. He works at a bar down in Little Five Points called Gay Par-ee."

Eadie lost her roll and handed the dice to Nita. "Hey, I know that place," she said. "All the employees are female impersonators. They dress up like Marilyn Monroe and Liza Minnelli and Madonna and . . ." She stopped talking suddenly and looked at Grace.

Grace grimaced. She nodded her head slightly. "That's right," she said. "He goes by the name of Lola Fellatio."

Eadie's eyes were round as bottle caps. Her mouth was a perfect *O* of astonishment. "Oh my God," she said. "Larry Pearson is *gay?*"

Lavonne said, "Say it a little louder, Eadie. I don't think they heard you over in Dooly County."

Two tables over, Sally McBryde stopped

rolling. She said, "Little Larry Pearson that graduated in my brother Clay's class?"

"Here we go," Lavonne said.

"Little Larry whose sister plays the organ down at the Church of God?"

"That's right. The one who was married to Grace. His mama was a Stockett."

"What about him?"

"He's queer."

"So what? All the Stocketts are queer."

"No, not queer. Gay. You know."

"Little Larry Pearson is gay?" Sally said.

"Cooter Pearson is a transvestite?" Kaki said.

"Who needs another martini?" Eadie said.

Later, after she got them calmed down, Eadie leaned across the table and said to Grace, "I'm an idiot. Sorry about that."

Grace shrugged. "It's an old secret and I'm surprised it hasn't got out by now. It really doesn't affect me one way or the other. I'm just glad Larry's happy." They were rolling threes now. After a minute, Grace looked at Nita and said, "Speaking of secrets, how's Virginia?"

Nita didn't know what she meant. "Sorry?" she said.

Grace rolled a mini-bunco and kept going. "What is it you think Madame President has up her sleeve?"

Nita, still not understanding, said, "She's taken Whitney and some of her friends up to Atlanta to go shopping this weekend. I think that's real sweet of her. The girls were so excited."

"Nita and Virginia have turned over a new leaf," Eadie said to Grace. "They're good, good friends now."

"That's right," Nita said stubbornly.

"We keep trying to remind Nita of how Virginia made her life miserable for sixteen years but she seems to have forgotten all that."

Lavonne said, "Are you keeping score, or should I?"

"You keep score," Eadie said. "Remember, Nita. Once a rat, always a rat."

Lavonne rolled another set of threes. "What was that you said earlier about people changing?"

Nita frowned and shook her head. "There's a lot about Virginia y'all don't know."

Eadie and Grace looked interested. "Like what?" Eadie said.

"Game!" Lavonne said. They added up their points. Lavonne and Eadie put *W*'s next to their third round and Nita and Grace put *L*'s.

"Does she ever say anything about growing up on that island in the middle of the river?" Grace said. "Virginia, I mean. Does she ever talk about that with you?" Her face was splotched with color and her eyes were intensely blue. Blue like sapphires. Like bayonet points glittering in the sun.

Nita leaned over and pretended to count her losses. She didn't want to tell them what she knew about Virginia's childhood, not here anyway, in front of everybody. She felt oddly protective of the older woman. After all, Virginia had taken Whitney and her friends up to Atlanta, at her own expense. Who could ask for a better grandmother than that?

A pale sliver of moon hung over the shed like a tattered cloth. Fireflies flickered in the darkness. Grace said, "I've always wondered why Virginia didn't develop that property earlier. I guess I'm not surprised she and Redmon have set up that development deal. I guess I was a little surprised, though, to see that Jimmy Lee's involved, too."

Lavonne looked at Eadie and frowned. Nita looked blankly at Grace. "What development deal?" she said.

CHAPTER TWELVE

Virginia's revenge scheme was coming along nicely. It was going so well that sometimes Virginia had to wonder if she might have missed her calling as a war games planner or State Department strategist. She had convinced Redmon and Jimmy Lee to pay her a one-hundred-thousand-dollar finder's fee and had her attorney draw up the contracts so that she retained ownership in the island and only released the property one lot at a time. Flush with money, she began to regain some of the confidence she had lost when the stock market dropped and Boone & Broadwell collapsed, leaving her a pauper. She even managed to convince Redmon to let her redecorate portions of the house, starting with the kitchen and the dining room. They were still negotiating the Elvis Red carpet.

Redmon had more important things on his mind these days than interior design.

After overcoming his initial reluctance, he had thrown himself into the Culpepper Plantation project with all the zeal and determination he could muster. He left early in the morning and returned late at night, too tired for anything but dinner, a few hours in front of the TV, and bed. Exhausted, he was snoring within minutes of his head touching the pillow. Virginia was only sorry she hadn't cooked up the scheme earlier in their marriage. It might have saved her countless embarrassing episodes of the Cheerleader and the Coach or the Schoolteacher and the Naughty Schoolboy, not to mention her latest performance as a romping debutante.

And having Redmon distracted with work left Virginia with more time to spin her web around the pliant Whitney. The girl was an easy mark, with her love of clothes and adolescent luxuries, not to mention the possible gift of a new automobile that Virginia dangled in front of her like a piñata. (She had warned Whitney to keep it between them for the time being; she had promised to bring Nita around to the idea eventually.) The process of winning Whitney's loyalty had been as easy as cutting butter with a hot knife, as her daddy used to say, and all Virginia had to do now was wait until the time was ripe to strike.

There were moments when Virginia was amazed at her own genius, at her own capacity for treachery and deceit. There were times when it seemed her whole life had been nothing but a dress rehearsal for this one climactic expression of vengeance, a righting of all the wrongs and slights she had suffered throughout her solitary childhood, her loveless marriage, her lonely ascent to the top of the Ithaca social ladder. But there were other times, less frequent, when Virginia wondered if she might not be missing something important, moments when she questioned whether vengeance was the pinnacle of happiness or the slough that separated her from it. In those brief moments of self-awareness, she realized that she missed her sexual escapades with Redmon, she was conscious of the fact that she enjoyed the time she spent with her granddaughter, she understood that she might have been a better mother to a daughter than she had been to a son, had fate and circumstances not worked to her disadvantage. These moments, however, were fleeting.

Most of the time Virginia just thought about how clever she was.

■ ■ ■ ■

Ashley and Louise were spending spring break with Leonard and his new family in Florida, and Eadie had flown up to Bald Head Island to meet Trevor, so Lavonne had the whole week to herself. She spent as much of it as she could with Joe, who was leaving on Wednesday to fly up to Chicago to see his daughter. On Monday and Tuesday, Lavonne took some time off from work and they packed picnic lunches and rode their bikes down to the Riverpark. In the evenings they had dinner and saw a movie or ate in and watched TV.

After he left, he telephoned every day. She looked forward to his calls the way a cheerleader looks forward to a call from the captain of the football team. It was corny, but it was true. She was forty-seven years old and she felt like a high school sophomore. They laughed and talked on the phone for hours. When she wasn't talking on the phone, Lavonne stood in front of the bathroom mirror looking at her naked body. *It's not too bad,* she decided, turning this way and that. She'd lost a lot of weight but the skin was still firm. Her nipples might not stick straight up but they were still more horizontal than vertical. All in all, she was pretty pleased with herself. If she'd looked this good twenty years ago, it wouldn't have been just Eadie Boone streaking across the Wal-Mart parking lot and jumping naked into the Courthouse fountain.

So far her physical relationship with Joe hadn't progressed much beyond kissing and snuggling. Any time things got too intense, Joe would pull himself away, take a deep breath, and go into the kitchen to grab a beer or make a bowl of popcorn. He seemed to be just as willing as she was to take things slow.

Maybe it was because he wasn't pushing it that Lavonne began to fantasize about what it would be like to sleep with him. She wasn't one of those women who found beefy twenty-year-old hard-bodies appealing. She liked a man with a few wrinkles in his face, a little gray at his temples. Someone who could discuss the intricacies of postperestroika Russia, but still knew who Monty Python was. Someone who appreciated an imported beer but kept himself in the well-toned, muscular shape of a college swimmer. The more she thought about Joe Solomon, the more she appreciated the fun that could be had by two unfettered, consenting adults.

But other times she thought about how great it was to have a friend to watch movies and television with, someone to laugh with and go out to dinner with. Then Lavonne was determined not to blow it by sleeping with him. She knew from experience she could go without sex, but she wasn't sure she could go without his friendship. She had grown too accustomed to having him around.

On Saturday Leonard called to say that he and Christy and the boys were driving up from Florida and wanted to stop in to pick up some furniture that Lavonne no longer wanted. Ashley and Louise had flown back to New Orleans the day before and Lavonne really didn't want to see Leonard, but she figured money must be tight if he was willing to take her cast-offs. She had forgiven him long ago for being a shitty husband, and she found it best to maintain a cordial relationship with him, if only for the girls' sake. Now that she had fallen for Joe Solomon, she could afford to be generous with her ex-husband.

"Sure," she said. "Come on. I'll be home all afternoon."

Leonard had remarried soon after their divorce, before he moved to Atlanta to practice law. He married Christy, his thirty-something, ex-secretary. She was everything Leonard had ever wanted in a wife — young, slim, pretty, and subservient in that coy, false way that Leonard so admired in Southern women. Christy lost no time getting pregnant with twin sons who were born eight months after Lavonne left Leonard.

"Congratulations," Lavonne said, when he told her. "Are they yours?"

"Of course they're mine," Leonard said irritably, followed quickly by, "they were born a little early. I never actually slept with her until after the firm party."

"Well, technically, we were still married at that time," Lavonne said. "Which makes you a bigger asshole than I originally thought."

"I may need to borrow some money," Leonard said.

"Good luck with that," Lavonne said.

Leonard had somehow managed to hang on to the beach house during the financial melee that followed Boone & Broadwell's dissolution, although Lavonne had insisted he mortgage it and put the money into a college trust fund for the girls. It was at the beach house that Leonard, Christy, and their sons had spent spring break with Louise and Ashley. The girls affectionately referred to their half-brothers as the Devil's Spawn. The twins' real names were Preston and Landon.

"Landon threw the cat off the balcony," Ashley told Lavonne when she had called two days earlier. "Christy got hysterical and while she was downstairs checking on the cat, Preston stuck a fork in the toaster and set fire to the kitchen."

"Where was Daddy when all this was going on?"

"He was playing golf. But Christy says his golfing days are over."

Lavonne laughed all afternoon. When Joe called, she told him and they laughed together. But when Leonard pulled up in front of her little house in a brand-new, bright-yellow Hummer, Lavonne decided she might have to rethink the generosity thing.

"What'd you do, Leonard, pillage your clients' trust funds?" she said, pointing to the urban assault vehicle in her driveway.

Leonard, who had just spent five hours in an enclosed space with Preston and Landon, not to mention a wife on the cusp of a PMS meltdown, was not amused. "Where's the furniture?" he said, all squinty-eyed and sullen. His face was sunburned and he'd lost a substantial amount of hair in the last year.

Lavonne tried not to stare at his sad comb-over and pointed with her thumb toward the shed.

"It's in there. Be careful not to mess with Eadie's stuff."

"Eadie?" he said. "What's she doing here?"

"She's visiting. You might need a bigger trailer than that," she said, looking at the U-Haul attached to the bumper.

Leonard didn't say anything. He put his head down and trudged toward the shed. Inside the Hummer, Christy was screaming at the boys to leave the cat alone. Landon had figured out how to unbuckle his seat belt and he'd sprung his brother, too, and now they had the unfortunate feline cornered in the luggage compartment. The passenger door opened and Christy swung down over the running board like she was rappelling off a vertical cliff face. Lavonne was surprised to see she had put on some weight. She stopped and stared sullenly at Lavonne. Behind her there was a flash of brown followed by a squalling sound, and Christy turned in time to see the family cat disappearing under the neighbor's hedge.

"No, kitty," Christy screamed. "Here, kitty-kitty. Here, kitty-kitty." But kitty had streaked across the neighbor's yard and was halfway down the block. With any luck, he'd make Florida by nightfall. Landon stuck his cherubic face around the edge of the opened door. He saw Lavonne and grinned. "Landon, you stay in the truck," Christy said over her shoulder, hurrying after the escaping cat. "Stay in the truck, Landon."

Landon swung down out of the Hummer like a monkey in a banyan tree. Preston, the more cautious of the two, turned around and slid out of the vehicle backward, the way he had been taught to safely come down a flight of stairs. They were loose by the time Lavonne reached them but she squatted down and pretended to be looking at something in the grass, and when they circled back, she caught one in each arm. They were dressed in identical outfits and probably weighed about forty pounds each. Lavonne was breathing heavily by the time she set them down in her living room.

Winston came out of the kitchen and stood there, looking at her sadly.

"Kitty!" Landon screamed. They were developmentally advanced for their age, the way mathematical geniuses and serial killers are apt to be. Winston had once gone up against a rottweiler in the street, but he took one look at Landon and Preston and headed for the back bedroom. Lavonne found him later, cowering under the bed.

She handed each of the boys a pair of wooden spoons and two cooking pots and when Leonard came in later they were beating on the pots with the steady precision of jazz musicians. "You might want to invest in a couple of drum kits," she said loudly. She was sitting on the sofa reading the newspaper.

Leonard stood in the doorway looking at his sons with the same expression Winston had used. "I need a drink," he said.

"How about some sweet tea?" she asked, rising.

"How about a beer?" he said, mopping his brow with the back of his hand.

She stepped around the boys. Stopping in the kitchen doorway and turning around to ask Leonard if he wanted a lime in his Corona, she caught him.

He was staring at her ass like he'd just seen the eighth wonder of the world.

Christy appeared later, empty-handed, looking tired and despondent. She shook her head when Lavonne asked her if she wanted something to drink. "Whiskers done flew the coop," she said to Leonard.

Leonard, who sat on the sofa looking like a man on the edge of something dangerous, lifted his beer and said, "Free at last, free at last, thank God Almighty, I'm free at last."

Christy, who had no appreciation of Martin Luther King, in particular, and irony, in general, said, "First thing I'm gonna do when I get back to Atlanta is get me a new cat."

"No more cats," Leonard said. "They all run off. They're too smart to stay." He burped loudly. "We've had four goddamn cats," he said, holding up three fingers. Lavonne, who had not failed to notice the way he was tossing back Coronas, began to worry she'd have to offer them a place to spend the night.

"How about some sandwiches?" she said, rising. "Before you head back? Or maybe a pizza?"

Christy stood over by the bookshelves, pretending to recognize some of the titles. "Naw, we got to get going," she said.

"Sure," Leonard said. He stared at his ex-wife appreciatively as he sipped his beer. Landon, who had mastered the four-four beat, moved on to a syncopated rhythm. Preston, tiring of the whole thing, leaned over and rapped his brother on top of the head with one of his spoons.

"You know I can puree the boys some vegetables or fruit in the blender if you like,"

Lavonne said to Christy. "I can sliver some carrots and celery."

"Naw," Christy said. "They won't eat that shit."

"Well, maybe if they'd learn to eat that *shit* they wouldn't need Ritalin by the time they start preschool," Leonard said morosely. He couldn't believe the way his life had turned out. When he left her, Lavonne had weighed two hundred ten pounds and had an ass as big as a Yugo. He'd figured she'd spend the rest of her life alone, shut up in some dark, decaying house filled with cats. Now she looked like one of those attractive women on those TV make-over shows, the ones where plastic surgeons and experts turn hopeless middle-aged ugly ducklings into sexy swans. Not only that, but he was pretty sure Lavonne had a six-figure retirement account, not to mention what she was bringing down annually with the Shofar So Good Deli, while he was struggling to make the payments on the beach house, the Hummer, and the new condo Christy had insisted they buy. Not to mention Christy's weekly shopping sprees at the mall and her recent decision that the boys would need to attend one of the most expensive private preschools in Atlanta.

If Leonard could have looked into a

crystal ball a year and a half ago and seen what his future held now, he might have made some different decisions. He might have lived his whole life differently.

"I'll make some sandwiches," Lavonne said.

"You got any more beer?" Leonard said. After a year and a half in Atlanta, he had begun to lose his false, carefully cultivated Southern accent and spoke now in the hard, clipped tones of his Ohio youth. He sat there looking despondently at his sons.

Lavonne said, "I can make up some goody bags for the boys, if you like."

Christy, fearing Lavonne might try to load the twins up with contraband like apples, carrots, or celery, asked suspiciously, "What kind of goody bags?"

"How about handcuffs and duct tape," Leonard said.

"I've got some road games the girls used to play with when we traveled," Lavonne said. "The boys are pretty young but the games might keep them occupied and quiet."

"Oh, those boys are *angels* in the car," Christy said. She had a doting mother's capacity for selective amnesia and had already managed to forget the torturous drive from Florida.

"We'll take the travel games," Leonard said. "And any Darvon you might have on hand."

"You can't give Darvon to babies," Christy shrilled, looking at Leonard like he was stupid.

"You can give it to me," Leonard said morosely.

Preston dropped his spoons, staggered over to the ficus plant, and began to methodically strip the leaves. Lavonne went into the kitchen and came back out with an old phone book that she set on the floor. "Hey, Preston," she said, bending over. "Look at this." She began to tear the pages, one by one into long strips. Preston, entranced, toddled over and squatted down on his haunches. He pushed Lavonne's hands away and began to tear the pages himself.

Leonard watched Lavonne sentimentally. "I'd forgotten how good you were with children," he said.

Lavonne thought, *I ought to be good with children. I was married to you for twenty-one years.* Christy looked at Leonard the way George Washington might have looked at Benedict Arnold after he surrendered West Point to the British.

Too drunk to sense danger, Leonard

284

continued on. "You look great, Lavonne. How much weight have you lost anyway?"

"Ham sandwiches okay?" Lavonne said. "Or I can make tuna."

"Tuna gives me gas," Christy said sullenly.

"Ham it is then," Lavonne said.

Christy patted one of her ample hips. "I'm still carrying the baby weight," she said to Lavonne.

"It's been ten months," Leonard said. "How long you planning on carrying it?"

Christy's sharp little eyes sliced through him like surgical scalpels. "As long as it takes you to regrow some hair," she said.

"I can pack a cooler," Lavonne said, "if you'd rather eat on the road."

"I'll have another beer," Leonard said to Lavonne, sucking despondently at his Corona. Before they were married, Christy had called him Sweet Cheeks. Now she called him Hey you. *Hey you, the cat just barfed on the carpet* or *Hey you, the baby needs a diaper change.*

"Sorry, I'm out of beer," Lavonne lied. She hoped he hadn't noticed the old Philco out in the shed stocked with Coronas. "Joe's coming over later and maybe he'll bring some with him but you'll be gone by then."

Leonard set his empty bottle down on his

leg. He looked at Lavonne with a dazed expression. "Joe?" he said.

CHAPTER THIRTEEN

Virginia invited Nita to go to the beach for spring break and Nita almost accepted. Redmon had a condo in Destin, the Redneck Riviera, and Virginia was taking Whitney and one of her friends on a "girls' trip."

"It'll be fun," Virginia said, clapping her little hands together. "We'll go out to dinner and go shopping and maybe even play some tennis."

"Well, it does sound like fun," Nita said. "But I promised Jimmy Lee I'd spend some time with him. Maybe next year."

She felt a little guilty about turning Virginia down after she had been so nice to Whitney, even though Nita didn't exactly agree with the way Virginia went about showing her love. Virginia's fondness for her granddaughter revealed itself in overtly materialistic ways: shopping trips for Whitney and her friends, new clothes, a decorator hired to redo a spare bedroom in Virginia's house where Whitney slept when she visited. Virginia had even promised Whitney a new car once she turned fifteen, which, of course, Nita had immediately vetoed, incurring the everlasting wrath of Whitney. Virginia, contrite, had apologized repeatedly to Nita over this. "I am *so* sorry, Nita. I know I should have asked you first before promising the child anything so *extravagant.*" She sighed. "It's just that I never had a little girl of my own so of course I have a tendency to want to spoil my only granddaughter rotten. She is *such* a lovely girl." Nita found it hard to stay angry with Virginia after this confession.

"Maybe Virginia just wears an evil mask to protect her inner child," Nita said to Loretta one sunny afternoon after Whitney had left for the beach with her grandmother. She'd been reading some of her psychology books again, trying to get a handle on Whitney. "Maybe she's just trying to get over a bad childhood."

"Virginia's inner child is about as helpless as Attila the Hun," Loretta said. They were sitting in Nita's small kitchen, peeling potatoes for supper. "Her inner child makes Vlad the Impaler look like Cinderella."

"Now, Mama, people can change."

"A snake by any other name would still

be a snake," Loretta said darkly. Loretta James had grown up in Vienna, Georgia, and she had her own way of talking. Most of the time Nita understood what she was trying to say. She figured her mother had trust issues when it came to Virginia Redmon. Nita herself had once had trust issues, but they were being slowly eroded away by Virginia's newfound warmth and friendliness. Still, it had taken some work on Nita's part, too. When she first found out that night at bunco that Jimmy Lee had gone into business with Redmon and Virginia on the Culpepper Plantation project, she had felt sick to her stomach and had stayed in bed the next day.

When she finally worked up the strength to talk to him, she asked Jimmy Lee, "Why didn't you tell me you were going into business with them?"

He was distraught. This was the first time in their relationship he hadn't been honest with her and the guilt had nearly killed him. "I didn't tell you, honey, because I was afraid you wouldn't lend me the money. I knew it was a good deal. I knew we could make some money, but I had to have some capital, too, or they would have found somebody else. It was a once-in-a-lifetime chance, and I just had to take it." He tried to stroke her hair but she turned her face away. "Just tell me the truth, Nita. If I had told you who it was I was going into business with, would you have lent me the money?"

Nita thought about the six hundred thousand dollars she had put away in her bank account as insurance against Charles filing for child custody. She shook her head. "No," she said coldly. "I wouldn't have."

"See?" Jimmy Lee said, spreading his hands like he was trying to make her see reason. "I knew you wouldn't. And you were so caught up trying to finish your paper and all, and you didn't really seem to want to discuss it, so I just made the decision by myself."

That much was true. She had been too distracted to think about anything else. She had given him the money without asking any questions, and it was too late, now, to go back and regret her decision.

Still, she was relieved that things seemed to be going so well with the project. The bridge was in and the surveyors had begun plotting the lots. The asphalt road was laid. The utilities were going in over the next few weeks and with any luck, and good weather, they'd begin the foundation of the first spec home sometime in June. Jimmy Lee went around the house whistling, just like he had when they first fell in love and the world had seemed bright and full of promise. He worked hard, from sunup to sundown, making sure the subs showed up and the work progressed ahead of schedule. When her bank account got down to twenty-two thousand dollars, Nita stopped checking it. The dwindling balance made her feel abandoned and fearful. It reminded her of a reccurring nightmare she'd had as a child, one in which she'd found herself alone on the prairie with a tornado coming and no place to hide, just miles and miles of flat, unprotected country. Jimmy Lee put his arms around her and told her everything would be all right. They'd be starting on the first house soon and once it sold, Nita would get back a big chunk of her investment. And it might even be sooner than that if Redmon was able to work out the complicated leveraging deal he was trying to swing with the bank.

Outside the kitchen window, a hummingbird hung motionless. Cypress and mimosa trees reflected in the slow-moving water of the Black Warrior River. Nita giggled. She was thinking about what her mother had said earlier. "Vlad the Impaler?" she said.

"Just watch your back, is all I'm saying," Loretta said grimly. "Around Virginia, you got to be as careful as a toupee wearer in a windstorm."

Down the hallway, Logan picked up his electric guitar and began to practice a song he had written for his ex-girlfriend.

"Cut me with your stiletto eyes," he growled.

Loretta dropped a peeled potato into a ceramic bowl. She indicated Logan's room with her thumb. "He still going out with that Gilley girl?"

"No," Nita said. "They broke up."

"Stab me with your lies," he sang. When the Gilley girl broke up with him, Logan had decided to get revenge the only way he knew how. He had decided to become a musician.

"You know her grandmama was a Starr from over by Vienna," Loretta said.

"Really?"

"Beat me with your discontent," Logan crooned.

"Her granddaddy's people come from over by Oostanaula. James Edward was his name."

Behind them the guitar wailed like a banshee. Logan's voice rose above the guitars. "Slash me with your indifference," he sang.

"He had red hair and freckles."

"Crush me with your loathing," Logan growled.

"He was a good-looking man, but bad to drink. Had a brother with a clubfoot by the name of Stump."

The guitar shook the rafters. "Kill me, you bitch!" Logan screamed.

Nita shrugged and looked at her mother. "It's a love song," she said.

"Naturally," Loretta said.

On Saturday, Nita went out to the nursing home to see Leota Quarles. She was not in her room when Nita arrived but the nurse was making up her bed. "Miz Quarles is still at lunch, but she'll be back any minute."

"Oh what lovely flowers," Nita said, looking at an arrangement that sat on the bedside table.

"Aren't they pretty?" the nurse said. "Mrs. Redmon had them sent over yesterday."

"Virginia Redmon?"

"Yes. She comes to have lunch with Miz Quarles every Friday, but she couldn't come this week because she's down in Florida."

Nita sat down by the window to wait. Sunlight splashed the red-brick façade of the building and rolled across the neatly manicured lawn like a carpet. Traffic passed busily in the street. In the top of a tall fir tree a wren built a nest. Nita heard Leota's voice and she turned her face to the door just as a young orderly wheeled her into the room. Her eyes were clear and bright and she was giggling at something the orderly had said. She seemed surprised to see Nita. "Is today Tuesday?" she said.

Nita stood up. "No, Miss Leota, remember, I had to move our appointment from Tuesday to Saturday. Is that okay?"

"Oh, yes, honey, of course."

The orderly helped her stand. She indicated with her hand that she wanted to sit by the window. "Shouldn't you be in bed?" he said.

"I've been in bed," she said. "I want to sit where I can see the sun."

He got her settled in her favorite rocking chair and then he went out. Leota listened while Nita read back what she had so far. Then she turned her head toward the window and began.

"After that first night at the movies, Miss Virginia and Hampton Boone starting going around together. He'd wait for her at the landing in his mama's big Chrysler New Yorker and she'd have one of the colored hands row her across the river and she'd meet him there.

They were quiet about it, at first, but it was a small town and word got out pretty quick. Maureen Hamilton went to see Miz Boone, his mama, and she put her foot down, but you know how it is when a mama puts her foot down — any boy worth his salt will do just the opposite. Mr. Boone had been dead for years by then, and it had been just the boy and his mama, and he was used to doing as he pleased. He was good to me, always speaking to me respectfully if he run into me in town, always sending me little presents through Miss Virginia. But I could see the kind of man he was behind his handsome face and manners. He was the kind of man used to having his own way. When he went back to school at the end of Christmas break, Miss Virginia laid in her little bed and looked at the ceiling and wouldn't talk to nobody."

Leota pulled a Kleenex out of a little box on the bedside table and blew her nose.

"We can stop now if you're tired," Nita said, but the old woman shook her head, no. She looked out the window at the traffic passing in the street and after a few minutes, she went on.

"And then it was summer again, and Hampton Boone was back from college and Miss Virginia was a new person. She went around laughing and singing and her face glowed all

the time and she was prettier than any of the actresses you saw up on the movie screen, the kind of girl who could make your heart ache just looking at her. She and Hampton would drive around town in his big car and go swimming at the country club and have picnics on the river. You never saw a girl as crazy in love with a boy as Miss Virginia was with Hamp Boone. She came home late one night and I was sitting on the porch waiting for her. I'd heard her go out, soon after her mama and daddy went to bed. She came home later, walking down the sandy road in the moonlight, carrying her shoes in her hand. When she saw me she run up on the porch and hugged me and said in her fierce little voice, 'Leota, I'm going to marry that boy or die trying.' It made me sad, hearing her talk like that and seeing her little bare feet so pale and fragile-looking. The week before he went back to school, I held her in my arms again and this time she was crying and saying, over and over, 'Leota, what am I going to do? What am I going to do? I love him.' And I said, 'You have to tell him,' and she said, 'I can't unless I know he loves me.' "

Leota sighed and blew her nose again. The sun had reached its zenith and under the noonday glare the landscape looked flat. Bees moved in lazy circles among the azaleas. A white cat stretched out on its side in the shade of a boxwood hedge. Leota looked tired and Nita knew she should stop her, but she couldn't. She had to know what happened.

"After he left, she stopped eating and she got so small and frail I was afraid she had whatever you call that disease that Mary Lee Hamilton died from."

"Anorexia nervosa?"

"Yeah, that one. I tried to get her to eat but she was sick all the time and all I could do was make her lie down so I could put cold cloths on her forehead like I'd done when she was a little girl and the town kids had teased her about not having indoor plumbing. She went by the post office every day after school but the letters didn't come as often as they'd come before. Then in December, two weeks before he was supposed to come home for Christmas, there was an announcement in the paper that Hampton Boone was engaged to be married to Maureen Hamilton. They were getting married in April. It was to be the social event of the county. Miss Virginia never said a word, she just clipped the article and took it up and put it in her little cigar box where she kept all her other treasures since she was a little girl, the pottery pieces and spear points she'd dug up on Big Ridge, the corsage she'd

worn to her first cotillion, all her love letters from Hampton Boone. Later, I went into her room to hug her and try to get her to cry about it, but she never cried, her little face was flushed and hot to the touch and her eyes glittered like shards of broken glass, but she never cried. Something gentle had gone out of her and something hard took its place.

"When she went away in January I was crying, and her mama was crying, and her daddy was crying and saying, 'Poor little Queenie, poor little Queenie,' over and over, but her eyes were dry and hard as bone. She sat down in the bow of the boat and held on to the sides with her little gloved hands and looked straight ahead like a woman who knows what it is she has to do."

Leota was crying now. Tears streamed down her cheeks and dripped over the edge of her chin into her lap. She wiped her face and blew her nose, and Nita got up and hugged her for a long time. Her shoulders shook for a while and then slowly subsided. Nita could feel the old woman's brittle bones through her clothes, like kindling wrapped in burlap, and for some reason Nita felt like crying, too, although she couldn't say why.

CHAPTER FOURTEEN

Two weeks after Eadie met him at Bald Head Island, Trevor showed up at Lavonne's house unannounced. She had talked to him nearly every night on the telephone, and she liked that, but when she heard the rental car pull up in the drive and, a few minutes later, he came through the back gate shouting "Anybody home?," she felt more than a little annoyed. It was one thing to communicate with him via telephone; it was something else entirely to find him encroaching physically on her newfound creativity and freedom.

Trevor saw her and stopped. "Hey, baby," he said, grinning.

"What are you doing here?" she said flatly.

She was working back in her garage-shed studio. "Is that anyway to greet your husband?" he said, strolling toward her. He didn't seem to notice her annoyance. He put his arms around her and kissed her hungrily.

"You'll get paint on your shirt," she said.

"I don't care."

"I thought we agreed no visits while we're working."

He shrugged and let her go. "I missed you," he said.

It was a warm sunny day and Eadie had the studio doors thrown open to catch the light. She was working on one of the canvases she had started when she first moved in with Lavonne. Trevor stood in front of the easel looking at her work. "This is wonderful," he said. "It reminds me of one of Modigliani's Jeanne Hebuternes."

Eadie dropped her brush into a jar of turpentine. "Just what every artist wants to hear," she said. "That she paints like someone else."

"I meant it as a compliment," he said.

"Would you take it as a compliment if I told you that you write like Hemingway?"

"Hell, yes," he said, kissing her again.

Later, they went out to dinner with Lavonne and Joe. Joe and Trevor got along like they'd known each other all their lives. They had the same dry sense of humor and both counted Lewis Nordan as one of their favorite writers.

"*The Sharpshooter Blues* is just about the

best novel ever written," Trevor said. They were at the Pink House Restaurant and had just ordered their fourth carafe of martinis.

"I don't know," Joe said. "It's pretty hard to beat *Music of the Swamp.*"

"Y'all need to slow down on those martinis," Eadie said. "That shit'll eat right through your liver."

"This coming from the Tequila Queen of Ithaca County," Trevor said, lifting his glass for a refill.

"Bite me, Trevor."

"I intend to, my dear."

After the restaurant closed, they took a cab out to the country club and slow-danced to Perry Como and to Nat King Cole singing "Mona Lisa" and "A Blossom Fell." Eadie had to admit, it was nice having Trevor's arms around her again. When he kissed her neck, she almost forgot about all this foolishness, this separation that she had insisted on. When he sang "When I Fall in Love" in her ear, she knew she could never be happy without him, and it seemed then that her own need for success and independence didn't matter at all. But when the music stopped and she stepped away from him and her mind cleared, she realized her marriage could not continue unless she figured out some way to carve out a separate existence for herself. She could never be happy submerging herself in Trevor's life, painting herself into the background. She just wasn't that kind of woman.

"Take me home," she said to Trevor.

She had loved Trevor Boone from the moment she first set eyes on him, even though she'd known it wouldn't be easy, even though his mother was dead set against it. Maureen Boone died soon after the wedding, from shame, it was said by some. By others, it was surmised that her heart, atrophied from years of disuse, had simply shriveled into a knot so small and hard it could no longer pump. Whatever the reason, Eadie did not mourn her passing. When Trevor graduated from law school and they returned to Ithaca, they moved into the Boone mansion and Eadie set about getting rid of Maureen's heavy ornate furniture. Instead she filled the rooms with her fertility goddesses, using the dining room as her studio. The plan was for Trevor to practice law for a few years, save as much money as possible, and then give up his law practice to write full-time. But gradually he began to write less and less as the law claimed more and more of his time. Eadie's goddesses, which had started out small, grew monstrous, until they began to fill the entire house like an army of Chinese tomb soldiers. Trevor, frustrated and bored, embarked on his first affair, with a cocktail waitress out at The Thirsty Dog. Eadie, in retaliation, began sleeping with one of the bartenders. Years later, Trevor moved in with his legal secretary, Tonya, and Eadie took up with a personal trainer named Denton Swafford. By this time their twenty-one-year marriage had settled into a predictable pattern of betrayal and reconciliation. But Eadie, tiring of the game, had finally put her foot down. She refused to take him back unless he agreed to stop practicing law and finish his novel, and they both agreed to remain faithful to their wedding vows. No more infidelity.

And Trevor had been true to his word. At least, technically. As had she. Technically.

But now their marriage wasn't about cheating, it was about work, and for the first time Trevor could work and Eadie couldn't. She'd had dry spells before, periods when her creative energies went dormant, but never for eighteen months. And now that she had figured out how to work again, although she didn't know why it had to be in Ithaca, she didn't want anyone or anything to jeopardize that.

"Take me home," she said again to Trevor.

"Listen, you guys stay at my place," Lavonne said. "I'll stay at Joe's tonight and for the rest of the time Trevor's in town."

"He's here only for tonight," Eadie said. "He's leaving in the morning."

Lavonne and Joe exchanged looks. Trevor stared at Eadie like he was trying to figure out who in the hell she was. "You know," he said coldly, "I don't have to stay at all."

"Suit yourself," she said.

All the way to Joe's house, Lavonne was quiet. It occurred to her that she had been the one to jump at the chance to sleep at his place, and he hadn't said much of anything. When he finally did speak, he said, "Wow. They're intense."

"Who? Eadie and Trevor?" She was relieved that the awkward silence between them had had more to do with the Boones and less to do with Lavonne forcing a sleepover. "They've always been like that. It's a fight to the death, no holds barred. They have an odd marriage and it wouldn't work for everyone, but don't kid yourself. Those two are crazy about each other."

He grinned and reached for her hand. "Yeah, I got that." They held hands all the way back to his place.

Joe lived in a brick ranch house close to

where Nita had grown up. It was a neighborhood of 1950s and 1960s houses with neat, manicured lawns and large trees. Young couples had begun to move in and fix up the houses and now it was one of the hottest real estate areas in town. Joe had redone his house soon after moving in, taking down walls, refinishing floors, raising the ceiling to the rafters so that it felt like a California beach house, open and uncluttered.

He switched on the lights and went into the kitchen to make them a drink. Lavonne sat down on the overstuffed sofa in the living room and turned on the TV. Jon Stewart was interviewing Harrison Ford on *The Daily Show.*

"This is a rerun," Joe said, setting two martini glasses down on the coffee table.

"I know." She leaned over and picked up her drink and then sat back with one foot tucked under her. "I think Jon Stewart's adorable."

"Really?" He sat down beside her and leaned to pick up his glass. "I find myself oddly jealous over that comment."

She grinned and sipped her drink.

He tasted his martini and said, "Not bad. Not as good as Eadie's, but not bad."

"Not bad at all."

"What's her secret? How does Eadie make

her martinis so good?"

"If I told you, I'd have to kill you."

He kicked his shoes off and stretched his feet out on the coffee table, crossing them at the ankle. "You know," he said, smoothing his shirt over his flat stomach. "There are ways I could make you talk."

"Really?" She arched one eyebrow and looked at him over the rim of her glass.

"Did I ever tell you I was a wrestler?" He set his drink down and flexed his arm. "Nineteen seventy-five New York State Wrestling Champion, one-hundred-sixty-five-pound weight class."

"Wow." She squeezed his bicep lightly with her fingers.

"Want me to show you some of my wrestling moves?"

She shrugged. "Maybe," she said. "It's pretty entertaining stuff."

She sipped her drink and thought, *So this is what love feels like. Like falling down a flight of stairs or jumping from a tall bridge.* She said, "I didn't have time to pack a bag. Do you have some jammies I can borrow?"

He took her glass from her and set it down on the table. "You won't need jammies," he said. He leaned over and kissed her. His eyes, so close to hers, were a brilliant green. A small jagged scar stretched beneath his lower lip. "Are you sure you're ready for this?" he said.

She smiled and ran her finger along the scar. "I've been ready," she said, and kissed him back.

Trevor and Eadie went back to Lavonne's place and argued for nearly an hour. Then they went to bed. In the morning, Eadie woke up to find him gone. There was a note pinned to Trevor's pillow, along with a sprig of forsythia that he had obviously pulled from Lavonne's front yard. The note read, "Dear Eadie — I love you. I'm sorry you're unhappy and I'm willing to do whatever it takes to see you through this, even if it means sleeping alone and not seeing you for weeks at a time. I'll call you tonight. I'm going to London the end of the month and I hope you'll go with me. Love, Trevor." Underneath this, was a hastily scrawled note. "P.S. Don't sleep with anyone else."

Eadie grinned and yawned, and rolled over in bed. She had to admit, even after twenty-two years the sex was still good. She knew there were more than a few women who might look at her and think she was crazy for sending Trevor away.

But then Eadie had never cared much for what other people thought of her.

When Lavonne got home late that afternoon, Eadie was sitting out on the deck smoking a cigarette.

"I hope you're not picking up bad habits staying with me," Lavonne said, sitting down at the table. She had just climbed out of the shower and her hair was wet. Joe had dropped her off, but he didn't stay. It was Saturday and he was leaving on Sunday morning for a business trip to Boston. "In case you don't know this, cigarettes kill."

Eadie put her head back and blew smoke rings into the blue sky. "One bad habit at a time," she said. "I gave up Mondo Logs but don't ask me to give up cigarettes yet."

A lawn mower hummed in the distance. The air was fragrant with the scent of honeysuckle and barbecue. Lavonne slumped in her chair, tired but happy.

"So?" Eadie said. "How was it?"

Lavonne grinned and shook her head. "I can't even begin to tell you," she said. "I had no idea what I was missing."

Eadie pursed her lips and blew smoke over her shoulder. "Better late than never," she said.

In the alley behind the house, a group of

children played tag. The evening sun dipped slowly behind a line of ragged purple clouds. "We're out of vodka," Eadie said. "All you've got is beer." She stubbed her cigarette out in one of the potted plants. "What's with all the Coronas in the refrigerator?" she said, nodding with her head toward the garage. I never took you for a beer lover."

"Eadie, I grew up in Cleveland, Ohio. The only way I could be any more of a beer lover is if I'd grown up in Cincinnati."

Bats flitted in the darkening sky, swooping above the trees. Lavonne went inside to get a box of matches and came back out with two glasses of sweet tea. She bent to light the citronella candles. Eadie sipped her tea and thought about Trevor.

"You're kind of quiet tonight," Lavonne said. Eadie's face, in the candlelight, was lovely.

"I'm tired, is all."

"Didn't get much sleep last night?"

"Nope. Did you?"

"Nope." They grinned at each other. "I guess we do all right for a couple of old broads," Lavonne said.

"Old broads?" Eadie said. "Speak for yourself."

The soft evening closed around them. Tree frogs chanted in the shadows of the box-

309

wood hedge. A few faint stars sprinkled the night sky. "You know, it's funny," Eadie said. "But I keep dreaming about my mother. It's the same dream, and she's trying to tell me something, but when I wake up I can't remember."

"Recurrent dreams are important," Lavonne said.

"She's been dead twenty years but she visits me constantly in my dreams. And the funny thing is," Eadie put her glass down on the table and turned toward Lavonne. "The funny thing is, she's become some kind of wise woman."

"What do you mean?"

"Well, you never knew my mother. She was a pretty simple person. I never gained much knowledge from her other than what I learned from watching her fuck up and deciding I wouldn't do the same." Eadie grinned. "Don't look so shocked, Lavonne. It's okay to speak ill of the dead. She doesn't mind. She knows I loved her. Always." Eadie sipped her tea carefully and then set the glass down again. "But somewhere on the other side, she's picked up some kind of knowledge. She's trying to tell me something, and in the dream I realize what she's saying is important, but when I wake up I can't remember."

"Maybe you don't want to remember," Lavonne said. "Maybe it's something painful that you're not ready to face yet."

"Hey," Eadie said suddenly, putting her feet down. "I'm hungry. Are you hungry?"

"I guess. But I don't feel like cooking."

"Me neither. Let's go out to eat." Lights came on in the house next door. Moths as big as butterflies fluttered against the window screens. "Let's get dressed up and you can take me out and show me what this town has to offer in the way of entertainment now that it's gone all grand and upscale."

The restaurant was packed. It was a new place out on the river and was called, of all things, The Grotto. It was run by a chef out of New York who had tired of the rat race of Manhattan and moved south a little over a year ago. The menu was primarily seafood and southern Italian cuisine.

"Damn," Eadie said, looking around. They'd had to wait at the bar for a table, and were working on their second shaker of peach martinis. The hostess called their name and then led them to a small booth near the kitchen. "I don't know a soul in this place," Eadie said, looking around as she slid into the booth. "Who are all these

311

people?"

"The Sunbelt is growing," Lavonne said. "Everyone's moving south."

They ordered and then sat looking around the crowded restaurant. Candles flickered on tables and in sconces set into the thick stucco walls. One wall had been painted with a mural showing an outdoor market scene in Trapani or Palermo, the Tyrrhenian Sea sparkling in the background. Two young couples with a fussy toddler arrived and were seated at the table next to them. Soon after being strapped into his high chair, the child set up a relentless, high-pitched wail that the couples seemed oblivious to.

"Oh great," Eadie said. "We go out for a nice quiet dinner and we've got to sit next to a screamer." She looked around the crowded restaurant but couldn't see any empty tables where they could move.

Lavonne sipped her martini. "What does it mean when young mothers start looking like teenagers?"

"It means you're older than shit."

"That's what I thought."

"Hell," Eadie said, eyeing the young couple with the screaming baby. "For all we know, they *might* be teenagers."

The baby, whose name, unfortunately, was Caldwell, raised his voice an octave and began to kick the table with his feet. "Now, Caldwell," his mother said in a cheerful voice loud enough to be heard by most of the restaurant. "I know you don't want to sit in that high chair, but Mommy and Daddy are trying to have dinner with our friends and we'd appreciate it if you could be patient. Can you be patient, Caldwell?"

Apparently not. Caldwell opened his arms wide and turned his tear-streaked face to his mother. "I just love it when he makes that face," she said. "Isn't he the cutest thing?" she gushed.

"Adorable," the other woman said.

Caldwell's screams took on a tinge of rage.

"You know," Lavonne said to Eadie, "when my kids acted like that, one of us got up and took them out of the restaurant. There was a period of about six years when neither Leonard nor I ever got to sit through a complete meal."

"I always thought your girls were well-behaved."

"It's not that they were well-behaved. They were awful at times. It's just that we didn't feel it was right to inflict them on innocent bystanders. Mothers today seem to think they can *reason* with toddlers. There's no reasoning with a two-year-old."

As if to prove her point, the young mother

at the opposite table said loudly, "Caldwell, I can appreciate your frustration. I wouldn't like it either if I was strapped into some wooden chair. And I know, if you could talk, you'd express your frustration more reasonably than you're doing right now."

Caldwell began to throw himself violently against his restraints.

"Now that," Eadie said, clutching her martini glass and pointing with one finger, "is why I never had children."

"Actually, I always thought you'd make a good mother."

"Tell the truth, Lavonne." Eadie raised one eyebrow and sipped her drink. "Don't you miss having babies around?"

Lavonne looked at Caldwell. "No," she said. "I mean, don't get me wrong, I loved being a mom, I still do, but I wouldn't go back to those toddler days now. I've got the rest of my life in front of me to do with as I please. I'm not picking up after anyone but myself. I'm not wiping anyone's backside but my own."

Eadie grinned. "Speaking of wiping other people's backsides," she said. "How's Leonard?" Lavonne had told her about the visit with Christy, Landon, and Preston. They'd laughed about it for days.

"I haven't heard from him since he got

back to Atlanta. Since I told him about Joe."

At the next table, Caldwell's mother refused to give up. "Look, Caldwell, what shape do you see here?" She held up a cocktail napkin. "Is it a square? Is it a square, Caldwell?" She picked up a votive candle. "Look at the candle, Caldwell. It's round. Can you say round?"

Eadie said, "Look at the martini glass, Lavonne. It's round. Can you say round?"

Lavonne said, "Look at the cocktail shaker. It's round."

"And speaking of round," Eadie said, waving down the waiter. "We'll have another one."

After a while, Caldwell's father tired of the baby's screams. He picked him up and carried him around the restaurant nestled in his arm, standing in front of the opened kitchen so the baby could watch the employees work. Their food came and Eadie and Lavonne settled down to a quiet dinner. A few minutes later, Eadie's cell phone rang. She looked at the caller ID, and then turned the phone off.

"It's Trevor," she said. "I'll call him later."

"How are things going with you two?"

Eadie twirled her pasta with her fork. "As well as can be expected," she said. "Something's wrong but I don't know what. It's frustrating. He's starting to lose patience with me."

Lavonne hesitated, trying to pick her words carefully. "Maybe this isn't about you and Trevor." Eadie looked at her, but kept eating. "I've been thinking about what you said earlier. You said you'd been dreaming about your mother, right? And she's trying to tell you something, only you can't remember in the morning. Maybe your subconscious is trying to tell you something. Your shadow."

"Goddamn it, you sound like Trevor. I'm not crazy, Lavonne. At least I don't think I am."

"Crazy is a subjective term."

"I'll try and remember that when they're hauling me off in a straitjacket."

"Look, Eadie, I went through something similar a couple of years ago. I started seeing my dead mother. Everywhere. I saw her on street corners waiting to catch a bus; I saw her in crowded supermarkets, as real as you are sitting across from me now. I was beginning to think I had some kind of hormonal imbalance. I was beginning to think it might be time for a trip to the psychiatrist. But what I realized sometime during all of that craziness, is that middle age is a time when we have to face our

316

childhood demons. We have to slay those dragons, and then move on."

Eadie drank steadily and then put her glass down again. "Who said anything about dragons?" she said. "I don't buy into that blame-your-parents-for-your-problems-as-an-adult mentality. People have to be responsible for their own lives."

"I'm not saying to blame anybody. I'm just saying acknowledge what happened and then move on."

"My mother did the best she could," Eadie said stubbornly. "Given the circumstances. She had a hard life."

"I know that, Eadie, but from what you've told me, you had to grow up fast. You had to be the parent because your mother wasn't capable of being one. You had to lock up that child persona and take on the responsibilities of adulthood."

They ate in silence, their spoons clanking against the ceramic pasta bowls. Eadie hated talking about her childhood. Not that hers had been all that bad. She'd talked to plenty of people who'd had it worse than she had. And after Eadie figured out a way to stop Reba from bringing home any more stepdaddies, things had gotten a lot better. She'd done it by giving her mother something to concentrate on other than a bunch of sorry men. She'd done it by becoming a beauty queen. She'd let Reba and the girls down at Miss Eula's House of Hair enter her in Purvis Auto's Little Miss Mag Wheels Beauty Pageant and Tire Sale. Eadie promptly won a set of tires and was crowned Little Miss Mag Wheels. In quick succession she won the coveted crowns of Miss MoonPie Deluxe, Miss Waycross Watermelon Festival, and Miss Tishimingo County Fairest of Them All.

During the week Eadie was Queen of the Goths at Ithaca Public High School, wearing thick eyeliner and black lipstick; on weekends she was a beauty queen collecting trophies and glittering tiaras as casually as if she were picking daisies in a field. It was the kind of dyslexic contradiction that only the South can produce. By the time she was a junior Eadie had made enough money through modeling and endorsements to buy Reba a little house over on the south side of town, and by the time she graduated she had enough money saved to make it through two years of college.

So all in all, her childhood really hadn't been all that bad.

Lavonne finished her spaghetti con polpettini. She was determined to help Eadie get through this anyway she could. She figured she was entitled to act as a psychological counselor on account of what had happened to her two years before and the fact that she loved Eadie like a sister. "You know I love you like a sister and I don't want to hurt you," she said, pushing her empty bowl away.

"Good," Eadie said. "Then don't."

"But remember: depression is anger turned inward."

Eadie put her fork down. "Who said anything about depression?" she said.

"Look at your art." Eadie groaned and put her head in her hands, but Lavonne went on. "Look at what you make for yourself. You create an army of giant goddesses the same way a Chinese emperor creates an army of tomb soldiers."

"So? A lot of artists create female shapes. And in case you haven't noticed, Lavonne, I've been painting a lot of cherubs lately." Lavonne stared at her as if this might be significant, and Eadie flushed and lifted her martini.

"You have to ask yourself, do these images mean something to you? Do they symbolize something important?"

Eadie put her glass down. "Okay, Lavonne. You tell me. Obviously you think they symbolize something." She was feeling belligerent. It seemed everyone in her life felt like they had the right to psychoanalyze her whether she needed it or not.

"The female figures are totems," Lavonne said. "Powerful female figures to compensate for the powerful female figure you never had — your mother."

"Oh my God, you've been reading Jung again."

"Just think about it, Eadie."

Eadie grimaced and shook her head. She wished now she was drinking something a little stronger than peach martinis. If she'd known Lavonne had analysis on her mind, she'd have ordered a bottle of tequila instead. "What are you suggesting?" she asked in exasperation. "That I spend countless hours and thousands of dollars in therapy. That I give up my goddesses and paint still lifes?"

"No. The answer is simple. And cheap."

"I'm all ears," Eadie said morosely. She picked up her glass and looked down into the bottom like she was trying to read leaves in a teacup. The father walked by with a complacent Caldwell nestled in his arms. The child sat facing out with his chubby legs stuck straight out in front of him, his back resting against his father's chest. He looked at Eadie and smiled vaguely. "I'm listening," she said. "What's the answer?"

Lavonne leaned forward and rested her arms on the table. She smiled at Eadie's sullen expression. "Forgiveness," she said.

CHAPTER FIFTEEN

The week before Mother's Day, Nita went out to the nursing home with an orchid and a small present she had wrapped for Leota Quarles. She was not in her room, but the nurse was, arranging items on the bedside table. The room looked different. "Is Leota at lunch?" Nita asked, standing in the doorway.

The nurse, startled, looked around. "Miz Motes, didn't you get my message?" she said.

"What message?"

"I left it with your daughter last week."

Nita flushed and held the plant awkwardly out in front of her. She shook her head slightly. "She must have forgotten to tell me."

"I thought you knew. I'm sorry. Miz Quarles died in her sleep last Tuesday night."

■ ■ ■ ■

On Wednesday afternoon, Logan stayed after school for band practice so Nita went by the middle school to pick up Whitney. She was still shaken by the news of Leota Quarles's death and by the knowledge that she had not known about, and therefore hadn't attended, the old woman's funeral. She couldn't see Whitney when she pulled up in front of the school, so she parked in a spot close to the flagpole to wait. A few minutes later, a girl climbed out of a truck across the parking lot and leaned in the passenger's window to collect her book bag. She wore a skirt short enough to show off her long lovely legs and also her black thong underwear. The girl stood up and Nita, shocked and curious to see who had allowed their daughter out of the house dressed like that, craned her neck to see.

It was Whitney.

She watched her daughter saunter across the parking lot toward the car. She opened the rear door and threw her backpack in and then climbed into the front seat beside her mother. Nita sat for a few minutes, staring at the flagpole.

"What's wrong?" Whitney said.

Nita turned her head slowly. "Last week. Someone called me about a Mrs. Quarles. You were supposed to give me a message."

Whitney snapped her gum and rolled her eyes. "What about her?" she said.

"She died."

Whitney slouched down in the seat, putting her knees up on the dash. Nita started the car and backed up slowly, eyeing her sullen daughter with an expression of disappointment and concern. "Did your father see you before you went to school today? Did he see the way you were dressed?" Whitney had been spending the week with Charles.

She blew a bubble. "Christ," she said.

"Don't say 'Christ.' And don't sit like that."

"Why not?" Whitney turned her face to the window but kept sitting the way she was. She plucked idly at her hair.

"Because it's not what a nice girl would do."

"I don't care about being a nice girl. I don't want to be a nice girl," Whitney said, pushing herself upright.

"Seat belt," Nita said. Whitney slammed the belt in the buckle and Nita put the car in drive. She drove slowly past the pickup truck, trying to catch a glimpse of the driver. Then she circled the lot and came back up on the other side of the truck.

"What are you doing?" Whitney said, her voice edging toward panic as Nita slowed down. "Mother, what are you doing?" She put her hand over her eyes and turned her face to the window.

Nita stopped beside the truck and put her window down. "Excuse me," she said loudly.

"Mother," Whitney groaned.

"Yoo-hoo," Nita said, her little hand fluttering. The driver, a young man with long sideburns and a goatee, poked his head out the window.

"Hey, how you doing?" Nita said.

He looked at her and smirked, stroking his chin. "Not too bad," he said.

"Good," Nita said. "Hey, what's your name?" Whitney pushed herself back against the seat, trying to blend in with the headrest.

"Darrell," he said.

"Well, hey, Darrell, I'm Whitney's mom. You may not know this but Whitney is twelve years old. Now I don't know how old you are, but I'm guessing, since you're driving, that you're at least sixteen, and probably a lot older than that. Whitney has an older brother who's sixteen and I feel sure he would have told me about you, if he knew you. So I'm guessing you're older than that."

She grinned at him and he grinned back.

"Now you may not know this, Darrell, but the statutory rape laws in Georgia are pretty severe. Whitney's daddy is a lawyer and I can guarantee that if he finds out about you, he will make it his sole mission to see that you spend most of the rest of your life in prison. Whitney's two uncles played football at Ithaca High School and her granddaddy has one of the finest gun collections in the county, mostly shotguns and hunting rifles, and more recently a .40-caliber Glock semi-automatic that he takes out faithfully every weekend for target practice. He's a real good shot. You see, Darrell, what I'm trying to do is get you to see the big picture. Well, do you see it? Do you see the big picture, Darrell?"

Obviously, Darrell did. He put his window up and started the truck's engine. They watched him roar out of the parking lot and fishtail onto the highway with his tires squealing and a black plume of smoke following in his wake like a trailing tornado.

Whitney slumped against the passenger door. "I hate my life," she said.

"Of course you do," Nita said cheerfully.

She drove straight to Charles's office.

"Now what," Whitney groaned.

"I want Daddy to see how you went to school today. I want him to know how you looked when you left his house this morning."

Whitney took a napkin out of the glove box and quickly began to wipe her face clean of rouge and lipstick. She tugged at the hem of her skirt until it grazed the tops of her knees.

"Don't bother to roll down your skirt. I'll just make you roll it back up," Nita said.

Charles's new office was in the front of a rambling Victorian house that had been cut up into a warren of small offices, rented mostly by attorneys and court reporters. Nita and Whitney went up the bricked front steps and through the double doors into a small receptionist area. Mrs. Corley looked up and smiled. "Hello, Mrs. Broadwell," she said, coloring slightly. "I mean, Mrs. Motes."

"Hello, Mrs. Corley. Is Charles in?"

"He just got back from court."

He had heard her voice and he hurried out of his office, rubbing his hands together nervously. "Hello, Nita."

"Hello, Charles." She was always a little embarrassed when she first saw him. They had been married for sixteen years and he had ruled her life and the children's lives like a petty tyrant. Charles was one of those people who could not be happy and could not bear to have people around him be happy. Still, she had loved him once, a long time ago. Nita nodded for Whitney to sit down in one of the chairs in the waiting area. "I'll be just a minute," she said. "I want to talk to your father alone." Whitney scowled and slumped down into a chair, picking up a magazine.

Charles followed Nita into his office, closing the door softly behind him. She looked lovely, with her hair pulled up on the back of her head and small tendrils curling around her face and the nape of her neck. He would think he was over all that and then he would see her, or pick up an article of clothing that held her lingering scent, and then it would come flooding back to him. "Please sit down," he said nervously, indicating one of the chairs in front of his desk.

"No, I can't stay," she said. It was always so awkward between them. Nita tried to keep their face-to-face meetings to a minimum. "I have to get home and make dinner." She hadn't stopped to think how that would sound, but seeing his face tighten, she hurried on. "It's Whitney," she said. She told him quickly about what had occurred in the parking lot. "You have to be careful when she stays with you. She may look presentable when she's heading out the door to school, but you've got to check her backpack. She usually hides her makeup and an extra pair of clothes in there."

Charles started to speak and then closed his mouth. He was determined to convince Nita that he had changed. That he was a new man. "None of this would have happened if she hadn't gone to public school," he said. There. It had slipped out despite his best intentions.

"It has less to do with public school and more to do with parental supervision," Nita said firmly.

"And who was this boy?"

"I don't know. Darrell somebody. But I don't think we'll have to worry about him anymore."

The desperateness of the situation came gradually over Charles. He slid down into his chair with his arms resting stiffly on his desk. "Oh my God, she's capable of anything," he said.

"Well, Charles, she's a teenage girl, so technically that's true."

"Oh my God," he said.

"It's not that bad. She's just a little rebellious. She just needs a firm hand."

Charles sighed. He stared bleakly out the window. "I'll talk to my mother," he said.

Nita blinked. She opened her purse and took out a Kleenex and then closed it again. "This is not something your mother needs to get involved with, Charles. This is something you and I need to handle. Together." She blew her nose and threw the Kleenex in the trash.

"Yes, yes, of course, I didn't mean anything by that," he said quickly. Trying to win Nita back was like trying to coax a timid little bird. He had to be patient. And clever. "It's just that she's been spending a lot of time with my mother."

"Yes, I know," she said. "But you're still her father. And Virginia doesn't seem to be much of a disciplinarian."

He saw her expression and said, "You don't mind, do you? Them spending time together?"

"No, of course not."

"They haven't seen each other in a while and Mother was anxious to reestablish a bond," he said. "A connection."

"Tell your mother to check her backpack before she drops her off at school," she said, moving toward the door.

"Oh, right," he said, rising.

"Good-bye, then."

"I can have Mother pick her up here, if you like." He tried to take her arm but she moved ahead of him quickly and opened the door.

"No, that's okay. I'll drop her by your condo on my way home."

On the ride over to his condominium, the girl was sullen and quiet. With her scrubbed face and skirt tucked demurely around her knees she looked more like a girl again, and less like an adolescent sex kitten.

"Next time I get a phone call and you answer, I expect you to give me the message."

"Whatever," Whitney said.

"And I told Daddy to check your backpack for makeup and extra clothes before you go to school." Nita slowed down and pulled into the parking lot of Charles's condominium. "And Grandmother, too, if you're staying with her."

"Great," Whitney said, gathering her belongings. "She's the only one who doesn't treat me like a *criminal.* She's the only one who doesn't treat me like a *child,* and now you've ruined that, too." She opened the door and slid out.

"If you don't want to be treated like a criminal then don't act like one," Nita said, but Whitney had already slammed the door and was running up the stairs with her backpack bumping against her hip. Nita sighed and turned off the car. She couldn't very well just leave Whitney alone. Not after what happened in the parking lot. She would have to stay until Charles got home. She looked up at the window of Charles's condominium and was surprised to see a figure standing there. Nita leaned forward to look and the figure lifted its hand and waved.

It was Virginia. Relieved, Nita lifted her hand and waved back.

By the end of June they had finished laying the utilities to the Culpepper Plantation project, and by the middle of July they were set to begin work on the first spec house. Virginia and Redmon had a cocktail party at their house to celebrate. It was a small group. Nita was there with Jimmy Lee, Whitney, and Logan, and for some reason Virginia had insisted on inviting Eadie and Lavonne, so they were there, too. Redmon stood in the corner discussing business with Jimmy Lee. Lavonne, Nita, and Eadie stood over by the French doors overlooking the backyard. Della Smurl, with Whitney and Logan's help, passed around trays of stuffed mushrooms, bruschetta, and smoked crab.

"Hey, Della, how's Martha doing?" Nita asked. She'd gone to high school with Della's daughter, who'd graduated with honors and gone to college at Sewanee, and later, to law school at Vanderbilt.

"She's doing okay," Della said. "She's practicing out in Los Angeles, some kind of law where she represents all them rappers and singers with funny names who talk like they were raised without a mama. Just talking trash all the time and singing about it, too."

Lavonne said, "Entertainment law?"

"Yeah, I guess." Della stood there looking glumly out the French doors at the dying sun that disappeared slowly behind the trees and distant rooflines. Her bottom jaw jutted out from the severe plane of her face like a cliff. "My mama wouldn't have allowed such trash talk in our house. My daddy was an elder, you know. I was raised with the Temptations." Her face brightened suddenly. "Now there's some boys who could sing and dance," she said. She was holding a tray of smoked crab but that didn't stop her from showing off a couple of dance moves, taking a few tiny steps forward, a few tiny steps backward, and sliding to the side on one leg.

"Della!" Virginia said sharply.

Della stopped dancing. She dropped her head between her shoulders and swung around to face Virginia. "Yeah?" she said sullenly.

"Did you check the cheese toasts?" Virginia said. She smiled, showing her sharp little teeth. It was one of the things she was most proud of, the fact that at her age, she still had her own teeth. Lavonne, looking at that blinding row of gleaming enamel, was not surprised. She had read somewhere that rats lose several sets of teeth over a lifetime and then promptly grow new ones.

Della said, "No, I haven't checked the cheese toasts, have you checked the cheese toasts?" and turning she moved off, slow and ponderous as a battleship.

Virginia giggled nervously. "It's so hard to get good help these days," she said, but quietly, so Della wouldn't hear.

"I'm surprised you don't look into getting yourself some Guatemalans," Eadie said. "You could bring a whole family up and pay just one but have the rest of them work like slaves, even the children."

"Really?" Virginia looked interested. It took her a minute to realize Eadie was kidding. "Excuse me," she said, patting her smooth hair. "I'll just go check on things in the kitchen."

"I think you had her going there," La-vonne said to Eadie, as they watched Virginia swagger toward the kitchen in her high-heeled sandals.

"If I'd known this was going to be a dry party, I'd have brought my own giggle juice," Eadie said gloomily, lifting her iced-tea glass.

"Virginia's trying to wean Redmon off the Jack Daniel's, so I hope y'all don't mind going without alcohol for an hour," Nita said. "I hope you can hang in there another forty-five minutes without a drink."

"Damn, girl, do I sense a bit of sarcasm in your voice?" Eadie said.

"Just look at that poor slob," Lavonne said, nodding her head at Redmon, who stood slumped against a wall, awkwardly clutching a glass of soda water. He was dressed in a dress shirt opened at the collar and a pair of khaki slacks. His hair was slicked back off his face and she'd made him remove his gold chains and rings. The overall effect was that of a cuffed dog who'd just had his ass shaved. "Do you think Redmon had any idea what he was getting into when he married Virginia?"

"She's whittled him down pretty good," Eadie said, shaking her head. "Another

335

couple of years with Virginia and he'll be nothing but a stick of kindling and a little squeaky voice."

Even Nita giggled at this. Across the room Logan set his tray down on the coffee table. He glared at his grandmother as she stuck her head out the door and called to Whitney. Virginia hadn't said two words to him all night. He made her nervous and she overcompensated for this by chattering on in a bright cheerful voice and never allowing him to say a word. Under this barrage of false gaiety, Logan became more and more sullen and morose. Charles treated him pretty much the same way, only he spoke in an affected masculine voice and asked Logan serious questions about his future. Things like, *Have you thought about college?* or *What do you think you'd like to major in?* Logan, of course, answered these as smart-ass as he could. He had not yet forgiven his father for his childhood. *Forget college. I'm thinking about going to tattoo school and opening up my own parlor right here in Ithaca,* he told his dad once, and Charles's right eye began to flutter and he looked like he might be on the verge of a stroke. *Or, hell, clown school's a possibility. I hear there's always a market for clowns. You can't beat the clown business for job security.*

The problem with Virginia and Charles was that they didn't get Logan's sense of humor. They got caught up in the way he looked, six-foot-three with a Mohawk and Doc Martens adding another four inches, black eyeliner and a lip ring, and the truth was, he did look a little scary. But deep down inside he was a poet with a sense of humor, as the lyrics of his latest love song, "Kill Me," could attest.

Nita waved at Logan across the room and he waved back and went to stand with Jimmy Lee.

"This place reminds me of a haunted castle," Eadie said, glancing around the big room with its cathedral ceiling and tall windows and gaudy masculine decor. "It's kind of creepy."

Nita smiled. "You should have seen it before Virginia redid the kitchen and dining room and got rid of the red carpet. She told me she's planning on redoing the whole house but she has to do it slowly so Redmon won't freak out."

"Myra must be spinning in her grave," Lavonne said, noting the Elvis photo collage and the Naugahyde seating arrangement with built-in beer cooler that Redmon was proudly showing off to the other envious males. "She had one of the nicest houses in our old neighborhood."

"I think that's part of the problem," Nita said. "When Myra was alive, Redmon had to live the way she wanted, and when she died he just went wild and bought himself the swinging bachelor pad he'd always wanted."

"Well, I can't believe Virginia agreed to live here," Eadie said. "This place gives me the creeps. I wouldn't be surprised to see Boris Karloff step out of one of the closets."

"Oh look, there's Boris now," Lavonne said, and when they all turned to look, she said, "Nevermind. It's just Redmon." Eadie snorted and poked Lavonne with her elbow.

"Behave," Nita said.

"And I still don't get why Virginia invited us," Eadie said. "I mean, I know she and Jimmy Lee are business partners, which is kind of weird in itself if you ask me, and she's Whitney and Logan's grandmother, so that explains why you and Jimmy Lee were invited. But why did she ask us to come? What's she got up her sleeve?"

"Maybe she's just trying to be nice," Nita said, ignoring the look Eadie and Lavonne gave each other. Lavonne folded her cocktail napkin into a tiny square. "Y'all should give her a chance. You never know what it is that

338

makes some people act the way they act." Nita clutched her glass and tried not to think about how foolish that had sounded. She hadn't told a soul about what she'd discovered about Virginia's tragic childhood, not even Jimmy Lee.

Lavonne and Eadie stared at her. Eadie said, "What do you know that we don't know? Come on, Nita. Spill it."

Virginia came out of the kitchen with her arm around Whitney's shoulders. They were giggling and sharing some secret moment, drawing the attention of everyone in the room. Nita was glad to be spared a discussion of Virginia's childhood. She was glad to see Whitney had found a family member she could confide it. Adolescence was a tough time and all the child-rearing books she had read said it was important for girls to have a strong female role model they could rely upon. A teacher, a counselor, an older friend or family member. Rarely a mother, the books said. But that was normal. All teenage girls are locked in a love-hate relationship with their mothers, but that would change over time, the books promised. Nita could not remember ever hating her mother. Loretta always insisted that Nita had been "sweet as a watermelon's heart" as a girl, but that was beside the point.

The dying sun caught in the tops of the distant trees, shimmering the glass of the tall windows and filling the room with a warm glow. It occurred to Nita that the people she cared the most about were here in this room, with the exception of her brothers and her parents, and no one expected Virginia to invite Loretta to anything. It would be like sticking two pit bulls in a kennel crate and telling them to *be nice.* Everyone in this room was connected in one way or another. They were like one big family. She was glad that Virginia had finally understood this, too. Still, she wished Charles could be here to enjoy this moment of family togetherness. She wished he could be here to witness how far his mother had come.

She walked over to where her daughter and ex-mother-in-law stood, arm in arm, still giggling. "What's so funny?" Nita asked, trying to get in on the joke.

Virginia lifted one eyebrow and looked at Whitney, who immediately stopped giggling. "Nothing," Whitney said. She yawned and wandered off to talk to Lavonne and Eadie.

"We were laughing at something that happened to one of her friends at school," Virginia explained.

"Oh," Nita said. She smiled and sipped her tea. "Why isn't Charles here?"

"Well, of course I invited him, but he has to be in court early tomorrow. He's getting ready for a big case," she lied. She had told Charles two days ago about her plans and he had reacted quite unexpectedly, refusing to go along with her scheme. She had, of course, proceeded anyway. She had spent hours today making discreet phone calls to several professors at the University of Georgia, to an official at the Georgia Bureau of Indian Affairs, and to a Creek activist named Leonard Twohorses. Then she had called her attorney.

"I hate that he's not here to see the children and everybody together," Nita said.

Virginia looked at her curiously. After a moment she shifted her gaze across the room to where Whitney stood talking with Lavonne and Eadie. It was too late to start wallowing in forgiveness and goodwill at this stage of the game. The plan was already in motion and Virginia was determined to see it through to the end. As her daddy used to say, *She would see it through even if it meant hairlipping the governor and every mule in Georgia.*

341

"I hate that he's not here to share in the celebration," Nita said, still talking about Charles.

"Well, I'm sure he'll hear all about it," Virginia murmured, staring at her granddaughter.

Charles would thank her for this one day, she was sure.

CHAPTER SIXTEEN

One week later, Jimmy Lee rose early and drove out to the island. He was whistling, happy as any man who has just left the arms of his sleepy wife can be. He had brought her a gift the night before, a pair of emerald earrings. It was only the second gift of jewelry he had ever given her, besides her wedding ring, and when she opened the black box her mouth trembled and her hand flew to her throat. The note inside read, "These are not as pretty as your eyes. Accept them as a token of my love and a promise of the good things that are to come."

When she read the note, she cried, and he put his arms around her and kissed her tenderly. Her hair was damp and smelled of lavender. Her bosom rose and fell with her quick breathing, and when he put his mouth there, she moaned. He had meant the words he'd written. He had spent hours running the Culpepper Plantation projections through his cash-flow software and he foresaw a time when he'd be able to provide for her in a way he'd never thought possible back when he was a poor carpenter hired to fix her pool house. Back when he was a struggling handyman and she was the beautiful Mrs. Broadwell, mistress of a house so large a family of four could go for days without running into one another. And now, if his luck held, he'd be able to buy her a house just as grand as the one she'd given up when she abandoned her husband and ran off with him to the wild shores of the Black Warrior River.

The sun rose insistently over the horizon, filling the truck with a warm hopeful glow. With any luck, the excavator would finish today and they could begin laying out the forms for the concrete pour. He drove with the windows down, letting the sweet humid air blow through the truck. It was early enough to be cool but by mid-morning the temperature would climb to ninety-five degrees and then he would have no choice but to close the windows and turn on the rancid air-conditioning. Sunlight glinted on the waters of the Black Warrior River as he crossed the small bridge, his tires clacking against the expansion joints. On the other side, the mason was putting the finishing touches on the stone entrance sign and Jimmy Lee raised his hand and waved as he drove past.

He turned left and followed the meandering asphalt road up the side of the ridge. They had decided to put the first spec homes up here, where they'd have the best view of the river and the heavily wooded opposite shore. At the top of the ridge he could see a car he didn't recognize parked along the road and beyond that the excavator's truck. The bulldozer was curiously quiet. Jimmy Lee pulled in behind the car and parked, wondering if Redmon might have brought some of the bank officials out, although it was hard to imagine Redmon or a bank official driving a Honda Civic.

Jimmy Lee turned off the truck and climbed out. He was still whistling as he began the gradual descent to the building site, catching his hands in the thick underbrush to steady himself. Beyond a grove of sweetgum and red oak he could see the bulldozer resting beside the lip of the excavated foundation like some giant sleeping insect. He heard male voices, and someone called out sharply, "Oh my God, look at this."

He reached the rim. A mockingbird sang

in the top of a poplar tree. He would remember this moment later, the sweetness of birdsong, the sun-dappled shade beneath the tall trees, the air swarming with insects but curiously still, too, as if all of nature held its breath in anticipation of his ruin. He would wonder, later, at the ominous stillness he had felt there in the forest, standing at the edge of the opened pit.

There were three men at the bottom, poking their fingers into the exposed red clay bank. One of the men, dressed in blue jeans and a plaid shirt, sported two long braids. His name was Leonard Twohorses, Jimmy Lee would learn later, and what he was removing, reverently, from the dirt bank were pottery shards dating from the Mississippian Period. The other two men, one a professor from the University of Georgia, and the other an official from the Bureau of Indian Affairs, crowded around eagerly examining the shards.

From the corner of his eye, Jimmy Lee caught a movement and he turned to see the excavator leaning against a fallen hickory tree, smoking a cigarette and watching the men with an attitude of feigned indifference and disgust.

Jimmy Lee raised his hand and waved. "Hullo," he shouted, his voice loud in the stillness of the dappled forest. The three men in the pit turned slowly. Leonard Two-horses returned his gaze, his eyes dark and steady. Pine pollen drifted in a wide shaft of sunlight and beyond the treetops the cold blue sky stretched endlessly.

It was curious, once disaster befell him, Jimmy Lee realized he had been expecting it all along. He was Icarus who, through pride and a desire for fame, flew too close to the sun in his wax wings. He was a simple carpenter who had thought he could play ball with the big boys, and the truly distressing part was the money hadn't been his to lose in the first place. It was Nita's. And now he had to tell her it was gone.

Redmon took the injunction filed by the State of Georgia in his stride. He was a veteran of many land development skirmishes and he knew it would take time and money, once the lawyers became involved, but eventually he would prevail. In the meantime he could live forever on the money generated by his investments, rental income, and bank accounts.

Virginia seemed even less concerned. True, she had gotten her finder's fee money up-front, but she didn't seem unduly concerned that any future income she might have made from the sale of the lots was now tied up in the courts indefinitely. She stood in the middle of Redmon's office, while Jimmy Lee sat with his head in his hands, and chattered on as if she had no idea what was going on.

"So you mean we've lost all our investment money?" she asked innocently. She was wearing a flowered Dior skirt and high-heeled sandals, and her little toes had been painted a deep blood red.

"No, Queenie, I've already explained this to you," Redmon growled. "We don't lose anything. We just have to postpone the time we actually *make* money on the project until the lawsuit is settled. Who knew your old family plantation was built on a goddamn Indian burial ground!"

Virginia giggled and waved her hand above her head like she was swatting at a low-flying bird. "In one ear and out the other," she said gaily. "I never did have a head for business."

Redmon smiled at her fondly. She was leaving to go to Florida with Whitney the minute this meeting was finished. The car was packed and Whitney sat in giggling anticipation in the waiting room with her friend Carlisle, who had been invited to come. Redmon was tempted to go with them.

"Oh no," Virginia said, when he suggested this to her. She widened her eyes and pointed to Jimmy Lee with her chin. "Someone needs to stay here with poor Mr. Motes. We can't all abandon him to run off to Florida, now can we?"

Redmon sighed and glanced at Motes who still sat with his head in his hands. He wasn't crying but he looked on the verge of a breakdown and Redmon wasn't sure what advice he might offer. Something along the lines of *If you're gonna run with the big dogs, son, be prepared to hike your leg in tall grass,* which is what Redmon's daddy used to say to him when he tried, and failed, at some major undertaking. This comment had always spurred Redmon on to new attempts at success but he wasn't sure it would have the same effect on Motes. The boy looked like he'd been pistol-whipped.

"I better get on the road," Virginia sang, twirling around so her flowered skirt frothed around her shapely knees. "We hope to be in Destin before dark."

"Well come on over here and kiss me, girl," Redmon said and, in front of the despondent Jimmy Lee, she had no choice but to do as she was told.

Jimmy Lee slumped in his chair, oblivious to all but his own pain and suffering.

"Aw, come on now, son," Redmon said, winking at Virginia as she went out of the room and closed the door quietly behind her. "We got a lot of stumps in the field but we ain't finished yet. This is only a slight detour not the end of the road, and once the lawyers get involved they'll get that injunction lifted and it'll be back to business as usual. In the meantime, all we got to do is sit tight." Redmon got up and went over to the cabinet where he kept a bottle of Jack Daniel's hidden from Virginia. He took out two small shot glasses and poured a couple of jiggers in each. "You want a drink?" he asked, and when Jimmy Lee didn't reply, he said, "I've never yet found a sickness that a little Jack can't cure."

Jimmy Lee lifted his head and slumped back in his chair with his hands hanging loose in his lap. His eyes were dull and glazed, and his face was the color of ash. After a minute he roused himself from his stupor.

"Sure," he said wearily, reaching for the drink. "Why not."

Nita was speeding toward Virginia Redmon's house when Jimmy Lee called. He sounded like he might be crying but she didn't stop, she didn't even slow the car down, racing down the busy streets clogged with rush-hour traffic and praying that she would get there in time, praying it had all been a terrible misunderstanding.

"Nita," he said. "I don't know how to tell you this."

She passed a slow-moving minivan, swinging over into the left lane and swerving back to the right, just in time to miss an oncoming truck. She turned left at one of the older neighborhoods, taking a shortcut, her tires squealing against the pavement. Live oaks rose against the darkening sky their branches draped with Spanish moss. In the distance, a line of ragged storm clouds rolled in, followed by the low rumbling of thunder.

"I've let you down," he said, his voice breaking. "I've let you down when you trusted me and now there's nothing I can do to make it right."

Her mind was racing. Her heart swooped and veered through her chest like some monstrous bird.

"The state's closed down the job site," he said. "They're shutting down the site until they've had a chance to excavate the ridge. There's Indian artifacts buried there and it might take years before we can develop the island and get our money out. Redmon says his attorneys are good and he'll fix it eventually but in the meantime I've lost everything." He breathed heavily. "Everything," he said.

There was a sound in her ears like the wind moving through a pine grove, a steady insistent noise, creeping through her head and drowning out the low-pitched radio, her own ragged breathing, the broken sound of Jimmy Lee's voice.

"I've lost everything you had," he said. "Everything you trusted me with."

She had been sitting on the screened porch, reading, when the sheriff's deputy served the Child Custody Complaint. He was an old friend of her daddy's and his face was solemn and apologetic as he handed it to her through the screened door. She took it and signed where he told her to sign, feeling a dull thudding pain in the pit of her stomach. She stared at the document without reading it as the deputy said his sad good-byes and drove away. A slight breeze, heavy with the scent of rain, blew softly across the porch. Gradually her eyes began to focus. She read the complaint, from top to bottom, and then read it again.

"I don't expect you to forgive me," he

said. "I'll never forgive myself."

All this time she had expected Charles to be the one who took her children away, and now it seemed it was Virginia who wanted them. Not both of them, just Whitney.

"I'll pay you back if it takes me the rest of my life to do it," he said fiercely.

She had tried to reach Virginia on the telephone but no one had answered at the house. Whitney's cell phone appeared to be turned off. They were probably on their way to Florida but Nita had to see for herself. She took a sharp right and swung back onto the highway. The sun broke sporadically through the clouds. Green forests rose on either side of the road shimmering like a mirage.

He said, "Please say something, Nita."

Waves of heat rippled off the asphalt, collecting in distant puddles that thinned and evaporated as she got closer. A putty-colored bird swooped above the highway.

"I can't talk to you right now," she said, and hung up.

Virginia, of course, was gone. Her Mercedes was in the drive but her house was deserted. She had most likely taken Redmon's Volvo convertible to the beach as it was the car most likely to impress two adolescent girls. Too late, Nita had caught on to Virginia's ploy. She tried to call Redmon but his secretary said he was in a meeting with his lawyer. Desperate, she called Charles, and his secretary said yes he was in, and yes he would see her if she would come now. Charles picked up the phone then as if he were afraid she'd change her mind. She told him she'd be there in ten minutes.

She drove slowly, slumped against the door, her cheek resting against her hand. The storm broke finally, lashing the trees and drumming against the windshield, but Nita drove on, numb to everything around her, even danger, weighed down by a fierce heavy sorrow that swung from her breastbone like an anvil.

Charles stood at the window in his office watching the storm and waiting for his wife. He refused to think of her as his ex-wife. He had been expecting her call but he had not expected the degree of suffering he heard in her voice. It had thrown him a little, and made him question whether he would have the courage to do what he had to do.

To steady his resolve, he thought of his wife in the arms of that shiftless carpenter. Rage welled up inside him, damp and heavy,

354

poised above his heart like an avalanche. He could feel it giving way, sliding and tumbling, a sudden sense of weightlessness and violent flight, falling past his heart, his liver, his spleen, and churning into his bowels. All his life he had fought against fate. All his life he had waited for his luck to change. Only child of the bold and sadistic Judge, he had fought tooth and nail for his mother's attention. Fought and lost. The old man had sucked it out of her, all the love and attention she was capable of giving, the small degree of tenderness, her meager capacity for self-sacrifice, leaving nothing for Charles. The marrow-sucked bones of a bleached carcass, that's what his mother's love had been to him. But then he met Nita James and he had felt his luck changing. He had seen her vast capacity for love, had immersed himself in it like a parched man, had dreamed of starting a new family with her, different from his own.

But fate had turned that dream to dust, had crumbled it in the time it took his wife and children to drive away from him on that gray November afternoon into the arms of an impoverished carpenter. In the time it took for his law firm to come crashing down around him amid rumors of moral turpitude and fiscal mismanagement. Charles had thought his life was over. He had mourned the loss of his wife the way an artist mourns the loss of his greatest creation.

And now she was on her way to see him, to beg him to take her back (oh, not in so many words, but surely she understood by now that in order to have the child, she must take him, too). She would throw herself on his mercy and he would make everything all right again. He would call off his mother and retrieve Whitney. He would make his family whole again.

He heard her come into the waiting room and he went to his desk and sat down, pretending to read a brief while Mrs. Corley did her best to comfort Nita. "Go right in, Mrs. Motes," he heard her say, and he cringed at the sound of that odious name. "He's expecting you."

He stood up and stepped around his desk as she came in, and he had just a glimpse of her pale, tearstained face before she threw herself into his arms. She sobbed for some time, her little head resting beneath his chin and her full round bosom heaving against his chest, and he thought how right she felt wrapped in his arms. Holding her again, he wondered how he had ever taken her for granted.

Her sobs gradually subsided and she

seemed to remember herself, and pulled away in embarrassment. She slid down into one of the chairs facing his desk and when he didn't release her hand, she moved it gently, and reached in her purse for a Kleenex.

"Sorry," she said, dabbing at her face.

"Now, what's all this about," he said briskly, moving around his desk and sitting down in his chair, facing her. He had decided earlier his manner would be that of a trusted adviser, courteous but emotionally distant.

She looked at him, her eyes swollen with crying. "Don't you know?" she said in a small voice. "Don't you know what's happened?"

"No," he lied. "Tell me."

She told him, beginning in a trembling voice that grew firmer and more determined as she went on. Her eyes hardened until they were small and red-rimmed, smoldering in the smooth flat plane of her face. Looking at his wife's fierce expression he was reminded of that time, right before she left him, when she discovered the truth about the annual Montana hunting trip and went around the house with a look of numbed outrage on her face. Charles, unaware of her discovery, had caught her several times standing behind him holding a gleaming kitchen utensil in her hand and looking down at him with the blank expression of an executioner gazing down at the neck of the condemned prisoner. He had been frightened of her then, and he was frightened of her now.

She blew her nose and looked at him. "So you knew nothing of your mother's plans?" she asked coldly.

"N-N-No," he said. *Goddamn it.* He always stuttered when he was nervous. To throw her off track he said, "She must have gotten her attorney to allow her a private hearing in front of the judge."

"Is that legal?"

He smiled, relaxing. He was on firmer ground now. "Not exactly," he said, tenting his hands in front of him. "And I don't know a lot about grandparents' rights, it's a relatively new phenomena, grandparents seeking custody of minor children. But remember, this is Ithaca, Georgia, and my mother was married to a judge and she has a lot of influence. I'm sure there is a hearing set for sometime in the next few weeks to give you a chance to voice your case."

"Two weeks," Nita said tersely. "August eleventh."

"Okay, well in two weeks you'll be able to

at least get all this out in open court. Although I'll tell you my concern." He frowned and put his tented fingers up in front of his mouth as if he were just now re-alizing this.

She waited and then said, "What? What is your concern?"

"I can't believe the judge would go ahead and grant Virginia custody unless he thought there was some kind of endangerment to the child." He was trying to sound like a trusted legal adviser, but instead he sounded judgmental and insincere. Referring to Whitney as "the child" had definitely been a misstep. Nita looked at him suspiciously.

"Don't be ridiculous," she said coldly. She looked down at her hands in her lap. After a minute, she looked up again and said, "Do you know something about this, Charles? About this endangerment thing?"

"Well." He wasn't sure how to proceed without giving away the fact that he'd been in on his mother's scheme. He hadn't ap-proved of it, but he hadn't stopped it, either. And if Nita got wind of *any* collusion on his part, the reconciliation would never occur. Never. "There is something Virginia, I mean Mother, mentioned some time ago. At din-ner. I really didn't think much about it at the time, of course, I'm sure there's no impropriety on Jimmy Lee's part . . ." He put his hands out in front of him, palms up, as if trying to reassure Nita of his belief in Jimmy Lee's innocence, but she motioned impatiently for him to go on. "Well, Virginia," he began, looking at her, and then changed course again. "Mother," he said firmly. "Mother told me that Whitney had mentioned to her several times that she and Jimmy Lee always play around. Those were her words. We like to *play around.* And when Mother pushed her on it, she admitted that sometimes Jimmy Lee puts his hands under her shirt, on her belly . . ."

Nita shot up out of her chair. "He was *tickling* her," she shouted. "Oh my God, what is Virginia implying? I don't for one minute think Whitney would ever accuse Jimmy Lee of anything improper. This is all Virginia's doing! Virginia has taken a perfectly innocent event and twisted it into something evil!" Charles had never seen her so angry. He sat in stunned amazement while she continued, leaning her hands against his desk. "She's made something evil out of something innocent because that's the kind of lying, coldhearted snake she is." She flushed, remembering suddenly that she was talking about his mother. She sat down rigidly, trying to compose herself.

Her lower lip trembled for a while and then got still. "I'm sorry, Charles," she said finally, sounding stiff and formal.

Charles, who had only recently compared his mother's love to the marrow-sucked bones of a bleached carcass, took no offense. He dipped his head politely, trying to regain his position of trusted adviser. "I'll make a few phone calls tomorrow," he said, pretending to write something on a legal pad. "And see what I can do."

"Thank you," she said, her voice breaking.

"Of course I'll do what I can," he began, wondering if it would be inappropriate for him to rise and take her in his arms again, wondering if it might not make her sullen and distrustful.

She wiped her face again with a Kleenex. "She's our child and we must work together in her best interests."

"Of course."

She blew her nose and rose, and he rose with her. "Any help you can give me will be much appreciated," she said. "And that includes calling your mother and talking her out of this foolishness before it goes any further and causes irreparable harm to our family."

"Yes. I'll try and call her tonight." He came around the desk, wondering if it might be all right to take her hand, to put his arm around her shoulders, or better yet, embrace her. With any luck, his touch would set off another flood of tears and he would have an excuse to comfort her. He put his hand up to her cheek but she moved slightly and the hand fell awkwardly to her forearm, where it rested like a bloated corpse.

"Of course I'll hire an attorney," she said. "I can't expect you to involve yourself legally."

He hadn't expected this. His breathing quickened and a fluttering sense of panic gripped his stomach. How would he thread the narrow tightrope between his mother and Nita, how would he maintain his duplicity with another lawyer involved? "Maybe that won't be necessary," he began hesitantly.

She looked at him, her eyes hard behind their wet lashes and her face set in the fierce expression he remembered so well. He dropped his hand to his side. "She's my baby," she said evenly, "and I mean to have her back. No matter what it takes. No matter what I have to do."

He cleared his throat, trying to think of something supportive to say. Something that didn't commit him one way or the other. "Look on the bright side," he said finally.

"When she's fourteen, which is only a couple of years away, she'll have the right to choose who she wants to live with anyway."

Nita's face clouded. She said, "After a couple of years under Virginia's roof, under Virginia's influence, who do you think she'll choose?"

She was clever to have realized this. Virginia was a formidable enemy, as Charles well knew. He had spent most of his life in skirmishes with his mother, determined to get the upper hand, and always losing. The only battle he had ever won was the one over his engagement to Nita, which Virginia had vehemently opposed. And now it was his mother's scheme, the one he had refused to participate in, that had brought Nita back into his arms, where she belonged. There could be no doubt, now, what he must do. He would promise to help Nita but he would allow his mother to go on with her revenge, unchecked. He would wait until Nita's marriage crumbled under the strain of Virginia's plot, and then he would make his move. The deceit of this decision posed no moral dilemma for Charles. He had been practicing law for twenty years and had long ago given up the illusion of morality. A man had to do what a man had to do, to get his family back. Once Jimmy Lee had gone and

Nita had returned to him, they would retrieve Whitney and settle down again as a family.

They would be one big happy family again.

Nita drove home through the rain-drenched streets. The storm had passed and the sun, wreathed in ragged clouds, dropped slowly behind the dark line of distant trees. She felt drained, lifeless. Nothing had ever mattered as much to her as her children, and now she had lost her only daughter to her heartless conniving ex-mother-in-law. She had built her defenses against Charles and instead it had been his mother who snuck around Nita's unguarded flank in the dead of night and stole her child. For the first time in her life, sweet Nita, former Homecoming Queen and Crusader for Christ, understood why one human being would kill another. She could understand why Angel Phipps's mother had poured antifreeze into her husband's oatmeal to protect her child. Once on this tack, her imagination veered off into uncharted waters. She spent the rest of the ride home with her mind crowded with images of Virginia shrieking in pain from arsenic poisoning, Virginia flopping down a flight of stairs like a broken rag doll, Virginia lying in a watery grave at the bottom of the Black Warrior River, food for fish and slimy gastropods. Caught up in her visions of vengeance, Nita could think of nothing else.

When she arrived home, Jimmy Lee was gone.

CHAPTER SEVENTEEN

Lavonne and Eadie arrived an hour later. The house was dark except for the kitchen. Nita sat alone at the table in a pool of light clutching a shot glass. On the table in front of her sat a bottle of tequila and two small glasses. Eadie hugged her and Lavonne sat down across from her and said, "Okay. Start at the beginning and tell us exactly what happened." Nita poured out three shots of tequila and told them.

"That low-life bitch," Eadie said, when she'd finished. "That slimy, backstabbing female Judas. You know why she's done this, don't you? She's getting even for what we did to fucking Charles. She found out what happened in Montana and now she's getting even with all of us, through Nita. She was pumping me at Nita's wedding, trying to find out what happened on the hunting trip, and I'll bet she finally figured out some way to get Redmon to spill the beans. Some way I don't even want to think about." Eadie made it a habit not to think about other people's sex lives, but she knew a dominatrix relationship when she saw one. Even if the dominatrix dressed in Anne Taylor suits and talked like Scarlett O'Hara on speed.

Lavonne patted Nita's hand and looked through the doorway to the darkened house beyond. "Where's Jimmy Lee?" she asked.

"Gone with the wind," Nita said bitterly, lifting her glass. She told them about the failed business deal with Virginia and Redmon.

"He'll be back," Eadie said, pouring another round of drinks. She was an expert when it came to hot-and-cold relationships, and she figured, given the right circumstances, Jimmy Lee and Nita's would heat up again.

"He should be here now," Lavonne said firmly.

"He's probably feeling humiliated and guilty."

"That's no excuse."

"I don't want to talk about Jimmy Lee right now," Nita said in a brittle voice, setting her glass down on the table. "I want to talk about how to get my child back."

"Did you get an attorney?" Lavonne said.

"I got Rosebud. She says it's going to be a long, expensive fight going up against Virginia and Redmon. She says his pockets are pretty deep and I have about six hundred and eighty dollars in my checking account." Nita looked like she might cry and Lavonne said, "Don't worry. I'll help you with the attorney's fees," and Eadie got out her checkbook and wrote her a check. "Y'all don't have to do that," Nita said. Then she began to cry in earnest and Eadie and Lavonne put their arms around her. After a while, Nita sat up and blew her nose. "I'll get a sinus infection if I don't stop," she said, sniffing.

"Go ahead and get it out," Lavonne said. "You'll feel better."

Eadie got up and went to the sink to wet down a paper towel so Nita could clean her face. "Does Loretta know?" she said, flipping the faucet on.

"I wasn't going to tell her but then one of daddy's old cronies down at the sheriff's department told him and now she knows. She's on her way over here now."

"Oh, Lord," Eadie said. "Is she armed?"

"Most likely. But Virginia's in Florida for another week so she can't shoot her, at least not until next Friday."

"That won't stop her from shooting out

Virginia's windows or maybe taking a few potshots at the Mercedes."

Nita hadn't thought of that. "Shit," she said.

"If I were you, I'd do my best to talk her out of any gunplay," Lavonne said. "The judge in your custody case might not take kindly to your mother taking potshots at Virginia and her belongings."

"Lavonne's right," Eadie said, sitting back down. "Let's try to talk her out of shooting Virginia until *after* the hearing."

The refrigerator rattled and hummed in the background. Nita stared despondently at her shot glass. She felt numb. She felt like she might be frozen inside and she didn't want to be here, sitting in the kitchen with Eadie and Lavonne talking revenge. Anger was sure to follow, flaring in her breast and melting the cold hard lump that had formed around her heart, and then she'd have no choice but to feel deeply what she'd been avoiding all day — the loss of her daughter and her husband. "The truly ironic thing is I'd actually begun to feel sorry for Virginia." Nita grimaced and shook her head, ashamed of her own naïveté. "I learned all that stuff about her childhood and I felt sorry for her. I trusted her the way I never trusted her when I was married

369

to Charles."

Eadie said, "What stuff about her child-hood?"

"I convinced myself she wasn't really a bad person, deep down inside."

"What stuff?" Eadie frowned and looked at Lavonne, who shrugged. "What do you know about Virginia's childhood that we don't know?"

Nita got up and went into the bedroom to get her notebook while Eadie poured another round of drinks. Nita came back out and handed the notebook to Lavonne. "Read the entries circled in red. Those are the ones I took down from Leota Quarles." Lavonne read them aloud and when she was finished, she laid the opened notebook down on the table. No one said anything. The moon came up and pressed itself against the window screen like a ghostly presence. Lavonne stared at the notebook, an expression of bemused astonishment on her face.

"So Virginia knew about the Indian arti-facts buried on the island all along," she said in a quiet voice. She picked up the notebook and read aloud, *"Miss Virginia never said a word, she just clipped the article and took it up and put it in her little cigar box where she kept all her other treasures since*

370

she was a little girl, the pottery pieces and spear points she'd dug up on Big Ridge, the corsage she'd worn to her first cotillion, all her love letters from Hampton Boone."

Eadie said, "I'll bet she even called the state herself. I'll bet she's behind the injunction that shut the job site down. She knew Jimmy Lee didn't have the money to invest. She knew he'd have to go to Nita, and once she figured Nita's bank account was drained, she called the authorities."

"Oh my God," Nita said as the truth slowly dawned on her.

Lavonne whistled and shook her head. "And I'll bet Redmon didn't know about the Indian artifacts. He wasn't in on the plan. He cares too much about his pride and his money to let himself get strung out like that because of some revenge scheme Virginia cooked up." She shook her head solemnly and looked from one to the other. "Which means Virginia was willing to screw over her own husband just to get even with you, Nita."

The color drained out of Nita's face. On the wall behind her head, the clock ticked oppressively.

"Damn," Eadie said finally. "The woman's got balls." She lifted her glass and Lavonne lifted hers too.

"She's a Kudzu Debutante and doesn't even know it," Lavonne said. She tossed her drink back and grimaced. "I hate to say this, maybe it's the tequila talking, but I'm starting to feel a certain grudging admiration for Virginia. If the woman could just learn how to channel her energies for good instead of evil, who knows what she might accomplish?"

Eadie nodded her head in agreement. "I hear you," she said. "We're talking world domination here. We're talking CEO of any major corporation in America or, hell, who knows, maybe even postmaster general."

Nita was not amused. She gave them a quick dark glance and then shifted her eyes again to her shot glass. "Excuse me if I can't feel any admiration for the woman who just stole my child."

"Of course you can't," Lavonne said, putting her arm around Nita and patting her shoulder.

Eadie said, "Hold on a minute." She sat up straight, the trembling light from the tequila bottle reflecting in her eyes. "Virginia was in love with Trevor's dad. That means, if they'd married, she could have been *my* mother-in-law, Nita, not yours." She shuddered and took a long drink and then set her glass down on the table. "And I thought

Maureen was bad," she said.

"No, no," Lavonne, the logical one, said. "That would never have happened, because if Virginia and Hamp had had children, then they wouldn't have had Trevor. Trevor could only have come from Maureen and Hamp, not Virginia and Hamp."

Nita looked at her glumly and lifted her glass.

Eadie got up and began to pace the floor. Pacing helped her to focus. Another thought occurred to her and she stopped suddenly and said, "Hey, you don't think Virginia and Hamp carried on after they were married do you? You don't think they had an affair later on?"

"Let's ask Loretta," Lavonne said, hearing Loretta's car in the drive. Headlights flared suddenly through the kitchen window and then dimmed. "She'd know."

"Let's not do anything to get her any more riled up than she already is," Nita warned. "In fact, let's try to mention Virginia as little as possible." She got up to get another shot glass out of the cupboard.

"You're right," Eadie said, moving her glass to the middle of the table so Lavonne could pour another round. "Let's just offer Loretta a drink and try to get her calmed down. We can figure out what to do later."

Lavonne poured the drinks and then put the cap back on the bottle. "You might want to make sure Loretta's unarmed before you offer her tequila," she said.

"Good thinking," Eadie said.

The back door banged opened and Loretta stalked in. Her hair stood up around her head in stiff peaks and her face was the color of dried blood. She was wearing a bathrobe and slippers made to look like Tweety Bird.

Nita put her hands up. "Now calm down, Mama," she said.

Loretta scowled and swung her head back and forth. "What in the hell's going on?" she said.

"If you'll calm down and take a seat, I'll tell you."

Loretta stomped over to the table, her slippers snapping at her heels like a pack of angry Chihuahuas. She yanked a chair out and sat down.

Eadie said, "You don't have anything in your pockets do you, Loretta?"

"Like what?" Loretta growled.

"Like a handgun."

"No. Why?"

Eadie relaxed and poured her a drink. "We wanted to make sure you weren't armed before we plied you with tequila. We wanted to make sure you hadn't planned on going over to Virginia's and shooting up the place."

Loretta tossed her drink back and set the shot glass down on the table. "I hadn't thought of it, but now that you mention it, that's a damn fine idea."

"Good job," Lavonne said to Eadie.

Loretta said, "You got any limes?"

"No, Mama, I'm fresh out."

"Where's Jimmy Lee?" Loretta said. "I didn't see his truck in the driveway."

"He's gone," Nita said. "And Logan's gone to get a hamburger with his friends."

Nita told her everything. While she talked, Loretta sucked her top lip and stared at the shot glass in her hand. If Loretta had been the kind who liked to say "I told you so," she could have had a field day with Nita. But "I told you so" wasn't Loretta's style. She listened quietly and when Nita finished, Loretta leaned over and hugged her fiercely for several minutes. When she sat back, Nita's eyes were moist.

"I'm disappointed in Jimmy Lee," Loretta said, letting Eadie pour her another drink. "I would have thought he had more backbone than to skip town when you needed him most." Loretta had the gift of speaking what everybody else was thinking.

Eadie said, "Virginia pretty much fixed it that he wouldn't be able to hold his head up from shame. I wouldn't be surprised if she hadn't sabotaged Nita's marriage on purpose." She ignored Lavonne, who shot her a warning glance. She'd always liked Jimmy Lee and didn't like to see him blamed without at least sticking up for him a little bit. Even though he shouldn't have run off like he did.

Loretta nodded fiercely as if this thought had occurred to her, too. "What are we going to do about that old buzzard?" she said. "What are we going to do about Virginia?"

Lavonne said, "What can we do?"

Eadie said, "We're open to suggestions."

Loretta shook her head ominously and looked at her glass. "I don't know," she said. "You girls are pretty smart and what you did to get back at the husbands before was pretty clever. But going up against the husbands was one thing; going up against Virginia is something else entirely. Charles Broadwell couldn't drive a nail into a snowbank, but his mother's two shades meaner than the devil himself. We better be ready for trouble if we're going up against her."

"What do you mean, *we?* Look, Mama, I want you to let me handle this," Nita said, putting her hand on Loretta's arm. "I've hired Rosebud Smoot and she says it'll take time and money but eventually I'll get Whitney back."

"The courts take too long," Loretta said, her stiff little curls twitching. She poured herself another drink. "Just say the word, Juanita Sue, and I'll take care of things my own way." The way she said it left no question as to her intent.

Eadie looked interested. She leaned over and rested her chin on her palm. "How would you do it, Loretta?"

Loretta tossed back her drink, grimaced, and set the glass down. "Pig sticker to the heart," she said.

Eadie and Lavonne snickered softly. Nita watched them with a sullen expression.

"All I'm saying," Loretta said, "is you better have a backup plan in case the courts don't work."

"I trust Rosebud," Nita said stubbornly. "I have faith in justice."

"Justice?" Loretta snorted. "How much justice are you going to get in a court of law when Virginia can afford the best legal counsel in the state?"

Eadie and Lavonne stopped snickering. This thought had already occurred to both of them. "Let me handle it my way," Nita said tersely.

Loretta played with her glass and frowned. "When's the hearing?"

Nita shook her head. "I don't think it's a good idea for you to show up for that, what with your violent temper and all."

Loretta drew herself up to her full seated height, which might have been all of four-foot-two. She watched her daughter steadily. "She's my grandbaby and you're my child and I'll be damned if I'll let you go into that courtroom without me."

Nita sighed. She spread her hands on the table like she was trying to bear up under a weight that was too heavy to carry. Her mother had been fighting her battles for her all her life and it didn't look like she was ready to relinquish that post anytime soon. "Two weeks," Nita said. "August eleventh. And just so you know, there's a metal detector at the door so don't be getting any ideas about handguns and pig stickers and vigilante justice."

Loretta smiled fiercely and lifted her glass. "Give me credit for more sense than that," she said.

"I have faith in Rosebud," Nita said. "I have faith in justice."

"If I was to punch Virginia's ticket to the hereafter," Loretta said grimly, "I sure as hell wouldn't do it in front of an audience."

Virginia sat under a beach umbrella sipping a mai tai and watching the cabana boys scurry about carrying trays of tropical drinks. Far out in the pale green waters of the placid gulf, Whitney and Carlisle lay on a couple of rubber floats, their bodies undulating with the gentle waves like a couple of sea anemones washed up after a storm. Virginia stretched her pale legs along the lounger and laid her head back. Her straw hat tipped slightly above her forehead. The sound of the lapping waves was hypnotic, and after a while Virginia closed her eyes.

It was quiet here at this end of the beach, which is one of the reasons she liked coming here. Farther up, closer to Panama City, the budget motels and sprawling condominiums that catered to college students and the middle class crowded the beach with throngs of noisy tourists. But here, in the secluded private beach in front of The Beau Mer Resort, all was quiet and elegant. A long line of brightly colored beach umbrellas stretched along the white sand, each one placed at a discreet distance from its neighbor. Young families dotted the beach like clumps of exotic flowers. All was quiet and indolent except for the harried cabana boys who moved between the poolside bar and the guests like a stream of marauding ants. Virginia knew they would not be called cabana boys in this age of political correctness, but she was at a loss as to what they should be called. Umbrella attendants? Sand waiters?

Reynaldo, the boy assigned to her, stuck his head around the edge of her umbrella. "Another mai tai, Meesis Redmon?" he said. Virginia sighed and opened her eyes. He wore a white short-sleeved shirt with epaulets and white Bermuda shorts, something a British sea captain or a cruise ship director might have worn. She lifted her plastic glass. It was still half full.

"Not now," she said. "Check back with me in five minutes."

He nodded slightly and moved off, his sandaled feet sinking deep into the sugary sand with each step. It had been Virginia's experience that Hispanic men were either as devilishly handsome as movie stars, or as dark and squat as gnomes. Reynaldo unfortunately fell into the latter category.

Her cell phone rang insistently and Virginia rummaged in her beach bag to find it. She squinted to read the caller ID. It was Redmon. She was tempted not to take the call. It had been such a pleasant day so far, and she didn't want to ruin it. But if she didn't answer, he'd simply call the bar and have Reynaldo run a message down to her, or worse, get in the car and drive to Destin to deliver the message himself.

"Hello," she said sweetly.

"Queenie, what in the hell's going on?" he said shortly. "That girl's mama has called my office three times already today. She's called the house off and on all night. You got to talk to her. I tell you, this just ain't right, you running off with her kid like that."

"Now, darling, we discussed all that," Virginia said, trying to keep the irritation out of her voice. "My hands are tied until the judge makes his decision. Until then, we just have to sit tight and wait."

"I don't want her calling the house. I don't want her calling my office."

"Don't answer the phone! There's no law that says you have to pick up."

"You tell that girl to call her mama."

"Let me handle this," Virginia snapped. "She's my granddaughter. This is my family business, not yours."

She could hear him breathing heavily. When he spoke, his voice was hard and resentful. "Well it's my money paying the goddamned attorney fees, so I guess I got a say in what happens."

Damn it. She hated to do it, but when all else fails, you do what you have to do. She bit her lower lip, hard, and thought about Snowball, the puppy she'd had as a child. Snowball was a white spitz, the only pet Virginia had ever had, and he'd been bitten by a copperhead soon after Virginia's eighth birthday. A lump formed slowly in the back of her throat, swelling like a tumor.

"She's my only granddaughter," Virginia said. She thought of little Snowball lying in the dirt, stiff and frozen as a starched shirt left out in a freezing rain. Her eyes misted.

"And she's Nita's only daughter," Redmon said stubbornly.

"I don't want to lose her," Virginia sobbed. Tears rolled down her cheeks. She'd buried Snowball beneath a camelia bush in the backyard. The colored children sang hymns while she fashioned a cross out of two pieces of driftwood, and afterward she'd given a sad sermon and they'd all cried together. "I love her so and I've just gotten to know her and now you want to take her away from me!"

"Aw now, Queenie, are you crying?" His voice softened. He cleared his throat several times. "Don't cry, Queenie."

"I feel just terrible about what happened

on the island. I was just trying to make things right, to give Nita's husband a chance to make some money, to make us all one big happy family and now I've ruined everything."

"Now, Queenie, it's not your fault."

"You'll never forgive me!"

"I don't blame you for what happened, honey. You know that. How could you have known your family place was nothing but an Indian boneyard?"

Virginia took a Kleenex out of her beach bag and blew her nose. "Nita will blame me. She'll think I did it on purpose, and she'll never let me see my granddaughter again! Don't you see, Bob, I had to do it. I had to get the judge involved or I'll never see Whitney again! Nita will keep her from me for spite!"

"Now, sweetheart, I don't think she'd do that."

"Trust me," Virginia said. "I've known her longer than you have. You have to trust me, Bob. I'm not trying to keep the girl from her mama, I'm just trying to make sure I get to see her, too!"

"Okay, honey, we'll let the judge decide. I just don't want the girl to go without calling her mama. She's a good mama."

Virginia clenched her teeth and stared out

at the gulf. "And what am I?" she said. "Aren't I a good grandmother?"

"Well, of course you are, honey. No one's saying you aren't."

"I have to go now," Virginia said. "I'll call you later." She hung up. Out in the water, Whitney stood up and began to walk slowly toward shore, dragging her float behind her like a limp blanket. Virginia wiped beneath her eyes with the Kleenex. She readjusted her sunglasses and snapped her fingers.

"Reynaldo!" she said, waving her glass. "Another mai tai."

Whitney walked slowly up the beach. When she got a few feet from her grandmother, she stopped and dropped the float at her feet. She stood squinting at Virginia, her hand raised above her eyes to shield them from the sun. "I need to call my mother," she said. "Can I have my cell phone now?"

Virginia smiled amicably. She finished her mai tai and then set the empty glass in the sand. "Of course you can, dear," she said. She leaned over and took Whitney's cell phone out of her beach bag. She watched as the girl walked a few paces down the beach, and then frowning, turned around and shouted, "It won't turn on. It's not working!"

Of course it wasn't. Virginia had removed the battery that morning.

"Oh no," Virginia said. "Bring it over here and let me see it." Whitney gave her the phone and Virginia pretended to fiddle with it for a while. "It may just need to be recharged. Did you bring your charger? No? Well, that's okay. You can use the phone back at the condo, if you like." Virginia smiled brightly.

Whitney frowned and kicked her foot in the sand. She put her hand over her eyes and squinted at her grandmother suspiciously. "This isn't about the fight you had with Mommy, is it?" Virginia had told her briefly about the custody battle this morning, while Carlisle slept. Virginia had done her best to make it sound like it was nothing more than a simple argument over how many nights Whitney got to sleep at her grandmother's house and how many at home. More like a friendly disagreement than an argument. That's how Virginia had explained it. A silly argument that would be decided by a nice, kindly old judge. But Whitney wasn't stupid. She'd watched enough Lifetime for Women movies to know what a custody battle was. Her grandmother had made her promise not to tell Carlisle any of their "family business," so the first thing Whitney did once they got down to the beach was tell her. "Oh my God," Carlisle squealed, "custody battles are the best! That means they both want you, which means you get to have anything you want, and do anything you want to do because no one wants to tell you no." Carlisle went to the Barron Hall School. She'd been one of Whitney's friends back before Nita left Charles and ripped Whitney out of Barron Hall to enroll her in public school. "No one wants to piss you off because they want you to like them best. Kara Stockett's parents got into a custody battle over her and she got a Kate Spade purse for Christmas and a trip to Paris. Oh my God, Whitney, that's awesome!"

Yes, it was indeed, awesome. Whitney had watched enough reality TV about rich California kids living in Orange County not to appreciate the potential drama of the situation. Only instead of parents or boyfriends fighting over her, it was her mother and her grandmother.

"You said I could call Mommy whenever I want," Whitney said sullenly. "You said I could go home whenever I want."

"Well, of course you can, darling." Virginia clapped her tiny hands and then opened her arms wide to Whitney, making room for her at the foot of the lounger. Whitney sat down and let her grandmother hug her. "You can go home just as soon as the judge makes his decision about where you're going to stay. But for the time being, we'd like you to stay with me and Papa Redmon because we can take care of you best. We can buy you dresses and take you shopping and pay for you to go back to the Barron Hall School, if you like. And just as soon as your mother gets back some of the money that Mr. Motes took from her, then you can go back to live with her. Of course, you can visit her whenever you want. And if you'd rather stay with her, even though she can't give you new dresses or take you shopping or send you to the Barron Hall School, that's all right, too." Virginia watched her closely to see if her gamble had worked.

Whitney said, "Jimmy Lee stole Mommy's money?"

"Well, he didn't steal it. He just invested it unwisely." Virginia took off her hat and fluffed her hair, watching two seagulls fight over a dead crab on the beach. "Of course," she said archly, "money isn't everything. You know that. And I'm sure your mother will be able to find a nice place for you all to live, maybe an apartment over close to the public high school. Then you won't need a car. You can just walk to school."

Whitney squinted and looked out at the water. Being poor wasn't something she'd planned on. None of the kids out in Orange County were poor. As if reading her thoughts, Carlisle sat up on her float and waved. "Can we have some money to go shopping?" Whitney said dejectedly. "Me and Carlisle?"

"Of course, darling," Virginia said gaily, rummaging in her beach bag to retrieve her wallet. "How much do you need?"

CHAPTER EIGHTEEN

Jimmy Lee had tried to call her several times. He had left messages on her cell phone, which Nita ignored, and later he began to call without leaving messages. He never called the house, only her cell. Nita never called him back. Since that rainy day when she discovered her daughter had been kidnapped, a chilling sense of déjà vu had settled over Nita and she had been unable to think of anything except getting Whitney back. She had spent her whole life running from the specter of loneliness and now that it had caught up with her, Nita discovered she could stand it after all. She understood that loving someone and living without him, although painful, was possible.

Still, she was glad for Logan's company. Like any sixteen-year-old boy, he had his own life, but he seemed determined to help Nita deal with hers. He began coming home early from his rock-and-roll band practice to help with the laundry and the housework. He mowed the grass and made dinner while Nita occupied her time getting ready for the custody hearing. Despite her assurances to the contrary, she dreaded the hearing and felt nervous about the outcome. Virginia wouldn't have started something she couldn't finish and she must have known, before she filed the custody petition, that she had the upper hand. It wasn't like her to miscalculate anything.

Whitney was still in Florida but Nita had spoken to her twice by telephone. Both times she had sounded distant and restrained, and Nita guessed Virginia was probably in the room. During the second call, Nita heard a slight tremor of homesickness in Whitney's voice and Nita's throat tightened and she said brightly, "Don't worry, honey, you'll be home soon. I promise."

In between the drudgery of her daily life, Nita spent time with Rosebud Smoot, planning their strategy for regaining custody of Whitney. The case had, unfortunately but no doubt with manipulation by Virginia, been assigned to Judge Lamar Drucker, an old fishing buddy of Judge Broadwell's. He was the last of the old-school judges who believed the practice of law to be as clear and precise as the practice of aeronautical engineering; things were either black or they were white. There was no room in Judge Drucker's courtroom for subtle shadings of gray. He also believed that women, due to their inability to think in a logical, precise, and orderly manner, had no business practicing law. When Rosebud Smoot graduated number one in her class at Georgia in 1958 and returned to Ithaca to practice, she had been offered a position as a legal secretary in Judge Drucker's law firm. When she turned him down, he had seen to it that no one else offered her a job. Years later, she reciprocated by feeding information secretly to a young reporter by the name of Grace Pearson, who had written a series of scandalous newspaper articles on Judge Drucker and his crony, Judge Broadwell, who Grace sardonically dubbed The Hanging Judge. Whether or not Judge Drucker or Judge Broadwell ever figured out it was Rosebud who fed the crusading young reporter her information was unclear. Rosebud had actually won several jury trials in Judge Drucker's court, although rarely did she prevail in nonjury cases. She comforted herself with the knowledge that as the older judges died off, the younger ones seemed more willing to accept female attorneys in their courtrooms. There was even a chance that at some distant point in Ithaca's future, female attorneys might be treated as equals of their male colleagues. Rosebud hoped she would live long enough to see this.

Still, she was a realist, and despite their barely concealed dislike of each other, Rosebud thought it best not to oppose Judge Drucker hearing Nita's custody case. She had practiced law in a small town enough years to know that to ask a judge to recuse himself was like declaring war on the entire Kingdom of Judgedom itself. This was not a step to be taken lightly. Rosebud decided to play the conflict of interest card only as a last resort.

Besides, Judge Drucker had already announced his retirement next year, and with any luck, he'd drop dead of a heart attack or a stroke before then.

The day of the custody hearing, though, the old judge appeared in fine form. He walked into his courtroom like an actor walking onto the stage. His long white hair was swept back from his face, and he wore a stern forbidding expression that made him look like Jehovah perched on his throne on the Day of Judgment. He liked to begin questions to counsel or witnesses with "Well, I'm just an old country boy, of course, so maybe you can explain it to me," a ruse that fooled no one but always brought a few titters from the gallery. Most judges liked to sit quietly, weighing the arguments of counsel, but Judge Drucker liked to talk as much as possible, using the captive audience in his courtroom to showcase his wit and mental acuity.

The day of the hearing, there were only a few people in the courtroom. Besides a few bored spectators, the court reporter, the judge, and his staff, there was Rosebud and Nita, Virginia and her attorney, Whitney, Logan, Lavonne, Eadie, Loretta, and a spidery little man Nita didn't recognize. He sat over by Virginia's table and was obviously here to testify on her behalf. Charles was noticeably absent.

Judge Drucker wasted little time. He read over the Petition and Answer, allowed the parties' counsels a few brief words, and then, raising his hand irritably to silence Rosebud, began to drill Nita.

"Are you currently separated, Miz Motes?"

Rosebud immediately responded with, "That's irrelevant, Your Honor."

The judge's fierce eyes rested on her for a brief moment, and then slid back to Nita. "Just answer the question," he said.

Nita glanced at Rosebud and then spoke hesitantly. "Not legally, no."

The judge grimaced and looked at the ceiling. He sighed and looked at his hands. "All right, Miz Motes," he said with exaggerated courtesy, "let me put it another way. Is your husband currently residing at 308 River Road?"

"No."

"That wasn't so hard, now was it?" He looked around the room to see if they appreciated his sarcasm, but no one smiled except for Virginia. The judge rounded his shoulders and thrust his head forward. "Let's try another one," he growled. "Okay, Miz Motes, how much money is in your bank account right now?"

Rosebud jumped to her feet. "I object, Your Honor. This is ridiculous and has absolutely no bearing on the case."

"You wait your turn, Miz Smoot," he warned, wagging a thick hairy finger. "I'm trying to determine whether Miz Motes has the financial wherewithal to support her two minor children."

"Your Honor, my client has supported her minor children for the past year and a half. She receives child support from her ex-husband in sufficient amounts to support her children."

"Child support that Miz Motes will not receive if she loses custody." He waved his hand as if this was relevant and Rosebud stared at him a moment and then slid down into her chair.

"And where is the minor child's father?" Rosebud said loudly, looking around the courtroom. "He should be here to testify."

The judge ignored her. He leaned back in his seat and set his elbows down, tenting his hands in front of him. "Do you work, Miz Motes?"

"No, Your Honor."

"And I understand you have had a recent financial reversal due to a bad business investment?"

Rosebud didn't even bother to stand. She slung one arm around the back of Nita's chair and eyed the judge contemptuously. "As you are well aware, Your Honor, if parental custody was limited to those who had not made bad business decisions, then no one in this room would qualify. I daresay even the petitioner" — she looked pointedly at Virginia — "has had her share of financial reversals, although I don't hear Your Honor asking her to account for them."

"Another outburst like that, Miz Smoot, and I'll hold you in contempt of court!" He picked up his gavel and looked as if he might fling it at Rosebud, and she stared at him as if daring him to do so.

Virginia's attorney stood then, and politely asked if he might address the court. He was a tall, elegant gentleman from a very old and prominent family. His name was Dawson Henry and he spoke in a refined, Plantation South drawl that flowed through the courtroom like soothing music. Even the judge, entranced by the timbre and cadence of his melodious voice, fell silent. Dawson assured the judge that his client was only concerned with her grandchildren's welfare, that she only filed her custody suit because of her ex-daughter-in-law's current financial situation and marital instability. He explained that his client had her granddaughter's best interests at heart, that she was paying for Whitney's expenses, including tuition for her return to private school, out of her own pocket. She was willing to have her grandson returned to her custody also, but he had made it clear that he wished to remain with his mother. Dawson assured the judge that it was his client's hope that the custody would only be temporary, he asserted that his client loved Nita like a daughter and hoped that their relationship would return to normal once the issues in Nita's life had been resolved.

At this point, Loretta had had all she could take. She stood up and said loudly, "If you believe that crock of cow confetti, Your Honor, I've got some swampland in Florida I'd like to sell you." The judge did his best to reestablish order but by now Loretta, inflamed by a slight smile from Virginia, had attempted to climb over three rows of seats to get to her, and after being restrained by one of the deputies, had to be forcibly removed from the courtroom. "I'm gonna snatch you baldheaded!" Loretta was shouting as they carried her out. "You better give your soul to Jesus, Virginia, 'cause your ass belongs to me!"

Virginia sat through the entire ordeal looking small and terrified, with her little hand fluttering at her breast, and afterward her attorney requested that "due to the potential violence of the Respondent's family members, his client be given a police escort from the building after the hearing." This brought a loud and sustained outburst from Eadie who, after being threatened with removal by the judge, eventually managed to calm down.

Nita sat through the whole exchange with her head buried in her hands.

The judge gave Rosebud a few brief moments of rebuttal, which she handled with the calm resigned demeanor of one who realizes that this skirmish is lost but who stubbornly refuses to give up the fight. After that, the judge asked Whitney a series of questions, and the girl admitted that she loved her mother and wanted to visit her frequently, but she felt comfortable at her grandmother's house and was excited about the prospect of returning to the Barron Hall School in two weeks.

Judge Drucker had heard enough. He raised his hand and glowered at the small audience. "I hereby grant the Petitioner temporary custody, with the Respondent to receive weekly unsupervised parenting time to be worked out between the parties. We will schedule another hearing in ninety days, at which time we will revisit the issues and decide permanent custody, with the understanding, however, that Respondent will get a job during said ninety-day period." He nodded briefly at the bailiff and adjourned the hearing.

Loretta waited outside, stalking stiff-legged up and down the hallway. "Well?" she said, when she saw Nita's sullen face. "What happened?"

"Virginia got temporary custody," Eadie said, when Nita didn't respond. "But only for ninety days. Nita has to get a job and she gets weekly visits with Whitney, and then in ninety days the judge will award permanent custody."

Loretta's jaw dropped. "You have got to be kidding me," she said.

Lavonne shook her head slowly.

"So much for justice," Loretta said. She stood up on her tiptoes and tried to see over Eadie's shoulder into the room, and when this didn't work, she tried to push her way through the thin flow of people who were exiting the courtroom.

"Hold up, Loretta," Eadie said, grabbing her arm.

"Where is that crooked, conniving egg-sucker?" Loretta said, struggling to free herself.

Lavonne, not sure which egg-sucker she meant, said, "Virginia went out the back way and the judge is in his chambers."

Loretta stopped struggling. She swung around suddenly and would have scurried out the front door had Nita not stepped in front of her and grabbed her by both elbows.

"Mama, stop," Nita said, giving her a little shake. "You're only making things worse for me."

Rosebud came out of the courtroom carrying a big black briefcase. She was a tall, heavyset woman who walked with a pronounced limp. She stopped beside Nita and said, "Well, that didn't go as well as I planned, but we'll be ready for them next time. At least the psychiatrist didn't get a chance to speak."

Nita faced her but kept a tight hold on her mother. "Was that the little skinny guy?"

"Yes." Rosebud nodded grimly. "Virginia's got her seeing a child psychiatrist, but we'll get our own expert witness before the next hearing. Don't worry," she said to Nita. "We'll prevail in the end. Until then, just hang in there." She clapped her once on the shoulder, nodded at the rest of the group, and then limped off. They watched her as she went out through the double glass doors, and past Logan, who stood on the courthouse steps smoking a cigarette.

"The only one who needs a psychiatrist is Virginia," Eadie said.

"She'll need more than a psychiatrist when I'm through with her," Loretta said.

Nita nodded at Eadie and Lavonne. "Y'all go on," she said. "I need to talk to my mother."

"What is it?" Loretta said nervously, after they had left. "Look, if it's about me trying to kick Virginia's ass in the courtroom, I'm sorry." She sniffed and tugged at the end of her sleeves and you could see she wasn't sorry at all. "Something came over me and I just lost it for a moment there, that's all."

"Mama, it doesn't help me if we're trying to prove how stable our home life is and then you climb over three rows of seats and try to strangle Virginia in front of ten people. That kind of defeats the whole stability thing, if you know what I mean."

"I saw the way she was sitting there, smug as a cream-licking cat, the way she always is when she thinks she's pulled the wool over everybody's eyes. Like we're all too stupid to figure out what's going on."

"I'm not stupid, Mama. I've figured it out."

Loretta's face softened. "Well, I know that, honey." She put her hand up and smoothed the hair off Nita's face. "But you're my own little girl. I can't just sit back and let someone walk all over you like that."

Nita took a deep breath. "Mama, I'm a grown woman," she said gently, not wanting to hurt Loretta's feelings. "And you've been fighting my battles for me all my life. I love you, and I know you just want to help, but it's time I stood on my own two feet. I know what I have to do and you have to trust me and let me do it my way."

Loretta stared rigidly at her daughter. A muscle moved in her cheek. Gradually, her expression changed. After a few moments, her shoulders slumped. She looked suddenly tired and infirm, as if the knowledge that Nita no longer needed her protection had aged her twenty years. She looked down at her feet and Nita could see her scalp shining through her thinning hair, speckled and fragile as a robin's egg. Nita leaned and put her arms around her mother and kissed her.

"I love you, Mama."

Loretta patted her back. "I love you, too, honey," she said. "All I ever wanted was to shield you from pain and sorrow."

"I know, Mama, but you can't." Nita stood back but kept her hands on her mother's shoulders. "Pain and sorrow are part of life. It's what builds character."

Loretta shook her head sadly. "Yeah, well, just remember: what doesn't kill us, maims us for life."

"Mama, you're a closet pessimist."

"No, honey, I'm a realist."

Outside the glass doors, Logan had finished his cigarette. He motioned for his mother to come on, and Nita smiled and put one finger up. Loretta took a tissue out of her handbag and blew her nose. "Well," she said. "Rosebud's a good lawyer. I guess she knows what she's doing."

"I guess she does," Nita said.

On the ride home, Nita let Logan drive. She sat with her head resting against the window glass, watching the long rows of pecan trees that stretched away from the highway like the spokes of a giant wheel.

Logan cleared his throat. "Look, Mom, I've been thinking," he said, and she turned and looked at him. He had combed his hair for the hearing and although it still glinted with purple highlights, it lay neatly against his skull. He had removed his lip ring and wore only a small conservative nose stud.

Nita tugged lightly at the sleeve of his dress shirt with her fingers. "What have you been thinking?" she asked fondly. It was only when you got up close that you noticed the pattern on his tie was actually rows and rows of cannabis plants.

"I've been thinking that I know how to get Whitney back. If you really want her back, that is." He raised one eyebrow and glanced at her, and Nita smiled faintly and looked at him with a weary expression.

"Don't you worry about Whitney," she said, smoothing his tie with her fingers. "You let me and Rosebud worry about getting her back."

"It came to me while I was sitting in the courtroom listening to Virginia's lawyer spouting all that bullshit about how she only

403

wanted what was best for her grandchildren. It came to me in a flash, what I had to do."

Nita was curious. And it was sweet, the way he wanted to help, the way he wanted to step in like the man of the house to rescue his mother and sister. She stopped fidgeting with his tie. "I'm listening," she said.

He looked at her and grinned, and Nita thought how handsome he was despite his purple hair and metal-studded face. He looked a lot like his father, like the kind of boy Charles might have been if he hadn't had Virginia for a mother, if he hadn't been trapped by birth and circumstance and culture. "Well," Logan said. "Virginia wants one grandchild. She wants Whitney. Right?"

"Yes." She felt guilty admitting this but Logan didn't seem bothered by it.

He glanced at her and then back at the road. "I wonder how she'd feel about having two."

Nita said, "What do you mean?"

"I mean, I'll pack my bag and show up on her doorstep. Tonight."

Nita looked at him for a few moments, her eyes filled with sadness. "But, honey," she said gently, "Virginia doesn't want you living with her."

Logan gave her an evil grin. His hair

glinted like a crow's wing in the sunlight. "Exactly," he said.

Despite the tragedy of the situation, Nita put her head back and laughed. It *was* funny imagining Virginia's face when her Mohawked grandson showed up on her doorstep.

"I can keep an eye on Whitney and make Virginia's life a living hell at the same time," he said reasonably. "And with all that bullshit she fed the judge, about only caring for her grandchild's well-being, she won't dare ask me to leave for fear it'll look bad in court."

Nita had seen enough of their interactions to know that Logan did make Virginia nervous. And she knew, too, that Logan was more than a match for his grandmother. But at the same time, who knew what Virginia might be capable of pulling out of her sleeve? "I don't think so," she said finally, wiping her eyes with a Kleenex. "Virginia's a scary person. I won't send a child to do battle with her."

Logan stopped grinning and his face took on a hard, determined look. When he looked like that, he reminded her again of Charles. "First of all," he said. "I'm not a child. I've made my mind up to do this no matter what. Second, I'm not afraid of Virginia.

She's more afraid of me than I am of her. And third, this won't take long. Trust me, after a few weeks of me, after a few weeks of me and my *friends* hanging out at her place, Virginia will be calling you and begging you to take your kids back."

The prospect of sending another child into Virginia's lair should have filled Nita with dread, but somehow it didn't. Somehow, when things were looking their bleakest, Nita was beginning to recover her faith and belief in the future. She was daring to hope that everything was going to turn out okay.

"I don't know," she said. She watched the long flat peanut fields stretching into the distance. Beyond the fields a pine forest rose and above the blue rim of the trees, a hawk soared against a gunmetal sky. "I'll have to think about it. I don't know if I can stand losing both you and Whitney."

His grin spread slowly across his face. His nose stud shone like a hollow point casing. "Trust me, Mom," he said cheerfully. "We'll be home by Christmas."

CHAPTER NINETEEN

On a Wednesday evening in early September, Lavonne and Eadie sat out on Lavonne's deck drinking Cosmopolitans. "I'm a little disappointed," Eadie said, looking up at the soft purple sky. A pale sliver of moon rested on the top of Lavonne's garage like a scimitar. "I was really hoping we'd be able to come up with some way to get even with Virginia for stealing Nita's child."

" 'Hope' and 'Virginia' don't belong in the same sentence."

"Yeah, you're right. Virginia sucks hope out of a room the way a vacuum sucks dust."

"Nice analogy."

"Thanks. I haven't talked to Nita this week. How's she holding up under the strain?"

"As well as can be expected," Lavonne said. "She keeps busy working and visiting with her kids. She's substitute teaching, when she can. It keeps her occupied until the next custody hearing." She'd given Nita a part-time counter job down at the Shofar So Good Deli so she could fulfill Judge Drucker's employment requirements.

"It sure has been fun being roommates," Eadie said, tapping her fingers against the side of a citronella candle. "I've had a great time."

"You say that like you're getting ready to leave."

Eadie shrugged. "I've got to go home sometime. Before Trevor gives up and throws me out for good."

"What about staying to support Nita? What about the Kudzu Ball?"

Eadie frowned and passed her finger back and forth over the candle flame. "When's the final custody hearing scheduled?"

"Sometime the first week of December. And you can't miss the Kudzu Ball. It's the third weekend in September and you can't miss it again this year. Come on, Aneeda. You know how much fun we always have."

"Well, Ima, maybe I can go home and then come back for the ball and the custody hearing."

Lavonne looked up at the glittering stars. "If you go home you won't come back," she said.

She got up and went inside to get a

sweater. Eadie sipped her drink and watched the moon rise over the yard. She wondered what Trevor was doing right now. He was off on the West Coast somewhere, at a writing conference, and she was supposed to meet him in San Francisco for the weekend. They were still meeting every other weekend at exotic places, where they holed up in various four-star hotels like a couple of adulterers, making love and arguing and living off room service. In between, they lived separate lives; Eadie working on her canvases, and Trevor writing when he could in New Orleans and jetting off to writers' conferences and speaking engagements. He was quickly losing patience with their arrangement and the only reason he hadn't pressured her to come home now was because his book was doing well, and he was traveling a lot. She had promised him, last time they met, that she'd be home by the middle of September.

Lavonne came back out carrying a sweater in one hand and a shaker of Cosmopolitans in the other. She handed the sweater to Eadie, and Eadie smiled, said "Thanks," and put it on.

Lavonne sat down and poured two fresh drinks. "This is my new favorite cocktail," she said, leaning back and putting her feet up on the empty chair in front of her. "I think I like it better than a martini. I like it better than a margarita."

Eadie smiled and sipped her drink. "You're pretty fickle when it comes to alcoholic beverages," she said. "You'll change your mind in a week or so and then Sex on the Beach will be your new drink du jour. Or maybe a Tequila Slammer, Back Street Banger, Tahitian Tongue Tickler . . ."

"Wow," Lavonne said.

"Test Tube Baby, Paralyzer, Tetanus Shot, Baltimore Blow Job."

"You know, Eadie, if this art thing doesn't work out, you might consider work in the glamorous field of bartending."

"Maybe," Eadie said. She looked up at the sky with its dome of glittering stars. "Was that Joe who called earlier?"

"Yeah. He's in Boston on business but he's coming home tomorrow." Joe was doing a lot of traveling for DuPont. It was his last-ditch effort to prove himself loyal to a job he didn't really want anyway. He figured he had about three months before the ax fell and then he'd be a man unencumbered by a job, free to set off for the south of France with his bicycle and his notebooks and Lavonne, too, if she'd agree to go. "Did you ask Trevor about his father and Virginia?"

Eadie shook her head. "He doesn't believe any of that is true. He says they may have dated, briefly, but he's pretty sure they didn't carry on an affair after their marriages. His dad died when he was small and he doesn't remember him too well, but he says his dad and mom went together from the time they were freshmen in high school."

"Oh well," Lavonne said. "I was hoping there might be something there we could use to help Nita get Whitney back."

"I think it's all up to Rosebud."

"I think you're right."

At the house next door, a light came on. A door opened and then slammed, as Fergus, the neighbor's dog, was let out into the yard. He barked twice, a dry, snuffling sound more like a cough than a bark, and then went about his business. Winston, who was sleeping at Lavonne's feet, lifted his head, sniffed the air, and then went back to sleep.

Lavonne said, "I've been trying to talk Nita into going with me to the Kudzu Ball. She needs something to take her mind off Jimmy Lee and the custody hearing. She needs a good throw-down to take her mind off her problems."

"Don't we all," Eadie said.

"She thinks she'll be the only one there without a date, but I told her I'd go solo."

"Hell, we'll all go solo," Eadie said.

"Does that mean you're coming?"

Eadie sighed. She looked at Lavonne and grinned. "I suppose so," she said.

Lavonne said, "Good. It's settled then. I'll call Nita and we'll go down to the Baptist Thrift Store tomorrow and see if we can rustle up some ball gowns." She zipped the front of her fleece jacket and settled down in her chair with her drink resting on her stomach. The Cosmo had definitely gone to her brain. She was feeling happy and relaxed. There was a pleasant buzzing sound in her head, like a downed high-voltage wire. She lifted her glass and pointed at the garage. "How's the work coming along?" she asked Eadie.

Eadie had done her best to try to paint still lifes but that hadn't done a thing except give her insomnia. She had quickly gone back to her cherubs and goddesses, working with an intensity that bordered on mania. She worked from early morning to mid-afternoon and the canvases filled the garage like stone tablets, like bones in a catacomb, like firewood stacked on a funeral pyre.

"The work is going fine," Eadie said. "I

412

got a call from the gallery up in Atlanta and they said they'll take six or seven of my canvases in addition to the pieces they already have. They're talking about letting me have a show in the spring."

"That's great, Eadie," Lavonne said, lifting her drink. She sipped and set it back down on her stomach. "Actually, though, I wasn't talking about your art. I was talking about your interior work." Lavonne had left a book on Jungian theory on Eadie's bedside table a couple of weeks ago. After their conversation that night in The Grotto, she figured it was the least she could do.

Eadie groaned and laid her head back on the chair, staring up at the wide starry sky. The moon dangled over her head like a fiery sword of Damocles. "If we're going to talk about unintegrated negative complexes and the collective unconscious then I'm going to need something a little stronger than vodka to drink," she said. "If we're talking psychic crucifixion, then you better get out the tequila."

"So you did read the book." Lavonne was not discouraged by her attitude. Resistance before a breakthrough was common. "You're an extroverted sensate, Eadie, which means your neglected inferior function is intuition — a distinctly female emotion. I think anyone who knows you would agree that your animus is definitely more developed than your anima."

"My what?"

"Your animus. Your male soul image. The hard-drinking, rational-thinking, warrior that exists in every woman."

Eadie grinned and raised her glass. "You're a pretty hard-drinking warrior yourself, comrade."

Lavonne pulled on her drink and set it down. "Whatever the ego resists will persist," she said, wiping her top lip.

"Is this a free session or will you be expecting payment?"

"Your animus is highly developed but you've got to come to terms with your anima, your female image, your goddess image. She comes out in your work but you've got to accept her in yourself."

"Hey, I love being a woman," Eadie said, "and I can tell you why in two words."

"Free drinks?"

"Multiple orgasms."

They were quiet for a while, sipping their Cosmopolitans.

"I know you're trying to help but I can tell you right now I hate all this pop psychology shit," Eadie said, running her finger around the rim of her glass. "Maybe the reason I can't work in New Orleans is because I'm bored. Maybe it has nothing to do with depression but everything to do with boredom. I hate weak, whiny women who blame all their problems on their shitty childhoods. Or their parents. Or even their husbands. Women need to stand on their own two feet and take responsibility for their emotional baggage."

"I agree," Lavonne said. She pulled on her drink, grimacing. "Jung said the same thing. But being female isn't all about being weak and whiny, Eadie. It seems to me you're projecting."

Eadie poured herself another drink and topped off Lavonne's. "I mean, anyone can bitch and moan to some overpaid psychiatrist, but it takes a real hero to carry around his neurosis and shut up about it."

"See, there you go again. Identifying with your animus."

"You got any peanuts?" Eadie said.

Lavonne set her drink down. The buzzing in her head was louder now. She leaned forward and flattened her palms against the table like she was pushing down on some kind of antigravity force. "You can't keep ignoring this, Eadie. It won't just go away."

"Look," Eadie said, sticking her finger in her drink and then in her mouth. "How do you know this isn't just some physical problem? How do you know it's not just my biological clock ticking down to doomsday?"

"Well of course, that could be part of it."

"Maybe it's like that dancing baby on the TV show about the anorexic lawyer."

Lavonne looked surprised. "Do you want to have a baby, Eadie? Do you see yourself as a mother?"

Eadie thought about it for all of two minutes. "No," she said.

"Well then, at least entertain the idea that all this might be a shadow projection, your suppressed anima trying to break through to consciousness."

Eadie snorted and stirred her drink with her finger. "Okay, Dr. Phil, and what am I supposed to do about it?"

"Listen to your dreams. Your mother is trying to tell you something important."

"Like what?"

"I don't know. You have to figure it out. Maybe she's trying to tell you to forgive yourself. To let your anima flower. You can only bring forth the Divine Child by allowing both the animus and anima to flourish."

"Look, Lavonne, let's just drop the inner-child shit. I told you. I don't want children."

"Not the inner child. The Divine Child. The symbol of self."

Eadie looked at her like she might have sprouted hair on her face, like she might have something black and slimy trapped between her two front teeth. "What in the hell are you talking about?"

Lavonne shrugged. She chuckled and shook her head. "I don't know what I'm talking about," she said. "Pour me another Cosmo and let me see if I can figure it out."

Eadie grinned and picked up the cocktail shaker. "I don't think the analyst is supposed to drink during sessions."

"Neither is the patient."

They raised their glasses and touched them lightly.

"To middle-age neurosis," Eadie said.

Two weeks later, Eadie awoke with a start. She had been dreaming about her mother again, some dream about water, a lake or a river, or maybe the sea. Reba was sitting in the bow of a small boat wearing white gloves and a hat and she was calling to Eadie across the water, something faint and insistent. Eadie had turned her head and was straining to hear her mother's voice, which was like the rustling of dry leaves.

She sat up. Late-afternoon sun flooded the room. The clock read five o'clock. Across the room, in front of an opened

417

window, a stack of papers flapped in the breeze. She got up and went into the kitchen, where Lavonne was sitting at the table reading the paper and drinking a cup of coffee. Looking up, she said, "What's wrong? You look like you saw a ghost."

"I did." Eadie picked up the phone and dialed Nita's house but there was no answer. Then she dialed Nita's cell phone.

"What's going on?" Lavonne said. She and Eadie and Nita had spent the afternoon at the Kudzu Festival where Loretta had taken first place in the Betty Crocker Cook-Off for her recipe "Elvis's El Wienie Mexicano." They had hung around for the Hubcap Throw, Bobbing for Pigs Feet, and Hillbilly Jeopardy but had left before the recliner race, NASCHAIR, because it reminded Nita too much of Jimmy Lee. He'd taken fourth place two years ago with his blue velour Barcalounger, right behind the Pickett brothers with their plaid La-Z-Boy outfitted with a beer cooler, a remote control carry case, a crude steering wheel, and a drop-down table tray onto which had been glued a plate, a NASCAR beer coozie, and a fork on a chain.

Lavonne folded up the newspaper. "What in the hell is going on?"

"I think I may have figured out what my

mother was trying to tell me." Eadie held up one finger for her to be quiet. "Nita," she said, when Nita finally answered. "Where are you?"

"I'm at my folk's house," Nita said. "The children are here and we're having dinner."

"Where's your notebook? The one you used to take notes about Virginia's tragic childhood?"

"It's at home. Why?"

"You're going home later to dress for the Kudzu Ball, right?"

Nita hesitated. "Listen, Eadie," she said. "I've been thinking about that. I don't think I'm going to make the ball this year."

"Oh yes you are," Eadie said. "Come on, Nita. I stayed in town just for this. We've already bought our ball gowns."

"I paid two dollars and fifty cents for mine so it's not a big loss."

"Nita, you need to get out. You need to have some fun to take your mind off all the shit going on in your life right now. Don't make us come over there and get you."

Nita sighed. "All right," she said. "I'll go. Just a minute." She put her hand over the receiver and then came back on. "Mama says she's coming with me. She says she's pretty sure you two will need a designated driver to get home. We'll meet you over there."

"Don't forget to bring the notebook," Eadie said.

"Tell me what's going on."

"I'll tell you when you get there." Eadie hung up and sat down at the table. She chewed her bottom lip and stared blankly at the wall clock. Her leg bounced up and down like it was attached to electrodes.

Lavonne watched her steadily. "Okay," she said finally. "Spill it."

"Not yet." Eadie shook her head slowly. "I want to read the last few entries in Nita's notebook first. I want to make sure I've got this right before I say anything."

"Does this have anything to do with Nita getting Whitney back?"

Eadie looked at her. "Maybe," she said. "If I'm right. If we can figure out how to use it."

Lavonne tapped her fingers against the table. A shaft of sunlight fell through the French doors, illuminating Eadie's face. "What time do you want to go to the ball?"

Eadie shrugged, her eyes still fixed on the wall clock. "I don't know. Maybe around nine. Grace won't be crowned until ten o'clock and I want to be there to see that." Grace Pearson was this year's Kudzu

Queen. She was going as Miss Velveeta Gritz. Eadie and Lavonne had decided to return in their roles as Aneeda Mann and Ima Badass.

"What do you say I make up a batch of Cosmos and we start celebrating a little early. We can take a taxi to the ball."

Eadie slid her eyes from the clock to Lavonne's face. She grinned. "Damn, Miss Badass," she said. "You're a mind reader."

They arrived at the ball just as Queen Velveeta Gritz was arriving in the Kudzu Kruiser. The Kruiser was the brainchild of Clayton Suttles, who covered his Bonneville convertible in chicken wire and parked it every year at the edge of a large stand of kudzu. At the end of the summer he went in with a metal detector to retrieve it, cutting away large clumps of trailing vine but leaving the car swathed in greenery. The overall effect was that of a long flat topiary on wheels.

A large crowd waited outside the huge striped circus tent set up in the Wal-Mart parking lot. Vernon Caslin, this year's master of ceremony, stood at the end of a long roll of red carpet covered in peanut shells waiting for the queen's arrival. His name tag read *Hi, My Name's Spud Daddy,*

What's Yours? As the Kruiser pulled slowly into the lot, the crowd went wild. Vernon walked up to the Kruiser and gave Grace his hand. She stood up. She was dressed in a truly hideous white satin number covered in black polka dots. The dress was ankle-length and had a sweetheart neckline and leg o' mutton sleeves. She wore a white veil and a kudzu vine wreath that stood up around her head like a crown of thorns.

"Damn," Eadie said when she saw her. "Where'd you get that Mother of the Bride of Frankenstein dress? It's hideous. Did you have it specially made or did someone else actually wear it first?"

"Salvation Army Store in Atlanta," Grace said proudly. "I saw it and knew no one else could possibly have one as tacky. Although yours is close," she said, appreciatively eyeing Eadie's puff-sleeve, white satin bodice with a ruched black velvet skirt cocktail dress. "And I love what you've done with your feet."

"Thanks," Eadie said, holding one leg out for her inspection. She was wearing combat boots and a white sailor hat sprigged with kudzu that she'd picked up down at the Army & Navy Store.

"And speaking of hideous, Lavonne, look at you."

"It takes a lot of work to look this bad," Lavonne said proudly. She'd found a floor-length, gold lamé, Grecian-style dress down at the Baptist thrift store in Valdosta. On the back of Lavonne's exposed shoulder, Eadie had drawn a tattoo in Magic Marker that read, *Born to Party.* Underneath it was a crude drawing of a grinning skull resting in a martini glass.

"The tattoo's a nice touch."

"Thanks," Lavonne said. She'd done her hair up in a Grecian roll with a headband made of kudzu vine. She wore bedroom slippers on her feet. They were spray-painted gold and had sequins and faux fur glued to the tops.

They followed Grace into the tent that had been strung with colored lights in the shape of shotgun shells. Round tables sporting camouflage tablecloths were set up on the left side of the huge tent and the buffet tables to the right. The Kudzu Ball was open to anyone with a sense of humor who understood that Southerners like to poke fun at themselves but don't much like anyone else doing it, by God. That being said, this year's theme was Trailer Park Cuisine. Each table sported a miniature trailer along with recipe cards for such delicacies as Pearl Purdy's Slutty Pups,

Baptist Beans, Jethro's El Grande Sausage Balls, Sister Wahneeta's Old Rugged Cross Cake, and Flaming Possum. The buffet tables held samples of these and other trailer park favorites such as Engine Block Pork, Velveeta Fudge, Ima Pornstar's Hussy Dip, and Roadkill Potatoes. As Grace and Vernon entered the tent, the band, the Appalachian Groove Boys, launched into their hit single, "Talk Dirty."

Eadie saw Nita and Loretta sitting alone at a table and she steered Lavonne in their direction. Nita was dressed in a high-waisted calico gown, the kind of thing a hippie bride might have worn in 1974. A bottled water rested on the table in front of her.

"Don't tell me you're drinking bottled water," Eadie said to her, as she sat down. "Where's the Kool-Aid?" Kudzu Kool-Aid was the featured beverage of the Kudzu Ball and was rumored to be made from a number of ingredients, including various over-the-counter cold medicines as well as generous amounts of Curtis Peet's homebrewed whiskey. It was guaranteed to be strong enough to "suck the chrome off a bumper."

"Y'all, I can't drink that stuff," Nita said. "Last time I drank it, Jimmy Lee had to carry me home."

No one wanted to talk about Jimmy Lee right now, so Eadie just nodded at Loretta and said to Nita, "Did you bring the notebook?"

Loretta was wearing a high-collared pink taffeta number and faux diamond studded librarian glasses. "What's this all about?" she said, leaning toward Eadie. Nita had told her about the notebook on the way over.

"First, I need a drink," Eadie said. She waved her hand at Banks Hollowell who passed carrying a tray of drinks. He was dressed in overalls and a camouflaged baseball cap that read, *A Mind Is a Fun Thing to Waste.*

"Hey," he said, smiling so they could see his plastic Billy Bob teeth, "do y'all need a drink?" He swung his tray down theatrically and Lavonne and Eadie each took a plastic cup. Banks had been an associate at Boone & Broadwell before it folded and Lavonne was surprised to see him here.

"Shouldn't you be over at the Cotillion Ball tonight?" she said, taking a sip of Kool-Aid. It burned like battery acid down the back of her throat. The first sip was always the worst. After that, you didn't notice much.

"Naw," he said, grinning. "This is more

fun." He moved off into the crowd and Nita set the notebook out on the table.

"Whatever it is you have to say, say it quick," she said to Eadie. "We're not staying long."

"I thought you were our designated driver," Lavonne said to Loretta. Her tongue stuck to her teeth like a sea slug. She was beginning to realize the preparty shaker of Cosmos might not have been such a good idea.

"I'll take Nita home and then come back for you," Loretta said, squinting. "But from the looks of you girls, you might want to go easy on the Kool-Aid. I got a bad back. I'm not carrying anyone out of here tonight."

"We'll keep that in mind," Eadie said. She tapped her finger against the top of the notebook. "Read that last section," she said to Nita. "The part where Virginia goes away after she finds out Hampton Boone is going to marry Maureen Hamilton."

"He had too much sense to settle on Virginia," Loretta said.

"Read it," Eadie said.

Nita picked up the notebook and read, *"When she went away in January I was crying, and her mama was crying, and her daddy was crying and saying, 'Poor little Queenie, poor little Queenie,' over and over, but her eyes were dry and hard as bone. She sat down in the bow of the boat and held on to the sides with her little gloved hands and looked straight ahead like a woman who knows what it is she has to do."*

"Okay," Eadie said, her eyes flashing. "Now read that part right before. Where she's saying she needs to tell him something but only if he loves her."

Nita frowned and followed the page with her finger. "You mean this?" she said, and began to read. *"The week before he went back to school, I held her in my arms again and this time she was crying and saying, over and over, Leota, what am I going to do? What am I going to do? I love him. And I said, you have to tell him, and she said, I can't unless I know he loves me."*

Eadie grinned and slapped the table, looking from one to the other until Lavonne, losing patience, said, "What? What is it?"

"Don't you see?" Eadie said, grabbing Nita's arm and giving it a little shake, but Nita only looked annoyed. "Virginia had something to tell Hamp Boone that summer. Something important." She picked up the notebook and read, *"When she went away in January I was crying, and her mama was crying, and her daddy was crying . . ."* She put the notebook down and looked at Lavonne but Lavonne only stared at her with a blank expression on her face.

"I don't get it," she said.

"Virginia was pregnant! She was carrying Hamp Boone's child and that's what she had to tell him that summer, and that's why she went away in January. To have the baby!"

Loretta said, "What in the hell are you talking about?"

Nita and Lavonne looked at Eadie like she was crazy. "It doesn't say that," Lavonne said stubbornly, picking up the notebook.

"Read between the lines," Eadie said impatiently. "If she got pregnant in June, then she'd be about six months pregnant by December and probably showing. That's why she had to go away."

"Who got pregnant?" Loretta said.

Nita frowned. "But why didn't Leota just say that? Why didn't she say Virginia was pregnant?"

"Maybe she forgot why Virginia had to go away. Or maybe she was trying to protect her."

"Let me see that," Loretta said, reaching for the notebook.

Lavonne shook her head slowly, still looking puzzled. "But Virginia was in high school. If she got pregnant, somebody would know."

"She graduated early," Nita said quietly. "She's always bragging about how she was smart enough to graduate from high school early and then went to work at Roobin's Department Store to save money for college. Only later she met the Judge, and got married instead."

"Don't you see, it all makes sense," Eadie said, throwing herself back in her chair. "Maureen Boone *hated* Virginia. And when I asked Trevor later, after his mother died, he said it was because of something that happened a long time ago. Some bad blood between them. His mother would never tell him what. He just assumed it had something to do with the law firm."

"And that would explain why Virginia married the Judge in the first place." Lavonne was beginning to catch on. "Because he was Hamp Boone's law partner and marrying him kept Virginia as close to Hamp as she could be."

Nita's expression changed again. Her eyes widened and her lower lip trembled. "If it's true that Virginia had a baby with Hamp Boone, a baby that she gave up for adoption, then we could use that. If we could prove it. That's not the kind of thing Virginia would want to get around town. We could use it to bargain with her. To get Whitney back."

"But how do we prove it?" Lavonne said.

"Easy!" Eadie said. "We go out to the nursing home and ask Leota Quarles."

Nita's face fell. "Well, that might be a problem," she said. "Seeing's how Leota is dead."

Eadie said, "Shit."

Lavonne said, "If Virginia had a baby out of wedlock and gave it up for adoption, it would be about forty-nine years old. If only we could figure out some way to find out who it is."

Grace Pearson danced by in Vernon Caslin's arms. The Groove Band launched into a toe-tapping version of "The Walleyed Boogie." Grace saw them and shouted, "Y'all get up and dance! If I have to make a fool of myself, you do, too!"

Eadie said, "Maybe we could get access to adoption records."

"How do we get access to adoption documents that are probably sealed?"

"We start with the Internet," Nita said. "We figure out where she might have gone to have a baby and then we narrow it down from there."

Lavonne shook her head. "I'm pretty sure there are laws about that. I'm pretty sure only the birth mother or adopted child can access that information."

Eadie was too excited about the prospect of exposing Virginia to let a few rules and regulations get in her way. "Hell, if we have to we'll hire a private investigator," she said. "Maybe we should just do that to start with."

"No," Nita said grimly, shaking her head. "This is something I need to do."

No one said anything for a few minutes. Lavonne stared fixedly at the camouflage tablecloth and then looked up. "Loretta, I've got a question for you," she said.

Loretta stuck her finger on the page to keep her place. Her eyes, behind her sparkling glasses, were wary. "Shoot," she said.

"In your day, if a girl got pregnant out of wedlock, where would she go to have the baby?"

Loretta frowned. "Listen, girls, I think you might be jumping the gun a little bit here. You got to remember these were the ramblings of a ninety-year-old woman who may or may not be remembering things correctly."

"Humor me," Eadie said. "There must have been adoption agencies up in Atlanta and some of the major cities," she said, trying to encourage Loretta. "Places where a

431

girl could go."

"Well, sure there were. But those places kept records. If you were trying to keep it quiet, you most likely went to one of those homes for unwed mothers. They didn't keep too many papers. They didn't ask too many questions. I had a good friend who got knocked up and she went up to some place in north Georgia and had her baby."

"What was it called?" Lavonne said, getting out her Daytimer. "The home, I mean."

Loretta looked up at the strings of colored lights. She sighed and scratched her head. "I can't remember the name of the place, but it seems like it was run by the Catholics. There was another one, over in Valdosta, but it was run by the Baptists and you had to sign a paper saying Jesus was your Lord and Savior before they'd take your baby away from you." She watched Lavonne write this down and then she said, "Hey girls, I don't want to rain on your parade, but it seems to me you're getting excited over something that might not be worth getting excited about."

Nita shook her head slowly. "I've got a feeling about this," she said. It was true, she did. Just when things had looked their bleakest, a thin shaft of light had broken through the dark clouds. She felt like she had that day in the car with Logan driving home from the custody hearing, that anything was possible, that hope was not dead. "I think we might be on to something."

"I just hope Loretta isn't right," Lavonne said cautiously. "I just hope all this reading between the lines is not a wild-goose chase."

"Promise me something," Nita said, looking around the table. "Promise me you won't say anything about any of this to anyone. I want to keep it quiet until I figure out how to go about checking this story out. I don't want Virginia to get wind of what's up. I want to be just as dirty and underhanded with her as she's been with me."

"Now you're talking, girl," Eadie said, sipping her drink. "We have to be careful though. Virginia's pretty wily. She's pretty subtle."

"Virginia's about as subtle as the business end of a cattle prod," Loretta said. "And just as dangerous."

"Count me in," Lavonne said. "I'll help anyway I can."

"I still say you girls got the wrong dog by the tail," Loretta said. "Virginia's too self-centered to have ever loved anybody but herself. She's too clever to have ever made a mistake as big as Hampton Boone."

The day following the Cotillion Ball, Virginia awoke early and hurried down to get the newspaper. She swung the front door open and stepped out onto the porch. The day was gray and overcast. Virginia picked up the newspaper, her hands trembling with excitement, and stepped back inside, flipping on the hall light. She always looked forward to reading about the Cotillion Ball, to seeing her photograph displayed so prominently among the cream of Ithaca society, some of whom had refused to speak to her in high school.

But today, looking down at the front of the Lifestyle section, Virginia felt a swelling sense of disbelief and outrage. The paper had covered both the prestigious Ithaca Cotillion Ball and the lowbrowed Kudzu Ball on the same page. And to make matters worse, the Kudzu Ball was listed at the top. Virginia stared down at the large photograph crowning the page, her sharp eyes glittering like spear points.

There, in all her glory, was the behemoth Grace Pearson, looking drunk and foolish in her kudzu crown and leg o' mutton–sleeved ball gown. Underneath the photograph, in large bold letters, larger than those captioning the Cotillion Queen, it read "Seventh Kudzu Queen Crowned — Miss Velveeta Gritz (a/k/a Grace Pearson) Takes the Throne." Beneath this photo there were several others, fully half the page, as well as several interior pages that were devoted to coverage of the Kudzu Ball.

Virginia had been trying to get the Kudzu Ball closed down for years. It irritated her that people would make a mockery of the Cotillion Ball, would ridicule what had taken her years of scheming and hard work to achieve.

She recognized Lavonne Zibolsky and Nita and Eadie Boone, and also several prominent couples who, just a few years ago, wouldn't have been caught dead at the Kudzu Ball. They all looked drunk and ridiculous, decked out in tacky prom dresses and camouflage leisure suits and a couple of the men sported mullet wigs and Fu Manchu mustaches. By comparison, the Cotillion Ball Debs looked bored, the Queen looked less virginal than in years past, and the King looked dusty and ancient and maybe even a little senile. There was a larger photograph of Virginia and Redmon, and she noticed with dismay that the camera lights had accentuated her sagging cleavage, which her expensive dress did little to hide. Redmon wore his stunned-deer-in-the-headlights expression. He clutched his soda water and stared miserably into the camera and Virginia noted (again, those damn lights) that his tuxedo did not fit him properly and he needed a haircut.

She closed the paper in disgust. It would do no good to complain to the newspaper about their coverage of the Kudzu Ball. One of their own journalists had been named Kudzu Queen and most of the staff had, no doubt, attended, so they could not be expected to help her close down the ridiculous affair. Virginia felt sure the event would die out if the publicity surrounding it stopped. She wondered if she might be able to talk Redmon into buying the newspaper. The first thing she would do, of course, is take over the editorial department, fire any left-wing writers, including the renegade Grace Pearson, and see to it that future coverage of the Cotillion Ball would figure prominently in the society pages, and coverage of the Kudzu Ball would cease entirely.

This thought, planted in the fertile soil of her imagination, took root and spread like the kudzu vine itself, until her mind was a veritable jungle of twisted vines and suffocating greenery and she could think of nothing but her desire to acquire the *Ithaca Daily News* and punish those who needed punishing.

She stood in the hall tapping her little slippered foot angrily against the parquet floor. When Redmon came downstairs later, she was still standing there among the scattered newspaper, lost in thought.

CHAPTER TWENTY

Almost two months after he lost all her money and ran off to parts unknown, Jimmy Lee Motes walked into the Shofar So Good Deli where Nita was working. It was in the middle of the lunch rush on a Friday and the place was crowded, so Nita just nodded at him once and indicated a small, unoccupied table close to the window. She brought him a glass of sweet tea and a menu.

"I'm real busy right now but can you wait thirty minutes?" she said. "We need to talk."

"Sure," he said. His face was still tanned from the summer and he'd let his hair grow long over his ears. Across the room a table of office girls smiled and eyed him boldly.

"Can I get you something while you wait?"

He shook his head. "I'm not hungry." She turned to go and he reached out and took her arm. "You look good, Nita."

"Thanks." She smoothed her hair behind

her ears and moved off. She couldn't even remember if she had brushed it this morning; she had other things on her mind these days. When she wasn't working, she spent long hours on the Internet or on the telephone, searching for homes for unwed mothers that had existed in the 1950s. She entered the data into a spreadsheet, and although many of the homes had operated illegally and had only kept the first names of the mothers, she didn't lose hope, concentrating on women who had given birth in the first few months of 1951. She followed up these slim leads with telephone calls or e-mails or letters. She gave some of the leads to Lavonne and Eadie, who were desperate to help, but Nita kept most for herself. She felt intuitively that this was something she had to do on her own.

Nita moved mechanically through her lunch routine. She could feel him watching her as she went about her duties, but it didn't make her nervous. She was used to the job by now and was learning to enjoy interacting with the customers, most of whom were tourists down from Atlanta. She had rehearsed what she had to say to him a hundred times but she went over it again in her head, briefly, while she took orders at the counter and walked around to refill drinks. A group of businessmen sat at a big table near the counter and one of them smiled at her as she refilled his sweet tea. "Hey," he said, "didn't you use to be an actress? Didn't I see you in some Hollywood movie about stewardesses gone bad?"

"Sorry," she said. "That wasn't me."

"Maybe it was a soap opera. Don't you play a vixen on daytime TV?"

"Don't tell anyone," Nita said. "I don't want people knowing what my real job is."

They left her a twenty-five percent tip. Later, when she went over to sit down with Jimmy Lee, he said, "What did that fat fucker want?"

Nita said, "Why are you here, Jimmy?"

"I don't think this job is such a good idea," he said. He was clearly agitated. He played with the salt and pepper shakers, tapping them steadily against the table. She rose and went over and got a pitcher of sweet tea and brought it back to the table, pouring each of them a glass. The lunch crowd had thinned considerably. The new girl, Marjorie, had no trouble handling the few tables that were left.

Nita sat down. She crossed her arms on the table and leaned forward. "So, where have you been?"

Jimmy Lee stacked the salt and pepper

shakers like he was building a wall. "I've been up in Bowling Green, Kentucky, working with my cousin. He's building a house for some couple and I stayed with him just trying to get my head clear."

Nita picked up a spoon and stirred her tea. "How'd that work out?"

"It didn't." Jimmy Lee looked like he might take her hand, but then thought better of it. He lowered his voice and said, "All I could think about was you, Nita. All I could think about was how bad I fucked everything up."

Nita stirred slowly. She took the spoon out of her tea and laid it on the table. "Who told you I was working here?"

"Your mother. When I hadn't heard from you, I got desperate and called her. She told me. Everything."

"I'm sorry I didn't call you back," she said. "I just needed some time. I've had a lot on my mind lately." In between her Internet searches and work schedules, Nita drove around interviewing nurses who might or might not have worked at various underground homes for unwed mothers in the 1950s. She was thankful for the distractions. It kept her from thinking about Whitney, from wondering whether her marriage to Jimmy Lee would ever work out.

"I didn't know anything about the custody thing until Loretta told me yesterday. I didn't know about any of this."

"I know."

"Goddamn it, Nita, why didn't you tell me?"

She frowned and counted the ice cubes in her glass. "After you left, I was pretty pissed off."

"I didn't know," he said stubbornly, shaking his head. "I didn't know anything about her taking Whitney."

"Yeah, but you didn't stay around long enough to find out, did you?" she said, glancing up at him and then back down at her glass.

He leaned forward and took her hands in his. She let him hold her hands but she kept her fingers curled into tight little fists. "I figured you hated me. After I lost the money I figured you'd never want to see me again."

"It's not about the money, is it?" she said. "It never was, for me anyway."

He took a deep breath, looking down at her balled fists. "I was crazy," he admitted, "getting caught up in all of that."

"I wasn't angry at you about the money," she said, slowly letting her fingers uncurl. "I was angry at me. I should have asked more questions. I should have kept the money out of our marriage. I wouldn't have even *had* the money if Lavonne and Eadie hadn't made me take it from Charles when I got the chance."

"You deserved it."

"Yes, I deserved it but that's not the point." She frowned, trying to remember her rehearsed speech. It was hard saying what she had to say when he sat across from her looking tanned and handsome and contrite. "All my life I've been passive. I've let others push me into making decisions I should have been making for myself."

Jimmy Lee frowned and tugged at her fingers. "I've been sending you checks to pay you back but you haven't been cashing them."

She wasn't going to let him distract her. Nita felt for the first time in her life she was seeing things clearly. She pulled her hands away, gently, and folded them on the table in front of her. "I went from my father's house to Charles's house and then to yours, and now for the first time, I'm alone. I'm learning to stand on my own two feet and take responsibility for myself."

Jimmy Lee didn't like the way this was going. "It wasn't my house," he reminded her. "It was ours."

"You know what I'm saying," she said.

"Don't pretend like you don't."

"Just tell me what I can do to make things right, Nita."

"You can pay the utilities. At least until I get this custody fight settled. And help me with the car insurance."

"And you can cash the checks I already sent you," he said sullenly.

"All right, I will. As long as you know this isn't about the six hundred thousand dollars. I don't expect you to try and pay that back."

An awkward silence fell between them. Across the room, Marjorie bused her last table, glancing at them from time to time. The table of office girls got up and left, giggling loudly.

"Can I move back in?" he asked finally. She looked at him and he sighed and leaned back in his chair stretching one leg out in front with the other resting against the table leg. "Okay," he said. "I'll call one of my high school buddies and see if I can stay with him a while."

"Right now I have to concentrate on getting my daughter back. That's all I can think about." Whatever was wrong with her marriage would have to wait until after she brought Whitney home. She had made up her mind and there was no turning back.

He turned his face to the window and cocked his head as if listening to distant music. When he turned back to face her, his eyes were steady. "I love you, Nita," he said. "I just want it to be the way it used to be."

She stood up. Outside the window, a group of schoolchildren passed, swinging their backpacks like weapons. "It won't ever be that way again," she said, and reaching out to touch his shoulder lightly, she left.

A few weeks after Logan moved in, Virginia had had about all she could take. If she made it through to the next custody hearing without having a stroke or a heart attack, it would be a miracle. In all of her careful scheming, Virginia had failed to foresee this clever trick; it had never occurred to her that Nita would dump *both* grandchildren on her. And with her high-priced lawyer's tender outpourings in court, his assurances that Virginia cared only about the welfare of her grandchildren, Virginia's hands were tied as far as kicking her juvenile delinquent grandson out of the house. Unless he got arrested or stole something from the house, which was always a definite possibility, she was stuck.

It seemed she had underestimated her meek ex-daughter-in-law.

Sometimes it felt like her whole life was closing in around her like a thick black cloud of billowing smoke, and in those moments Virginia had to wonder if revenge was all it was cracked up to be. She had to wonder if it wasn't more trouble than it was worth. She had been surprised, leaving Judge Drucker's courtroom, that she hadn't felt more of a feeling of triumph and joy. Instead, a vacuous emptiness had spread through her like an oil slick. She had rushed home and tried, unsuccessfully, to fill the void with a pitcher of martinis. Even the memory of Loretta James being dragged out of the courtroom by a thick-necked deputy did little to raise her spirits.

The truth of the matter was, she missed Leota Quarles. The woman had been more of a mother to her than her own mother, and Virginia missed going out to see her every week. Never mind that Leota's mind had begun to go there, at the end. She slipped in and out of the past as easily as a car switching gears on a mountain slope. She would begin some story with "the young Mrs. Broadwell came to see me and asked me about the island," and Virginia, thinking she was talking about herself as a young matron, would discreetly change the subject. Leota's mind would wander alone down dusty corridors, along secret passageways hung with cobwebs while Virginia twittered on about the weather or the price of tomatoes or today's lunch menu. Still, despite the decline of those last few months, Virginia missed her. She missed the only mother-daughter relationship she had ever known. Leota's death had left a big hole in her heart that nothing seemed to fill.

And in the weeks following her grandson's arrival, Virginia's depression had only deepened. He stayed up all hours of the night, had table manners like a field hand, dressed and talked like a reality-show drug addict, and humiliated Virginia every chance he got. Just yesterday he had crashed her bridge group, coming downstairs wearing nothing but black eye liner, a metal lip ring, and a pair of obviously soiled boxer shorts pulled down so low in front you could see the beginnings of his dark thatch of pubic hair.

"My grandson is home sick from school today," Virginia had explained nervously to the stunned bridge group. She hadn't even realized he was in the house. "Y'all know Logan, don't you?" she said in a bright, hopeless voice. Over by the window, Worland Pendergrass and Lee Anne Bales snorted and giggled into their hands.

"How y'all doing?" Logan said, waving from the doorway. He grinned in a friendly manner and put his hands on his narrow naked hips. "Is this what y'all do when your husbands are off at work? Gamble and drink and talk about everybody who's not here?"

Virginia rose and walked over to where he stood, putting herself between him and the room of slack-jawed women. She put her tiny hand on his chest and said tersely, under her breath, "In the kitchen. Now." Over her shoulder, she smiled at the bridge group and said loudly enough for them to hear, "Honey, would you like some breakfast?"

Logan grinned his wide, lopsided grin. "Sure, Grandma," he said, and Virginia winced. She hated being called that. She preferred Grandmother, or Miss Virginia. "Breakfast would be swell," Logan said, showing her that he could act as well as she could.

He followed her into the kitchen. She swung around on her heel and hissed in a voice just above a whisper, "How dare you embarrass me in front of my friends? How dare you skip school and show up half-naked in front of my entire bridge group?"

He crossed his arms over his chest and leaned against the breakfast bar. "I guess you're getting a little more than you bargained for, huh, *Grandma?*" He wasn't grinning now.

Her face went rigid. She pointed at him with her index finger. "You will go upstairs and get into bed this minute," she said, "and you will not come downstairs undressed again. Not while you're under my roof."

He said, "Your roof?"

It was the first real exchange they had ever had. They stood facing each other over the new breakfast bar, and there was something in his sullen, stubborn expression that reminded Virginia suddenly of her dead husband. The boy had inherited his grandfather's bold temperament and, realizing this, Virginia felt a chill come over her.

He leaned toward her, his palms leaving damp marks on the new granite countertop. "You can stop this anytime you want," he said in a reasonable voice. "You know how." He swung around, and padded out of the kitchen on his bare feet, waving at the women in the living room as he passed. Lee Anne Bales waved back. "Y'all don't drink too much!" he shouted, disappearing up the stairwell.

Since then, Virginia had been unable to dispel the chilling sense that things were spiraling quickly out of control. She had avoided Logan as much as possible since the incident in the kitchen, and had been glad to see his car leaving this morning as he pulled out of the driveway and headed for school. She had decided that, in the future, she would avoid being alone with him, and in public she would put on her brave cheerful face and go about her business as usual. If Logan and his mother thought they could intimidate her into showing her hand, into allowing her carefully constructed façade to crack, then they had another think coming. Virginia had been wearing a mask all her life. She was good at it.

She would continue in her portrayal of naive grandmotherly goodwill and concern, at least until the final custody hearing, until Nita's life came crashing down around her the way Virginia's had when Boone & Broadwell folded. She had made her plans and she would not be swayed from her course.

Still, it was hard, at dinner the following evening, to keep her cheerful façade intact. She sat at the dining room table with Redmon and Whitney waiting for Logan to join them. He was downstairs, practicing with his rock-and-roll band in the basement.

"Them boys are getting good," Redmon

said, cocking his head to listen.

Virginia thumped the table irritably with her fingers. "Della," she called, repeatedly, until the black woman stuck her head through the kitchen door. "Did you tell Logan to join us at five-thirty?"

"I told him," she said. "He says he won't eat if his friends can't eat, too."

"Them boys are welcome," Redmon said. He'd taken a special interest in Logan and his friends, spending large amounts of time with them down in the basement. Virginia suspected he was providing them with beer and regaling them with tales of his happy boyhood in the Alabama swamplands. Redmon waved his hand at his step-granddaughter. "Sugar, run on downstairs and tell your brother and his friends they can come on up for supper."

"Whitney, stay where you are," Virginia said sharply.

Whitney snapped her gum and rolled her eyes at the injustice of being used as a pawn. She slid back into her chair.

Virginia slowly regained her composure. "Really," she said, unclenching her teeth and smiling at Redmon. "Della has only made enough dinner for four. We can't just ask her at the last minute to provide for two additional guests. Two *uninvited* guests."

Della called amicably from the kitchen, "I can fix another couple of plates." She stepped through the doorway, wiping her hands on her apron. She looked at Virginia and grinned. "That won't be no trouble at all," she said.

Virginia glared at her above the floral centerpiece. Della stood there wiping her hands and humming something that sounded suspiciously like "We Shall Overcome." A tinny, thumping sound filled the room and Whitney leaned over quickly to answer her cell phone. Virginia's eyes left Della and swung over to her granddaughter, where they rested like a load of steel girders.

"I'll call you back," Whitney said sullenly, and hung up.

Virginia set her teeth and smiled in a pleasant manner. "What have I told you, darling, about talking on the phone at the table?"

Whitney rolled her eyes toward heaven as if calling upon God to witness what she was made to suffer on a daily basis. "Oh, who cares?" she said. "Logan's not here anyway. We're just sitting around waiting on him so what difference does it make if I talk on the phone?"

Whitney often behaved like a spoiled brat,

which was something Virginia had not picked up on when she only saw the girl a few times a week. "It's not polite to talk on the phone at the table," Virginia repeated, for what might have been the twentieth time.

Whitney yawned and plucked at her hair. "Oh, who cares?" she repeated in a tired voice.

Virginia's hand slapped the table so hard the silverware jumped. "Go and get your brother," she said sharply. She lifted her glass and sipped her water, struggling to regain her composure. Whitney stared at her and then stood up, threw her napkin on the table, and slouched toward the basement door, swinging her hips in an exaggerated, insolent manner.

Watching her leave the room, the unfortunate Redmon chuckled.

"What are you laughing at?" Virginia said. Her sharp eyes pierced him like arrow points.

He recovered quickly. His face went slack. He had, after all, been married to Virginia for close to nine months and he was an expert now at defensive strategies. "Nothing, honey," he said mildly.

After dinner, Virginia and Redmon sat in the living room drinking coffee and watching CNN on the big-screen TV. Charles was supposed to join them later for dessert. Whitney had gone upstairs to study for an English test and Logan and his posse had retreated to the testosterone charged confines of the basement where they were putting the finishing touches on "Kill Me." Redmon wanted to be down there, Virginia could tell, watching the way he listened to them tuning their guitars, his head turned expectantly toward the basement door. He loved having male company in the house. Despite Virginia's admonitions to the contrary, Logan had brought his friends to the dinner table. Redmon had thoroughly enjoyed himself, joining in the teenagers' noisy banter and grinning from the end of the table like a doting mafia don gazing upon his dangerously dysfunctional family.

Only Virginia had sat quietly, putting in a cheerful word here and there, trying to ignore the fact that Whitney sat at the table with her knee up or that Logan's table manners seemed deliberately bad. He kept smiling and glancing at her as if daring her to say anything as he speared his pork chop with his fork and tore off large chunks of flesh like a heavily mascaraed Henry VIII wolfing down a leg of lamb.

Virginia ignored him.

After a while she stopped paying attention to the table and its ill-mannered occupants. Instead she focused on the room around her. She noted all the changes she had been able to accomplish through desire and careful planning. She looked proudly around the dining room that had been redone in a sand-and-taupe color scheme, complete with plantation shutters on the windows and new furniture in an English Chippendale style. It had taken several months of pleading and sexual fantasy to bring the transformation about, but it was worth it now, she thought, looking around. It would showcase nicely in a television spread. She felt a little tremor of excitement, remembering.

She had tried for years to get the *Gracious Southern Living* television show to come and do a segment on her home and they had steadfastly, but politely, declined. She had watched jealously over the years as homes less spectacular than her own, as hostesses less accomplished than she, were showcased in the entertainment segments. It was not until she married Redmon, and he, upon hearing of her unsuccessful attempts to lure them, had made a few phone calls, that the news had come that *Gracious Southern Living* would be happy to photograph a holiday gathering at the Redmon house.

Redmon's exact words had been, "Honey, them snotty *Gracious Southern Living* people will be happy to do a spread on a family throw-down at Casa Redmon!"

Virginia looked at him in horror. "Oh, for heaven's sake, you didn't call the house that, did you?"

"Why not?" he said, slapping her fondly on the rear end. "That's what it is. Casa Redmon."

Remembering, Virginia shuddered. They were coming two weeks before Thanksgiving to film a show that would air Thanksgiving weekend. She had decided to host a buffet and she would invite not only family members but also various society guests as well (at least those who looked presentable on film). She frowned, wondering how she would be able to pull it off with Logan here. Perhaps she could bribe him. Perhaps she could offer to send him and his bandmates down to the Florida condo for the weekend. She would get Redmon to offer him a thousand dollars, in cash, to go. Logan would, no doubt, up the ante but she would pay him whatever he wanted. She would allow nothing to spoil her triumphant *Gracious Southern Living* segment. It was the one thing in Virginia's life, besides her laborious crawl to the top of Ithaca society, that made up for the childhood humiliations she had suffered at the hands of her small-minded provincial classmates. It was a joyous affirmation that she had lived her life the way she was meant to live it.

The only thing that had come even remotely close to giving her the same sense of joy and accomplishment had been the look on Maureen Boone's face the day Virginia married the old Judge.

That, too, had been priceless.

Charles was late, and when he finally arrived his face was flushed and he spoke in a breathless, agitated manner that made Virginia suspect antianxiety medication.

"I'd offer you a bourbon, son, but Queenie's got me off the hard stuff," Redmon said. He was leaning back in one of the reclining parts of the sectional with his booted feet up on the footrest, clicking through the channels with his oversized remote control shaped like a bikini-clad female torso. It was next on Virginia's list of things to go, right behind the reclining sectional sofa with the built-in beer cooler.

She slid her eyes over to Redmon. "I'm sure the boys in the basement could offer you a beer," she said archly to Charles.

Redmon tightened his hold on the bikini-clad remote but other than that betrayed no sign of nervousness. Charles appeared not to have heard her. He sat down on a chair and then rose and went to stand at the windows overlooking the back lawn. A high-flying gaggle of geese passed slowly overhead. Charles had just come from a meeting with Nita and he was so excited he couldn't sit down. They had met for coffee and Nita had pleaded with him again to help her get the children back. She had also let him know, in a casual, offhand way, that the redneck carpenter had moved out of the house. Charles had felt an immediate sense of relief and optimism wash over him. He had barely been able to keep himself from wrapping his arms around Nita and picking her up in an exuberant bear hug. Caught up in the ecstasy of the moment, he had promised her he would talk to his mother about dropping the custody case.

Looking at his hulking shape reflected in the window glass, Virginia said suspiciously, "Charles, what is it?"

He continued to face the window. He cleared his throat several times. "Mother, I've been thinking. This custody battle might not be the right thing."

"Let me guess," she said flatly. "You've

been talking to your ex-wife." Virginia made a scornful sound, but before she could say anything else, Redmon spoke.

"I think your boy might be right, honey," he said, watching her peripherally, the way a cautious man might watch a rattlesnake coiled and ready to strike. "She's a sweet, pretty little thing that never meant a bit of harm to anybody."

Virginia shifted her steely gaze to Redmon. "What does being sweet and pretty have to do with anything?" she asked icily.

Redmon's left eye flickered like a bad circuit. "Nothing of course," he stammered. "Only she's a good mama, too."

"Good enough to take her children and run off with a man thirteen years her junior just because she *felt* like it. Good enough to destroy a sixteen-year marriage." There was a flapping sound in Virginia's head like a flock of startled bats. Her face felt warm.

"She wasn't in her right mind," Charles said stubbornly, still not turning around. "He enticed her to leave. That carpenter made her leave."

"Oh for heaven's sake, Charles, don't be such a fool." It was hard, sometimes, believing he was her child. It was enough to make Virginia question genetic probabilities and long-established theories on nurture versus nature.

Redmon swung his grizzled head around and looked at her with a strange expression on his face. His eye stopped fluttering. His defiant cowlick stuck out behind his head like a bird-dog's tail. "If I didn't know better, Queenie, I'd say you had a hard streak the size of Alabama running through you," he said gruffly. "I'd say you was coldhearted as an ex-wife's lawyer."

The sound in her head was a roaring clamor of flapping, black-winged creatures. Virginia ducked and scurried back inside herself. She wasn't ready to reveal that much of her true nature to Redmon. At least not yet. She decided on a different tact. "What choice did I have?" she asked, raising her little hands helplessly. She turned her pleading eyes on her husband. "I told you before. Once the deal with Mr. Motes fell through she would have taken the child and I would never have seen her again. She would have blamed me for what happened with the State of Georgia," she noticed him looking at her curiously and she hurried on, "although, *of course,* it wasn't my fault. She would have blamed me anyway. She always blamed me for everything."

Redmon set his jaw obstinately. "She's a

sweet girl," he said, shaking his head. "I don't think she would have done something like that. Keep the grandkids away from you, I mean."

Virginia stared at him with a look of utter disdain. She appeared to be on the verge of a full-blown seizure. "Sweet girl?" she said scornfully. "Have you forgotten what that sweet girl and her sweet friends did to you and Charles and that idiot Zibolsky out in Montana?"

That shut him up.

"That was more Eadie Boone's and La-vonne Zibolsky's doing," Charles said, swinging around from the window. "Nita would never have done any of that on her own."

Virginia snorted. "Well, if you want to believe that, go ahead."

"You never liked her," he said.

"I knew she wasn't the right girl for you."

"She was the right girl then, and she's the right girl now," Charles said, scowling.

"Don't be ridiculous," she cried. "Nita's not going to come back to you just because you retrieve her children. Any idiot can see she's not in love with you."

Charles chose to ignore this comment. He thought it best not to tell his mother he had invited Nita to Virginia's televised pre-

Thanksgiving buffet and she had accepted.

Redmon picked up the shapely remote and turned the sound up on the TV. "Damn, Queenie, why don't you just drive a stake through the poor bastard's heart? Why don't you just cut off his legs at the knee and feed him to the hogs?"

Virginia took a long series of deep breaths. A commercial for Fast Eddie's Auto Sales came on the TV. "No credit, no problem," Fast Eddie promised. Virginia panted like a rabbit caught in a trap. Her bosom rose and fell until it gradually grew still. Her top lip quivered and then lay flat. "I know it seems cruel, darling." She let her eyes mist over for effect. The flapping in her head had subsided now to a mild fluttering. "But sometimes a mother's got to do what a mother's got to do." She smiled gently at Charles. "Like a badger. She protects her young at all costs."

"I thought badgers ate their young," Charles said sullenly, but his mother had already turned away, and apparently didn't hear him.

CHAPTER
TWENTY-ONE

Somewhere around the end of October, Eadie and Lavonne began realizing just how hopeless their task of hunting down Virginia's phantom baby was. They checked and rechecked every lead revealed by Nita's magic spreadsheet, but nothing panned out. They were all dead ends. Eadie didn't give up easily but it was beginning to look like they'd have better luck finding the Holy Grail than hunting down a baby Virginia may or may not have had. But Nita refused to give up. She put her head down and proceeded with her county-by-county search. Lavonne and Eadie became steadily less encouraged.

And then, just when it seemed things were completely hopeless, Nita got a break. She was surfing through Internet websites featuring archival photos of long-defunct homes for unwed mothers, and she came across a photo that made her stop. It was taken at the Brainerd Home for Unwed Mothers in Chattanooga, Tennessee, and it showed a group of solemn-looking young women gathered around a long table. They appeared to be sewing. The photo was black and white and grainy with age. It was difficult to make out the faded background, but it was one of the young women's faces that had caught Nita's attention. She was in profile, and appeared to be turning away from the camera when the photo was snapped. The date scrawled across the bottom of the photo was March 5, 1951.

A week later, Nita called Lavonne and Eadie. When they showed up thirty minutes later, she had already made a shaker of Cosmopolitans.

"What are we celebrating?" Eadie said, when she saw the shaker and three martini glasses in the middle of the kitchen table.

"This," Nita said, handing her the photo she had printed. They huddled together under the overhead lights, studying the young women. Lavonne went to her purse and got her reading glasses. She put them on and peered at the photo again.

"What exactly are we looking at?" she asked.

"Here," Nita said impatiently, jabbing the photo with her index finger. "Who does this remind you of?"

"She looks oddly familiar," Eadie said slowly.

"Of course she does. She looks like Virginia."

"No." Eadie shook her head. "Not Virginia. Someone else."

"Oh for crying out loud, can't you see?" Nita said. "That's Virginia. That's her."

"You can't really see her face," Lavonne said. "She's turning away from the camera."

"Exactly."

Eadie glanced at Lavonne and raised one eyebrow.

"Here," Nita said, handing her a photo of Virginia and Charles as a baby.

Eadie compared the two. "I don't know," she said doubtfully.

"Look at the date," Nita said, jabbing again with her finger. "It fits."

"Were you able to come up with a list of names?" Lavonne said, handing the photos back to Nita. "Of the unwed mothers, I mean."

"They were only listed by first name and last initial," Nita said, rummaging around in a stack of papers on the table. "From what I gather this wasn't exactly a legal operation." She found what she was looking for and held it up. "Look at this. Jennie K."

465

They both looked at her with blank expressions on their faces. The clock on the wall ticked like a metronome. "Jennie K," she said, impatiently. "Virginia Kelly. It fits."

Lavonne looked at Eadie. Eadie sat down at the table and poured them all a drink.

"But how do we prove this?" Eadie said reasonably. "Most of those places didn't even keep birth certificates, much less birth mother records."

Lavonne sat down. "Eadie's right," she said. "A shadowy photograph and a first name aren't proof."

Nita sat down and crossed her arms on the table. "She's the only *Jennie* that was admitted the entire year of 1951."

"That still doesn't prove anything," Lavonne said.

Nita shrugged. "We're not going to have proof," she said. "Not legal proof, anyway. Not anything that would hold up in a court of law. But we don't need legal proof to bargain with Virginia. Don't you see? Just the fact that we know her secret, just the fact that we can spread the rumor is enough."

"Well, hell, then let's just make something up," Eadie said. "If all we're trying to do is threaten Virginia with a scandalous rumor campaign, we could just make it up." She grinned and touched her glass to Lavonne's.

"I've thought of that," Nita said seriously. "But I don't think it'll be necessary. To lie, I mean. I think we'll find all the proof we need in Chattanooga." Eadie and Lavonne stopped grinning.

Lavonne said, "How do you figure that?"

Nita pulled out another piece of paper and pushed it toward them. "They didn't keep birth mother records or birth certificates, but they kept employment records. This is a list of all the employees at the Brainerd Home for Unwed Mothers in 1951. I've been down the list and I've contacted everyone I could. Some are dead, and some I couldn't reach, but this lady here" — she pointed with her finger. "This Lorena Potter, she was a nurse at the home in 1951 and she remembers Jennie K well. And she still lives in Chattanooga. All I have to do is show her the photo of Charles and Virginia and ask her if it's the same woman she knew back in 1951."

Eadie frowned. "But there are laws about protecting confidentiality," she said.

"There are laws for legal adoptions," Lavonne agreed. "But illegal adoptions are something else."

"I told her I was a journalist," Nita said. "I told her I was writing a book on sex in

467

the 1950s and the shameful way they treated wayward girls. I told her I'd keep her name confidential, that I'd use her as an unnamed source."

Lavonne and Eadie stared at Nita in astonishment.

"Damn, girl," Eadie said, finally. "Look how you turned out."

"We're so proud," Lavonne said.

"Desperate times call for desperate measures," Nita said, gathering her papers. "Y'all want some supper? I can make some meatloaf sandwiches."

Eadie shook her head in admiration. "So you're going up to Chattanooga tomorrow to interview this woman?"

"Yes."

"Okay," Eadie said. "I'm going, too. I wouldn't miss this for the world." She looked at Lavonne.

"I can't," Lavonne said. "I've got payroll."

"Oh come on, Lavonne, it's a road trip. How long's it been since we had a girls' road trip?"

"Believe it or not, Eadie, some of us have to work."

"But not you. You've got employees. You've got a partner who can do payroll."

Lavonne tapped her fingers against the table like she was playing a keyboard, and thought about it. "Okay," she said finally. She lifted her glass and sipped her Cosmopolitan. "It's not every day a girl gets to act like a hero in a detective novel. It's not every day a girl gets to learn a lesson as big as this one."

Eadie said, "Oh yeah? What's the lesson?"

"Don't fuck with Nita."

"Y'all are crazy," Nita said. "Pour me another drink."

The next day they got an early start, leaving south Georgia around eight-thirty. The day was cool and sunny. Hawks wheeled lazily in the blue sky, gliding above the trees and empty fields. On the CD player, Mary Chapin Carpenter sang about love gone bad.

"I love this song," Nita said, tapping her fingers against the steering wheel. She had been telling them about how she and Jimmy Lee had started dating again.

Lavonne said, "That's great."

Eadie said, "Dating? Is that a euphemism for that other word you don't like to use, Nita?"

Nita smiled but watched the road. "We've been dating since he got back from Kentucky and moved in with his cousin Montel. We never really had a chance to date

469

before. I moved in with him right after the divorce."

Lavonne said, "His cousin's name is Montel?"

Eadie said, "Yeah, we know all that. But what's all this shit about dating?" She was sitting in the back and had her feet propped up on the seat.

"You know. Going out to dinner, to movies, bowling, stuff like that. Courting the way we would have done in high school. It's called Recommitting to Virginity. I read about it in a book. You and your partner recommit to being virgins and then you rebuild your relationship based on communication instead of sex. It's a growing trend."

"If you're going to read self-help books," Lavonne said, "you might want to try some Carl Jung."

"That's the stupidest thing I ever heard," Eadie said. "Recommitting to Virginity. Hell, if it were that easy I'd recommit to being twenty-two again. I'd recommit to having my nipples point skyward and my thighs be hard as rebar. Who writes this shit?"

Nita watched her warily in the rearview mirror. "Dr. Lucy Cloud."

Eadie snorted. "Dr. Lucy Cloud," she said. "That sounds like a made-up name to

470

me. I bet she's not even a real doctor. I bet she sent away for one of those Ph.D.s you can get over the Internet."

"So you and Jimmy Lee have been celibate since he got back from Kentucky?" Lavonne asked. Now that her own sex life was so prolific, she found it hard to imagine anyone going without. Now that she was dating Joe Solomon, it was easy to forget that she had spent eight years as chaste as a cloistered nun. Only instead of committing to Jesus, she had been committed to Peach Paradise and Rocky Road ice cream.

"Well," Nita said, appearing to consider this, "technically we're celibate."

"You mean *technically* as in Bill Clinton's use of the word? As in technically *I did not have sexual relations with that woman.*"

Nita giggled. "Something like that," she said.

"So what happened?"

Nita glanced at Lavonne and then back at the road. She giggled again. "Vodka," she said.

In the backseat, Eadie was still fuming about Dr. Lucy Cloud and her self-help book. "Recommitting to Virginity, my ass. That's just another way of trying to make women feel guilty about enjoying their sex lives. I thought we got rid of all that shit with the women's movement."

"Do y'all want to stop at the Cracker Barrel for lunch?" Nita said.

Eadie stared her down in the rearview mirror. "Quit changing the subject and get back to telling us what happened between you and Jimmy Lee last night."

Nita craned her neck, trying to see around a semi truck. "Y'all watch the signs and tell me when we get close to a Cracker Barrel."

Eadie said, "You heard me."

Lavonne kicked her shoes off and stuck her feet up on the dash. "So does this mean Jimmy Lee is moving back in?"

"No. I told him he can't move back in until after I get my kids back. As long as Charles thinks me and Jimmy Lee are separated, he'll help me with Virginia."

Lavonne stared at Nita. She shook her head slowly. "Let me see if I have this right," she said finally. "What you're saying is, you're shamelessly using your ex-husband to help you get back at your ex-mother-in-law. You're willing to use any trick necessary, no matter how dirty and underhanded, to get your child back?"

Nita slid her eyes over to Lavonne and then back to the road. "That's correct," she said.

A pickup truck swung around to pass

them. The driver honked and waved.

"All I've got to say," Eadie said, "is keep up the good work."

"Okay," Lavonne said, "now you're scaring me."

Nita shrugged. She glanced at the truck driver and then back at the road. "Sometimes I scare myself," she said.

After lunch, Lavonne drove for a while and Nita climbed into the backseat to take a nap. By three o'clock they had entered the foothills of the Appalachians. The afternoon sun was a deep yellow and rode just above the dark tree line to the west. Purple mountains rose in the distance, cloaked in fog. Eadie played with the radio, trying to find a station, but finally gave up and pushed in Mary Chapin Carpenter.

"Aren't you meeting Trevor this weekend?" Lavonne asked.

"In Chicago. We've got a suite booked at the Ritz Carlton."

"Do you guys come up for air or is it pretty much a three-day romp?"

"It's pretty much a three-day romp." Eadie didn't tell her how the last time, in L.A., they'd gotten into a huge fight. Trevor had yelled, "I can't live like this anymore!" and Eadie had gotten up and left in the middle of the night. She didn't tell how they hadn't spoken to each other for six days.

In the backseat, Nita snored softly. They topped a rise and came down into a long flat valley rimmed with mountains. Mary Chapin sang about passionate kisses.

"Just think," Eadie said, grinning. "You and Joe will have the house all to yourselves. You can play Hide the Lizard to your heart's content."

Lavonne focused her attention on a point on the distant horizon and tried not to blush. "Very funny," she said.

Eadie picked up a magazine and began to flip through it. "I really like him. Joe, I mean."

"Thanks. I like him, too."

Eadie fanned the magazine and dropped it in her lap. She yawned and then pulled the courtesy mirror down to check her reflection. "Is it serious?" she said to La-vonne, rubbing her finger over her front teeth to take off a lipstick stain. "You and Joe, I mean?"

Lavonne glanced at her blind spot and pulled into the passing lane. "We're not getting married anytime soon, if that's what you're asking." They passed an old barn with a "See Rock City" sign painted on the roof. A black-and-white cow stood in a pasture, watching the cars like a suicide waiting to jump. Lavonne wasn't even sure why she'd mentioned marriage, but now that she had, she felt a little embarrassed. Getting married to someone just because you were having sex with him wasn't always the answer. And it had taken her only twenty-one years of marriage to Leonard to learn this little tip. "How about you and Trevor? Is he still being patient?"

Eadie closed the courtesy mirror. She pulled one foot up under her with her knee stuck out at a right angle. She thought, *For all I know, my marriage might be over.* She said, "What choice does he have?"

"But don't you miss him? Don't you miss the physical closeness of seeing him every day?"

"You mean the sex? Don't I miss the sex?" Eadie glanced at her and grinned. "That's what the Love Monkey's for."

Nita's eyes fluttered open. She sat up, wiping the drool off her chin. "What's a Love Monkey?" she said.

Eadie tossed the magazine into the backseat. "Nothing a Recommitted Virgin needs to know about," she said.

Lorena Potter lived in East Ridge, Tennessee, a blue-collar suburb just north of the

Georgia state line. Nita called her to let her know they were on their way and to make sure they had the right directions to her house.

"I'm bringing two of my colleagues with me," Nita said.

"I'll get the coffee going," Lorena said.

She was a small spry woman in her late seventies. She greeted them at the front door of her tiny ranch house and led them back to the den, where she served them coffee and cookies on a silver tray. The house was like a sauna, but Lorena wore a sweater and rubbed her hands together to warm them. "Are y'all cold?" she asked.

"No," they answered simultaneously.

At the sliding glass door, Lorena's enraged terrier, Benjie, barked like a rusty weathervane spinning in the wind. "Don't mind him," Lorena said fondly. "He's really sweet. His bark is worse than his bite, if you know what I mean." On the other side of the glass, Benjie lifted his top lip and showed his teeth.

"Where's a good place to eat in Chattanooga?" Eadie asked, wondering if there was some other way Benjie might get into the house, wondering if there was a doggie door hidden somewhere in the kitchen Lorena might have forgotten to latch.

"Oh, any of those new restaurants down by the aquarium are good," Lorena said, stirring cream into her coffee. "They're expensive, but they're good. Chattanooga's come a long way since I was girl. It used to be just a railroad crossroads but now there's shopping malls and restaurants and the new aquarium and all those parks down by the river."

Nita was taking a folder out of her briefcase while Lorena talked. "It's grown a lot since the 1950s then?" she said.

"Oh, honey, yes. You wouldn't hardly recognize it now. It was just a sleepy little place back then."

Benjie scratched frantically at the glass door. Nita took a tape recorder, a notebook, and a pen out of her briefcase. "As you know, Mrs. Potter, I'm writing an article on unwed girls who got pregnant in the 1950s and had to give their babies up for adoption. We've agreed that anything you tell me today is confidential and you won't be named as a source in the article."

"That is correct," Lorena said formally, like she was being sworn in with her hand on the Bible.

They talked a while about the Brainerd Home for Unwed Mothers, how Lorena had started there as a young woman just out of nursing school and worked for a number of years until the place closed down in the early 1960s. "It was the birth control pill that did it," Lorena said, shaking her head. "Girls didn't get pregnant after that. At least not as many as used to."

Nita took out the photograph of Virginia and Charles as a baby and handed it to Lorena. "Mrs. Potter do you recognize this woman?"

On the other side of the glass, Benjie made a sound like a chipmunk trapped under a box. The elderly woman squinted her eyes and peered at the photograph. "I don't know," she said. "Maybe." She handed the photo back to Nita. "It was a long time ago. I probably nursed over a thousand girls in my time that came through the home for unwed mothers."

Lavonne glanced at Eadie. Lorena said, "Do y'all want some more coffee?"

"No, thank you, we're fine." Nita took out the photograph she had downloaded off the Internet and handed it to Lorena. "Mrs. Potter do you recognize this girl?" she asked.

"Which one?" Lorena took the photograph and stared down at the table of solemn girls. Nita pointed with her finger and Lorena brightened and said, "Oh, yes, Jennie."

"Jennie?" Nita said, trying to keep the

excitement out of her voice. She glanced at Eadie who raised an eyebrow and shrugged. Lavonne carefully studied Lorena's face.

"I'd never forget Jennie," Lorena said, rising. "She was a pistol." She left the room and came back in a few minutes carrying an old scrapbook. "She was what we used to call a 'white gloves girl,' " she said, sitting back down beside Nita on the sofa. "You know, the kind that seemed like she came from a good family. She kept to herself but she had real nice manners and talked like she might have come from some money. We didn't get many like Jennie, most of our girls were cotton mill hands or daughters of cotton mill hands, but every so often one would show up at the door." She laughed. "I guess even rich girls get tempted."

Lavonne leaned forward. "Where was Jennie from, Mrs. Potter?"

"Somewhere down in south Georgia. I know that because the family that took Jennie's baby was from down there, too. Of course, Jennie didn't know that. We never told any of the girls who got their babies back then. We just let them hold them once and then they were taken away and given to their new families."

No one said anything. Eadie leaned forward and picked up the photo of Virginia and Charles and the photo of the young women gathered around the table. "Mrs. Potter, do you think this might be Jennie?" Her movements seemed to set the dog off again.

"Benjie, hush," Lorena said. She compared the two photos and shook her head. "There is a resemblance," she said doubtfully.

"What family?" Lavonne said, and they all turned and looked at her. "What family from south Georgia took Jennie's baby?"

Lorena gave the photos back to Eadie and opened her scrapbook. "We didn't keep the mothers' full names but I kept the names of the people who took the babies. Unofficially, of course." She took out a piece of fragile typing paper and ran her finger down a long list of names. "Grantham," she said, finally. "Vienna, Georgia."

Nita leaned over her shoulder and stared at the opened scrapbook. She picked up a photograph and said, "Is this Jennie?"

Benjie was throwing himself at the glass now, his little claws clicking like castanets. "Yes," Lorena said. "I took that right after she got to the home. She was such a pretty little thing and had the nicest clothes. Always dressed like a movie star even up to the time right before she delivered."

Nita stared at the photograph. Her chin trembled. Slowly she passed it to Lavonne.

Lavonne said, "Oh my God."

Eadie said, "Oh shit."

Nita said, "Do you mind if I keep this photograph, Mrs. Potter?"

On the ride into Chattanooga, Nita called her mother. Lavonne was driving and Eadie was sitting in the front passenger seat, beating her hands on the dashboard and singing along to Mary Chapin Carpenter.

"Hey, Mama, it's me." Nita was shaking so badly she could hardly talk.

"Nita? Where are you?"

"I'm up in Chattanooga with Lavonne and Eadie."

"What in the hell are you doing up there?"

"It's a long story. I'll tell you when I get home."

"Y'all didn't go up there to hire a hit man did you?" Loretta said.

"Listen, do you know a family named Grantham?"

" 'Cause I told you I'd do it for free."

"From Vienna, Georgia. Do you know the Granthams?"

"Of course I do. I went to school with Pinky Grantham and Vera, too. She was a

481

Ledford before she married Pinky and her mother was a Hambright from over by —"

"And they had a daughter? The Granthams, I mean."

"Say, what's this all about? Does this have something to do with getting Whitney back?"

"Mama, just answer my questions! I'll tell you all about it when I get home."

"Sure," Loretta said. "Pinky and Vera had a daughter. An only child they adopted after Vera kept having miscarriages. They never had any other kids, which is a shame because they were both from big farming families and they are the nicest people you could ever meet."

"Do you know her?"

"Who?"

"Goddamn it, Mama. The daughter. Do you know the Grantham daughter?"

"Juanita Sue, you watch your language. Of course I know the Grantham daughter and you do too. Pearson."

Nita said stupidly, "Pearson?"

"That's her married name. You know who I'm talking about, I must be getting the Alzheimer's, I can't believe I've forgotten her first name. The newspaper woman. That was at your wedding."

Nita said, *"Grace?"*

"That's it," Loretta said. "Grace. Grace Pearson."

"The whole town's a goddamn Dickens novel," Eadie said later that night, on the ride home. The moon hung over the expressway like a golden Ferris wheel. The lights of faraway farmhouses twinkled in the darkness. "I mean, think about it. Virginia gets pregnant with Hampton Boone's child, goes up to Chattanooga to deliver it, and the baby gets adopted and winds up growing up fifteen miles from where Virginia lives now. Grace is Trevor's half-sister. She's Nita's ex-half-sister-in-law. She's my half-sister-in-law. I mean, goddamn. Trevor's wasting his time writing all those legal thrillers. He should be writing about his dysfunctional family and their sad heritage in this crossbred little backwoods place that is Ithaca, Georgia."

Nita was still in shock. Not about Virginia having an out-of-wedlock baby, but the fact that the baby was Grace Pearson. "Do you think Grace knows? I mean, she must know she's adopted, if my mother knows, everybody knows, but do you think she knows about Virginia?"

"No way," Eadie said. "Have you seen the way those two look at each other? The last time they ran into each other, I thought we were fixing to have a catfight right there in the middle of Nita's wedding reception."

Nita laughed quietly. "I can't wait to see Virginia's face when she finds out the woman who wrote all those articles exposing Judge Broadwell is her daughter. Her own flesh and blood. I can't wait to see her face when she realizes her own long-lost daughter is this year's Kudzu Queen."

Lavonne was quiet, studying the road in the headlights. She was sitting in the passenger seat beside Nita. "Who do you think it'll upset more, Grace or Virginia?"

"I'll tell you who it *won't* upset," Eadie said, "and that's Trevor Boone. He's always loved Grace."

Nita gripped the steering wheel. She shook her head slowly. "We can't tell Trevor unless we tell Grace." She looked at Lavonne. "Can we?"

Eadie said, "Look, y'all, I like Grace too much to tell her that Virginia's her birth mother."

"That's the kind of news that might make someone suicidal," Lavonne said.

Eadie said, "Let's don't tell Grace. If Virginia wants to tell her, fine. If Trevor wants to tell her, fine. But I don't want to be the one to ruin Grace's life by telling her that her birth mother is actually Virginia Redmon."

Lavonne watched the moon through the trees. Van Morrison sang softly on the radio. "Now that that's settled, how are we going to tell Virginia?"

"I've been thinking about that," Nita said. "Charles told me his mother is having a big pre-Thanksgiving dinner party and, get this, *Gracious Southern Living* is coming to televise the whole affair for their 'Holidays in the South' program."

"Oh my God," Eadie said. "Virginia must be in heaven."

Lavonne stopped looking at the moon. She turned slightly with her back to the door. "But how does that help us?" she said.

Nita's face was lit by the dim light from the dashboard. "I'm thinking that would be a perfect time to spring the news about Virginia's past. I'm thinking that might be the perfect time to bargain for my child's release. If we threaten to go public, she's sure to drop the custody suit. Especially in front of all those TV cameras."

"What are you suggesting?" Eadie said, warming to the idea. "That we crash the party?"

"Charles invited me," Nita said. "But that shouldn't stop y'all from crashing if you want to."

Lavonne thought about it for a moment, and then she said, "Of course the other, less dramatic thing we could do is just call Virginia on the phone and tell her the jig is up. It might be more effective if we threaten her in private."

Nita and Eadie looked at each other in the rearview mirror. "Naw," they both said simultaneously.

"There's something about crashing a *Gracious Southern Living* television event that appeals to me," Eadie said. "I like the potential drama of the situation. Virginia will be on her best behavior in front of the cameras. The hostage family will be gathered together in a false gesture of togetherness and communion. The guests will be dressed in their most extravagant finery trying to prove to the viewing audience that they're not a bunch of redneck losers. There's a certain train-wreck quality to the scene that I find appealing."

"Besides," Nita said, "if we give her a private warning, I'm afraid Virginia will figure out some way to turn this situation to her advantage."

Lavonne said, "That's settled then." She said to Eadie, "What're you going to wear?"

Nita adjusted the rearview mirror.

"Charles said we're all supposed to wear dark sedate colors. Nothing too showy or over the top."

"Isn't that just like Virginia to give everyone a dress code." Eadie sat up suddenly and leaned into the space between the two front seats. She put her hands on each of their shoulders. "I'm thinking my Kudzu Ball gown might be just the thing," she said. "I'll bet *Gracious Southern Living's* never done a spread with real Kudzu Debutantes in attendance." Her teeth gleamed in the darkness. "I'm thinking Aneeda Mann and Ima Badass might be just the thing to liven up Thanksgiving dinner at the Redmon house." She pumped Lavonne on the shoulder. "What do you think, Ima?"

"I'll dust off my tiara," Lavonne said.

CHAPTER
TWENTY-TWO

Eadie hadn't meant to fight with Trevor when she called him to tell him about Grace Pearson. She'd meant to surprise him. She'd expected to find him excited and eager to learn he had a long-lost sister. She'd expected them to share a good laugh together about the unpredictability of life, in general, and the irony of fate, in particular. What she hadn't expected was to call his cell phone and then his hotel room, repeatedly, over a six-hour period and get no answer. What she hadn't expected was the blind rage that welled up inside her around three o'clock in the morning when she realized that her husband wasn't where he was supposed to be.

He was supposed to be on a solitary book tour through the Midwest. He was supposed to be in a lonely hotel room in Dubuque, Iowa. She left a message with the front desk of the Hyatt Regency.

"Tell him his wife called. Tell him his wife says he's an asshole. Did you get that? Yes, asshole. Okay good." Eadie hung up and tried, unsuccessfully, to get some sleep. She lay awake watching the clock as it ticked steadily toward dawn, imagining Trevor drinking in a bar with a gorgeous young blonde, Trevor wrapped in the arms of a leggy brunette, Trevor rolling around in the sheets with a buxom redhead. Somewhere around five-thirty Eadie fell asleep and dreamed of Trevor having sex with her mother. Every time they climaxed, Reba would shout *Order up!,* and she would lean over and slap her palm against the top of a strange-looking alarm clock that rang like the starting bell at Pimlico. This went on incessantly until the ringing sound in Eadie's head felt like an electrical current vibrating against her skull.

She awoke to the sound of her cell phone vibrating against the hardwood floor. It was clear across the room where she had thrown it last night after talking to the lonely desk clerk in Dubuque. Eadie clicked on the phone and said, "Of course I'll marry you, Richard. I'll tell my deadbeat husband about us tonight."

Trevor said, "Very funny. Now listen, Eadie, before you get all bent out of shape

489

about last night . . ."

Eadie hung up, turned off the phone, and went back to sleep.

Two hours later, Lavonne stuck her head in the door. "Eadie, wake up. And talk to your husband. He's called about twenty times on my house phone and he's threatening to get on a plane and come down here if you don't talk to him. I'm meeting Joe at the park and I'm not going to be here to take messages, so for Christsake get your ass out of bed and talk to the man."

Eadie got up and made herself a pot of coffee. The phone rang twice while she was in the kitchen, and she went over to check the caller ID. It was Trevor. She called him back about thirty minutes later.

"Goddamn it, Eadie, I'm getting real sick of the drama." He sounded like he had a cold. "My plane got delayed in Phoenix and then I missed my flight in Denver so I spent the night at the airport."

"Why didn't you call?"

"There's something wrong with my goddamned cell phone. The battery keeps dying on me."

"Well, it sounds like you have an excuse for everything. It sounds like your alibis are airtight."

Trevor sighed. "Don't do this, Eadie," he said.

"I called because I had something to tell you," she said. "Something I thought you might find interesting." She told him about Virginia and Grace Pearson. When she finished, he was quiet. She could hear him breathing, slow and heavy.

"That is unbelievable," he said finally. "I guess I'd have to see a DNA test to believe it completely, but that is fucking unbelievable. Grace Pearson is my half-sister. No wonder I always liked her."

"You both laugh the same," Eadie said. "You have the same laugh."

"And I guess that would make my father a lying, cheating scoundrel. Or at least it would make him an unprincipled Don Juan."

"The apple doesn't fall far from the tree."

"Oh, come on, Eadie," he said. "I'm happy. Try not to ruin my happiness."

"I'm your wife. That's my job." She thought of the first time he cheated on her, with that waitress out at the Thirsty Dog. She remembered how she had felt, seeing them together, like someone had driven a spike through her chest. And years later, when he left her for Tonya, his legal secretary, she had covered her pain and despair with anger and alcohol. And Denton Swafford, her personal trainer.

"I can't wait to see you in Chicago," he said.

She didn't want to see him. She realized this suddenly. Her anger went beyond a missed plane flight to Dubuque, it went deeper than his earlier infidelities. It was something more painful and infinitely more humiliating than all of that.

"I can't make Chicago," she said. "Something's come up."

She could hear him breathing. His voice, when he finally spoke, had a hard metallic ring. "Don't do this, Eadie," he said.

"I'm glad about Grace. I'm glad you have a sister. A family."

"You're my family. I need to see you. I'm tired of living like this."

She was alone. Her mother was dead, her father was gone, and for all Eadie knew she didn't share a single blood tie with any other human being on the planet. It was a desolate feeling, realizing this for the first time.

"I've been lonely my whole life," she said.

"I know, baby."

"Everyone I've ever loved, let me down. Even you."

"I know. I'm sorry. I love you."

"Talk is cheap. Words don't mean a thing."

"Forgive me, Eadie."

"I'm trying," she said, and hung up.

Later, she took her sketchbook and went down to the creek bank behind the Shangri-La Trailer Park and sat where she used to sit as a child, dreaming of a life better than this one. She sat quietly beneath the slim sheltering branches of a willow tree, sketching, filling page after page. Thunder rumbled in the distance. The sky darkened. A breeze, heavy with the scent of fish and fermenting apples, blew across the creek. Her drawings looked like something out of a nightmare. She drew a succubus sitting on the chest of a dreaming woman. She drew a mermaid becoming a tree, becoming a butterfly. She drew a whale with a harpoon quivering in its flesh and she thought suddenly of Frank Plumlee exposing himself to her in the darkened kitchen all those years ago. She remembered how she had tried to tell her mother but all Reba did was look around wildly and say in a panicked voice, *What are you saying, Eadie? What are you saying?* when Eadie thought it was pretty clear what she was saying and any mother worth her salt would have known, too. She thought of all the times in her life when people had been willing to think the worst

493

of her, just because she grew up without a father in a trailer on the wrong side of town. She thought of all the ways they had misunderstood her rebellious nature, not understanding it was the only way she had of protecting herself. She remembered how Principal Sully had looked at her that day in his office after the home ec fire when Lee Anne Bales had blamed her and cried like a baby and Eadie, too proud to explain it had been an accident, stared fixedly at the wall just beyond his shoulder.

The rain came suddenly, splattering the dense canopy above her. It drummed against the hard-packed ground but could not reach her beneath the sheltering willow. Thunder rattled the sky. Lightning flashed. A blustery wind blew from the east, swaying the trees. Gradually the rain subsided to a gentle drumming, and then stopped.

After a while Eadie began to cry, softly at first, so softly she wasn't even aware she was doing it until the tears began to flow down her cheeks and wet the pages of her sketchbook. And then loud sobs that came from somewhere deep inside herself, heavy sobs that splintered her chest the way lightning had splintered the sky. She cried for the time she missed the bus after kindergarten and waited for three hours outside the school for her mother, who never came. She cried for the time she overheard Worland Peet telling a group of girls that Eadie Wilkens's mother was trash and her daddy was a drunk who left home before Eadie was even born and might not be her daddy anyway. And she cried for her mother, too, for the loneliness and longing that had permeated their sad lives like a bad smell they could not wash away no matter how hard they tried.

Eadie held herself and cried. She cried until her throat felt grainy and her heart felt sore and swollen in her chest.

Later, she rose and walked around the place where their trailer had once stood. The sun peeped from behind a line of ragged clouds like a shy child. A mockingbird sang in the top of a walnut tree, its song sweet and tender as a lullaby. Eadie sat on the stump of a fallen cottonwood rocking herself back and forth. After a while she opened the sketchbook on her lap. She felt weightless. Drained. She sat for a while and sketched until the sun dropped below the tops of the pines and the air turned cool and it was too dark to see.

When she got home, she showed Lavonne her sketches.

"Hey, those look like mandalas," Lavonne

495

said, pointing to the pages she had finished last. "Are those mandalas?"

"Yes," Eadie said, and hugged her. "They are."

Lavonne hugged her back, patting her with the palm of her hand. "I love you, Eadie."

Eadie didn't have blood sisters but she had Lavonne and Nita, and that was good enough. "I love you, too," she said.

"Everything's going to be all right."

"I know."

Lavonne let go of her and stepped back. "I thought I'd make fettuccine for supper."

"That sounds good." Eadie closed up her sketchbook. She felt different. She felt like a woman without a past, only a future. Anything was possible. She might even have a child. It wasn't so far-fetched now. Somehow she could imagine her and Trevor counting out change and holding a little one's hand on the way to the St. Charles streetcar, or tucking a blanket around a small sleepy face.

"Why don't you go pour us a couple of glasses of red wine and then you can make a salad while I fix supper."

Eadie smiled, sliding her sketchbook into her bag. "I will in a minute," she said. "But first, I have to call my husband."

■ ■ ■ ■

It took him two days to call her back and that's how she knew how pissed off he was. She left him two messages. When he finally called, he sounded angry and distrustful.

"You make it hard to love you, Eadie," he said.

"The greater the hardship, the greater the reward." What else could she say? He was right.

"That sounds like a promise. Are you promising me something?"

She went into the bedroom and closed the door. "I'm promising you a new beginning."

He was quiet. He said, "Just like that." He said, "What made you change your mind?"

She told him everything. She told him about Luther Birdsong and Frank Plumlee. She told him about Reba and her lost childhood. And finally she told him about her breakdown in the Shangri-La Trailer Park, how she had confronted the old ghosts and demons and wept herself clean of the regret and despair of forty years of living. She described to him the spirit of forgiveness that had flowed through her like clear, sweet music. When she finished, he was quiet.

Finally he said, "You could have told me.

You could have told me about your step-fathers. You could have told me about your shitty childhood. I wouldn't have judged you. I wouldn't have blamed you."

"I know," she said simply. "But you have to understand, Trevor. A lot of this stuff just came up. I'm not even sure where it came from. And just so you know," she said. "I don't blame you, either. I don't blame you for my sleeping all day, or the Mondo Logs, or my not being able to work."

"Well, I appreciate that, honey."

"Whatever was wrong with me had nothing to do with our past. Yours and mine. Well," she said, frowning. "Maybe a little bit. But mostly it had to do with my childhood. With forgiving my mother. It had to do with setting my shadow free, with embracing my anima."

"You never mentioned therapy." Trevor sounded surprised. "When did you start?"

"About six months ago."

"Dr. Jordan?"

"No, Dr. Zibolsky."

He got quiet again. Eadie laid on her back on the narrow bed and looked at the ceiling. "I can live with that," he said, finally. "I can live with the fact that you've spilled your guts about our marriage to Lavonne. If it makes you feel better. I can live with anything you've done if it makes you feel better about yourself."

She knew then that she still loved him.

"I've been thinking about what you said the other night." He took his time, picking his words carefully. "I want us to be a family, Eadie. I want it to work, I really do. But if it's going to work, you have to forgive me. You have to forget about the waitress at the Thirsty Dog —"

"Lucy," Eadie said.

"You have to forget about Lucy and Tonya, and I have to forget about the bartender and the goddamn personal trainer."

"Bobby," she said. "And Denton." She put her knees up and set one foot across the opposite knee, resting it at right angles. She could hear Lavonne in the kitchen, banging pots and pans around.

"Right," he said, evenly. "Bobby and Denton." He coughed and cleared his throat. "We have to forget all that shit that happened before. What's past is past, and we have to move on from here."

"That's what I want, too."

"Will you come home?"

"Will you stop going off and leaving me alone?"

"Yes," he said.

"Then I'll come home. But first I have to do something for Nita. And then I have to finish what I started down here, I have to get my pieces ready for my show. But then I'll be home."

"Before Christmas?"

"I think so."

"I can't wait until then. I can't wait to see you."

"Just so you know," she said. "It wasn't about the infidelities. It was about the pain. I've pretended my whole life that people can't hurt me, but they can."

"I know that, honey," he said. "I know."

CHAPTER
TWENTY-THREE

From the beginning, things went badly. Despite Virginia's well-laid plans, the *Gracious Southern Living* crew arrived early to shoot the pre-Thanksgiving dinner and had to be entertained by Redmon in the living room while Virginia hurriedly dressed. By the time she got downstairs, Redmon had broken into his hidden stash of Jack Daniel's and, despite Virginia's earlier repeated admonitions to "keep sober and keep quiet," had begun to entertain them with tales of his wretched childhood spent in the snake-handling hills of Alabama. Several of the crew hauled in TV cameras and lights while others sat around the room, politely watching Redmon. One of them, a nice-looking young man with a ponytail, held a tumbler of whiskey in one hand and appeared to be taking notes with the other. Virginia shuddered and hurried into the room, greeting everyone effusively. The young man, a direc-

501

tor of photography named Porter, stood up and shook her hand. She shot Redmon a warning glance, but he ignored her, settling himself down on the sofa beside Porter. The Lifestyle producer, a heavyset young woman named Carlin, and her assistant, Rose, shook hands briskly with Virginia.

"Oh my, this looks so *professional*," Virginia said, feigning an interest in their gear.

"Do you mind if we go ahead and set up in the dining room?" Carlin had a masculine haircut and a brusque, efficient manner that left Virginia feeling a little uncertain of herself.

"Of course," she stammered. She showed Carlin and Rose into the dining room, leaving Porter behind with Redmon. He was a film school graduate with dreams of Oscar glory. The *Gracious Southern Living* gig was only temporary. After ten minutes with Redmon, he was envisioning a documentary on snake handlers and faith healers in the rural South.

In the dining room, Carlin snapped her fingers and said loudly, "Come on, Porter, get a move on. We need to get set up."

"The buffet looks nice," Rose said shyly and Virginia blushed with pleasure and said, "Why thank you. The silver service came from my great-grandmother on my father's side — is it okay if I mention that in the interview? — and the silver serving pieces on the sideboard . . ."

"Porter!" Carlin barked, interrupting her, and Virginia fell silent. Porter downed his drink and stood up with his equipment bag banging against his hip. He took out a light meter and began to take several readings around the room. "Listen, there won't be any interview," Carlin said to Virginia. "This is supposed to be natural, not staged, just as if we'd dropped in on a dinner party. Everyone needs to act natural and don't stare at the camera. We'll add any details we want mentioned later in the voice-over. All you have to do is eat and act natural. How many guests are you expecting?"

"It's a small group," Virginia murmured. "Maybe fifty or sixty." She didn't tell Carlin how an invitation to the buffet had become the hottest ticket in town. Really, it was disgusting the way so many of Ithaca's finer citizens would practically prostitute themselves just to get a chance to show up on regional television. Still, it had been fun culling the wanted from the unwanted. Mrs. Astor, putting together the New York 400 couldn't have enjoyed herself more than Virginia, putting together her final guest list.

"Excuse me," she said, "I'll just go check

on the turkey." Virginia walked into the kitchen expecting to find Della scurrying about. Instead, the black woman sat at the kitchen table reading a newspaper with her slippered feet propped on a chair. Her starched uniform hung on the pantry door.

"My God, why aren't you dressed?" Virginia said, trying to keep her voice down.

Della lowered the paper and looked at her. Her lower jaw jutted like a battering ram. "I am dressed," she said.

"In the uniform, in the uniform," Virginia hissed, pointing at the pantry door. She stamped her high-heeled shoe against the hardwood floor as quietly as she could.

Della slowly creased the newspaper and laid it down on the table. She crossed her arms over her chest. "I ain't wearing no uniform," she said sullenly.

Virginia said in a stage whisper, "What do you mean you aren't wearing the uniform? I paid you to wear the uniform. You have to wear the uniform."

Della shook her head slowly. "You didn't pay me enough," she said.

It took Virginia a minute to catch on. When she finally did, it felt like a blood vessel had burst in her head and was slowly thumping the side of her skull like a convulsive water hose. "How much?" she said finally, between clenched teeth.

"One large," Della said. She was addicted to *The Sopranos.* Everything she'd learned about extortion and bargaining, she'd learned watching Tony Soprano do business with the New Jersey mob. She figured that was good practice for dealing with Virginia.

"One large what?" Virginia said.

"One thousand dollars."

"One thousand dollars?" Virginia said, her voice squeaking with the strain. "You must be crazy. You must be insane."

"Cash," Della said.

In the dining room, Carlin said, "Porter, set up over here where we can get a shot of the buffet before everyone gets here." Virginia and Della faced each other across the large kitchen. Virginia's steadily rising blood pressure flooded her face like a geyser. The turkey, a twenty-pound organic bird flown in from someplace where they let birds roam wild before killing them humanely, sputtered in the oven, wafting its delicious aroma. Dishes of corn bread dressing, squash casserole, and sweet potato soufflé rested on the stove, covered in aluminum foil. A spiral-cut ham sat on a silver serving platter and another one waited in the warming oven.

Virginia hissed, "That's highway robbery!"

Della shrugged. "Reparations," she said.

Giving in to the inevitable, Virginia nodded curtly. Della, understanding they had a deal, rose ponderously and went back to work. Virginia spun around on her heels and stalked into the living room. She stopped on the threshold, staring in openmouthed amazement at her grandson, who had steadfastly refused his grandmother's bribe of fifteen hundred dollars to spend the weekend at the beach. Instead he was here, dressed in an ill-fitting navy blue suit he'd picked up at the Baptist Bible Thrift Store, and a pair of red Converse high-tops. Obedient to his grandmother's order "to do something about your purple hair," he had shaved his head. And to make matters worse, there appeared to be a tattoo on his scalp, something that looked unsettlingly like the number 666. He saw Virginia and waved.

"Hey, Grandma," he said.

Behind her, Carlin came into the room, followed by Rose and Porter. "Oh hello," Carlin said, giving her hand to Logan.

"Hello," Logan said. He stood there staring at his grandmother, daring her to say something. Virginia clicked her mouth shut with a sound like a bullet being loaded into a chamber.

"Who are you?" Carlin asked.

Logan grinned. "I'm the grandson."

She pointed at his feet. "Cool shoes."

"Thanks." He nodded at the French doors. "Okay if me and my band set up on the deck? We've written a song to perform for the occasion."

Virginia thought, *Over my dead body!* She said, "Oh no, darling, I don't think we'll have time for any live performances. Maybe some other time."

"Sure," Carlin said. "Live music would be great. Talk to Eddie over there. He's our sound guy."

Virginia stood there trying to imagine what her life would be like once the *Gracious Southern Living* segment aired. She imagined cocktail parties, and bridge groups, and bunco groups giggling behind their fingers. She saw in her mind's eye televised images of her ruddy-faced, intoxicated husband; images of her bald grandson, marked with the sign of the Beast, in his thrift store suit and red tennis shoes. She imagined her surly maid, who watched too many mafia TV shows, parading into the scene carrying a steaming turkey on a tray.

As if to authenticate this vision, Della did appear suddenly in the living room carrying a small silver tray of stuffed mushroom caps.

She had hastily put on the maid's uniform, with the result being that the buttons were done up wrong and the cap rested at a jaunty angle on her thick hair.

"Oh, Della, you've brought the hors d'oeuvres," Virginia said brightly, trying to hide her dismay.

"Oh, yas'm, yas'm I done brought the appurtizers just like you done ordered me to." Della dipped her head and lifted one shoulder, walking with an exaggerated limp. She was laying it on thick. The result was an uncomfortable silence that seemed to billow through the room like smoke. The three producers, all of whom had attended various Southern prep schools, exchanged horrified glances. Across the room, Redmon and Logan snorted and snickered behind their hands.

Virginia took the tray from the wincing Della and served the camera crew herself. Della humped and limped her way out of the room.

"Mrs. Redmon, we can't have an African American woman dressed in a maid's uniform," Carlin said in horror. "This is the new South. My executive producer would fire me on the spot if I taped something like that. And even if we taped it, the editors would edit it out anyway."

"Fine!" Virginia said. She set the tray down on the coffee table and followed Della into the kitchen. "Change your clothes," Virginia said shortly. The thumping in her head had taken on the high-pitched whine of a dental drill at full speed.

Della eyed her suspiciously. "I still get the price we agreed on," she said, humping her shoulders like a linebacker. "The price you agreed to pay me to wear that raggedy-ass uniform. Or I quit."

Virginia clenched her teeth to keep them from chattering. She couldn't very well walk around the room carrying a tray herself, at least not on camera. "Oh all right," she said finally. Satisfied, Della went off to find something to wear. Virginia stood for a few moments trying to compose herself. The whining in her head gradually subsided until it was more like the hum of wild bees clustered around a sunflower. She listened to the frenetic activity going on in her living room and dining room. She rearranged her face into a pleasant expression and then wandered back into the living room in time to catch Redmon pouring himself and Porter another stiff drink from a bottle of Jack Daniel's he had obviously hidden behind the new flat-screen TV. She gave him "the look," which normally would have stopped him dead in his tracks. But today, of all days, Redmon seemed to have achieved intentional blindness through a sheer act of will and stamina.

"Speaking of editing," Virginia said to Carlin. "How exactly does that work?"

Carlin popped one of the mushroom caps into her mouth. She chewed for a moment with her finger up in front of her face. "Well, we'll tape the entire party. However long it lasts, probably two hours or more, but then the editors will edit it down to a thirty-minute segment that we'll run during our holiday show."

"And will I have a chance to help with that?" Virginia said sweetly. "The editing, I mean."

The producer laughed and shook her head. "Oh no," she said. "That's their job. You signed a release when we booked you, allowing them to edit it any way they see fit."

"I see." Virginia smiled bleakly. She went to the bar and poured herself a glass of wine. Across the room, several of the crew laughed loudly at something Redmon had said. He gestured wildly, spilling his drink on the new Oriental rug. Della crossed the room wearing a garish red-flowered print dress and red pumps. Outside on the deck,

Logan and his juvenile delinquent band-mates cheerfully set up their massive equipment. Despite her best-laid plans, this whole party was definitely beginning to feel like a runaway horse. Virginia was on board, sawing desperately on the bit, but despite her best efforts the deranged horse was galloping recklessly and relentlessly toward the hedgerow.

An hour later, most of the guests had arrived and had been instructed by Carlin to ignore the cameras and just act as if they were at any other normal party. They stood stiffly in small groups scattered around the large living room, clutching glasses of wine and trying to keep their best profiles presented at all times to the wandering cameramen. Virginia had invited the brightest and most attractive people she could think of, with special preference going to those she thought would look best on camera. She had invited some of the dusty old aristocracy, too, although they had mostly declined her invitation. Which was a good thing, Virginia decided, as they were the ones most likely to dress down and drink too much, the ones who inevitably tried to monopolize the conversation, standing in the middle of the room, regaling the crowd in their Plantation South accents so that no one could get a word in edgewise. It was bad enough she'd had to invite that old bore, Judge Drucker, and his equally boring, twittering wife, Eulonia. There was, of course, a method to her madness. She had thought it best to show the judge, firsthand, the advantages Whitney had living in the privileged bosom of Virginia's family. Although now, given Redmon's obvious inebriated state and her grandson's crafty expression (she knew he had something dirty up his sleeve, hadn't she seen that expression a million times on her dead husband's face), she wondered if inviting Judge Drucker might have been a mistake.

Virginia began to feel better once Whitney appeared. The girl, dressed in a Nicole Miller knockoff they'd found in a little boutique in Palm Beach, was stunning. Virginia could see from the special attention the camera crew gave her that most of the scenes would feature Whitney. Virginia relaxed a bit. *This might turn out well after all,* she thought. And then, just when she had begun to feel that things were indeed looking up, Charles arrived with Nita in tow.

She was dressed in a tasteful blue suit. Looking at the pretty, demure woman, Virginia had to wonder just what it was about Nita that had made her dislike her all those years she was married to Charles. Surely her own daughter would look much like Nita did now, and it amazed Virginia that she had never considered this before, that she had never actually thought of Nita as a daughter until this very moment, when it was too late.

Because it was too late. Virginia could see this, even if Charles couldn't. Even if he was still so besotted with his ex-wife that he would do anything to win her back, even if it meant going up against his own mother to do it.

Well, poor Charles. He would learn his lesson the hard way. Virginia leaned toward her crafty ex-daughter-in-law and said, "Nita, bless your heart, how wonderful to see you." She kissed her lightly and insincerely on the cheek. Nita stared at her and said nothing.

Logan saw his mother and came over and hugged her. "How's my boy?" Nita said, standing on tiptoe to kiss him. Whitney moved up behind her shoulder.

"Hello, Mommy," Whitney said. Her mother looked so small and pretty that for a moment Whitney felt a trembling homesickness in the pit of her stomach. But as she leaned to hug Nita she remembered that

Virginia had promised her a new BMW and a shopping trip to Paris, and when she stepped away from Nita, her eyes were dry.

Nita smiled and touched her lightly on the cheek. Carlin, who had watched the family greet each other, and had assumed Nita to be Charles's second wife, was confused. "Excuse me," she said, extending her hand to Nita. "I'm Carlin Benwood. Are you the children's mother?"

"Yes," Nita said firmly. "I am."

Carlin frowned. "But they live with their grandmother?"

Virginia, who was old-school Southern down to the last molecule of her being, stepped forward. She would rather be drawn and quartered than air the family dirty linen in front of strangers. Especially strangers with a camera. "The children are just staying with me," she said brightly, "just a vacation, of sorts. While Nita finishes up some unfinished business."

Nita stared at Virginia as if contemplating a pistol-whipping. She said, "I'm working on an article on domestics working in the South prior to the civil rights movement."

"Oh," Carlin said.

"You'd be amazed at the secrets you can learn," Nita said, staring deliberately at Virginia, "listening to these women talk about the families they worked for. Troubled marriages, love affairs gone bad, babies born out of wedlock, it's all there."

Virginia forced a stiff smile and said to Carlin, "Oh, you can't trust half of what you hear. People make up all kinds of stories to relieve the boredom of these small towns. My goodness, if only half of it were true, Ithaca would be worse than Babylon!"

"I could write a book," Nita said. "I could tell a story no one would believe."

"Yes, I daresay you could," Virginia snapped.

Charles glanced uncomfortably from Nita to his mother. Porter, sensing a rising tension between the two women, quickly swung his camera from one face to the other. He had already forgotten the documentary on snake handlers and was envisioning a reality TV show involving a dysfunctional modern family and their symbolic American holidays. *Dinner at Casa Redmon.*

"Does he have to point that camera at me like that?" Virginia said sharply.

"What are you afraid he'll see?" Nita said.

"Y'all just try to act normal," Carlin said, and then blushed fiercely. "I mean, just pretend we're not even here. Just continue on as you normally would, as if you didn't have a room full of strangers documenting your every move." Even she realized she was treading dangerous waters. "I'll just check with Della in the kitchen," she finished lamely.

Across the room, Duckie Bradshaw and her husband, Harris, had arrived fashionably late. Virginia, glad for a distraction, turned her back on Nita and said, "Yoohoo, Duckie! Hello!" She was this year's president of the Junior League, so Virginia couldn't just not invite her. Virginia hadn't spoken to her since Duckie had the brilliant idea of holding a League luncheon out at the new Ithaca Zoo Monkey Annex that the League had helped fund through one of its community outreach programs. Duckie had stood up there in her Prada suit and Fendi pumps and droned on and on about the "darling monkeys" and their new "darling habitats" while in the cage behind her, Bobo the Chimp slowly masturbated. *And don't tell me that monkey didn't know exactly what he was doing,* Virginia thought savagely, remembering his crafty expression and obvious delight at the shocked faces and nervous gigglings of the all-female audience. She hadn't been able to think of dumb animals in the same way since.

Behind her, Celia Banks let out a little cry

of alarm. "Oh my God, who is *that?*" she said.

Virginia swung around. Nita and Charles had moved off to get a drink. Virginia followed Celia's horrified stare to the deck where Logan stood tuning a guitar strapped to his chest. "My grandson," Virginia said. "And some of his bandmates." She noted, with dismay, that some idiot had opened the French doors so they would be able to hear the music clearly.

"Oh," Celia said, lifting her artificially sculpted little nose. "*Public* school boys."

Virginia held her smile, aware that the cameras were rolling. Really, who did the woman think she was? Her father had driven a delivery truck, for goodness sakes. Until she married Franklin Banks, Celia had been poor as a lizard-eating cat.

"And how is your father?" Virginia said pleasantly. "Still driving his route between Oak Grove and Valdosta?"

"Excuse me," Celia said. "I think I see Lee Anne. Lovely party."

Logan stepped up to the mike. He lifted his head and looked out over the crowd until he spotted Virginia. "Hey, Grandma," he said, waving. Everyone giggled. Virginia forced a smile. "This song's for you," he said, opening his arms wide to include his band members. "It's called 'Colla' Poppa'.' "

" 'Colla' Poppa'?' " Virginia said to Whitney. "What's that? It sounds like a flower," she said, hoping against hope that it might be some kind of a soft ballad, a love song perhaps, or maybe a bluegrass number.

Whitney looked at her like she was stupid. "Collar Popper," she said, pointing to her neck. "You know. Like those poseurs who walk around in Polo shirts with the collar popped up in the back and a sweater tied around their shoulders. There's a lot of them at my school." Her voice carried loudly over the quiet room.

Virginia smiled and looked around nervously at her guests, many of whom had children and grandchildren at the Barron Hall school. "Whitney, dear," she said. "Go and find your grandfather and ask him to see if the band can't play *after* we eat dinner. Or maybe later in the evening. Much later."

Just then, a red-faced Redmon lifted his glass above the crowd and shouted, "Hey, Queenie, wait till you hear this song. It's awesome."

Logan said *"One-two-three-four"* and the band was off, a sudden, raucous, three-chord wall of sound that would have made the Sex Pistols proud, that would have made Johnny Rotten stumble around the stage and projectile vomit for joy.

> Hey, Colla' Poppa', where'd you get that shirt?
> Your front's tucked in, but your buttons don't work.
> Hey Colla' Poppa' those teeth are gold,
> Bleach them yourself, or is that how they're sold?
>
> You hang around town in you pink Po-los,
> Axe Bodyspray burning up my nose,
> Talking about shit that you don't know,
> If you're at the bar in sandals then I'm stepping
> On your toes!
>
> Hey Colla' Poppa' —
> Driving daddy's car,
> Drinking in a college bar,
> Think that you're so cool?
> You're a fucking tool!

"Oh my God," Virginia said. The whole scene was like a nightmare, one of those where you know you're dreaming but can't wake up.

Hey, Colla' Poppa' who's that chick you're
    with?
I think I know her, let me give her a kiss.
Hey, Colla' Poppa' don't you have no fear,
I already fucked that slut last year!

High on coke, you're up all night,
Can't get laid so you look for a fight,
Head on home and pummel the pipe,
Your only true friend is Xbox Live!

Hey Colla' Poppa' —
Daddy get you a job?
You act like a snob.
Daddy turned you away?
When he found out that you're gay!

"Dinner is served," Virginia shouted helplessly, trying to make herself heard above
the wailing guitars and foot-thumping base.
She turned to her guests who clustered like
stalagmites at the edge of her Oriental rug,
their faces frozen into various expressions
of horror, outrage, and suppressed mirth.

Hey Colla' Poppa'! Hey Colla' Poppa'! Hey
    Colla' Poppa'!
Oy! Oy! Oy! Oy!

"You know," Carlin shouted beside her,
"they have kind of a Beastie Boys thing go-

ing on." She and several of the television crew were dancing around with their hands in the air, their fingers curled into some kind of cryptic gang symbol, not the kind of thing they would have learned in prep school, at least not in Virginia's day. The cameras, she noted dismally, were rolling.

The music stopped suddenly on a three-chord riff. Lee Anne Bales dropped her glass. No one moved. The silence was almost as deafening as the noise had been.

"Reaganomics!" one of the boys shouted.

"Socialism!" another one said.

"Hey, do y'all know 'Blue Suede Shoes'?" Redmon said. "Or how about 'Up Against the Wall Redneck Mother'?"

"Dinner is served," Virginia said brightly, opening her arms wide and attempting to herd her stunned guests into the dining room, the way Jesus might have done that evening at Mount Zion, the night he was betrayed by Judas Iscariot and his band of wine-guzzling, backstabbing dinner guests.

Once she saw that her own guests had begun to recover from "Colla' Poppa' " and were lined up obediently at the sideboard buffet, Virginia followed Carlin into the kitchen. She was afraid to leave her alone in a room with Della. There was no telling what the black woman might say or do if she wasn't watched carefully. The stress of the situation was beginning to wear on Virginia. Her stomach ached and she could feel a familiar thumping against the top of her skull, as if something was trapped inside the brain-pan and was trying desperately to get out.

Carlin leaned against one of the granite countertops, her legs crossed at the ankle. "Everything smells so good in here," she said to Della. The black woman grinned but then, seeing Virginia enter the room, the grin faded. She quickly lapsed into her female impersonation of Morgan Freeman in *Driving Miss Daisy.* "I'se trying to get it on the buffet, Miz Redmon," she drawled.

"Well of course you are," Virginia said quickly, trying to put a stop to this nonsense.

Della ducked her head and lifted one shoulder. "I'se trying but there's only one of me and my back's still bothering me from all that heavy cleaning you had me to do yestiddy."

This, of course, was a bald-faced lie. Virginia did not expect Della to do, nor would she ever have done, any cleaning around the house. She was lucky if she could get Della to clean the kitchen before she went home. There was many an evening when Virginia finished up the dishes herself, after Della left.

"Listen, you let us carry the dishes out and put them on the sideboard," Carlin said to Della.

"Oh that won't be necessary," Virginia said sharply, and then, remembering herself, "I mean, I'll help Della serve. There's no reason for you to bother." She tried to recapture her jovial pose but no one was buying it. Carlin went out the swinging door into the dining room.

Virginia looked at Della and drew her finger slowly across her throat. "Enough with the Butterfly McQueen routine," she said. "No one's buying it."

Della straightened up and put one hand on her hip. "Oh, they're buying it," she said.

"If you ruin this for me, I'll never speak to you again."

Della lifted her lip. She smiled, showing her teeth. "I can live with that," she said.

The door swung open and Porter, Carlin, and Rose came in. Carlin quickly motioned for the other two to take the side dishes out. "Set everything up on the sideboard," she said. "And let's get a few shots of the food before everyone eats." Della leaned and took the turkey out of the oven. It was cooked to perfection, a lovely golden brown. She slid it onto a bed of wild lettuce on a silver serving tray.

"That looks wonderful," Carlin said.

"Where are the radish roses?" Virginia asked.

Della pointed with her chin. "In the refrigerator," she said.

"Listen," Carlin said, while Virginia went to get the radish roses. "Della, I've been thinking. Once the food is out, why don't you join the guests?"

"What?" Virginia said. She stood there in front of the open refrigerator with the cold air prickling her cheek. The thumping at the top of her head was as loud and insistent as a jackhammer.

"Well, I guess I could," Della said. She slid her eyes coyly at Virginia. "If Miz Redmon won't get mad."

Carlin stared at Virginia. Virginia said nervously, "Well, of *course* I won't get mad. What a silly idea!" She laughed unconvincingly, looking from one to the other. "Of course, you're welcome to join us Della, but then who will keep the buffet stocked?"

She raised her hands and shrugged her shoulders as if this settled the matter but Carlin said in a brittle voice, "Actually, once we film the sideboard, there's no reason why everyone can't serve themselves. I'll get my staff to bring out what needs to be brought out. Once the buffet is filmed, everyone can just relax and enjoy themselves."

"Whatever you think is best," Virginia said flatly. Really she didn't know why she had even bothered to plan this event if the producers were simply going to do things their own way. She poured herself a third glass of wine and then swung around on her heels and went out through the swinging door.

Grace Pearson stood slumped against the far wall, a notepad in her hand, sullenly watching the festivities.

Virginia put her hand up to her temple to steady herself. Then she hurried over. "What are you doing here?" she said, trying to keep her voice low.

"Lumineria's sick. She asked me to come." She had on a pair of baggy brown slacks and an oversized sweater that did little to enhance her figure.

"Lumineria didn't call me," Virginia said suspiciously. "She didn't tell me she couldn't come."

The big woman regarded her with a pair of bloodshot eyes. Her nose and cheeks were red and it appeared she had been drinking. "Lumineria's sick," she said stubbornly. "She asked me to cover for her. We work for the same newspaper. What, do you think I'm not capable of writing a column for 'The Town Tattler'? Did you or did you not ask the paper to cover this party?"

"Yes, but I wanted Lumineria to cover it."

"Well, we don't always get what we want, do we, Virginia? You should know that by now. Life's nothing but one big fucking crapshoot." She was clearly intoxicated and spoiling for a fight. She crossed her arms over her big chest and stared at Virginia. "What's the matter?" she said evenly. "Don't you want me?"

"Oh fine," Virginia said. "Write the article. I really don't care." She would probably write an exposé similar to the ones she used to write about the dead Judge, but Virginia didn't care. She refused to be blackmailed. By anyone. "Say whatever you want to say."

"Oh, trust me, I will."

"Good."

"Fine."

"Knock yourself out."

"I intend to."

"I have to check the buffet," Virginia said.

"What's a girl have to do around here to get a drink?"

"There's wine on the sideboard," Virginia said, waving her glass carelessly. Across the room, an inebriated Redmon was entertaining the crowd with an a cappella version of "I'm Just a Psychobilly from Philly." This party couldn't get much worse.

"You got any whiskey?" Grace said.

The main topic of conversation, of course, was the fact that Charles Broadwell had come with Nita Motes as his guest. Virginia noted the way her guests twittered behind their hands, the way they watched surreptitiously as Charles tried to maneuver Nita away from the crowd like a cowboy trying to cut a rogue cow out of the herd. She saw the way they smiled and rolled their eyes with glee when Nita, just as determined, made her way back into the throng of guests. Intent on damage control, Virginia hurried over to where Charles, Nita, Whitney, and Logan stood awkwardly balancing their plates and trying to make small talk.

"How nice you look," Virginia gushed to Charles, ignoring Nita. She noted the way Duckie Bradshaw and Celia Banks had moved up closer so they might overhear the conversation. Celia's youngest daughter, Casey, had been kicked out of four boarding schools and was rumored to be living in a halfway house in Jacksonville, a rumor Celia never acknowledged or discussed. Instead, she immersed herself in the tragic histories of other unfortunate families. If there was a case of adultery, drug abuse, sexual addiction, or compulsive gambling within a sixty-mile radius of Ithaca, Celia would sniff it out. She collected tragic stories the way some women collect dolls.

"Thanks," Charles said. He knew he was still a good-looking man. Women threw themselves at him all the time, and he had dressed carefully today in a dark blue suit, blue-and-white-pinstripe shirt, and red silk tie.

"And you, too, Whitney," Virginia said.

"Hey, what about me?" Logan said. "Don't you like my shoes? Don't you like my haircut?"

"Nita, you look a little pale," Virginia said. "Have you been feeling under the weather?"

"Can I have a glass of wine?" Whitney said. "French kids get to drink when they're little."

"Are we French?" Virginia said, looking at her as if this settled the matter once and for all. She noted the way Celia had one ear turned their way. She had ears like a bat, big and hairy, and no doubt able to hear a pin drop from twenty feet away.

"I never get to have any fun," Whitney said. "This party blows."

Celia sputtered red wine down the front of her dress. Duckie helped her dab the spill with a cocktail napkin. Neither one made any effort to move toward the bathroom door, standing there with the horrified fascination of spectators who've just happened upon a particularly grisly highway accident scene. Logan, who had noticed Judge Drucker standing just a few feet away, said loudly, "I don't know why you won't let us drink some wine when Grandpa Redmon lets us drink all the time!"

Duckie let out a nervous little twitter. Virginia's face looked like it had been carved out of granite.

"Are you telling me you let my children drink alcohol?" Nita said tersely, staring at Virginia.

"No, Nita, of course not," Charles said. "Mother wouldn't allow something like that. The children are just teasing, of course." He laughed nervously. This wasn't going like he had planned. His dreams of a happy family, reunited, seemed to be dissolving like chalk in the rain.

Virginia said to Nita, "Whatever bad habits those children have, they picked up from you, not me."

"I'll have a Kamikaze," Logan said gaily. "With a beer back."

"Make mine a double," Whitney said.

"One more word out of you two and you'll go to your rooms," Virginia said.

Nita swiveled her shoulders like a gun turret sighting an enemy target. She said, "Don't talk to my children like that."

"I'll talk to them any way I like when they're living under my roof."

"That won't be for much longer."

"We'll see about that."

"Yes, we will."

Across the room, Redmon finished his song to a slight smattering of drunken applause. He'd been on a whiskey-free diet for nearly eight weeks so the Jack Daniel's was definitely having an effect. He was feeling better than he had felt in months, better than he had felt, in fact, since he married his sweet little Virginia and brought her home to their happy love nest complete with traditional Elvis décor. Redmon frowned, looking around the fuzzy room. Speaking of Elvis décor, what had happened to the Elvis Red carpet and the lighted curio cabinet? And where in the hell was his reclining sectional sofa complete with built-in beer cooler? Redmon walked over to Virginia as steadily as he could, given the circumstances. She looked up at him and said in a low voice, "You've had enough. Don't drink any more." He pretended he couldn't hear her.

"This boy is a singer, by God," he said, throwing his arm around Logan's shoulders. The drunker Redmon got, the more he lapsed into Alabama hill country dialect. Another couple of shots and they'd need an interpreter. "This here boy needs to be a musician when he grows up. Hey, boy, sing your daddy that love song you wrote."

"You mean, 'Kill Me'?"

"Yeah, that's it."

Logan said, "Well, as you can see from the expression on his face, my *daddy* doesn't want me to sing him any songs."

"Naw," Redmon said. "He's just got a little indigestion is all."

Charles ignored them. It was apparent he was going to have to put his foot down. He had put up with the black clothes and the dyed hair and the lip ring, thinking it was just a phase, but the idea of his son becoming a musician struck him like a kick to the kidneys.

Logan said, "He wants me to go to college and be an accountant or a doctor or a deadbeat lawyer like he is."

"Is that how you talk to your father?" Charles said, his nostrils flaring. His dream of a happy family caught fire and went up in a full blaze. "Is that the respect you show your father?"

Logan squared his shoulders. "I only show respect to those who deserve it," he said. He and his father stood there, glaring at each other like gladiators awaiting the first blow.

Whitney yawned. Nita stared at Virginia. Virginia looked at Celia and Duckie, who had moved up so close they were practically touching Charles's shoulder. Redmon grinned like a monkey and looked fondly around at his sullen and depressed family. "Goddamn," he said, "this is what it's all about." He raised his amber-colored rock glass in a toast that no one bothered to join. "To family," he said, misty-eyed. "It don't get no better than this, by God, and if it did, I couldn't stand it and the sheriff wouldn't allow it."

"Ha, ha," Logan said, still looking at Charles.

"Can I leave early?" Whitney said, stifling another yawn. "I have to meet some friends at the mall."

Redmon felt like singing. It was an old family tradition in the Redmon family, everyone gathered around on the front porch after dinner to sing gospel songs while the searing sun broke over the distant line of pine trees like a giant yolk. "Speaking of singing," Redmon said. "How about we do a few gospel numbers?"

"Why don't you make yourself a plate of food?" Virginia said to him.

"Do y'all know 'Bringing in the Sheaves'?"

"You better get some turkey before it's all gone," Virginia said.

"How about 'Rock Me in the Arms of Jesus'?"

"I know that one," Della said. She had materialized suddenly at Redmon's elbow like a bad ghost.

"We're not singing any goddamn gospel songs at my party," Virginia snapped. She glanced around the room and crimsoned, adjusting the sleeves of her dress. She hadn't felt that outburst coming on, which was dangerous, because Virginia always kept a tight rein on her emotions. It wasn't good to show yourself in front of strangers or enemies. Or family either, for that matter. Perhaps it was the wine, or the clanging racket that was going on in her head. Perhaps it was the way Nita kept looking at her, like a cat watching a fishbowl, as if waiting for just the right moment to strike, that had thrown her off-balance. Perhaps it was Grace Pearson, glaring at her from across the room while she clasped a tall glass of whiskey to her bosom, her poisoned pen moving rapidly over the pages of her little notebook.

Della said, "How about 'He Is My Shepherd in a Land of Wolves'?"

One of Virginia's eyes appeared to have crossed. Whatever it was that had been trying to escape had finally pushed through the top of her skull. She could feel a slight breeze there, where the hole was. She considered striking the woman but then decided it would not be wise. Della probably outweighed her by a good eighty pounds.

Oh, what the hell, she thought, looking around the room at the guests who had begun to crowd her sad little pantomime of a family like a flock of buzzards waiting out a roadkill. The room spun softly. The faces of her guests rose up and down like grisly carousel horses. Virginia got dizzy looking at them. Looking around, she thought, *Who are these people and why are they here?* Franklin Banks's face swam slowly into view and Virginia saw again the red-haired freckle-faced boy who had teased her and called her a swamp hick in second grade. Milly Craig floated by and Virginia saw the evil child with the golden ringlets who had plotted with Mary Lee Hamilton to make her life miserable. What was it about these people that had made them important to her? What was it about their good opinion that had held her captive all these years?

And that Carlin is a hypocrite, Virginia thought savagely. Her eyes fell suddenly on the young producer who stood next to Della talking to the older woman like they'd been friends all their lives. Virginia sipped her wine, watching the producer deliberately over the rim of her glass. She had asked Carlin what boarding school she'd attended, and Carlin had told her. Virginia knew the school, she knew the annual tuition for a boarding student was $35,000, which meant that Carlin was a "rich kid" and had probably grown up with black servants. Or Mexican. Or . . . whatever. Who was she to judge Virginia's insistence on the damn maid's uniform?

The more wine she drank, the more abused Virginia began to feel.

"I need to go," Whitney said. "I told Shannon I'd meet her at the mall."

"You're not going anywhere," Virginia said.

"Get your stuff," Nita said. "We'll leave now."

"You're welcome to leave," Virginia said to Nita. "But the girl stays."

Whitney said, "You can't talk to my mommy that way."

"Hey," Redmon said, "what do you call twenty lawyers skydiving from an airplane?"

"I think I'll get another drink," Charles said.

"Skeet," Redmon said. He and Logan snickered and thumped each other on the arms.

Charles stepped closer to Redmon. "Better a lawyer than a crooked redneck contractor," he said.

"Who you calling a redneck, you high-domed pencil pusher."

"Cheating scoundrel."

"Lying bastard."

"Who's ready for pumpkin pie?" Virginia said, lifting her glass.

After that, things could only get worse. And they did.

Redmon broke out the Bloody Marys. Virginia figured her social life was pretty much over by now anyway, so what difference did it make? Whatever faint dreams of glory she had once had, had evaporated, seeping up through the hole in her head like a punctured gas line.

Thirty minutes later Lavonne and Eadie arrived. Redmon and Della stood at one end of the room singing a sloppy rendition of "Open Up Them Pearly Gates," accompanied by Logan on the guitar. Charles watched them like a man trapped by bad odors. Nita and Whitney huddled together with their heads bowed while Nita talked quietly. Most of the guests, happy to move from wine to something more substantial, hoisted their Bloody Marys and filled the room with their raucous laughter, having long since forgotten about the television cameras. A few joined in the singing. The more sedate among them stood like hostages, unable to look away from the tragic Shakespearean quality of this televised gathering. Virginia leaned against the new armoire and sipped her Bloody Mary, wondering how hard it would be to move to Palm Beach and start a new life.

Eadie stuck her head in the front door and shouted, "Where's the party?" When no one answered, they made their way toward the noisy living room. Virginia looked up and saw them standing in the doorway in their tacky Kudzu Ball gowns. She grimaced and lifted her drink. "Perfect," she said. "Just perfect."

Lavonne said, "I hope you guys don't mind us barging in like this, crashing your pre-Thanksgiving dinner."

Eadie said, "Hey, are y'all drinking Bloody Marys?"

Redmon stopped singing to pour more drinks and Lavonne and Eadie mingled for a few minutes and then wandered over to say hello to Virginia. Virginia watched them with a look of sullen resignation. Lavonne was wearing a gold lamé dress that looked like something Donna Summer might have worn back in 1978. Eadie had on a ridiculous-looking puffy-sleeved cocktail dress and a pair of scuffed combat boots. They both wore kudzu wreath crowns, stuck with feathers and plastic beads, kind of like Mardi Gras Indian princesses.

"Well I guess there's nothing you two won't stoop to," Virginia said, stirring her drink with a celery stick. "I never would have taken you for party-crashers."

"Sorry," Lavonne said. "We just couldn't help ourselves."

"You know, I could call the police and have you arrested for trespassing."

"Now that would look good on camera," Eadie said. "Can't you just see it? An outside shot of your house, me and Lavonne being carried out in our Kudzu Ball gowns, kicking and screaming, by a couple of burly policemen. The interview with you, Virginia, under the klieg lights. Kind of like *COPS* meets *America's Funniest Home Videos.*"

"Don't think I won't do it," Virginia said glumly, looking around the room. "This party couldn't be any more of a fiasco than it already is."

As if to prove her wrong, Riley Weeks let out a rebel yell and broke into a kind of impromptu rap. On his sober days, Riley was a stockbroker at the local Smith Barney office. Many of the guests, who had obviously never seen a live rap performance, clutched their drinks nervously and edged away from Riley, who looked like a palsy victim trying to thread a needle.

"Now that's just sad," Eadie said.

"White people shouldn't rap," Lavonne said. "And white people like Riley shouldn't dance, either."

"Someone changed the music," Virginia said, scowling. She had carefully planned the music for this party, loading the CD player with Handel's Sonata #1, Pachelbel's Canon, and Mozart's Serenade #13. Someone had obviously sabotaged her musical arrangement. Across the room, Logan caught her eye. He grinned and raised his glass.

"I wish I'd worn my Kudzu Ball gown," Nita said, moving up between Lavonne and Eadie. Charles trailed behind her like a moth caught in a spider web.

"Yes, why didn't we all wear our Kudzu Ball gowns?" Virginia said bitterly. "Why didn't we all dress like freaks and sluts? I could have used it as a theme for the party." She swallowed her drink and looked around the room like a woman with nothing left to lose.

"A Freaks and Sluts Party," Lavonne said. "I like that." It was apparent to her that Virginia had been freely partaking of the wine and Bloody Marys. She was slurring her words and her hair stuck out at odd angles around her face.

"If I'd wanted to dress like a slut," Eadie said, "I'd have worn the black leather mini with the leopard-print halter top." She stuck out her hand to Carlin who had just come up behind Virginia. "Hey," she said. "Y'all must be the TV people."

"Have you been to some kind of costume party?" Carlin said to Eadie and Lavonne.

"Something like that," Lavonne said, sipping her Bloody Mary. She'd never had one before but she liked it. It tasted healthy. She munched on the celery stick garnish that Redmon had added as a decorative touch.

"They're Kudzu Debutantes," Virginia said, curling her top lip, and everyone tried not to notice how much trouble she was

540

having pronouncing her words.

Eadie looked at Lavonne and raised one eyebrow. Carlin said, "What's a Kudzu Debutante?"

"It's a woman who refuses to follow dress codes."

"It's a woman who likes to run her own life, her own way."

Virginia said, "It's a woman with no understanding of history or tradition." She had some trouble with *tradition.* She glared at Eadie and Lavonne, finishing up with, "A woman with no class or breeding."

"Okay," Eadie said. "The gloves are coming off."

"The Kudzu Ball is a parody of the Ithaca Cotillion Ball," Lavonne said. "It's a parody of the whole debutante tradition."

"Cool," Carlin said.

Nita stared at Virginia. "What favors has history or tradition ever done for you?"

"You watch yourself, my girl," Virginia said, waving her celery stick like she was swinging a machete. "You just watch yourself."

"What have you ever done with your life except make people around you miserable?"

"Now, now," Redmon said fondly. He had come up carrying a pitcher of Bloodies. He went around the circle and poured everyone a fresh drink. The tension in the room didn't bother Redmon at all. He was from Alabama. He was used to family gatherings that ended in violence.

"Oh, look who's talking," Virginia said. "Look at that poor slob standing there." She swung the celery stick around and pointed at the hapless Charles. "So sick with misery and love for you he can't move on with his life even though he isn't getting any younger. Even though you'll never take him back."

Charles blushed furiously. "Mother, let's check the buffet line, shall we?" he said, trying to take her elbow.

She shook him off. "Just look at him. Poor slob. The laughingstock of the whole damn town." She pointed at each of them with her limp celery stick. "Laughingstock of the whole damn town. All of you," she said.

"Why don't you have another drink and tell us about it," Eadie said.

"You shut up Eadie Boone. You . . . Boone! You're all alike, you Boones. You think you're better than everybody else just because you're a *Boone*."

Whitney's cell phone rang. "I'll call you back later," she said. "You won't believe what's going on here." She hung up and pushed the phone back in her pocket.

542

"I don't blame Charles for being the way he is," Nita said. "With you for a mother, how could he be any different?"

Charles shook his head in warning. Nita was treading dangerous waters here, although she didn't seem to know this, or to care. His mother was deadly. She could smile sweetly and disembowel an enemy at the same time; they'd never know what hit them until it was too late, until their entrails lay curled on the floor at their feet. Poor Nita didn't stand a chance.

"You nitpicked your son and made him so insecure about himself he could never be happy —"

"Uh, Nita," Charles said.

Porter focused his camera. He motioned for one of the other camera guys.

"No, Charles, let me finish." Nita put a finger up for him to be quiet. She pushed her face close to Virginia's, her eyes gray and ominous as thunderclouds. "You screwed up your son's life and now you want to screw up my daughter's life and I'm not going to let you. My children are mine, Virginia, not yours." Nita thumped her chest for effect. "You had your chance to be a mother. And you failed."

"Oh, well now, aren't you just the most perfect little thing?" Virginia said, showing her sharp little teeth. She twirled the limp celery stick around and then lifted it and took a bite off one end, chewing slowly. "Aren't you just the most perfect mother in the world, running off with another man and leaving your husband of sixteen years to pick up the pieces of his life."

Nita stared steadily into Virginia's face. She shook her head slowly. "You failed your son and you failed your daughter, too."

"Adulteress," Virginia said.

"Lunatic," Nita said.

"Hey, do y'all know 'Baby, Let's Play House'?" Redmon said, looking around his dysfunctional family circle. He and Myra had never had kids, and marrying Virginia and becoming part of her extended family had made him as happy as a pig in a peach orchard. Redmon came from a family of twelve siblings, although most had died before they reached fifty of alcoholism, heart disease, lung cancer, or various accidents involving farming implements or cotton mill machinery. He had once seen his uncle Rafe shoot his uncle Faris in an argument over a Plott hound, and more than one Redmon family gathering had been broken up by violence. That being said, Redmon felt perfectly at home in Virginia's family.

"How about 'Daddy Was a Preacher but Mama Was a Go-Go Girl,' " Eadie said.

"I'll get to you in a minute," Virginia said, cutting her eyes at Eadie and then back to Nita. Something bothered Virginia. There was something stuck in her brain, hung up like a scrap of cloth in a briar patch. What was it the woman had said, *You failed your son and you failed your daughter, too.*

"Y'all are gonna need some more Bloodies," Logan said cheerfully, taking the empty pitcher from Redmon.

Charles watched his mother's face change. He thought, *Danger, danger.* He thought, *This can't be good.* He said in a false, jovial voice, "Well, Mother, Nita and I need to get going. Thanks for a lovely afternoon."

Virginia bared her teeth. She shook her head grimly. "No one leaves until I say they can leave."

Daughter. So that was it, the threat Nita had been implying all along, the knowledge that had made her so bold as to go up against Virginia in her own house, at her own party. Nita knew about her lost daughter. She knew the secret Virginia had kept hidden for forty-nine years. And now she meant to blackmail Virginia just the way she had blackmailed Charles into going along with the divorce and keeping his mouth shut. Well, Nita had underestimated her enemy. What was it Eadie Boone had said, *The gloves are coming off.* Indeed they were.

"That's why they're here," she said to Redmon and Charles, pointing at Nita, Lavonne, and Eadie. "These Kudzu Debutantes. That's why they've come. To make me pay. To blackmail me. They know I had a child out of wedlock . . ."

Charles blinked. "What?" he said.

Redmon said, "Hurry up with those Bloodies!"

Virginia set her teeth and smiled brightly. "A child out of wedlock with Hampton Boone," she said.

"What?" Charles said.

Virginia lifted her chin. "A love child with Hampton Boone that I gave up for adoption forty-nine years ago!"

The room got quiet. Redmon chewed a celery stick and blandly watched his wife. Charles stared at his mother with a look of dawning horror. One eye fluttered and wandered off on its own. His top lip spasmed and rose on the right side like it was being pulled by invisible strings. In the long silence that followed, Charles thought about moving out of state to open a new practice. He wondered how hard it would be to pass the Alaska bar exam.

"That's not all we know," Nita said grimly. She wasn't letting Virginia get off that easily.

"Yes, yes a daughter," Virginia said, squaring her shoulders like a prizefighter. It felt good to get it off her chest, the secret guilt she had worn for forty-nine years like a hair shirt. Virginia was overcome suddenly by a feeling of buoyancy and elation. She looked around the room and said loudly, "I gave up a daughter. So what? What do you know? You girls had birth control. Legalized abortion. What did we have? Shame. Homes for unwed mothers. I did what I had to do. I had my baby and I gave her up for adoption and I never looked back. It was the right thing to do, the only thing I could do. And I never told Hamp Boone. I never spoke to him again, after my wedding day. I kept it all inside and never told anyone." She lifted her head triumphantly. "So go ahead. Do your worst. Spread your rumors. I don't care. I've gone up against bigger villains than you three and survived." She put her hand over her heart and lifted her pointed chin, looking a little like Napoleon in that famous portrait by David, only with more hair.

Nita said fiercely, "I want my daughter back."

Virginia shook her head. She lifted her Bloody Mary like she might be going to throw it. "You shouldn't have tried to blackmail me," she said.

Nita looked desperately at Eadie and Lavonne. "I know something else you may not want to hear." Across the room, Grace Pearson stopped writing in her little notebook.

Virginia laughed. "Nothing you can say will make me give up now."

"I know who your daughter is."

Grace quietly closed up her notebook and slid it into her purse.

Virginia's mouth twitched. She kept her face blank. "I don't care," she said. "You can't blackmail me. Nothing you say will make me change my mind."

Nita stood there staring at her. Her knees shook. Her mouth trembled but she couldn't say it. She couldn't hurt Grace by telling her the truth here in front of all these people. She couldn't ruin her life that way.

"Well?" Virginia said, steadying herself for the blow. "We're waiting. If you know, tell us."

Nita tightened her hands into fists and stared helplessly at her feet. A blue shadow hung in the hollow of her cheek. Her lower lip trembled as if she might be talking, wordlessly, to herself.

"It's me," Grace said in a loud clear voice. She pushed herself off the wall and stood where they all could see her. She smiled gently at Nita. "I'm your daughter," she said.

It took Virginia a few minutes to collect herself. Her jaw sagged. She swayed slightly but remained standing. A tremor started in her feet and traveled up through her knees like an electrical current. She stood there swaying, slack-jawed and stunned, her face a mixture of outrage and disbelief. She knew it was true, though. Grace looked just like Virginia's father with her big hands and feet and red-gold hair. And she looked like Hampton, too, around the eyes and mouth.

Charles said, "I'm confused." He said, "Father must be spinning in his grave."

Redmon said, "Where's that boy with those drinks?"

No one else said anything. Eadie and Lavonne went over and stood on either side of Grace. Virginia watched them. Nothing stirred but her eyes, which seemed to blur as something feeble struggled in their depths. A look of gradual understanding came over her face. Her expression softened, and then went blank. The guests milled around and looked at each other over the rims of their glasses. They whispered to one another in low voices. A few pulled out cell phones and began to send frantic text messages. Virginia drank steadily and then set her glass down on a Chippendale table. She clutched the back of a wingback chair like she was standing behind a podium, facing the crowd.

The room got quiet. Everyone seemed to sense a cathartic moment and maintained a respectful silence not unlike that the ancient Greeks must have maintained while waiting for the sibyl to speak. Even Redmon stopped munching his celery stick and watched Virginia expectantly. She stood behind the wingback chair, swaying like a sapling in a fierce storm.

"No one knows what it's like to be me," she said, putting her hand over her heart. "To be Virginia." Everyone tried not to notice that she said *Vuh-shinya*. Duckie snorted again but Celia shot her a warning glance. Charles stared at his mother like a man about to be injected with the Ebola virus.

"Do you know what it's like to grow up in a town where everybody looks down on you? Just because you're poor? Where the kids at school all call you names just because your dresses are homemade?" She scowled and flung a malevolent look around the room.

"Actually, I do," Eadie said.

"Shut up, Eadie! This isn't about you. It's about me. Virginia." She thumped herself on the chest and went on. "Do you know what it's like to have to put up with snotty girls like Maureen Hamilton who everyone thinks is so *pretty,* so *nice,* just because her daddy owns the Chrysler dealership. Just because she can dress in department store clothes and lives in a big house and drives a new car." Virginia sniffed, glaring at the stunned spectators. She put her finger up against her nose and tapped. "Well," she said. "She wasn't nice. She was *mean.* She said things about me that weren't true. She spread rumors. When me and Hamp started going out, she went to his mama and she forbidded him, she forbade him — oh, what the hell — she said he couldn't see me anymore. Just because my daddy truck-farmed!"

Charles said, "Mother, I think you need to lie down for a while."

Virginia waved her hand like she was swatting at a gnat. "And later when he married her, she lorded it over me every chance she got. Coming into Roobin's and buying new clothes, making me wait on her, saying, *Oh, I wonder if my husband would like this, Oh, I wonder if my husband would like that, Oh, my husband he spoils me so!*"

"Della, maybe we can have some coffee?" Charles said, but Della just stood there. She wasn't going anywhere. This was better than *The Sopranos* and *All My Children* and *Days of Our Lives* all rolled into one. She'd pay good money just to see a performance like this one.

"But I fixed her," Virginia said in a harsh voice. "I married the Old Judge, her husband's own law partner, and then what choice did she have but to be nice to me?" She chuckled to herself.

Eulonia Drucker stood at the edge of the crowd looking like she might faint. "I don't understand," she said in her soft, fluttering little voice. "What's happening? What does this mean? Should we leave?"

"Hush," Judge Drucker said.

Charles began to back slowly out of the room, edging his way out of the family circle and pushing himself backward through the crowd.

Virginia pulled on her drink and looked around the room as if daring anyone to leave. "Do you know what it's like to have an old man touch you on your wedding night? Well, do you? His hands shook. His skin smelled like mothballs."

Charles stopped retreating. "Okay kids, Nita, get your things," he said firmly. "We're leaving."

Whitney, Nita, and Logan, who had come back in carrying a fresh pitcher of Bloody Marys, did not move. Virginia pointed at Charles with her Bloody Mary. "No one leaves until *Vuh-shinya* says they can go." Logan looked at his father and grinned, shrugging his shoulders. He went around to top off everyone's drinks. Virginia tried hard to concentrate. She was having trouble staying on track. She had a lot to say but the thoughts kept flying away before she could catch them. She pointed at Eadie, Lavonne, and Nita. "After they blackmailed the husbands, I lost everything. Everything," she said, clenching her fist and pointing down with her thumb, like water being poured through a funnel. "All gone," she said. "No money and no way to make any more. So I did what I had to do. Just like before. I got married." She stopped and looked at Redmon. "I married you for your money," she said.

He grinned. "I know that, honey," he said.

"That prenup," she said, tapping herself

on the forehead. "Very good idea. Very smart."

"Thanks, Queenie."

"And just so you know, it was me who called the state and got the project shut down."

"I figured it was."

She frowned and looked at Redmon. "You're a pretty good husband," she said as if this thought had just occurred to her. "You're a miser and a pervert, but other than that, you're a pretty good husband." Virginia nodded. Redmon blushed with pride. "Even though I didn't really want a husband. If I had to choose between poverty and disgrace, or marriage to you, I'd still choose you."

Redmon was too choked up to speak. He lifted his glass in a silent toast.

Virginia would have lifted hers, too, but it was empty. Logan leaned over and emptied the rest of the Bloody Mary pitcher into her glass. "I'll make another round," he said cheerfully, taking the empty pitcher and heading for the kitchen.

"Goddamn it, don't make any more drinks," Charles shouted.

"The vodka's in the second cabinet to the left of the refrigerator," Redmon called.

"If I had to choose between poverty and

disgrace, or marriage, I'd choose you," Virginia repeated to Redmon. "But my first choice would be freedom. Or no, no, my second choice would be freedom. My first choice would be Keanu Reeves." She put her hand over her mouth and giggled.

Whitney said, "Ew."

Eadie lifted her glass and said, "I'll drink to that."

Lavonne said, "It's a brave new world. Women don't have to marry for money anymore. They can make their own."

Virginia said, "Oh, ha, ha." She said, "Mind your own business, Lavonne."

"That's what the women's movement is all about," Lavonne said. "Choice."

Virginia pulled on her drink. She set it down and stared glumly at the mantel centerpiece, a tasteful arrangement of pumpkins, gourds, and English ivy, trying to remember what they were arguing about. "I don't believe in that women's lib crap," she said, finally.

"Mother, sit down," Charles said firmly.

Virginia shook her head. The hole in her head had opened up like a broken hive. Her thoughts buzzed around in her skull like a swarm of angry bees. She blinked. "I like a man to hold the door for me," she said.

Lavonne said, "So you're willing to give

up equality under the law in exchange for someone holding the door for you?"

Virginia leaned against the chair to steady herself. The droning in her head got louder. "You shut up," she said. "Vuh-shinya is talking. Vuh-shinya has something to say." She snapped her fingers, barely missing Lavonne's nose. "You been to college. You know what my daddy said when I said I wanted to go to college? He said, *You don't need college. You'll get married and your husband will take care of you.* Words of wisdom. From a man who went to eighth grade. So you know what I did? I got a job at Roobin's selling clothes and I waited until I figured out who I had to marry and then I caught him. I caught the Old Judge, *I run him to earth,* as my daddy used to say. He didn't like the Judge. He didn't want me to marry him. He wanted me to marry someone young. But I was tired of being poor. I was tired of watching Maureen Boone drive all over town in her new Chrysler New Yorker like she was some-body! Like she was the cat's meow! So I fixed her. I married the Judge."

Virginia laughed, remembering the way Maureen had been forced to attend the wedding, the way Hampton had held on to her elbow and dragged her down the aisle to the front pew. And Virginia's dress had come from New York. She had gone up there on the train with her mother to buy it, compliments of the Judge. Everyone said she was the prettiest bride to ever come out of Ithaca, and they said it in front of Maureen Boone, which made Virginia giggle with glee. It had been her crowning moment. But then the night came, and she was alone in a room with her new husband whose hands shook and skin smelled like mothballs. She wasn't laughing then. Virginia put her fingers on her forehead and squeezed, trying to squeeze that memory out of her head. She sighed, realizing it was useless. She dropped her hand and lifted her Bloody Mary. *Why did they call it that? Bloody,* she understood, *but Mary? Who the hell was Mary?*

"Mother, you've had enough to drink," Charles said sharply. First his wife, and now his mother. He had spent his whole life being disappointed by women.

Virginia made a vulgar noise. She clutched her drink and wagged her finger at him. "Don't you talk to me like that," she said. "Don't you talk to me like your father did. For twenty-six years he told me what to do and I had to pretend to do it. I had to sneak around like a thief in the night and do what

557

he said, *Yes, Judge, No, Judge, Whatever you say, Judge,* just like the coloreds had to do. That's all I was to him, a colored." She stopped suddenly and looked at Della. "Sorry," she said. "No offense," she said.

Della chuckled and shook her head. "Rich folks can't wait for trouble to find them," she said. "They have to go out and hunt it down."

"Where was I?" Virginia said, frowning. "Oh yeah. I've made some mistakes in my life." She looked at Grace and Nita when she said this. "I've done some things I'm not proud of."

"Mother, I think you might need to lie down for a while," Charles said.

"Go ahead and get it all off your chest," Lavonne said. "You'll feel better. Say what you have to say."

"Goddamn it, Lavonne, this is none of your business!" Charles said. He'd had three Bloody Marys and with each succeeding drink, the veil of illusion that had blinded him had slipped further from his eyes. He wondered now why he had brought Nita here. He wondered why he had not remarried and started a new family like Leonard Zibolsky had done, a family that would be loyal and supportive to him no matter what the costs. He wondered why he had spent the last year and a half pining for something he could never have and didn't want now anyway. Why remodel an existing family when it was simpler to start from scratch and build a new one?

Virginia squinted her eyes and glared at them. The room had gone hazy. The droning in her head had subsided to a dull hum, more like the cooing of doves now than the buzzing of bees. She lifted her chin and looked at Grace who watched her with an expression of futile detachment. "What I have to say is this. I did what I had to do. I survived a childhood of loneliness and prejudice. I survived twenty-six years of marriage to a man I didn't love. I loved another man who wasn't worthy of me, and I paid for that love every day of my life. I'm still paying for it. But, by God, I did the best I could do with what the good Lord gave me. I didn't lie down and let life run over me like a steamroller, I stood up to it the best I could. Before you judge me, walk a mile in my moccasins. And that's all I've got to say." She staggered around the wingback chair and sat down.

Redmon raised his glass to his wife in love and admiration. "Here's to you, Queenie," he said. "Goddamn, what a woman." Eadie and Lavonne lifted their glasses.

Lavonne said, "No one can say you don't have guts, Virginia."

Eadie said, "It doesn't excuse what you did, but it does explain why you've been such a whack-job all these years."

The antique clock ticked steadily on the mantel. Sun slanted through the long windows and fell over the scattered wreckage of the pre-Thanksgiving party, on the roving cameramen, on the stunned guests who woke up and stumbled around like toddlers learning to walk, like drunks uncertain of their legs. Judge Drucker looked at his wife. "Mama, get your coat," he said.

Whitney said, "This is embarrassing." She said to Nita, "Can we go home now?"

Charles tried to put a good face on it. He rubbed his hands together and looked around the room. "Thank you for coming!" he said. "Coats are in the foyer closet!" He wondered if he still had the phone number of the accountant with the thick ankles. He could get it from his mother if he had to, later, after she sobered up.

Duckie snorted suddenly and clamped her hand over her mouth as if she was just now catching the punch line to a joke. Celia hissed like the brakes of a runaway Winnebago. She said loudly, "She should have charged admission to this party. This is better than opening night on Broadway!"

Grace picked up her purse and slid it over her shoulder. "How's Casey liking rehab?" she said to Celia.

Caught up in the wonder of it all, Virginia smiled at her daughter. Her *daughter.* She had thought of Grace for so long as an enemy, it was hard to think of her as anything else. But now, miraculously, she could feel something growing inside her, a small, glowing ember of maternal feeling, like a tumor, like an ulcer eating away at the lining of her stomach.

She grinned and raised her empty glass. "Bring Mommy another cocktail," she said to Grace. "And let's see if we can't get reacquainted."

CHAPTER
TWENTY-FOUR

Virginia awoke the following morning to a dull thumping headache and a vague persistent feeling of nausea. It was her first hangover and she found it to be unlike anything she had ever seen depicted on TV. For one thing, she didn't crave strange beverages concocted with Alka-Seltzer and raw egg yolks. For another, she could remember everything that had happened the day before with perfect clarity. She remembered the pre-Thanksgiving dinner down to its smallest detail; her own rambling confession; her guests' sly, amused expressions; the cold, steady eye of the camera lens; her son's stricken face as he fled her house, alone, like a man escaping a tsunami.

She rose groggily to her feet, finding that the headache seemed less pronounced when she stood. She looked down at her toes and frowned. It was only then that she realized she was naked. Redmon groaned and rolled over in bed, flinging one arm wide. *Oh God,* he appeared to be naked, too. He opened his eyes, blinked, and then sat up on one elbow, grinning at her.

"Damn, Queenie," he said. "Who needs Viagra when we got Bloody Marys?"

Her ears got warm. It seemed there were some things she didn't remember after all. She decided this was probably a good thing. She swung around and headed for the bathroom, sidestepping Redmon who lunged suddenly from the bed. "Hey, where you going?" he cried.

She stood in front of the bathroom mirror brushing her hair. It appeared from the love bites on her shoulders that it had, indeed, been a wild night. Suddenly, without warning, Virginia giggled. Two bright spots of color appeared in her cheeks and her eyes shone. She giggled again and clamped her hand over her mouth.

"Hey, baby, come here. I've got something to show you," Redmon called on the other side of the door. She quickly put on her robe, opened the door, and walked past him with as much dignity as she could muster, given the circumstances.

Downstairs the kitchen was only partially cleaned. She had sent Della home soon after the *Gracious Southern Living* crew left.

Virginia hadn't felt like spending the evening washing dishes. Instead, she had helped her grandchildren pack. Later, when they left with Nita, Redmon had said, "Well, I'm gonna miss the kids." He added roguishly, "But now we got the whole house to ourselves." He was standing with his back to the front door, grinning at her, and Virginia, seeing his expression had said, "Oh for goodness sakes." He finally cornered her in one of the upstairs bedrooms, but when he started in on his impression of Maurice Chevalier singing "Thank Heaven for Little Girls," Virginia realized further struggle was futile.

She made a pot of coffee and went outside to get the newspaper. The sun shone brightly across the wet lawn and she had to shield her tender eyes as she bent to retrieve the paper from the azalea bed. Back inside, she poured herself a cup of coffee, pushed aside a stack of dirty dishes, and sat down at the table, steeling herself for what was coming next.

She opened the paper and found she could look, without flinching, at the grainy photograph of Grace Pearson. She couldn't, of course, think of her as a daughter. At least, not yet, not sober in the cold hard light of day. She wasn't certain how long it would take to openly acknowledge their kinship, to call Grace directly and talk about their shared past, but surely the fact she no longer despised the woman meant something. Surely a lack of repugnance was the first step toward a promising mother-daughter relationship. Virginia took it as a hopeful sign.

She flipped the paper open to "The Town Tattler" column. The headline read, *Local Hostess Featured in TV Special.* The article was straight-forward and informative, with Virginia featured by name, without the coy use of initials usually favored by Lumineria Crabb. There was no mention of Virginia's breakdown. Grace had tactfully skirted that event, which Virginia took as another hopeful sign for the future of their mother-daughter relationship.

Not that this would stop the town gossips and scandalmongers who were at this very minute, no doubt, spreading rumors about Virginia's sad but bawdy personal history. *Oh, what do I care?* Virginia thought savagely. What was it Rhett Butler had said to Scarlett? *Frankly, my dear, I don't give a damn.*

Two days later she got a phone call from Leonard Twohorses, the Creek Indian activist she had used to shut down the Culpepper Plantation project. It seemed that with the improvements made by Redmon and Jimmy Lee, the island was worth more now to the Creeks than just a burial ground. They had decided to buy the island from Virginia and turn it into a gambling casino called Tsali-wood. Although stunned, Virginia kept her cool. She had learned a thing or two about negotiation from watching Della Smurl operate, and in less than a week she had hammered out a deal that would pay her more than enough money to live on for the rest of her life. In addition, they agreed to pay Redmon and Jimmy Lee to waive their lien rights, an amount that would allow them to recoup a good portion, if not all, of their original investment money. Virginia did what she could to broker this second deal. She figured it was the least she could do.

For the rest of the week, she walked around the house like a tiny ballerina on point. She was so excited she couldn't eat; she couldn't sleep. With the money she'd receive from the sale, she'd be a free woman. She could travel. She could move to Atlanta or Savannah or West Palm Beach, shaking the red dust of this provincial town off her shoes forever. She could divorce Redmon.

Although, oddly, now that she no longer needed to stay married to him for the money, she found she did not really want to leave him, either. After all, he was the only man she had ever shown herself to, the true Virginia, and the fool still loved and worshipped her anyway. What were the odds, at her age, that she'd ever find another man who actually loved her for who she was, and not some idealized version of herself? And then there was Grace. They had spoken, shyly and tentatively, by phone a couple of days ago and had made plans to meet for dinner the coming week. Did she really want to leave her long-lost daughter before at least attempting to establish a relationship with her, did she really want to abandon her now just as she had done forty-nine years ago? Virginia had a lot of decisions to make. But strangely, she did not feel discouraged.

On the contrary, she felt as light and buoyant as a box kite dancing on the currents of a high-flying breeze.

Across town, Nita's little family was finishing up dinner. She had cooked chicken tetrazzini and homemade yeast rolls, and she'd made a fresh spinach salad with portobello mushrooms and a raspberry vinaigrette. She'd gotten word today that her paper on domestic servants was going to be published by the *Journal of Southern Historical Perspective,* and they were celebrating. Jimmy Lee had come for dinner and brought a bottle of wine with him. Whitney and Logan had set the kitchen table with a bowl of apples and silver candlesticks, and they'd eaten dinner by flickering candlelight.

Outside the windows, dusk fell. A high-flying wedge of geese passed, flying in perfect formation against the darkening sky. Otis, who was sleeping on the rug by the door, lifted his head and whined as they flew over.

"Poor old Otis," Whitney said fondly. "Don't you wish you could fly?" The dog looked at her and thumped his tail against the floor.

"He missed y'all," Nita said. "He was lonely."

Whitney leaned over and put her arms around her mother. "I was lonely, too, Mommy," she said earnestly. Her life had changed that fall, in ways that went beyond simply changing schools and being the celebrity pawn in a high-stakes custody battle. She had discovered drama. At her old school, the drama coach was also the wrestling coach and the plays had always centered on halfhearted, poorly attended productions of *Our Town* or *The Glass Menagerie.* At the Barron Hall School, however, drama was a Big Deal. Whitney had won the coveted role of Katherine in *The Taming of the Shrew,* beating out Michelle Campbell-Jones, a junior who had played the lead in various plays for three years running. Whitney was only in eighth grade but she could have warned Michelle Campbell-Jones not to even bother showing up for tryouts. Whitney had the part of Katherine nailed. She'd been playing it for most of her adolescence.

The drama kids at school provided Whitney with a whole new peer group. They went out together after practice and sat at The Waffle House smoking cigarettes and drinking black coffee and talking about anarchy and nihilism and Friedrich Nietzsche until it was time to climb into their big expensive SUVs and go home to their big expensive houses for dinner. There was something about being a prep school nihilist that appealed to Whitney's nature. She saw a bright future for herself at the Barron Hall School.

Whitney stood and began to clear the table. "I can't believe how spoiled the kids at Barron Hall are. I can't believe Sophy Shelton's parents bought her a brand-new

Volvo for her sixteenth birthday. And Ashley Butler's bought her a *Range Rover.*"

Logan said, "Well, that's pretty funny coming from a girl who was trying to get her grandmother to buy her a brand-new BMW just a few short weeks ago."

"I don't care about any of that stuff now," Whitney said carelessly. "I'm not a shallow, superficial person. At least, not anymore." She stood beside Nita and Jimmy Lee and put a hand on each of their shoulders. "Promise me you won't buy me a new car when I turn sixteen. Promise me you won't buy into all that bourgeois coming-of-age stuff like sweet-sixteen parties and gifts of expensive imported automobiles."

"I promise," Nita said.

"A 1976 Ford Pinto it is then," Jimmy Lee said cheerfully. He was wearing faded blue jeans and a navy blue sweater and Nita was having a hard time keeping her hands off him.

"You can get *me* a new car if you want to," Logan said. "I won't mind."

"You're funny," Jimmy Lee said.

"Materialism is the last refuge of scoundrels," Whitney said, quoting Nietzsche. She patted her mother on the shoulder. "Thank you for *not* raising me to be a spoiled rotten yuppie. Thank you for teaching me the pleasures of a simple life" — she lifted her hands and indicated the crowded kitchen around them — "in a simple house with simple food and very few material possessions to speak of."

"Now hold on a minute," Jimmy Lee said.

"Thank you for taking me away from Grandmother with all her riches and wealthy enticements."

"Listen." Nita turned slightly in her chair so she could see both of her children. "I want you kids to understand something," she said. "Whatever Grandmother did, she did it for the love of you two. I don't want you to blame her, or your daddy, either." Here she looked pointedly at Logan. "Don't blame them for the way they are." Logan scowled and looked at his feet but he didn't protest, which Nita took as a hopeful sign. "Daddy wasn't the best father in the world and he knows that. But sooner or later you'll have to forgive him and just move on."

"I don't really need a father," Logan said.

"Everybody needs a father," Nita said firmly. "You and your dad just need to figure out some way to spend time together without fighting all the time."

"Charles just loves himself," Logan said. "He doesn't care about anyone else. He doesn't care what I do."

"He's your father," Nita said, "don't call him Charles. If he didn't care about you, you wouldn't fight all the time. He wouldn't react no matter what you did. Indifference is much more terrible than conflict."

"So you're saying, because we fight, it means we love each other?"

"Yes."

"That's fucked up," Logan said, shaking his head.

"Hey," Jimmy Lee said.

Nita said, "You're a smart boy. He's a smart man. You two just need to figure out some way to communicate your feelings without letting all that resentment and rage get in the way."

"In the meantime, you've got me," Jimmy Lee said.

Logan grinned and they slapped palms. "Cool," he said, rising. "Hey, me and the boys are playing in that Battle of the Bands they're having next weekend over in States-boro. Grandpa Redmon called a couple of people he knows and got us on the bill. Are you coming?"

Jimmy Lee said, "Is a pig's butt pork? Of course I'm coming."

Nita said, "You have to figure out some way of forgiving Daddy and Grandmother. Both of you. It's important." She had given up reading how-to-be-a-good-parent books and was just winging it now.

"Oh, I forgive them," Whitney said airily. "Daddy is sweet as can be. He really is. And Grandmother, well, Grandmother is just Grandmother. Living with her was not nearly as much fun as I thought it would be. She's so damn picky. It's always, 'Sit up straight,' or 'Don't talk with food in your mouth,' or 'Don't put your elbows on the table, my goodness what will people think.' "

"You know who I feel sorry for?" Logan said. "Grandpa Redmon. What's he gonna do now that me and the boys aren't there to protect him?"

"Old Virginia rides him pretty hard, does she?" Jimmy Lee grinned and winked at Nita.

"He enjoys every minute of it," Nita said, grinning back.

"He's like a whipped dog," Logan said. " 'Yes, honey,' this and 'no, honey,' that. Like a lovesick teenager, always following her around and slapping her on the butt every chance he gets."

"Ew, don't remind me," Whitney said. "It's disgusting. They're both so *old*." She shuddered at the disturbing notion of people over forty having a sex life.

Nita smiled gently at Jimmy Lee. "Y'all

go ahead and stack the dishes in the dishwasher," she said. "And then get your homework done."

"Okay, Mommy," Whitney said.

"Yes, ma'am," Logan said.

When the kids had finished cleaning up the kitchen and gone into their bedrooms to do their homework, Nita and Jimmy Lee sat at the kitchen table in a companionable silence. "This is nice," Jimmy Lee said, taking her hand.

"Yes, it is."

"It's funny, what Whitney said about living a simple life and all that. She's right."

"Out of the mouths of babes."

"How long do you think her change in attitude will last?"

"Maybe two weeks."

He laughed. "This is all that matters, right here." He looked around the kitchen and back at his wife. "Everything I care about is right here in this little house." Otis raised his head and thumped his tail on the floor. Jimmy Lee played with Nita's fingers, gently pulling each fingertip. "I want it the way it was before. I want to appreciate it this time."

"We can't go back. We can only go forward."

"That's true," he said. He leaned over and kissed her, soft and slow, and she could feel everything there was between them in that kiss — all the love, regret, and above all, hope. When he pulled away, he kept his face close to hers. His breath was sweet. His eyes were round and dark as river stones.

"I want to come home," he said.

Nita leaned and kissed him back. "What are you waiting for?" she said.

Three weeks before Christmas the ax finally fell and Joe Solomon lost his job. He had been dreading it for so long that when word finally came, it was almost a relief. He showed up on Lavonne's front porch carrying a bouquet of pink roses and a bottle of champagne. When she opened the door, he just stood there grinning. "I got fired," he said finally.

"Well try not to look so depressed," Lavonne said, opening the screen.

She'd been making pad thai for supper and he kissed her and followed her into the kitchen. He put the roses in a vase of water and rummaged around in the cabinet for a couple of champagne flutes. "Where's Eadie?" he said, over his shoulder.

"She's out at the art supply store."

She stood at the stove and he leaned over her shoulder and looked down at the smoking wok. "That smells good," he said. He kissed her again and she said, "Why don't you set the table and we'll celebrate the demise of your sorry-assed corporate job."

She was surprised to find him in such a cheerful mood. Most men she knew who lost their jobs in middle age lapsed into bitterness and despair, but Joe had the cheerful demeanor of a reprieved death-row felon. He was whistling as he set the table and he looked like he had lost about fifteen years of age and worry.

"So what's next?" she asked, halfway through the meal. The thought that he might have to look for a job elsewhere hovered always at the edge of her consciousness like a bad dream.

"I think you know the answer to that," he said, pouring them both another glass of champagne.

She said, "Atlanta? Detroit? Chicago?"

He frowned. "Oh come on," he said.

"The Big Apple?"

"I was thinking more like Provence. Saint-Tropez or maybe Marseilles."

Lavonne put her fork down. "Were you serious?" she asked. "You mean all that talk of biking through the south of France was for *real?*"

He looked hurt. "Of course it was for real," he said. "Why do you think I've been working my ass off for the last twenty-five years? Why do you think I've been saving every penny I could for the last fifteen?"

"But do you have enough?"

"Sure. If I economize. I got a good severance package from DuPont and Katie's education is already paid for. I set up a trust fund years ago. I need some time away from the corporate rat race to work out a business plan for my bike shop. And Provence seems like the perfect place to do it." He laughed and pinched her cheek. "I mean, we won't exactly be living a life of luxury but we'll get by."

Lavonne said, "We?" She said, "Provence?"

He pushed himself away from the table and got down on one knee. She shook her head but he just laughed and took her hands. "Come on, girl, run away with me to the south of France."

"Get up off the floor before you hurt yourself."

"Let's live the Bohemian life, if only for six months."

"I'm not getting married again anytime soon."

"Who said anything about marriage?"

"But what about my business?"

"What about it? Hire somebody. Hell, I've

seen your balance sheet. I've seen your profit and loss. You can afford to hire a manager, or even a whole management team. Both you and Mona deserve some time off."

She smiled in spite of herself and shook her head. "You'll throw your back out if you don't get up."

"Come on, Lavonne," he teased. "What are you afraid of? You always said you wanted to travel. You always said you wanted to write a book for women looking to protect themselves financially from bad husbands."

"If I promise to think about it, will you get up off the floor? You're not a damn twenty-year-old, you know."

He grinned and pulled her toward him. "Then why do I feel like one?" he said.

Since the cathartic pre-Thanksgiving throwdown, Eadie had pretty much worked nonstop painting a series of large female nudes for the gallery up in Atlanta. She had given up on abstract expressionism and had returned to her first love, classical realism. Her females now looked less like geometric body parts held together by paint and more like Botticelli angels. She rose early every morning and went out to Lavonne's little shed to work, sometimes painting steadily for five or six hours before taking a break. Now that Nita had her family back, now that Lavonne was happy in love, now that Eadie had banished whatever demons haunted her from her childhood and gone back to work, her job here was nearly done. She wanted to go home to New Orleans. She wanted to spend Christmas with her husband.

Later that afternoon, he called. He had cut short his tour of the Midwest and was home waiting for her. He had taken to calling her daily, as if the harassment alone might be enough to make her jump on a plane and head back to the Big Easy.

"I'm making Cosmopolitans just the way you like them," he said, when she picked up the phone. "On the veranda. It's a beautiful day. The sun is slanting through the ironwork making lacy patterns on the old bricks. The banana plants are swaying in the breeze. It smells like New Orleans."

"Like mud flats and jasmine? Like garbage and gardenias?"

"That's right."

"Goddamn, I miss it."

"So come home."

"I can't just leave in the middle," Eadie said. "I've got to finish what I started."

Trevor sighed. Eadie wiped her hands on a rag and went outside into the yard. It was sunny here, too, and the air was cool and dry. Not like New Orleans, though. Not soft and balmy and sweet with decay.

"I thought you had finished helping Nita. I thought your job there was done."

"It is," she said. "Almost. I have to finish what I'm working on and get the canvases up to that gallery in Atlanta."

"I talked to Grace yesterday. I invited her to come up and spend some time with us in New Orleans. I told her I had a lock of my father's hair that I'd be happy to have DNA tested if she so desired."

"You're a good brother."

"I'm a good husband, too." When she didn't say anything, he chuckled and said, "So, I've been looking at some of the pictures I took with my digital camera last Christmas."

"How'd they come out?"

"Odd."

"What do you mean odd?"

"There's one of you in the bedroom. You're sitting on the edge of the bed. It looks like you've been napping and you've just woken up."

"Oh shit. Destroy that one."

"And here's the odd thing," Trevor said.

"There's this light just beyond your right shoulder."

"Maybe it's a reflection off the window."

"I thought of that. It shows up on several of the shots and then gets darker. But when I checked the shots immediately before and immediately after, it's gone. It's like it appears on one frame, gets larger, gets darker, and then disappears."

"What does it look like?"

"A head. The shadow of a head."

"A small head, right?"

"Yes. A small head. And small shoulders. And a small body."

"Like a child?"

"Yes."

"I told you I wasn't crazy," Eadie said. There was a drumming sound in her head, slow and steady as a heartbeat.

"The thing is, now I'm kind of spooked. I'm kind of scared staying in this big house all by myself."

"Now you know how I felt."

He chuckled and said, "Promise me you'll be home for Christmas."

"I can't make any promises about the future. I'm living one day at a time."

"That sounds ominous."

"No it doesn't."

"But you're coming home?"

"Yes."

"I need you here. All I have for company is a group of fawning flatterers."

She laughed. "You must be in heaven then."

"I'm lonely in this big old house all by myself."

"You're not by yourself. There's a ghost."

"Thanks for reminding me."

"I'll send you a Ouija board so you'll have someone to talk to."

He was laughing when she hung up. Smiling, she went back to work.

Two weeks before Christmas and several days before Eadie was scheduled to return to New Orleans, Lavonne had a going-away party. It was a small affair, just Lavonne, Nita, Grace, and Eadie. They sat out on the deck under a leaden sky, watching the neighbor's colored Christmas lights twinkle merrily. It had rained all day, a slow, steady drizzle that stopped just as evening fell.

"Three days from now I'll be home," Eadie said, looking around the table. Clouds of fog rolled in under the lights. "What are y'all gonna do for fun once I'm gone?"

"Give my liver a vacation," Lavonne said.

"Count the days until you come back," Nita said.

"Plan a trip to the Big Easy," Grace said.

"Y'all should do that. Come up and see me in New Orleans. We could get into all kinds of trouble and I know the police commissioner so it's nothing that would show up on our permanent records."

Lavonne chuckled and shook her head. "Speaking of trouble, do you want me to mix up a shaker of Cosmopolitans?" Nita and Grace shook their heads.

"No, thanks," Eadie said. "I think I'll lay off the hard stuff for a while. I feel a health binge coming on."

"Sweet tea it is, then." Lavonne went into the kitchen. She came out a few minutes later carrying a pitcher of tea and a tray of baked brie and crackers.

"Did Trevor call me on the house phone?" Eadie said to Lavonne. "I've been trying to reach him all day."

"No. I checked messages when I came in from work."

Nita said, "How long's it been since you saw him?"

"Three and a half weeks. That's the longest we've ever been apart, except for the two trial separations." Eadie poured herself a glass of tea and then sat back in her chair. "He thinks I'm coming in next week. He doesn't know I'm coming home early. I thought I'd surprise him."

"Better warn the neighbors," Lavonne said.

"Very funny."

"Are you blushing?" Nita said, giggling. "I don't think I've ever seen you blush, Eadie."

"Speaking of blushing, how's that recommitting to virginity thing working out for you and Jimmy Lee?"

Nita took a long, slow sip of tea and then set her glass down on the table. "It was a pretty stupid idea anyway," she said.

"Yeah, that's what we thought."

Grace cut a thick wedge of brie and spread it on top of a cracker. "So what's the deal with Charles?" she said to Nita. "I hear he's leaving town."

"He's moving to Atlanta. He was offered a job working for Coca-Cola back when Boone and Broadwell folded, and now he's decided to take it."

"I'm not surprised," Lavonne said, "after that blowout at his mother's house. I mean, how much humiliation can one guy take?"

"Don't tell me you feel sorry for that asshole," Eadie said. "He's only getting what he deserves."

Grace said, "Hey, that's my half-brother you're talking about."

No one knew what to say to this. They

hadn't asked Grace about her relationship with the Broadwells. They figured she needed time to come to terms with it before speaking about it openly.

"And don't tell me he wasn't in on Virginia's little kidnapping and land fraud scheme from the beginning," Eadie said.

Nita shrugged. "Maybe," she said. She didn't care about any of that now. She was happy and that was all that mattered.

Lavonne poured everyone some more tea. She leaned back in her chair and looked at Nita. "So how're things with you and Virginia?"

Nita helped herself to the brie. "She dropped the custody suit, of course. I've agreed to let Whitney see her, but only if I'm present. She and Redmon are coming for Christmas dinner. I believe in letting bygones be bygones. Up to a point."

"You're a hell of a lot more forgiving than I am," Eadie said. "I know she's turned over a new leaf and everything but I still wouldn't let her within ten feet of my child."

"I thought you admired Virginia," Lavonne said.

"Yeah, well, admiring her from a distance and welcoming her into the bosom of my family are two very different things. You might admire a grizzly bear in the zoo but that doesn't mean you'd bring it home for tea and cookies."

"She's trying hard to change," Grace said. They all looked at her. "I talked to her a few days ago. She's agreed to counseling. We think it might be the best way to rebuild our relationship."

"Damn," Lavonne said.

"Good luck with that," Eadie said.

"I think that's sweet," Nita said.

The sky darkened into evening. A damp mist hung over the yard. Lavonne got up to light some candles.

"Just tell me one thing," Eadie said to Grace. "When did you find out about Virginia being your mother? And how?"

Grace shrugged and looked at her hands. "I'm an investigative journalist," she said. "It wasn't all that hard. I knew I'd been adopted. My parents never tried to hide that from me, and for a long time it just wasn't important. But when I turned forty-eight, I started thinking about it. All the time. I wanted to know who my real parents were and I wanted to know why they gave me up. My parents told me everything they knew and I kind of worked backward from there."

"So you've known for a couple of years?"

"No. I found out the truth a few weeks before Nita's wedding. It was a shock, I can tell you. It took me a while to assimilate. Everyone knows Virginia and I never got along too well. And I had no idea about Hampton Boone until the day of Virginia's pre-Thanksgiving throw-down." She looked at Eadie and grinned. "That was a complete shock."

Lavonne patted her on the shoulder. "Well, you seem to be handling it all pretty well," she said.

"I'm adjusting," Grace said. "Virginia's asked me to come over next week when they air the *Gracious Southern Living* holiday segment. She says she needs me there for moral support."

"Does she have any idea what exactly it is they're going to air?"

Grace shook her head. "She has no clue," she said.

Eadie snorted. "Well, it might be interesting. You know that producer, Carlin, called me to talk about filming a segment on next year's Kudzu Ball. She thought it might be just the kind of thing their viewers want to see."

"Hell," Lavonne said. "Maybe we should pitch it to the networks as a new reality series."

Nita giggled and put her hand over her mouth. Eadie looked at Lavonne and grinned. Grace chewed a cracker and gazed at the twinkling Christmas lights, still thinking about her newfound mother.

"I mean, I'm not saying Virginia and I are ever going to be close," she said. "There's no telling what kind of relationship we'll be able to forge through counseling. My feeling is, if we can get to the point where we can sit in a room without physically assaulting one another, that's a good thing."

"I think that's the best you can hope for with Virginia," Eadie said.

"You have to take love where you can find it," Nita said, smiling and looking around the table. "It's not always pretty."

There was a scent of wood smoke in the air, rolling in with the fog. The lights of the neighborhood houses glowed cheerily. Distantly, the strains of "God Rest Ye Merry Gentlemen" wafted on the cool damp air.

"Speaking of love," Eadie said to Lavonne. "Have you decided whether or not to run away to the south of France with Joe?"

Lavonne sighed and looked at the Christmas lights. "I don't know," she said. "We're such good friends and I'm kind of scared to ruin that. What if we hate each other after living together a month? What if it turns into a relationship like the one I had with Leonard?"

"You've got to get back in there, Lavonne. You can't be afraid of what might happen. You have to go for it."

"Well, I know I can't stay for six months. Not with my business and the girls coming home for summer break."

"If you're over there long enough, you'll learn to speak French."

"Hey, will you teach me how to curse in French?" Eadie said. "I've always wanted to do that."

There was a sudden thunderous knocking on the front door. They all jumped and looked at one another. Eadie frowned. "Joe?" she said.

Lavonne shook her head, rising. "He's still in Chicago."

"Maybe it's Christmas carolers," Nita said.

"If it is, send them back here," Grace said.

They waited, listening for Lavonne's footsteps as she crossed the kitchen and into the front room. She opened the door and a deep, masculine voice said, "Evening, ma'am. I'm Officer Tater Hogburn. We've had a complaint about a disturbance coming from this residence, something about some vodka-crazed women and a troupe of high-flying circus midgets."

It was Trevor doing his best redneck accent.

"Well, good evening Officer Hogburn, come on in. The midgets were just leaving." Lavonne grinned and stepped back so he could enter. "Eadie, get your clothes on," she said, swinging her head over her shoulder. "You've got a visitor."

But she was too late. Eadie had already jumped up and was running for the door.

ACKNOWLEDGMENTS

I want to thank my editors, Charlotte Herscher and Dan Mallory.
Thanks also to my agent, Kristin Lindstrom, for her tireless work ethic and unceasing good humor.

ABOUT THE AUTHOR

Cathy Holton, the author of *Revenge of the Kudzu Debutantes,* was born in Lakeland, Florida, and grew up in college towns in the South and the Midwest. She attended Oklahoma State University and Michigan State University and worked for a number of years in Atlanta before settling in the mountains of Tennessee with her husband and their three children.

The employees of Thorndike Press hope you have enjoyed this Large Print book. All our Thorndike and Wheeler Large Print titles are designed for easy reading, and all our books are made to last. Other Thorndike Press Large Print books are available at your library, through selected bookstores, or directly from us.

For information about titles, please call:
(800) 223-1244

or visit our Web site at:
www.gale.com/thorndike
www.gale.com/wheeler

To share your comments, please write:
Publisher
Thorndike Press
295 Kennedy Memorial Drive
Waterville, ME 04901